Kissing ADRIEN

Siri L. Mitchell

HARVEST HOUSE PUBLISHERS

EUGENE, OREGON

Published in association with the literary agency of Alive Communications, Inc., 7680 Goddard Street, Ste #200, Colorado Springs, CO 80920

Cover by Garborg Design Works, Minneapolis, Minnesota

KISSING ADRIEN
Copyright © 2005 by Siri L. Mitchell
Published by Harvest House Publishers
Eugene, Oregon 97402
www.harvesthousepublishers.com

Library of Congress Cataloging-in-Publication Data

Mitchell, Siri L., 1969-
    Kissing Adrien / Siri L. Mitchell.
        p. cm.
    ISBN-13: 978-0-7369-1636-3
    ISBN-10: 0-7369-1636-9
    1. Triangles (Interpersonal relations)—Fiction.   2. Inheritance and succession—Fiction.
    3. Americans—France—Fiction.   4. Apartment houses—Fiction.   5. Paris (France)—Fiction.
    I. Title.
PS3613.I866K57 2005
813'.6—dc22

2005001902

Printed in the United States of America

05   06   07   08   09   10   11   12   / BP-MS /   10   9   8   7   6   5   4   3   2   1

To Tony, because kissing Adrien
could never compare to kissing you.

Acknowledgments

To Carolyn McCready and Terry Glaspey, for taking a chance, and to Chip MacGregor, for giving me one. To Kim Moore, for her uncanny ability to edit. To Pastor Scott Stearman, for not being afraid to think about God and for encouraging the rest of us to do so too. To Noreen Riols, my first mentor, for brutal honesty and unswerving faith. To Lissa Welch, for jamming a stick under the ball and jumping up and down to start it rolling. To Mick Silva, for cheering from the trenches. To Andrew Hecker, for graciously answering my questions about doing business in France. To Michelle Bayer, my first reader, for her sharp eye and friendship in a foreign land. To Tony, for being my biggest fan. To Kaiya, for taking long naps. To Dad and Mom, for love. To my friends in France, for teaching me how to live well. To God, for this adventure we call life.

And most of all, to Paris.

My name is Claire and I used to be nice. In fact, nice was the all-purpose description of my life: nice girl has nice boyfriend, nice job, nice house, and nice car.

So what happened?

Cynthia and Mademoiselle. Adrien and Paris.

Me.

I happened. If I were being completely honest with myself, I would place all the blame on me. Because if I'd done something different the summer I was 17, if I'd majored in history at college, if I'd gone to work as a teacher instead of as an accountant, then maybe I could have been kissing Adrien.

But I didn't.

So I wasn't.

But I sure needed to.

Chapter 1

❧⟨❧⟩

*N*ice girl gone bad. That's me: Claire Le Noyer.

When I left my home and job in Seattle, my original plan had been to fly to Florida. Period. Not that Florida was my idea of paradise, but I had been lured there by an ingenious trick of my parents'. They moved there when they retired. And then my father broke his back.

Exactly how is still a little unclear to me, but I think it might have involved a throw rug.

My dad isn't a big man, but he makes a poor invalid, so Mom asked if I could come and help her. It was the end of July. I still had nine days of annual leave left, and several weeks of sick leave, so I asked for some time off from my budget coordinator job at the University of Washington and bought an unbelievably expensive ticket to Florida by way of Denver, Chicago, and Miami.

Mom picked me up at the airport, drove me home, and delivered me straight into the hands of Satan: my father. Normally, he's a very nice Americanized Frenchman, but when he's sick, he reverts.

Fortunately, Mademoiselle Dumont chose the evening I arrived in Florida to die. In Paris. We found out about it the next morning. She had been a distant relation through a web of second and third cousins, and when she died at the age of 82, she left Dad her entire estate.

For some reason my parents were imagining treasure chests filled with jewels. I was thinking more along the lines of half-eaten cheeses left in cupboards growing bright colors of mold. But that just shows how obsessively tidy I am.

Within half an hour, my parents had it all planned. I would be dispatched to France to claim the family's new fortune. Mom hurried off to the bank and returned with a wad of euros. Three thousand of them, just in case. Too bad they weren't dollars; they would have gone a long way toward putting a new roof on my house.

The next day, I found myself tamped into seat 35E on a 777 airplane bound for Paris. The combination of those two sets of numbers meant that I was seated at the dead center of economy class. I had a toddler kicking the back of my seat and a baby screaming in my left ear all the way to France.

And I'd already seen all the movies.

Adrien was supposed to pick me up at the airport; our mothers had arranged it before the Delaportes left on vacation. I'd been waiting almost an hour, but I had no doubt he would find me. Which was why I didn't mind sitting on a hard vinyl-covered bench just inside Charles de Gaulle Airport, even though I had to flick away the cigarette smoke of the stranger sitting beside me.

At least I was keeping myself occupied. In between flicks I was trying to scrape back my shoulder-length walnut brown hair into a ponytail. It had started out that way in Florida, but somehow, now that I was in the capital of fashion, locks of hair kept springing out and slipping down my face. I finally pulled the elastic band off and let it all hang loose.

I wished I could have done something about my clothes, a worn pair of jeans and a navy blue T-shirt, but the only clothes I had to choose from were the clothes I'd packed for Florida. At least I looked good in jeans—I had my father's long, slender legs. I also had my eyes. Gray-green cat eyes.

Legs and eyes.

They are all I had to offer.

I'd just have to do what my mother had taught me for instant confidence: Stand up straight, pull your stomach in, and throw your shoulders back. Which had the same effect as "thrust your chest out," but she would have died before saying that, even though we both knew I could have used a little help in that department.

I just wished I looked a little better. For Adrien. Not that he would notice, of course. Or even care.

I did some more flicking and glanced at my watch. Closed my eyes and tried not to breathe too deeply; tried not to fall asleep. But then it seemed, through my closed eyelids, that something about the airport was changing. There was an extra energy in the air.

The trolley wheels were still squeaking; the voices were still whispering. The smoker was still exhaling. But there was something else.

A sort of background hum.

That's when I knew it was Adrien. He was always humming. And when he wasn't humming, he was prone to break out into song. As long as he was humming, things were looking up.

I slit my eyes open and watched as he made his way through the crowd.

Little boys were gazing at him, puzzled, as if they were certain he was an actor, or maybe a soccer star. He had that casual confidence which could only be gained by countless victories. He paused beside a woman and placed a hand at the small of her back to move her so he could pass by. Except that he stopped a minute to chat. Another minute to smile and flirt.

Me? I scrambled to my feet, threw my purse-sized backpack over a shoulder, and yanked up the handle on my wheeled suitcase. In my experience, when Adrien stopped to talk, it could be a while.

I could appreciate his charms, but before today I hadn't watched him use them on a female of his own age. My mother and her friends, yes. Me and my friends, yes. But to see him flirt for real was an experience.

The interesting thing about Adrien was the synergy of all of his parts. He was tall and lanky. Lithe and energetic. He had dark hair, bright blue eyes, and a perpetual tan. A largish nose and nice white teeth. But what pulled it all together was his personality—part clown, part diplomat—and the strange desire he created in those he talked with to want to make him laugh.

And that woman had just done it. The way she smiled at him said that his laugh was a reward in itself.

Then he glanced beyond the woman's shoulder and saw me. So he touched her back once more, bowed, and pushed off in my direction.

When he was close enough, he grasped me by the shoulders and held himself back a little so he could look at me, doing a big brother imitation. His mouth turned up in a half smile. "Claire! *Ma petite poule.*"

Hearing him call me his "little chicken" made me smile. He's called me that since I was a child. But by that time, he was kissing me on both cheeks and I was getting an up close look at both of his ears.

They were very nice. And clean. You can't say that about everyone's ears.

Then he took the suitcase from me and tucked my hand under his arm. Fresh lime-scented cologne wafted from his skin as he moved. He'd rolled up the sleeves of his wrinkled yellow buttoned-down shirt, but his khakis were neatly pressed. His loafers had been shined, but he was wearing no socks. Not that I blamed him. August in Paris could be stifling.

I used to have a crush on Adrien. I'll admit it. But I hadn't seen him in ten years, so I had a pretty realistic opinion of him. And of myself. Enough to recognize that in my wildest dreams my future still included a man who, although not Adrien, was vaguely dark-haired, blue-eyed, and irritatingly smart. Adrien was the big brother I'd never had, so it was no surprise that he had influenced my idea of the ideal man.

My fascination with Adrien began the summer I turned five. That's the first time I remember him. Practically my first memory ever. We were playing on the beach at Carcans-Plage, east of Paulliac, in southwest France. He was running in the spindle-legged way that 11-year-old boys do. His feet splatting in the hard wet sand left at the upper edge of a recent high tide. He was wearing white shorts. His dark hair had faded from the sun, and his skin was a sand-dusted bronze.

I remember him flinging out an arm, beckoning me forward, toward him. He slowed in his careening gait and then stopped and waited for me to catch up. At least, that's what I thought he was doing. By the time I caught up with him, he had planted his feet in the surf, and turned to face the ocean. A stream of golden pee was lifting in a perfect arc toward the sunset before dropping down to join the sea.

It's the sort of thing that little boys do in France where we spent our summer vacations. And I thought it was the greatest thing I'd ever seen.

Over the years Adrien became a golden boy. He proved to be above average in intelligence, especially in the subject of math so highly prized by the French. When he graduated from high school, he was accepted at "X."

X is Ecole Polytechnique. It was founded by Napoléon and is the MIT or Oxford of France. Most of France's CEOs are graduates. After four years at Ecole Polytechnique, graduates earn the right to list an *X* after their names, as if they had earned a master's degree or a Ph.D. Forget business school; everyone in France aspires to be an engineer. Laugh if you want, but it's the French way to fame and fortune.

And that is the track Adrien is on.

There was Adrien. And then there were the rest of us. It was always like that.

Except that I wasn't exactly part of the "us," being the youngest and considered the worst sort of pest. As a solemn, quiet child, my *modus operandi* was to shadow the group, find a piece of shade, and sit and stare at them. They were collectively responsible for my welfare, but being so quiet, I inevitably ended up being left behind. Or misplaced. Or, once in a great while, lost.

Adrien was the only one who could ever find me.

As we walked toward the terminal doors, there was a change in the atmosphere. It felt to me like disappointment. The French are always up for a good romance, so I'm sure they'd imagined Adrien striding through the airport, looking for his lover. What they were hoping for was a good kiss.

I was too.

But I was having trouble with my boyfriend, and Adrien might as well have been my big brother, and they were all just going to have to wait. But it did give me a secret satisfaction to know that Adrien was mine. That I was his. That he was there for me…because of me.

You know what I'm trying to say.

Chapter 2

ℬↃᏟℰ

"I am sorry that I was late, but the traffic was *difficile*. Do you mind if I speak English? My English teacher tells me that I must practice."

Adrien could speak whatever he wanted as long as he could get me to Paris alive. As it was, I had my doubts. We were whizzing down the autoroute in his sleek black Mercedes at a rate the speedometer said was 150 kilometers an hour. It felt like 120 miles an hour. Which would not have been so bad, except that everyone else seemed as though they were in slow motion. Adrien was weaving in and out of traffic, using the shoulder as his own personal speedway.

He tossed a glance in my direction and began to laugh. "You do not have fear?"

"Yes, I do. *Beaucoup*. Could you slow down?" I had pressed myself into the back of the leather seat and hunched down as far as possible, trying to lessen the percentage of my body that would come into contact with the car when it crashed. Which it would.

"*Impossible.*"

"But the signs say 120 kilometers per hour."

"And they also say *rappel*. Reminder. It is just a suggestion. Sometimes I drive more fast. Sometimes I drive more slow. It depends on the weather. And *regarde*. Today is sun, no rain, no wind." He shot another glance in my direction. I must have looked worried. "You do not think a policeman is going to stop me?"

"Maybe. Yes."

Laughing again, he shifted gears and revved the engine. "Not *possible*. How could he ever catch me?"

Good point.

"You must have more faith. Tell me about you. Tell me everything. I have not seen you for…"

"Ten years."

"Ten long years my heart has ached."

"No, it hasn't." I loved Adrien as though he were my own brother, but I had his routine down cold. He was a great guy if you could get past the flirtiness. That's why I put the lid on him. The sooner done, the better.

"*Oui.* You are my favorite. Why have you not come to see me before this?"

"Because I'm not so little anymore, Adrien. I graduated from college and I can't just spend all summer on vacation."

"Why not?"

"Because I work. And I only get 12 days of vacation a year."

He swerved, just missing a car on our right. Horns blared to life all around us, and he raised his hands above his head in a "What? What?" gesture that could be seen by the other drivers. One sped by on our right and threw Adrien an obscene gesture. He muttered something and then shot me a sheepish grin. "Twelve days? Just 12? And how long have you been working at this place? When do you get more?"

"I don't."

"*Jamais?*"

"Never."

"Why?"

"That's all anyone ever gets."

"This is *ridicule*. You work too much. You will get sick. *Alors*…find a new job. You must come to work in France. You must have 35 days of vacation a year. Then we can go again to Carcans and spend August at the beach."

Like I'll ever have a month again in my life to lie around in southern France doing absolutely nothing.

"This is what we must do. And your parents have this apartment now. This is *parfait!*"

Well, sure. In my daydreams it would be perfect. Except for my house, my parents, my boyfriend. My life was back in the States. "Good idea, but I can't. *Je ne peux pas.*" I said it in French just to make sure he'd understand.

"Then my heart must ache again."

"Sorry."

"You do not look it." He turned his head from me in a mock sulk. But a moment later it swung back in my direction with a teasing grin. "There must be someone else."

I didn't deny it.

"There is. I know this. I should have come to America and this would never have happened. And now my heart is broken. You break this." He placed a hand so tenderly over his heart that I couldn't help laughing.

"And Virginie? Solange? Véronique?" His parents had kept mine updated on his more serious romantic alliances.

For just a second he had the good grace to look guilty, but then he recovered. "I was waiting for you, *ma poule.* I did not know how long you would be, so I had some fun. Good thing. It takes you ten years!"

The best thing to do when he was flirty was to press on with the conversation. Sooner or later he'd drop it and become serious. "His name is Brian."

"Brian." It sounded much different in French. As if it belonged to a person I'd never met. "And you are in love?"

I shrugged. "Maybe." And maybe not. Someday soon I would have to decide because we were starting to get serious. At church we had already ceased to be "Brian" and "Claire." We had become "you guys." As in, "Are you guys planning on going to the potluck?" In fact, we had almost become "you." And that's what was worrying me. In still being "you guys," I could go to the potluck even if Brian couldn't. But once we became "you," I wouldn't have the option of being an individual. He would be Brian, the assistant pastor, and I would be Claire, Brian's fiancée, and then, eventually, his wife. I just didn't know if I was ready for that.

If I had been feeling less tired, I would have laughed at myself. Because I had been the one praying, pushing, pleading, and subconsciously doing everything I could to encourage Brian to propose. Trying to tackle, hurtle, or otherwise combat every excuse he'd thrown in my direction. The funniest thing is that I think he may have been on the verge of proposing. Finally. He was supposed to take me out to dinner last night. At the Space Needle.

But then Dad broke his back.

So.

Adrien was sitting forward in the driver's seat, gripping his hands around the steering wheel as if he were getting ready for some warp-speed driving. As if all the other 50 million illegal things he'd just done had been a warm-up. "Do not tell me—let me guess!" He was excited about this. Adrien loved games; especially ones in which he could display his cleverness. "He is tall and blond with sad blue eyes. He has a tan. He wears plaid shirts and shaggy hair and pants that are too big." His eyes turned toward me, triumphant. "Am I right?"

I had never been able to lie to him, and I wasn't about to attempt it now. "Yes."

He glanced back at the road, saw a six-inch gap in the lane to the right of me, and plunged the car into it. Miraculously, despite a chorus of honks, the gap expanded to fit the car. "Okay. Let me try one more. He has a beard just here." Adrien's long fingers had reached up to stroke the area around his chin.

"No." Not at this very moment. Brian *had* worn a goatee, but he shaved it off the previous month. Adrien didn't have to know that. It would just make his huge head bigger.

"*Dommage.* Too bad." Adrien shrugged and turned his head back toward the road.

Had our mothers been talking again? But that would have been impossible because my mother didn't even know that I was so serious about Brian. I hadn't wanted to get her hopes up. "How did you know that?"

"It is very easy. All Americans look alike."

This was news to me.

"Not in the face, but in the style. Most American movie stars and singers look the same. So this is what most of the men in America try to look like too. Right? But tell me more about this Brian. You have been dating how long?"

"For a while." Two years. Not two years' worth of actual dates. It was more like two years of parallel church attendance. Brian was a busy man. Overscheduled in my opinion, but it was probably a way of life for a pastor. I had promised myself that I could get used to it. But I was still waiting for a ring. I'd celebrated holidays with his family. We'd each seen the other sick. We'd even attended each other's high school ten-year reunions.

"So, you have been dating for a while, but you are not yet in love." He was pretending to be a detective.

"He has issues."

Adrien's eyebrows hooked together and his head reclined toward his shoulder. Thinking that he was hung up on the word "issue," I tried to think of a different way to explain it. Before I could, his eyebrows smoothed and then he pounced. "He is married."

"What? No!"

"He has another girlfriend?"

"I would never cheat with someone."

"Me too." He slid a look at me under his eyebrows. *"Normalement."*

I cocked an eyebrow at him and gave my best impression of his mother's Adrien-Jean-Luc-Delaporte-stop-that-right-now look. But it's hard to have a staring contest when the other person is dodging traffic at video game speeds.

"He has issues? So then he has not ever tried to kiss you?"

Did I really have to tell Adrien all the details of my maybe-maybe not relationship?

"Ma poule?"

"We've kissed."

He looked at me, an eyebrow raised.

"He's a pastor. An assistant pastor. We don't spend a lot of time alone." Because Brian needed to show exemplary character in every aspect of his life. We did hold hands. When we were alone.

"That is a shame. He is a coward."

"No, he's not."

"But he is. He is afraid to kiss you."

"No, he isn't. He wants our relationship to be about us, not about physical attraction."

"He is afraid because the man who kisses you will lose his heart to you." Adrien said it as if it were a fact.

"How can you know that?"

"Because I have kissed many people. And because I know you. How do you think I can always find you?"

In a strange way, it was the nicest thing anyone had said to me for a very long time.

Chapter 3

❧

As we neared the city, the stretches of grassy medians and open lots surrounding the airport gave way to big, boxy warehouse stores and structures that coalesced into ugly cramped apartment and office buildings made fuzzy by haze. If I took too deep a breath, I risked choking on diesel fumes made more potent by the relentless August sun.

It wasn't the Paris I had remembered.

But then we entered the *péripherique* ring road at Porte de la Chapelle and most of the ugliness was banished outside the city while glimmers of graceful beige limestone buildings began to break up the suburban landscape.

After playing hopscotch with other merging drivers, Adrien turned into a tour guide. "If you have not been here in ten years, you have forgotten our historic city. So, on the right, through the trees you see St-Denis. The *basilique* where most of the kings and queens of France were buried and where they were dug up during the Revolution. We assume that they have since been reburied. On the left you have the newest religious monument in France, the Stade de France, dedicated to the god of soccer. We know we make this god happy because in 1998 France won its first victory in the greatest sports event in the world, the World Cup."

World's greatest? Hadn't he heard of the World Series?

And then we went through a tunnel and the city disappeared.

When we resurfaced, Adrien made me look off to the left in order to see Sacré Coeur. "The basilica floats like a white celestial cloud over the dirtiest, most sinful part of the city. But this is very efficient because you can go and watch a naked girl dance and then you can hike up the hill and say your confession and be forgiven before you arrive back home. We French are serious about sinning."

As we turned southwest, Adrien pointed out a sign for Porte de Clignancourt. "There, in St. Ouen, is the largest flea market in Paris. You can find leather jackets, Levi jeans, and antique furniture, but not many bargains and not any fleas."

At Porte Maillot we stopped at a traffic light before entering the city proper. But Adrien wasn't quite ready for Paris yet. "To the right, you have La Défense, where French ladies picnicked during the Prussian War. It was a good spot because they could talk to the German soldiers who were camped on the other side. Quite amusing. Now you may see the skyscrapers and the giant square Grande Arche which is almost in line with the Arc de Triomphe and the Arc de Triomphe du Carrousel at the Louvre."

At this point the light changed and we raced left toward the round-about at Porte Maillot. "In the middle you have the Gallic Cross, which is a symbol for Charles de Gaulle. And a modern sculpture that is a symbol for I am not sure what. And a lot of very nice green grass."

And then I began to smile because looming at the top of the hill, at the end of avenue de la Grande Armée, was the Arc de Triomphe. The blinding white, grandiose monument Napoléon had built for his soldiers. It was always a site that stirred the French *esprit* in my soul.

"Bienvenue á Paris!" Adrien shouted as he challenged a bus to see who would be first at the roundabout. As far as I could tell, cars entering had the right of way. Since it was a 12-way intersection, it led to a homicidal stop-and-start reel as we jerked our way around the circle. Adrien was smarter than I had given him credit for—he let the bus run interference for him.

A quarter way around, I closed my eyes. There weren't any lane markings. There weren't any stoplights. It was a giant free-for-all I just couldn't watch anymore.

And then Adrien pointed the car right to plunge through traffic. "Avenue Marceau!" he cried as he hit the horn.

My eyes flew open and I couldn't believe what I was seeing. He was holding up three lanes of traffic, which all seemed to be coming straight at me, so that he could peel off from the traffic nearest the monument to attempt an exit at the far outside lane. It took lots of honks, but we finally made it through.

We coasted down a gradual hill as my heart retreated from my throat back into my chest. Went a dozen more blocks before veering left to the Place de l'Alma to wait for a light to cross the river.

"Here, you have a replica of the torch of the Statue of Liberty." Adrien gestured to his right at the corner of the Place. "This is a gift of the American people given to France to celebrate the centennial of the Statue of Liberty, which France gave as a gift to the American people."

The light changed and we crossed Pont de l'Alma. As Paris bridges go, it was disappointing because all the statues were below eye level. No gilded sculptures or floral curlicues. I remember thinking, as a child, that its streetlamps look like glowing alien eyes. But it does have a splendid view of the Eiffel Tower. We passed over into the posh seventh *arrondisement*, or district, and zipped up avenue Rapp, turned left on rue Saint Dominique and left down avenue Bosquet, doubling back toward the river.

We reached the Delaportes' apartment with all of our body parts still attached and the car in one piece. I thanked God for that because Adrien certainly had nothing to do with it. I didn't realize how nervous he had made me until I tried to thank him for coming to get me and found that my teeth were clenched.

He angled the Mercedes into a parking space on the street that I was sure he'd never be able to get out of. There was literally one inch of clearance between both the car in front of and the car behind him. It was too bad because if I hadn't enjoyed his driving, I had enjoyed his car.

My own car was a Subaru. I'd bought it long before it had become the sporty person's mobile of choice, and I had thought hard about trading it in for something else after I began to feel guilty about not spending my weekends foraging through the forest. The problem was that it fit my needs: It had four wheels and it was paid off. I never objected, however, to riding in someone else's cushy leather seats and looking at a dashboard carved from burled wood.

Standing in front of the Delaportes' nineteenth-century apartment building was like pausing before a door to my childhood. Our annual month-long vacations to France always began and ended at the Delaportes'.

The creamy cut stone building with its mansard roof, garret attic windows, graceful iron adorned balconies and French windows was as dear to me as my own childhood home. The broad-leafed plane trees that lined the street were taller than I remembered, but they still cast their cooling shade out over the sidewalk.

Adrien punched in the pass code while I stood staring through the glass-fronted wrought-iron door. When the lock clicked, I wrapped a hand around the brass handle and pushed. Walking into the dim front entry, I saw the opposing twin consoles with identical potted plants reflected back to each other in gilded Empire-style mirrors. The floor was still covered in broad tiles, the walls still painted a vague color of green. And the hallway still hushed the thump-thump-thump of the cars that raced across the *pavé*-covered street outside.

I closed my eyes and took a deep breath and…I could smell what the building's *gardienne* was having for lunch. As always, it smelled of cabbage.

"Madame Granvis…"

"…*est toujours ici.*"

Still here. After all this time.

Adrien had taken charge of my suitcase, so I followed him to the back of the hall and around to the right. Past the polished brass mailboxes and the tightly twisted spiral staircase. An oriental-style runner accordioned up its treads in a deep shade of red, and it was kept in place by brass stretchers that ran across the base of each step.

In the staircase's hollow center, custom-built to fill the space, was a cage elevator that dated to 1924. It was barely big enough for two people standing face-to-face. And even then they had to press themselves together to allow the pleated inner door to close. There was a modern elevator that held three, but it surfaced farther away from the Delaportes' apartment.

Adrien opened the door and ushered me forward.

I stepped in and then turned around and pressed my back against the cage. There was an awkward moment when Adrien realized that the two of us plus a jumbo-sized suitcase equaled four people. He solved the problem by calling the other elevator, shoving in the suitcase, and sending it upstairs ahead of us. I knew, from previous experience, that the elevators always stayed put until they were called into use again. It would probably park itself at the fourth floor until six that evening.

Adrien jogged back to me and then tripped coming through the elevator door. I reached an arm around his waist to catch him as he extended an arm to the back of the cage to catch himself. I heard the whir of the inner door as it started to close, and then it stopped and reopened.

It was caught on his heel.

I'm not sure how he managed to drape his arm over my shoulders when all he had to do was move his foot, but we ascended four floors like the best of buddies.

I closed my eyes, and by the time the elevator door opened, I think I actually might have been snoring on his shoulder.

At least I didn't drool on him.

Adrien wedged the front door of the apartment open with his foot as I walked by him, lost in a wonder world of nostalgia. It was the same. Everything was exactly the same. It was as if the whole building had been placed under a fairy's spell and banished for eternity to a time warp. I heard the door shut behind me, and then he was taking my arm and steering me down the hall, away from the kitchen, living room, dining room, and toward the bedrooms and the library. I wanted to protest and head in the opposite direction, toward the kitchen. I was really hungry. But I just couldn't get my feet to turn around.

So I sat down on the floor. In the hallway.

I couldn't walk anymore. Between the nightmarish flight and the twilight-zone car ride, I was finished. And the jet lag. There was that too.

Big mistake. As soon as I was seated, vertigo overcame me. I had the sensation that I was still on the plane, my body responding to the perpetual turbulence of flying.

Before I could do or say anything, Adrien had hoisted me into his arms, taken me to his room, and set me on his bed. Sitting on that bed was like pulling on my most comfortable college sweatshirt. I had always stayed in Adrien's room when I was little. My parents had slept in the library, I slept in Adrien's room, and Adrien slept on the floor of his parents' room.

"You sleep." He was patting my hand as if I were a frail invalid.

"No. *J'ai faim.* I'm hungry."

"So you stay here and I will bring you something to eat."

After considering his offer for a moment, I decided to accept. "Okay. I'll just lie here for a minute until you come back."

"*Bien sûr.*" He was on his way out the door, and something must have been funny because he was smiling. He paused in shutting it. "*Bonne nuit,* Claire."

My head was already on the pillow and my eyes were shut. "Goodnight, Adrien."

Those simple phrases recalled our days at Carcans when '*bonne nuits*' echoed between our families' vacation cottages.

"When will I knock you up?"

"Excuse me?" My eyes flew open.

"What time do I knock? On the door. This is not correct? This is what my English teacher tells me."

"In America, 'knock you up' means to get someone pregnant." But I could see how it might mean something different in England. Maybe. The British have all sorts of strange phrases.

"*La vache!*"

The cow? Why was he calling me a cow?

Adrien took pity on me and started to explain. "*La vache.* This means...sacred cow."

"Holy cow?"

"*Oui.* This one. But maybe the baby would have your eyes and my hair. Or your looks and my brain. Or your smile and my laugh."

I was too tired to deal with Adrien. "Let's try...ten?"

"In 15 minutes? *C'est fait. Alors, bonne nuit,* Claire."

"Make that eleven. *Bonne nuit.*" At least that's what I meant to say. I have a suspicion that the words never quite made it to my mouth.

My thoughts drifted while my brain tried to overpower the coffee I'd had just before landing at seven A.M. in Paris which was one A.M. in Florida.

Claire.

I'd never really liked my name that much. Among those in the know, it's the name of choice for Franco-American couples because it sounds the same in both French and English. In France, the name Claire is usually preceded by Marie. For decades Marie-Claire has been the most popular name for baby girls. There's even a women's magazine called *Marie-Claire.* The American equivalent would be a magazine called *Mike.* There's a million-dollar idea! Just before I fell asleep, I had an enlightening moment of clarity.

Get it? Claire, clarity?

When Adrien says my name, it feels better. It almost seems to fit.

I wonder if jet lag feels anything like being drunk?

Chapter 4

ᑫᑐᑫᑐ

I woke with a splitting headache.

At three in the afternoon.

Adrien must have heard my groans because a moment later, the door inched open. "Claire?"

"Hmm?" I was using my home remedy miracle cure for my headache. Put heel of hand against temple and press hard, cover head with pillow, close eyes and sleep until you wake up. Usually it worked. But then, usually there wasn't Adrien.

I felt a bottom corner of the bed depress and then my body rocked as something made its way up the bed and around my back. I used to have a cat that climbed onto my bed in the middle of the night and curled up between my shoulder blades. If she had weighed 170 pounds, that's what it would have felt like.

"Claire? *Tu as mal?*"

I lifted the corner of the pillow and pointed to my head.

"*La pauvre.*" He started to the take the pillow from me, but I clung to it as though it were my favorite childhood doll. He gave up and settled himself on the bed, his front to my back, and then I felt him take a lock of my limp, travel-worn hair and run his fingers the length of it. With the hypnotic rhythm of his fingers through my hair and the murmur of his smooth voice, I must have fallen back to sleep.

When I woke again it was six. My headache was gone, my will to live was back, and I was hungry.

Hungry? I was starving.

Somehow, during the nap, my hand had slid off my head and had come to rest on the pillow above me. Instead of facing the door, I was now facing Adrien. His eyes were the most stunning shade of blue. Not quite cobalt; too light for that. Not quite ultramarine. Sometimes it's hard to find depth in blue eyes. But his had flecks of white and of dark blue and they were ringed in gray and…they were looking right at me.

I blinked.

He smiled.

I rolled off the bed and tried to stand, but I was dizzy from the sudden change in position. I sat back down.

He yawned and then stretched. He must have learned how to do it from a cat because I recognized those satisfying moves from my own stint as a cat-owned person. "In the commode."

"Pardon me?"

"Your clothes. They are in the commode."

It was only due to lifelong tutoring by my father and his love of antique furniture that I didn't head straight down the hall to the bathroom, but instead I went to stand in front of the marble-topped three-drawer dresser. My shoes had already been pushed underneath it. I was hoping that Adrien had somehow managed to cram my whole suitcase into one of those narrow drawers.

No such luck.

He had removed my laundry-faded polo shirts, raggedy-hemmed shorts, sensible full-coverage ivory-colored cotton bras, and a pile of white-turned-grayish cotton panties from my suitcase and placed them, in small tidy piles, in two drawers.

At least they were bikinis.

I could feel my teeth clenching. I knew I should have taken advantage of Victoria Secret's 5/$20 perpetual panty sale. Too late, too late.

But what was I worried about? I had known Adrien back when he was wearing Astérix briefs. So there. Which reminded me. I jerked the remaining drawer open. It was empty.

"I do not live here anymore. I have an apartment across the river in the eighth *arrondisement*."

"You don't live here? Why not?" Picturing this apartment without Adrien was like thinking of heaven without God.

Adrien had always lived here with his parents. At least he had ten years ago.

He'd pushed himself onto an elbow, but he still looked stuck to the mattress. Putting a hand up to his forehead, he squinched his eyes up as if he were thinking really hard about how to answer my question.

I know how difficult it can be to spend a whole day speaking in a foreign language, so I just waited.

Finally, his eyes flew open and he held up a finger. "Because I am not so little anymore, Claire. I graduated from college, and I can't just spend all summer on vacation…oh, wait…yes, I can."

I threw a shoe at him for mocking me.

He caught it and laughed as he bounded from bed and tossed it back in my direction. "I will get us a *café*. Then we can go to dinner." He shut the door behind him and I heard him, still laughing, pad down the hall.

Standing in front of the commode, those golden feelings of nostalgia I'd experienced earlier disappeared. Adrien was right. He didn't live here anymore. Gone were the red, white, and royal blue PSG scarves and pennants that had honored Paris-St. Germain, his favorite soccer team. Gone were the stacks of books on every subject that had made climbing in and out of his bed a hazard. No more T-shirts, jeans, socks, or briefs in the drawers. And I didn't have to open the carved fruitwood armoire to know that his shirts, pants, and jackets were gone too.

It was still a very nice room. The black-and-cream toile bedspread was still sprinkled with picturesque trees, cottages, geese, and country maidens. The walls were still papered in thick black-and-cream stripes. The hardwood floor was still covered by the red oriental carpet with the same spark-eaten hole in the corner near the fireplace. The bed had the same feel. And it was still shoved against the wall opposite the door and flanked by two French windows hung with curtains in a red-on-cream striped paisley design. The commode and armoire stood sentry on the wall to the right of the door, just as I remembered. Opposite was the fireplace with its carved and molded mantel, a mirror hanging above.

Same room. But, *sans* Adrien, it had lost its soul. And sleeping there had held more appeal when it had been his room.

I wouldn't be here for long, however. As soon as I had the key to Mademoiselle Dumont's place, I'd be sleeping there.

I debated whether or not to jump into the shower before joining Adrien, but hunger trumped personal hygiene, so I wiggled into my shoes and then wandered down the hall. It looked as though the only thing that had changed was Adrien's presence.

Tasteful oil landscapes on the walls.

The living room, on the right, was decorated with white-painted, lemon-upholstered Louis XVI-style furniture. Straight round backs and columned legs. The spring green paint on the walls was outlined by white molding.

The Henri IV dining room on the left was still medieval, with dark blue-upholstered fringed chairs and a matching narrow table. A country scene tapestry still hung above the buffet.

Then the hall turned left, wrapping around the dining room. Down at the end of its length was the kitchen. It already smelled of espresso. The one thing the Pacific Northwest and France had in common.

Coffee.

The Delaportes' kitchen was very small and very plain without even a window for light. It had the same 12-foot ceilings as the rest of the house, but none of the charm. Apparently, the French don't believe all the hype about the kitchen being the new living room. No cooking islands or stool-equipped breakfast bars. No dining nooks or planning centers.

There was a black-and-white checkerboard tile floor. White walls, white glazed aluminum cabinets that looked like 1950s era. There was the white chest-high refrigerator I remembered from ten years ago, with a microwave perched on top. A stove and oven. No dishwasher. The only nod to the present that could be seen was a deep aluminum sink, under which, on a wire shelf, were stacked pots and pans. The sink wasn't even skirted with a bright Provençal floral or cheery plaid. Tucked behind the door were a stacked miniature washer and dryer. There was only enough room for two people to stand together shoulder-to-shoulder in that kitchen. Since Adrien was busy fixing a tray with espressos, I stood out in the hall and watched him. When he was finished, we took the tray out to the dining room.

I held the demitasse cup to my lips, took a small sip, made a big grimace, and it was gone. I'd drunk it all.

I had finished my espresso in one fell swallow, but that didn't stop Adrien from taking his time. I waited. And waited. And just about the time I had begun thinking that he owned the world's first bottomless demitasse, he set his cup down on the saucer.

Picked up his spoon, gave his coffee a stir. Smiled at me.

"You could pour it into a travel mug."

"Why?"

"So you could drink it while we walk."

"What is this travel mug? Why would I want to do that? Is this what Americans do?"

He was looking at me as if I were Martian. Was it really that strange of an idea?

"This is a *pause café*. A break. One drinks *café* to sit and talk. To relax." He raised his cup toward me. "So…relax."

It took him five more sips to finish.

I counted.

He must have been drinking atomic portions.

After we carried our cups back to the kitchen, I grabbed my backpack and we walked from the apartment toward the Eiffel Tower down rue Saint Dominique. He'd heard of a restaurant across the Champs de Mars, on avenue Suffren, that he wanted to try. I was still starving, and now I was high on caffeine, so anything would have sounded good to me.

Mademoiselle's apartment was supposed to be somewhere near the Eiffel Tower. At least according to Dad. He'd told me the address, but I had trouble remembering French street names. They commemorated people I'd never heard of and events I'd never studied, so they didn't gain any natural foothold in my memory.

Adrien strolled along humming while I speed-walked ahead of him.

A few moments later he grabbed my hand and made me walk beside him. That lasted for about a block.

I've never been one of those girls who can flirt as well as they breathe, who kiss their male friends hello and goodbye on the lips or hold hands with someone they've only known for ten minutes. Not that I think any of that should be reserved until marriage. I was born in the twentieth century, but I think you ought to at least be officially dating someone before you do things that make people think you are.

And, anyway, Adrien's hand over mine was sending feelings through my body that I'm sure he never intended. Fluttery feelings in my stomach, prickles on my scalp, and sudden perspiration behind my ears. So, I gave his hand a squeeze and then dropped it, sort of like the hand-squeeze at the end of a prayer.

Amen. Squeeze. Release.

But then I didn't know what to do with my hands. They seemed awkward. And chilled without the warmth of Adrien's palm. So I shoved them into my pockets. But that didn't feel right either. No one else was walking around with their hands in their pockets. In fact, no one else was walking around in jeans, except obvious tourists who were yelling to each other in English. So I pulled my hands out. But they kept dangling at the ends of my arms next to Adrien. I finally just folded them across my waist and used them to cup my elbows, as if I were freezing to death. Which looked ridiculous in August, but it was the best I could do on short notice with jet lag.

If I hadn't felt so odd and been so hungry, I would have enjoyed the walk. Parisians were returning home. The American-style coffee and sandwich shops were closing down. The tables at the cafés were starting to fill. The bars had been scrubbed. Smells of stale cigarette smoke drifted out of their open doors, but they didn't have any customers yet.

And through the streets echoed the clip-clop of heeled shoes, the cries of children running home for dinner, the distant honks of cars sitting in traffic along the *quais* lining the Seine.

We cut through the Champs de Mars halfway between the Eiffel Tower on our right and the Ecole Militaire on our left. There were several tour buses nosing down the street and several more parked along the sidewalk. A handful of people were jogging, some of them with dogs. A group of teenage boys were kicking a soccer ball back and forth as they walked up the dirt path that swung off toward Ecole Militaire. Another group was actually playing soccer on the vast lawn that stretches dead center between the two monuments.

Without warning, Adrien skipped away and broke into a run to intercept a soccer ball that had spun from the grass onto the dirt path. He went through a series of spins and kicks as he took the ball into custody and worked his way back to the group. But then he was leaping into the grass and running a crazy zigzag pattern toward what the group had marked out as the farthest goal.

The goalie faced off against him. After jigging this way and that, Adrien took his shot. And scored! You'd have thought he was a group favorite the way the other players surrounded him, cheering. A few high fives, a few pats on the butt, and he was sprinting back down the grass toward me.

And again, I felt an unreasonable sort of pride. I'm sure it was just jet lag and an attachment to a familiar person in a foreign place.

Adrien had gone from humming to singing. *"On est champion, on est champion, on est, on est, on est champion…"* At least it was under his breath. But I didn't really understand the words. It sounded like he was calling himself a mushroom. It wouldn't surprise me. With Adrien, you never knew. So I asked him.

He laughed, delighted. *"Non.* Not *champignons,* Claire. *Champions.* The winners. But you can be a mushroom if you want to be. I will let you. I will even sing a song for you." He cleared his throat and then belted out at the top of his lungs, *"On est champignon, on est champignon…"*

We heard a few distant jeers from the corner of the park, and then he relented, stopped singing, and quickened his pace. Within five minutes we were standing in front of the restaurant, La Giberne. They were only able to seat us on the sidewalk, but that was fine by me. A slight breeze was making the city's tendency toward stuffiness bearable. The evenings in this latitude were long in the summer, so Parisians strolled the streets until ten thirty or eleven.

"Quelque-chose à boire?" The waiter had come to ask for drinks.

SIRI L. MITCHELL

Adrien began to order two *kir royales*, but I stopped him. I don't drink.

"Of course, the *décollage*."

I looked down at my chest. What did my chest have to do with anything?

"*Décollage.* The jet lag." His eyes were glinting, and it looked as though he was trying hard to keep the corners of his mouth from turning up.

Of course. Not *décolletage*. He wasn't looking at my chest. If he were, he'd never have found it. He was talking about jet lag. Well, he could chalk it up to jet lag if he wanted to.

"Water?"

I nodded, my cheeks flaming.

The waiter left us alone with the *cartes*, the menus, and I scanned mine for something that would be easy to digest. They had a fixed-price menu for 15 euro and another for 23 euro, but the choices looked too rich for my stomach. I'd forgotten this about myself: When I travel internationally I become both ravenous and nauseous. I can only manage an *omelette* or *croque monsieur*, a toasted ham-and-gruyere-cheese sandwich, the first night. In a restaurant specializing in game and southwestern French cuisine, I was pretty sure I wasn't going to find anything lite or plain. The best I could do was to order *oeufs en gelée* for an entrée and *sole meunière* as a main course. The hard-cooked egg halves in gelatin and the flour-dusted butter-baked fish would probably satisfy my finicky requirements.

Adrien ordered an entrée of six different kinds of *foie gras*, a delicacy made from the livers of corn-feed geese. He followed it with a main dish of *magret de canard* and *pommes sautées* and a half-carafe of some sort of wine. The fat-preserved duck and sautéed potatoes were usually a favorite of mine. If we ever came back, I'd probably order what he had.

When Adrien's drink and my water came, we raised our glasses and drank to each other's health. He'd ordered *gazeuse* water with carbonation, and I must have made a face when I tasted it.

"It is good for the digestion."

Once I'd grown used to it, it wasn't really that bad. I finished the bottle before my eggs arrived, so Adrien ordered me another.

"*Alors*, who is this relative who died and left your father an apartment in the very best part of the city?"

"We don't know. Some sort of cousin."

Adrien waggled his eyebrows. *"Mystères et boules de gomme."*

I couldn't have agreed more. "Definitely a mystery."

He was intent on playing detective. "Who was Mademoiselle?"

"We hardly know anything about her. She was 82 when she died."

"So she was born in…"

"1919, 1920." I'm good. At least with numbers.

"Just after the Great War. You said she never married."

"Did I? She might have been. I don't know for sure."

"Yet you call her Mademoiselle…?"

Well now, I did, didn't I? There must be some reason I assumed she'd never married. "Let's pretend she was single."

Adrien shrugged. "Okay. She is your relative. No. Wait. I have a better idea. We shall pretend she was the Queen of France."

"That is not helpful."

Adrien was trying hard not to laugh. "So sorry."

"What we know is…she was born in 1919 and she was never married." Yep. That was about it. "Your turn."

"Yes. I agree. That is what is known."

"Come on. Do your thing. You're the one who's so clever."

"What do you want me to do with this information? Tell you her favorite color?" He closed his eyes. Put his fingertips to his temples. "Wait. It comes to me. Her favorite color, based on her date of birth and marital status, was…" his eyes sprang open "…I do not know what it was. I am not a magician."

"Just pretend. Pretend you're a detective."

"Ah. This I can do. Let me think, it has been…30 years since I have pretended to be Arsène Lupin, gentleman burglar. Which disguise shall I use as I investigate this mystery?"

"What are you talking about? Be serious, Adrien."

He stretched his arms out, pushed back his sleeves, and rubbed his hands together. "Yes. Okay. We have one Mademoiselle, 82 years old. Wealthy. We can say this because of her address. But she was also a recluse. We assume this because you do not know anything about her, and yet she left your father her estate. She never married, so she did not get her money from a husband. First question: How did she make her money?" He was looking at me as if I could provide an answer.

I couldn't.

"Your father knows nothing about her, so we can assume that she either hid her wealth from her family, or they were too ashamed of how she got this wealth to speak of her."

Hmm. Okay. That made sense. I guess.

"Second question: Why does no one know anything about her?"

"I have no idea."

"I think that is enough questions. If we ever find the answers to them, we will have solved our mystery. We will know who Mademoiselle is. Was."

And at that point, between the time we ordered and the time our entrées came, I wound down. One minute I was talking with Adrien, the next minute the *oeufs en gelée* arrived. And all I could think is that they were staring up at me, out of their molded oval gelatins, like giant eyeballs.

I guess I ate because after a while there wasn't anything left on my plate. I guess Adrien talked to me, because every once in a while I would find myself nodding. I hoped I wasn't agreeing to anything important.

After dessert—for Adrien, not for me—we drifted back the way we had come. I glanced at my watch and it said ten thirty, but I was sure I must have set it wrong, so I asked him.

"Ten thirty. *Oui.*"

"Wow." The last time I'd eaten a three-hour meal had been down in Carcans. Dinner for me in Seattle was usually microwaved leftovers with a side of that morning's newspaper and a diet coke. It wasn't very inspiring cooking for just one.

The sad truth was, I'd never been an inspired cook. Whenever we had group events at church, I'd swing by a wholesaler and pick up a tray of assorted cheesecake slices. Everyone likes cheesecake.

Except me.

So the good thing was that I never had to take any home with me. The other good thing was that I got credit for bringing something everyone liked. My name had become synonymous with cheesecake, and no one thought to ever ask me to bring anything else. At church, the planning for events went like this:

"And for dessert?"

"How about cheesecake?"

"Cheesecake? Sounds good. Claire?"

So how bad a cook was I? I wasn't terrible, but I wasn't good, either. Let's just say that I have never been able to get Jell-O to jiggle. A three-hour meal at my house would consist of chips and salsa, grilled cheese, and ice cream sandwiches. If I were reading a really good book, I could probably stretch the whole thing out to three and a half hours. My other specialty was grilled tuna and cheese. Sometimes I even added tomato slices for extra flair.

We paused at the center of the Champs de Mars.

The Eiffel Tower was glowing in the lingering twilight. I could see now why Paris is called a romantic city. For all the time I'd spent in France, I really didn't know the city that well. We'd flown in and out of it, but we had spent all of our time in Carcans. And thoughts of romance had been far from my mind as a child. If I wasn't looking forward to organizing Mademoiselle's apartment, at least this was a more exotic vacation than I would ever have planned for myself. And maybe, if I was lucky, it would allow Brian to resolve some of his issues.

He hadn't been that clear on what they were. They involved something about whether a pastor should date a member of his congregation. Like he should go to a bar to find a wife instead? And something about a previous girlfriend flipping out after they'd broken up. It's not as though I could make any promises about that sort of thing, but I generally wasn't suicidal, and we were both adults, weren't we?

Frankly, I felt as if I were being punished for the excesses of his previous relationship. I admired that he was being careful with my feelings, and with his, but there's careful and then there's gutless.

If I knew what my feelings were about the whole tangled mess, then

I might have asked Adrien what he thought. But then, I already knew what he thought about Brian, didn't I? Guess I was ahead of the game.

"I suppose that you wish Brian were here in place of me."

"No." My answer surprised even me. Because among all my many thoughts about Brian, that had not been one of them.

Adrien smiled, threw an arm around my shoulder, and, singing something about a black cat in the moonlight, walked me back to the apartment.

What did he have to be so happy about?

Chapter 5

A̶t the apartment building Adrien showed me the code for the door to the building.

"It is this one." I watched him punch a series of numbers into the keypad beside the entrance. "You try it." He stood aside for me.

I raised my hand, held up a finger and...nothing happened. "What is it again?"

He leaned in and reentered the code. "You see? It is a pattern: 05-26-42. A straight line and then two diagonals."

A straight line and two diagonals? I'd almost flunked geometry. But I'd gotten a 4.0 in calculus. Go figure.

"Try it."

I tried. I failed.

"There is no key for this door, Claire. The only way in is by code."

Couldn't we just figure out some sort of secret handshake? "Okay...06-52-24?"

Adrien sighed and pounded in the numbers once more.

There had to be some way to remember. "What is it again?"

"It is 05-26-42."

Six numbers, just like a date. May 26, 1942. May 26, 1942. Okay, but what was the significance of that date? A really nice day in spring during WW II. Wow. How depressing. Especially if your boyfriend...no, your fiancé...had been ordered to the front?...arrested?...accused of being a spy. Tied up, paraded to the center of your village in central France, and then executed. By a firing squad.

Yep.

That would be depressing. My fingers flew across the keypad. The lock clicked.

Adrien pushed open the door and held it for me. "Well done. You will not forget?"

May 26, 1942? Not a chance. I'd remember it for the rest of my life.

Once we got to the apartment, he gave me the key. "I have another. This one I give you is the spare." He dropped it into my open palm, and it nearly caused a hyperextension of the elbow.

"Thanks?" I was going to have to do some serious weight lifting if I was expected to tote that key around town.

He took a deep breath, puffed his cheeks, and let the air out in a sigh. "So. Tomorrow morning, I go to church. You would like to come?"

Adrien's always doing something unexpected, but this seemed a bit un-Adrien-like to me. "Church? As in *church* church? You don't have to go just because I do." I'd forgotten that the next day was Sunday.

"*Non, non.* This is not about you. Once one decides that there must be a God, then one is compelled to find out about him. Do you not think so? So you will come?"

"Yes."

I woke at six with a start, and it took me a moment to realize where I was.

Grabbing a handful of my toiletries, which Adrien had arranged on top of the commode, I lurched down the hall and stowed them in the bathroom. The one that had the bath, not the closet with the toilet.

I suppose it makes good sense to separate the two if you have guests often. It allows one person to use the bathroom—the one with the toilet—while another person takes a bath or shower. But in my opinion, as a guest, it was much more convenient to have everything in the same room to avoid having to alternate between the two in various stages of undress.

I wish I could say that I jumped into the shower and was done in ten minutes. But here's the thing: How do you take a shower in a bathtub that has no shower curtain or shower door and in which the shower head is stuck in its holder on the back wall about six inches from the top of the tub? I probably should just have taken a bath, but I wanted to be quick about things. And it had been quick in the old days, because my mother and I would take turns. I would hold the shower head for her and then she would hold the shower head for me. And then we would both mop up the bathroom floor together.

It was an entirely different experience showering solo.

But I did it, and then I wrapped a towel around myself and padded back down the hall. I opened my dresser drawers and put together a combination of a polo shirt and shorts. I had no idea what Adrien's church was like, but polo shirts and shorts were my only choice, so if I were underdressed, they'd just have to crucify me.

He came up to the apartment to get me.

As I was getting into the car, I noticed a guitar on the backseat.

He got into the driver's seat, started the ignition, and swung out into the street.

"I didn't know you played."

He flashed a smile. "Every adolescent boy plays the guitar. Growing old is inevitable. Growing up is not."

It was as good a motto for Adrien as anything I had ever thought of.

He drove through the lush Bois de Boulogne with its sinuous paths, past the Grande Cascade waterfall, the Hippodrome de Longchamps racing track, and the windmill that looked as though it had been transplanted from Holland. We crossed a bridge and drove through Suresnes and up the hill into Reuil Malmaison. There, tucked away on tree-lined rue des Bons Raisins, was the last thing I'd expected to find: an English-speaking church.

Adrien parked the car along the street a block away. As we walked toward the church, he waved at the occupants of passing cars and stopped to introduce me to people walking our direction. By the time we got to the church, our twosome had turned into a dozensome.

In the concrete courtyard in front of the church, he joined a group of people speaking English in various accents. There was a family he introduced me to from South Africa. A couple from Cote d'Ivoire. A woman from Germany. A man from Alabama. Adrien told a few jokes and asked a few questions. Offered a few kisses, clasped a few hands, and then drew me out of the group and into the building.

The pastor was standing by the door to the sanctuary, so Adrien introduced me to him too. The pastor reminded him about the following month's council meeting, and Adrien assured him that he would be there. Then Adrien held out his guitar case and gestured me into the church.

It was a rectangular room, finished in simple tongue-and-groove paneling painted a creamy yellow. The floors were covered in deep turquoise-blue carpeting. The "pews" were assembled chairs. The pulpit stood at the center of the front of the room, and a screen was pulled down behind it.

An old-fashioned hymn board listed two numbers.

A bearded man was playing the piano.

Adrien led me to a row near the front and then left me to set up his guitar. I smiled when he lifted it out of the case. Only Adrien would think of playing a star-shaped, heavy metal-style guitar in church. He plugged it in, played a tentative riff, and then launched into "Stairway to Heaven."

The teenage boy sitting behind the drum set laughed, loving it. Those still loitering outside ambled in.

Adrien smiled after he was done, bowed, and then raised a hand toward the boy on the drums, who launched into a drum solo that was notable only for its deafening loudness. Mercifully, it didn't last long, and when it was over, the pianist began playing something that everyone seemed to know the words to.

I rose to my feet when everyone else did. It was then that I discovered the reason for the smile that had hovered across my face since I'd set foot on the property. It felt like family. It felt like coming home.

Even more so after the service.

A petite blond woman zoomed right up to me. "Hi, I'm Cynthia. Haven't seen you before. You must be new." She held on to my arm with both of her hands as she spoke. The gesture sent a stack of colorful plastic bracelets clacking down her arm. Her hair was cut into a thick simple bob, and it bounced as she emphasized her words with animated gestures. The magenta shoes she wore somehow matched her orange dress.

"I'm Claire." Without wanting to be obvious, I tried to spot Adrien.

"So you live here then? In Paris?"

"No. Just visiting."

"Oh, that's too bad. I was getting ready to add you to the group. I'm always on the lookout for new B.S.ers."

"B.S.ers?"

"Bachelors and Spinsters. The B.S.ers." The woman winked. "That's what we call ourselves."

"They let you say that?"

"It's a lot better than being called 'singles' as if it were a terminal disease. As if we were just waiting around to transition to 'married couples' or 'parents.' Right, Adrien?"

I hadn't noticed his arrival and turned around to find him at my shoulder.

"Cynthia, *ma biche. Ça va?*" He leaned in to kiss her cheeks while she did the same. "You have met Claire, then?"

"Yes! Where'd you pick her up?" Cynthia's brown eyes darted between Adrien and me.

"In Carcans when she was about four years old."

"Our families are old friends."

Those quick eyes looked as if they were making calculations. "You know what they say about old friends: old friends, best friends. Anyway, are you coming over to the Chinese restaurant?"

"*Non.* Not today." Adrien placed a hand on my back, moving me toward the door.

But Cynthia put a hand on my arm. "Are you busy this week? Want to get together?"

I blinked. Surprised. "Um. Sure."

"How about tomorrow?"

I glanced at Adrien. He was looking down at me. He shrugged.

"Um. Yeah. Okay."

"Where should we meet? Where are you staying?"

"She is staying at my parents'. In the seventh."

"Have you ever been to the Rodin Museum?"

I shook my head.

"Me neither. So I'll meet you in front of Ecole Militaire at…"

Adrien cleared his throat. "Invalides is closer…?"

"Ecole Militaire, Invalides…I always get them mixed up. Okay. We'll meet at Invalides… let's say about ten. Sound good?"

She didn't wait for me to decide what it sounded like.

"Fabulous! I'll see you tomorrow. Bye!" She leaned in, kissed my cheeks, and then was gone like a figment of my imagination.

I hoped I'd be up for it. At least I wouldn't have to worry about making conversation. I was sure she'd do the work for both of us.

Instead of walking back to the car, Adrien hefted the guitar case over his shoulder and turned in the opposite direction. "There is a market just down the street every Sunday."

Sure enough, a block later, we came to Marché des Goddards. The one-story warehouse structure, hemorrhaging people, lay to our left. We walked through an opening protected by wide dangling strips of clear plastic. I was accosted by the smells: fruit, fish, and cheese. Fresh bread and fresh meat. Adrien made the rounds, collecting a baguette, several wedges of cheese, slices of proscuitto wrapped in paper. Several fruit *tartelettes* and a bottle of wine.

He told me his plan only after I'd noticed that he wasn't driving us back the way we'd come. "I thought we would picnic at Versailles."

"Versailles, the town?"

"Versailles, the château."

"You're allowed?"

"*Bah…oui.*"

He drove straight through the center of town and up to the outer gate of the château so that I could get the tourist's view. It was both more immense and uglier than I had imagined. Not castlelike at all. More of a palace or a very big official-looking government building. We got caught at the light. Stopped long enough to see that the guys peddling cokes from buckets filled with ice were offering a good deal. Then the light changed and Adrien drove right by.

"But—where are we going?"

"To the other side." He turned left when there was a break in the stone wall that surrounded the grounds. He pulled into a parking space in the lot outside the wall, walked around to open my door, and then gathered our picnic supplies. We walked through the shaded wood for a while before breaking out onto a small arm of a man-made waterway that had been cut from the surrounding park.

Adrien found us a suitable spot of not-so-patchy grass and then opened all of our packages and arranged lunch in a tempting display. He took a knife from the pocket of his pants and proceeded to cut the baguette into tartine-sized pieces, reserving a third of the bread for the cheese.

He used the knife to pry the cork from the bottle of wine and then looked at me, aghast.

"Claire, I must apologize."

"For what?"

"I had forgotten that you do not drink wine and I failed to bring any water." He looked very grave. As though he'd committed the worst crime in history.

"It's okay. I'll be fine. It's not that hot out."

He flashed his gleaming teeth and then got to work on making me a sandwich before making his own. Finished with that, he turned to his side and propped himself up on one arm. He took a swig of wine straight from the bottle. Sent a glance in my direction. "You do not want just a little?"

"No. Thanks."

We ate in companionable silence, watching baby blue-and-white rowboats navigate the thick green waters of the canal. An occasional bird flat-footed in for a landing.

"So tell me about church."

"When I first started coming? A couple years ago. I met the pastor at a reception at the Ambassador's Residence. For *la Rentrée*."

"What's that?"

"*La Rentrée?* The Return. In September, when everyone comes back from holidays, when school begins again. The *Assemblée Nationale* convenes. So, I meet him at this reception. I began to talk with him, and then before I even realized, the party was over. I had not known that Christians could be so smart. He is very intellectual, our pastor. A doctorate in philosophy. In any case, I began attending and have not stopped."

"And now you're on the church council?"

Adrien looked at me. He shrugged. "Yes. I am a member of the council. Guilty as you have stated."

"I never think of you as a Christian, Adrien."

He laughed. Teetered on his arm, lost his balance, and collapsed. He lay flat on his back on the grass. "Then we are even because I never think of you as a pagan."

"Ha-ha. I just never…you have to admit that you've never acted like a Christian before."

"What? I am a murderer? I cheat, I steal, I lie?"

"You're just not Mr. Christian, that's all."

"But has not God made us each with our own personalities? Knowing him should allow us to become even more like ourselves, not more like a stereotype. This is why I became a Christian. To be more me. Self-actualization."

That was an interesting reason for conversion. But was it an actual, legitimate reason? Was it on the approved list of reasons for becoming a Christian?

We watched the boats for a while longer.

"If one walked this canal, the Grand Canal, one would walk more than four miles. Louis XIV sailed ships on it; one of them had over 30 cannons. And nobles would float on it in gondolas brought from Venice."

"Mmm." I was lying on my back, watching the clouds swirl the cornflower blue sky into drifts of cotton candy.

"I cannot offer you a gondolier from Venice, but I can rent you a boat and I will row it. And I can sing. But not in Italian."

"If you row, I'll come, but only on the condition that you don't sing."

"You wound my heart, Claire." He grabbed me by the hands and pulled me off the ground. We carted our trash to the rowboat vendor and threw it away. Except for the wine bottle. Adrien had corked it and toted it along at his side. "In case you are dying of thirst."

What a gentleman.

He chose what looked to be a seaworthy boat. He got in first and then helped me in. I placed a hand on each side and slithered onto my seat. I might live in Seattle, I might savor an occasional view of Puget Sound, but I wasn't one who lived my life wishing I were a mermaid or the captain of a pirate ship.

The vendor gave us a shove, and then Adrien bent and leaned on the oars, rowing away from the pier and into the middle of the canal.

For a while I looked at the sites. Sunlight glinting off statues in the distance. The château at the end of the canal, never seeming to get any closer. Couples, dozens of them, sitting on the grass. Lying on the grass. All of them kissing.

What gave them the right?

Why should they be able to impose their romance on my life? Were they so absorbed in themselves that they didn't care about other people? The couple grappling on the ground over there. The couple feeding each other lunch over here. The couple standing, midpath, their bodies so close they looked like a single person with two heads.

Who kissed like that?

Brian didn't. Wouldn't have been caught dead doing it. Pastors can't go around groping their girlfriends in public. It's probably the first thing they teach you in seminary.

"You should visit the châteaux on the Loire."

I started.

The boat rocked.

I turned to see Adrien watching me. "Those châteaux are worth seeing."

"You don't like Versailles?"

He shrugged eloquently. One of those French shrugs that contains the beginning, middle, and end of the presentation of an opinion without uttering a single word.

"It *is* sort of…big."

"*Ah, oui.*"

"And it's not very…pretty."

"*Bah…non.*"

"I don't think I'd ever buy it."

He laughed. "I do not think that the président of the République could ever buy it. *Non.* What is needed in a château is grace, a defensive position, and a good story. A history. I would buy ten châteaux in the Loire before I would ever buy this one. We must go, while you are here."

"To the Loire?"

"It is not so very far."

He rowed on for several minutes and then finally pulled the oars in and stowed them. He uncorked the bottle. Took a sip. Replaced the cork. Leaning back, he slouched in his seat, and put his arms under his head. Closed his eyes. "It is too hot to work so hard."

It sure was.

I tried to follow his example, but if I slouched, my legs would have ended up tangled with his. Sighing in frustration, I sat up and leaned forward over my knees.

There was water in the bottom of the boat. Not a lot. Just enough to trap dirt and make gentle sloshes as the wind nudged us. I sat up. "Do you ever wish you had a boat?"

"*Non.*" He hadn't even cracked open an eye. "The two happiest days in the life of a boat owner: the day he buys the boat and the day he sells it."

"But you could drift around whenever you wanted to. Sail in the Mediterranean."

"If you were willing to work at it. You have to have someplace to store it. You have to have something to move it. You have to spend your free time cleaning it. *Non, merci.*" He sat up. "The best thing is to have a friend who has a boat. A very generous friend who has a boat."

"What *would* you like to have then? What's your pipe dream?"

"My pipe dream? But I do not smoke. Maybe one cigar from time to time." He paused. Pinned me with a stern look. "Do you speak of hashish? Because I do not smoke this. And neither should you."

"No! A pipe dream. It's a…dream you have even though it never has a chance of coming true."

"Ah. Yes, I see. *Un château en espagne.*"

"A castle in Spain?"

"The French kings used to reward their knights with a castle in Spain. The knight would travel with much anticipation to reach this castle, but in arriving he would find that it is already occupied. By a Spaniard who had not met the French king and who had not the least idea of the castle being given to someone else. And so the knight, unprepared to fight for this castle, would turn around and go back to France. *Un château en espagne.* The unattainable dream." He closed his eyes again. Settled back into his seat.

"So if you don't want a boat, what do you want…an airplane? A second home?"

"*Non.* Not really. Once I almost bought a motorcycle. It was beautiful. Really sexy. But then I realized it would probably sit in the garage all winter because I would not ride it in the rain. However, I would like to find a complete set of Victor Hugos. First editions. But mostly, I already have what I want. Good food, good wine. An apartment filled with things that I like. The only thing missing is someone to share it with." He opened one eye. "And this cannot be a *château en espagne.*"

The funny thing was that usually Adrien was surrounded by people the way he was at church that morning. He was a natural leader who drew people toward himself like gravity. He should have been married by now.

Easy for me to say, but it's true.

He should have been. Probably could have been a dozen times. To models or actresses, even. He was that kind of guy. Or maybe not. Suddenly, I realized I had made a discovery.

Adrien was lonely.

I could sympathize. I made my loneliness go away by plunging my nose into a book or a spade into my flower beds or my rear end into the couch to watch TV. But only on Wednesdays and Sundays. That's when my shows were on.

"And you?"

"Me what?" My mind was spinning its wheels on the thought of Adrien being lonely. I'd forgotten what we'd been talking about.

"What do you want? Why is it that you work so hard without taking any vacation?"

In fact, I was taking a vacation. And sick leave. And contemplating asking for leave without pay, but that wasn't what he was asking and I knew it. I pushed a strand of hair back behind my ear. "It pays my mortgage."

I was stranded at the University of Washington after graduation. The state economy, always lagging that of the rest of the nation, had been in a depression. I used my business degree to find a nice, secure, union-represented job as an administrative assistant for the French department, and gradually, through the university's professional development courses, had worked my way into a position as a budget coordinator. It was a low-stress job with a small, but dependable, wage increase every year. I'd never in my wildest dreams imagined life as a budget coordinator. Maybe as a ballerina or an astronaut. But once I'd grown used to it and become comfortable with the job, I'd found it wasn't a bad way to live. It entitled me to a subsidized bus pass, access to the university library system, and reduced prices for Husky football tickets. The benefits were good even if I never took advantage of them.

"So the house? This is your dream?"

Retirement without a house paid off seemed like the worst sort of nightmare to me. The kind you can never wake up from. So when I pictured my life, I pictured working. At least for another 28 years. I was trying to be sensible. If I had to go it alone through life, I figured the least I could do was pay my own way. But when the question was put to me so baldly, I had to admit that the answer was no. "Are you asking what would make me happy?"

Adrien pursed his lips. Thought a moment. *"Non.* We each make our own happiness. If one is not happy, then one is to blame for it and not a circumstance. Happiness is not something that can be put off for a future time or acquired like a new tie. One either is happy or one is not. That is an interesting question, 'Is Claire happy?' and I will ask it some other time, but the one I wanted was 'What do you want?'"

What did I want?

That was a more interesting question to me than "Is Claire happy?" What did happiness have to do with anything important?

What did I want?

I wanted a kiss. One of those kisses. The kind that didn't care if anyone was watching. That's what I wanted. But Brian would never be able to give it to me.

At least not in public.

Because he cared too much about what other people thought. I mean, what would they say if they saw him locked in a passionate embrace? Those people who might say something had been present in our relationship from the start, and I was getting really tired of them. Although they might have said lots of things, they never had. But even the threat of their unspoken accusations had a direct impact on our relationship. "They" always seemed to have a larger vote in our relationship than I did.

It's not that I didn't want my life to be an example. It's not that I didn't admire Brian for trying to treat me with respect. But I felt like the living room in the house I grew up in. It was beautiful, filled with gorgeous antiques. But I was never allowed to go in there; never allowed to sit on the furniture. In my opinion, there's no point in having a living room if you can't do some living in it.

And there's no point in having a relationship if there's no relating going on.

It's not as though I wanted him to jump in bed with me, but I felt like his pet dog. I was surviving with two pats on the head and a ruffle of my hair. I might as well be a dog. Then maybe at least I'd get a pat on the butt once in while.

I wished Brian cared about me more than he cared about what other people might say or think.

But the question was, would he ever be able to give me one of those kisses in private? Because he hadn't yet. We'd kissed, of course, but it hadn't been one of those kinds of kisses.

And it came to me then what I wanted. I wanted someone different than Brian. He was nice, and I could build a nice life with him, but it would never be filled with passion. And it wouldn't have been based on love. "Love." It leaped from my lips, and for a moment I didn't think I had spoken the word aloud.

But then a slow smile crossed Adrien's face and he sat up. "You see, I always knew that you were the daughter of your father. I knew that you were French. You just never admitted this to yourself before."

Suddenly, I was parched.

We drove back into town, parked in a free space near the Delaportes' and had dinner at an Italian place. Adrien walked me back to the apartment before going home.

"So. You know where is the telephone?"

"Yes. In the living room."

"*Oui.* I will give you my phone number. And you know the code? For the door?"

"Yes, 05-26-42."

"*Oui.* And you know the number for SAMU? Just in case?"

Samu? I was tempted to just say yes, but what if Samu was the local pizza parlor? I'd sure like to have that number around just in case. "No. What's SAMU?"

"*Service d'aide médicale urgence.* If you have a medical emergency."

"Oh. Like 9-1-1."

"*Bah…non.* It is the number 15. Can you remember this?"

Fifteen? Why 15? Why not 13? Or 16? Or even 17? The summer I was 17 was the worst summer of my life. "Yes. If I have an emergency, I will dial 15."

"And then call me."

"Okay. I'll dial 15. And if I'm not having a heart attack or choking, you'll be the next person I'll call."

"And if there is a fire?"

"Then I'll die in my sleep and never know."

"Claire. Pay attention."

"Adrien, just—write them all down and I'll put them by the phone. I'll be fine."

As soon as I got upstairs, I called Brian.

"Claire! How are you?"

"I'm fine."

"How's your dad? I've been praying for him."

"Thanks. He's getting better every day. Brian? The reason I'm calling you is that I'm in Paris."

"I thought your parents lived in Florida."

"They do. But there's been a death in the family, and since Dad couldn't fly, I had to come instead."

"Are you coming back soon?"

"I don't know. I hope so."

There was silence for a moment. "Um, Claire? You know that girl? The one from my last church?"

"The one you said you should never have dated? The one that flipped out?"

"Yeah. Well…she's in town."

"In Seattle?"

"Yes."

"She's not stalking you or anything, is she?"

He laughed. "No. It's not like that. Things are…she's better."

"That's great. I'm glad."

"And…well, the thing is—"

"Brian. I really need to say something before you say anything else." I told him then that it was time to move on.

For both of us.

Chapter 6

The next morning Adrien had to go to work. It was his last day before vacation. He left me with instructions to make an appointment with Mademoiselle's lawyer. And if the lawyer would give me the key, then Adrien would come with me that evening to see the apartment.

By the time I was done bathing and had dressed, it was eight thirty. I called the lawyer's office and found out he wasn't in yet. Left a message. Then I went through the kitchen cupboards trying to find something to eat. Adrien's mother was a wonderful cook, but she cooked from scratch, so there weren't boxes of macaroni and cheese or cans of SpaghettiOs. I opened the fridge to take a look. There wasn't any bread, but there was a loaf of not quite stale brioche, a slab of *pâté*, a bowl of jam, and a jar of *cornichons*, tiny sour pickles. And lots of eggs. But if I ate any more eggs, I'd probably sprout wings. So I decided to find a grocery store or eat out. Or maybe both.

I set off east down rue Saint Dominique. I passed several shoe stores and some small women's boutiques. A children's clothing store. It was only when I got to the church, St. Pierre du Gros Caillou, that I found what I was looking for: a bakery. There was a line, but I was so hungry that I'd run out of steam. I didn't have the energy to search for another. While I waited I tried to decide what to buy. All the choices lined up in the display cases didn't make it any easier.

There were *opéras* with alternating layers of cake and cream. Tiny strawberry and blackberry *tartelettes*. Cylinders of dark chocolate filled with chocolate mousse and dusted with cocoa powder. And there were

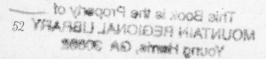

macarons in pastel colors with pistachio, raspberry, or lemon fillings to match.

And then there were my favorites: *religieuses.* One small chocolate- or *café*-covered cream puff stacked on a large one; both filled with chocolate or *café* cream. The shape brought to mind the silhouette of a nun, or *religieuse.*

Not, of course, that all nuns are fat. Or round.

Standing guard in the bins on the wall behind them were tall baguettes, thin *bâtards,* and, on shelves, fat rounds loaves of country and nut breads.

Even if I were able to get into Mademoiselle's apartment this after-noon, I didn't count on being able to do any cleaning; I'd be at the Delaportes' another night or two. Which meant at least two more breakfasts. So first on my list would be two baguettes. I liked them as *tartines* in the morning, cut into long pieces and then halved length-wise, spread with jam or nutella. Two baguettes should last four days. Two baguettes and…it was my turn.

Two baguettes, two *religieuses* (one for now and one for later), and two strawberry *tartelettes.* And another baguette. Because if we ate one for dinner, then I'd still have two left. Or maybe four, because if I had a sandwich for lunch tomorrow and the next day I'd need another…and if I did that, maybe I'd want something for dessert after. So I ordered two *opéras* as well.

I watched as the clerk wrapped the *religieuses* in tiny tents of paper and taped them shut. Then he set the other pastries in a box, put a lid on, and tied it with a ribbon. The box went into a plastic bag and was topped by the two tents. The baguettes were handed over the counter to me just as they were. And it cost about 20 euros, which, converted to dollars, was about…20 dollars!

Notice how fast I made that conversion? That's why I'm a budget coordinator. Twenty euros of my parents' money gone in a flash. At this rate, I'd be broke in…150 days. So I was fine. Everything was okay. Except for my guilt factor, which automatically added a "0" to every price tag. I'd skipped right over the "Spoiled and Loving It" chapter in the *How to Be an Only Child* handbook.

I rationalized the cost by telling myself that Adrien was giving up a lot more than 20 dollars to help me out. The least I could do was feed him. My parents would approve of that.

After I'd stepped out of the bakery, I had a little debate with myself: *religieuse* now or later? Since I had two, if one disappeared on my way down the street, it wouldn't make much of a difference, would it? Besides, I was in Paris.

Eat well for a week or two, diet for the rest of my life.

With that worked out, I drifted down rue Cler a ways before I found a seat on a curb on a quiet part of the street. I had started to take a tent out of the bag when I realized that I was receiving strange glances. Looking up and down the street, although I saw many people walking with bags full of food, none of them had sat down on the sidewalk to eat. Even the buildings seemed to lean in toward the street as the windows glared their disapproval.

When in Rome, right?

I plucked the top off the chocolate *religieuse* and popped it into my mouth, hoping it would quiet my mutinous stomach until I got back to the apartment. I stood and resumed my walk.

At the top of the block, across rue de Grenelle, were fruit and vegetable vendors, their stalls heaped with produce. There was a butcher, pieces of meat hanging from his shop's ceiling. There were restaurants filling the pedestrian-only street with sidewalk seating and, walking a bit farther, I found what I was looking for: a *fromager*. A cheese guy.

It was a shop flanked by two doors. Before I stepped inside, I began breathing through my mouth. Cheeses lined the walls of the small store and a single aisle made a loop that started at the first door and ended at the second. Much as I loved cheese, I hated the smell of lots of them piled together at room temperature.

I passed by the *fromages bleu* coursing with mold veins, the creamy goat cheeses rolled into logs and dipped in ashes or formed into bells or pyramids, the firmer cheeses like Cantal and the various Tommes.

And then I found the Brie. Small wheels of brand-name Brie were packed in boxes. A huge wheel of Brie de Meaux sat in the open air on a wooden board. Next to it were plastic-wrapped wedges. It was one of these that I poked for texture. I like mine slightly oozy. I selected one and carried it to the cash register.

After leaving the *fromager*, I found a *boucher* and went inside to buy some meat for dinner. They had small roasts netted in string, whole skinned rabbits complete with their white bunny tails, trays mounded with ground meats, legs of lamb, and chops of veal. But without a recipe to follow, I had no idea what I'd need to make a meal.

I left before anyone could ask me what I wanted and surfaced again next door at the *traiteur*. It was more what I had in mind. Like an upscale deli, it had things in its cases that were ready to eat.

My ungrateful stomach growled.

I asked for a small container of *tabbouleh* made of couscous mixed with lemon juice and mint, and four pork medallions stuffed with dates. On my way back down the street, I stopped at a produce seller to buy the ingredients for a green salad. I started to choose them myself, from the sidewalk area that was staffed by a worker, but then he frowned at me and confiscated my head of lettuce. I'm a quick learner. After that, I pointed. I chose what, and he chose which one or ones.

And then I had to figure out how to carry everything home.

The four baguettes I tucked under an arm. That was a good place to start. But then I had the plastic bag from the bakery, the wedge of cheese from the *fromager*, the paper bag from the *traiteur*, and another plastic bag from the produce seller. And I couldn't really set the baguettes down on the ground in order to rearrange the other purchases. So I set the paper bag on the ground. The cheese went in on top of the pork.

No. That wasn't right.

The pastries came out of the plastic bag. The *tabbouleh* and the pork went in. Then the box of the pastries and the cheese and *religieuses* on top.

That worked.

So I headed home. Baguettes under one arm and a plastic bag in each hand. Never mind that I started getting cramps in my armpit and the carrots and tomatoes barreled into my knee at every step.

I made it to the apartment and into the kitchen before the baguettes slid out from under my arm and onto the floor. I shoved everything else into the fridge. Small as it was, it instantly went from empty to full. I put the baguettes on the counter, and they took up all the counter space. Then I remembered that half-eaten *religieuse* and fished it out of the bag. While I nibbled at it, I found a knife and bisected one of the baguettes. By the time I'd spread jam on top, I was done with the cream puff.

And my entire breakfast, sad to say, was eaten in the tiny kitchen with my back against the sink. It seemed a shame to have to transport everything down the hall and into the dining room when it was only me.

By that time it was nine thirty, so I went into the living room and called the lawyer's office. He was out, but his secretary implied that he was a very busy man and probably would not be able to see me until the beginning of September since he was planning to go on vacation at the end of the week. I left another message stating my name, Mademoiselle's name, and the fact that if he didn't see me before he left on vacation, then he wouldn't have the chance to see me at all since I was planning on being back in America well before the beginning of September.

I got the feeling the secretary didn't think this would make a difference.

I went back to the kitchen and cleaned up my mess. Washed my plate and put everything back in the drawers and cupboards. Then took the broom hiding behind the door and swept up all the bread crumbs where the baguettes had fallen on the floor.

My eyes had been drooping and I had been yawning my head off while I was cleaning, so it seemed like a good time for a nap. But then I remembered Cynthia.

I was supposed to meet her.

In 15 minutes.

Not a problem. Ecole Militaire was just down the street. I walked along sun-speckled sidewalks straight up avenue Bosquet. Got to Ecole Militaire. Stood in front of the gate, staring at the Eiffel Tower.

I waited ten minutes before I realized something might be wrong.

And then I remembered the Ecole Militaire/Invalides mix-up at church. And that's when I realized that I was mixed-up.

I sprinted down avenue de la Motte Picquet, skidded around the corner to rue de Grenelle, and practically ran right into Cynthia.

She had been floating down the sidewalk, resplendent in a fly-away halter dress of deep purple and emerald green. "Hi! I was just thinking you might be waiting in front of Ecole Militaire. Which would have been fine. But anyway, how are you? It's so nice to have someone to do something with. I'm a teacher, so I have summers off. But I don't have the means to spend them along the Riviera. And everyone else is working or away on vacation. So anyway, you still want to see it?"

I nodded.

"Great! Let's go." We walked in front of Invalides and its gold-domed church. Rounded the corner to boulevard des Invalides and then turned onto the quieter avenue de Varenne. Paid our money at the gatehouse and stepped into the well-manicured garden of Hôtel Biron, host of the Musée Rodin.

And that's about all I remember of the outside of the museum. Cynthia plied me with questions about my stay in Paris, my job, and my life until we were inside.

I placed the conversation on autopilot and took a look around as we entered Hôtel Biron.

The building itself was something I could admire. It wasn't that much older than the Delaportes' building. In spite of how it was spelled, it wasn't a hotel, but a private mansion, built in a style typical of the mid-1700s. A grand, double-winged structure with the dignified air of a mini château.

Not meant to be representative of a particular era in history, it was furnished in a simple manner with Rodin's own furniture. And visitors were actually invited to sit on it.

I was eying a chair when Cynthia's words barged into my thoughts. "I'm not much into art. Rodin, Van Gogh, Picasso. They seem the same to me."

Really? A sculptor, a painter who cut his ear off, and an infamous womanizing weirdo? I really, really wanted to sit on the furniture. The opportunity caused my secret historian's heart to skip a beat or two. I surreptitiously took a try.

Oh, it was nice.

I got up and looked around. Cynthia trailed me, still talking.

We moved from room to room, posing here and there to pretend we were appreciating the art. My conscience niggled at me. I decided I'd better keep up my end of the conversation. "So how long have you lived here?"

"Me? Seven glorious years."

"Where did you come from?"

"Florida."

"My parents live there."

"Really? Where?"

"Naples."

"I was farther south."

"Don't you miss the beach?"

"I've never met one I didn't want to bulldoze."

"I know! The water's—"

"Too warm to be refreshing."

"And the sand's—"

"Too hot to even walk on."

"And the sun—"

"Burns my skin to a sizzle."

We stopped and grinned at each other as if we were long-lost sisters.

"Is your family still there?" It was quite a move, from Florida to France, if it were permanent.

"Mostly."

"And you don't think of going back?"

"Never. If they want to see me, they can come here. They complain all the time, but this is my city. This is where I belong."

She looked about my age. Give or take a few years. "So you've always been single?"

"Always. But not happy about it. Not until I moved here."

"Paris made you happy to be single?"

"No. Paris made me happy to be me. I like my life now. If someone comes along, that's fine. But I've quit looking. It takes too much energy. If there *is* a person for me, he'll just have to take out a billboard or send me an e-mail. I'm too busy to do the 'does he like me/doesn't he like me' routine. I mean, we're grown-ups. Let alone the 'you're the only single man in church over 30; you must be my future husband' thing. I am not going to contort my personality 43 different ways just to make myself the perfect person for some unattached guy just because he goes to church."

"You honestly don't care if you spend the rest of your life by yourself?"

"Me? I'm great company! Don't you think? I'm the most fascinating person I know."

Cynthia was my new hero.

"So what's with you and Adrien?"

"Nothing. Family friends."

"Are you sure? Because there's something about the way he looks at you…"

"I'm sure."

"And you've never wished there could be something?"

"Not never ever, but you've seen how he is. He's flirty with everyone. So you can't trust what you see. Or think you feel. Because he's never serious."

"Are you sure?"

"Trust me." She didn't look convinced. And she didn't look as if she were going to leave it alone. So I told her something I've never told anyone. "I'm speaking from experience. The summer I was 17, I had a huge crush on him. The whole schoolgirl thing. Couldn't eat. Couldn't sleep."

"Wrote Claire Delaporte on everything you owned just to see what it looked like?"

"Basically. Our families spent August together at the beach. Near Paulliac. I was 17 and he was 23, and I followed him around that summer like a lost puppy. But he flirted with me the whole time. It wasn't all my fault."

"I believe you."

"So I got it into my head that he liked me. My whole goal for the summer was to get him to kiss me. But then halfway through our vacation, he had to go back to Paris for the weekend. Before he left, he said, 'Don't go anywhere or my heart will miss you.'" I could still hear him whisper those words. Still feel him brushing my hair from my forehead. "And then he kissed me on the nose."

"Oh, no."

"Oh, yes. On the nose. So it was clearly a brother-sister thing, right?" Cynthia grimaced. Nodded.

"Okay. So I spent the next two days plotting. By the time he returned, I had it all planned. I put together a basket with supplies for a dune-side moonlit picnic. I left a note on his bed telling him where to find me. There were candles, a blanket, bread, cheese. Grapes."

"So you could pluck them from their stems and feed them to him?"

"One by one. You get the picture. So there I was, waiting in the dunes. Candles were planted in the sand. Flames were flickering. It was perfect. I waited two hours. And then I had to go to the bathroom. So I ducked into a valley between two dunes."

"And when you got back?"

"When I got back, Adrien was there."

"And?"

"He was with his girlfriend. And they were kissing in between grapes."

"So you never got your kiss."

"Never got my kiss. But I did learn my lesson."

I got back to the apartment at four and thought I'd take a half hour nap, wake up, and call the lawyer back. That might have worked if I hadn't slept until six.

When I woke, it was with the thought that I'd heard something. I couldn't say exactly what, but it seemed as though a sound was still echoing in my ears. I listened for a moment.

Heard nothing out of the ordinary.

Just cars thumping past the building, the occasional voice or honk. I slipped out of bed and cracked open the door. Listened some more. Then I crept down the hall toward the living room.

Nothing.

On my way back down the hall, I heard a doorknob turn. It was coming from the bathroom. I slipped a little farther back down the hallway.

As I watched, the door to the bathroom opened and Adrien appeared. "*Zut!* Claire! I was just working. I thought that you were sleeping."

"I was."

"I woke you. I am sorry. You have been well?"

Aside from not getting ahold of the lawyer? And meeting Cynthia at the wrong place? "Yes. I bought some things for dinner."

"*Bien fait. J'ai faim.*"

Chapter 7

𝄞

While Adrien went into the library to collect his papers, I fiddled with the CD player in the living room. The Delaportes' taste ran from classical to jazz.

And that was it.

It had been a warm but breezy day, so I wanted some lazy summer music. I chose a Vivaldi CD. Then I unlatched the windows and pulled them open toward me to welcome in the wind. I did the same in the dining room, hoping that it would provide some cross-ventilation. But those windows opened into the building's chimneylike interior courtyard.

No breeze.

But it did give me a good whiff of someone else's dinner. Smelled like garlic and green peppers. I decided to open the windows in my own room, but I found that Adrien had beaten me to it. He was just catching back the curtains when I entered.

"Sorry. It wasn't as stuffy when I started sleeping."

"It is nothing at all, *ma poule.*" He placed his hand at the small of my back and pushed me out the door ahead of him.

He was barefoot and dressed in a fuchsia polo shirt and jeans, but somehow, he looked much more presentable than I felt.

At least my hair was clean this evening.

He looked at me, clapped his hands together, and suggested an *aperitif.* A before dinner drink. I reminded him that I didn't drink. He shrugged. Didn't indicate it was a problem.

I trailed him to the kitchen and watched as he stopped midstride when he saw the baguettes.

"Three? And one half? Is this what you buy for dinner? Bread?"

"No. I bought other things too. And only one of the baguettes is for tonight. The others are for breakfast. *Petit dej.* Tomorrow and the next day."

"If you like wood for breakfast. They will be hard." He knocked on them with a knuckle. "Hard, like wood."

"In one day?" I hadn't known that. I'd thought I'd been efficient, getting everything I'd needed at once. "I got *tabbouleh*, pork, and salad for dinner. And Brie. And *opéras* and *tartelettes*. Two of each. Some for tonight and some for tomorrow night."

"By tomorrow night they'll be…" He must have seen something in my face that stopped him from finishing his sentence. "I had thought to go to a restaurant tomorrow night."

"We don't have to. I don't mind cooking."

"I do this *normalement*, Claire. Or I buy something on my way home. This is when I get my baguette for the morning."

"You buy one every day?"

He looked at me as if I'd asked a trick question. "*Bah…oui.* Yes. I eat one half with dinner and one half for breakfast"

He bought a baguette every single day? That seemed very inconvenient.

"You do not remember from Carcans?"

"No."

"Every morning someone goes to the *boulangerie* to get the bread. Or *pains au chocolat*. You do not remember?"

"No."

"But you were young, and then later, you slept late, so I guess you have no memory of this."

Memories of eating them? Yes. Memories of buying them? No. Being in France as a child was a whole different experience than being in France as an adult. I'd noticed that several times that day. Buying too many baguettes, when I sat on the curb to eat, and when I had tried to pick out my own head of lettuce. But then, I never needed to worry about etiquette or food when I was a child. I was forgiven my *impolitesses* because of my age and I had never had to fend for myself.

Why would I know that you couldn't keep a baguette out on the counter like a loaf of bread?

While I had been thinking, Adrien had found a box of orange juice, slit the top, and poured me a glass. Then he had put the slab of *pâté* and some *cornichons* on a plate and sawn off some pieces from a baguette.

"Claire?"

"Hmm?"

"What is happened to this?" In one hand he held a bread knife. In the other he was holding out the end of a baguette that looked as though it had been chewed off.

I'd forgotten about that.

It had happened in between the bakery and the curb-sitting experiment. I'd been ravenous, the baguettes had been clamped under my arm, and I had just torn off the end with my teeth and eaten it. I used to do it all the time as a kid.

That's how it had happened. But Adrien didn't need to know that. "It fell on the floor."

That part was true. My conscience was clear.

"And the end got bashed in."

Okay. That was not true, but I couldn't keep myself from saying it. I should have stopped while I was ahead.

"It fell on the floor." He said it as if he were a second-grade teacher and knew I was lying about finishing my homework. He turned back toward the counter and put the slices into a bowl. He handed me the glass of orange juice. Gestured down the hall with his chin and then picked up both the bowl and the plate of *pâté*.

While we were walking toward the living room, he said just loud enough for me to hear, "I too, Claire, was once six years old." There was laughter in his voice.

I stuck my tongue out at him.

Too bad he couldn't see it.

In the midst of all the eighteenth-century Louis XVI-style furniture in the living room, there was an incongruous modern glass-and-metal table in the middle of the floor. Adrien set our food on this and then stepped over to the *secrétaire*, pulled the key from the desktop, and used it to open the cabinet underneath. Never having seen it open before, I was surprised that it was filled with liquor and glasses. He selected a bottle of something and a glass and poured himself a drink. Then he locked the cabinet up again and stuck the key back in the top.

He settled onto the lemon-upholstered banquette couch beside me. "*Santé.*"

"*Santé.*" I might not drink, but I didn't mind toasting to our collective health.

Adrien cut off a corner of *pâté*, spread it on a piece of bread and handed it to me. Then he did the same for himself.

I remembered that it had been his last day of work. "Congratulations and welcome to vacation."

He smiled, raised his glass at me and took a sip. Then he turned his quizzical eyes toward mine. "Why do you not drink alcohol, Claire? Are you *allergique?*"

"Allergic? No."

"You do not like the taste?"

"I don't know. I've never tried."

"*Jamais?*"

"Never."

"Why not?"

I shrugged. I didn't know really. Growing up, I hadn't done it in high school because it was against the law. I started college with the same reasoning. I wasn't a party girl, so I didn't put myself in situations where alcohol was available. And by my senior year, when I turned 21, it was my identity: I was Claire and I didn't drink.

"Is this your religion?"

"No." Not exactly, but it had something to do with it, didn't it? People who drank got drunk. And when you were drunk, you lost control, and bad things could happen. So maybe it was like this: It wasn't wrong to drink, but it led to doing things that were wrong. That was probably it.

Adrien was looking at me as if more explanation was required, but

I didn't have anything else to tell him. I didn't drink. Besides, it wasn't his business anyway. "Why do you drink?"

He shrugged. "Why not?"

"Is work so hard? Is life so bad?"

"*Non.* It tastes good. Here. Try it." He was holding out the glass to me.

"No, thanks."

"Wine was made to go with food. It aids the stomach to digest. And it is nice. Like a fur coat or a good car. A Mercedes. You know."

"A luxury?"

"*Non.* Not this. It is like…it makes a good thing better. You have a nice day, the weather is perfect, and you come home and have champagne. You see?"

Substitute chocolate for wine and I could see his point.

"Or like *truffes* in an *omelette.* The *omelette* is perfect by itself: It is fluffy, it is hot. But, you put in a *truffe* and…*voilà!*"

Only a Frenchman would try to explain the finer points of an argument by using food as an example. And it was making me hungry. I took another piece of bread and slathered it with *pâté.*

"Does your Brian drink?"

"No. He's an assistant pastor. And he's not my Brian. Not anymore. I broke up with him."

"When?"

"On Sunday. I called him after you left."

"*Pourquoi?*"

"Because I didn't love him."

"*Evidemment.* But I am still sorry if you are sorry. Are you sorry?"

About Brian? No. About the idea of him? Yes.

"*Ma poule,* he did not break your heart, but did you break his?"

"No."

"Then he is blind or stupid. But explain to me why Brian does not drink."

"He's a pastor. He can't drink. Some people think drinking is wrong."

Adrien looked at me with his eyebrows raised.

Maybe it was the concept of "wrong" that he didn't understand. I tried to think of a different word. "Some people think drinking is bad."

Adrien brushed a hand through the air as if he were swiping at flies. "*Non.* This I understand, but it is not *logique.* Some people think that eating meat is wrong, but this does not stop me from doing this. They have one opinion, I have another. They do not try to make me eat vegetables, and I do not try to make them eat meat. Why do they think drinking is wrong?"

"People get drunk. They hurt other people. People get drunk and drive. They kill other people."

He sighed and rolled his eyes. "This is so American. You do not have to get drunk every time you drink. There is choice. One can decide. One can have five drinks or one can have two. This is not so difficult."

"Drunk drivers kill people every year."

"Yes. So you should not drive when you drink. This is a personal responsibility. Lung cancer kills people every year, but I do not go to church and say that no one can have lungs anymore. This is *ridicule.*"

Ridiculous. Maybe it was. Part of the problem I'd had with Brian was the importance he placed on what other people said about our relationship.

No. That wasn't right.

It was the importance he placed on what other people *might* say about our relationship. It just hadn't seemed right that other people had a stake in something that wasn't even theirs to begin with.

"Can I try some of that?"

"*Bien sûr.*" He handed me his glass.

I held it up to my nose. It didn't smell too bad. Kind of like cherry cough medicine. It tasted like it too. Only better. "What is it?"

"Pineau des Charentes."

I took another sip. Handed it back. My stomach felt pleasant. Warm. I took another bite of bread and *pâté.*

"So you tell me that in your church there are people who tell everyone else that they should not drink?"

"For some people it's part of their faith."

"Their faith? Do you really think so?"

"Or maybe a practice of their faith."

"Perhaps. But just because this is a practice of their faith, does it mean it must be a practice of mine? Or of yours?"

"No." If we worshiped the same God, then we had to agree about certain things. But not about everything.

"So you want some wine with dinner? I could open two bottles, a Burgundy and a Bordeaux, and then you could taste the difference. We will start with the Bordeaux. It tastes of pepper, olives, tarragon, and other *herbes*. Then we will have the Burgundy. It tastes of cherry and roses, prunes and earth. For Bordeaux, there are many fines wines, for Burgundy, not so many. But when you taste a good one, it is paradise."

I'd had a drink. It hadn't killed me. But I wasn't ready to jump into a wine barrel feet first. "Can we talk about something else?"

"What would you like to talk about?"

"I don't know. In America it's not polite to talk about politics or religion." Or wine. In some circles.

"But why not? What else is left to talk about?"

"The weather. Your job."

Adrien tsked. "*Non, non, non.* Not in France. We do not talk about jobs in France. *Pas poli.* Why would you want to hear about my job? It is the same thing every day. A meeting in the morning at which nothing gets decided. Lunch. A meeting in the afternoon at which more of nothing gets decided. And in between, I read papers and contracts and memos. I sign them and pass them on. And you?"

I shrugged. I wasn't a career woman. I never had been. If I could have a mulligan for my college years, I'd get a degree in history and teach high school. Instead, I got a degree in business and worked with budgets.

What had I been thinking?

A few years ago I ran across my college transcripts. Guess which classes I did well in? Sociology, history, geography. I did fine in accounting: mostly Bs with one small D. In my defense, it was in a course about bonds. Not stocks which, like economics, were intuitively obvious to me, but bonds.

I am a very rational person with logical thought processes. I actually took an Introduction to Logic course and got an A in it, but then again, it was taught by the Department of Philosophy, which is part of the College of Arts and Sciences. Same thing with economics.

But again, in my defense, how many people know themselves well enough at the age of 18 to make decisions about degrees which will affect the course of their entire lives? Is this why the French don't talk about jobs? Because everybody lives in a state of regret about what they do and what they might have done had they only been wiser?

"I review the budgets every morning. I tell people how much money is left in the budgets for certain things and whether or not their request is legitimate. I make reports to the budget office…that's it."

"*Bon.*"

He looked at me.

I looked at him.

The silence was becoming strained, so I felt I had to say something. "The weather was nice today."

"The weather is beautiful."

"It is. It's very sunny out. And windy."

"*Oui.* It is very windy."

"And tomorrow?"

"The same thing. Sun. Wind. Day. Night." He fiddled with his wine glass, rotating it by the stem. "No wonder Americans watch so much TV. You have nothing to say to each other. Just the work one does and the weather? This is all that you talk about?"

"We talk about people. And the news."

"This is not much better. What do you say about people and the news? These are facts. They either are or are not. Either something did take place or it did not. Or maybe, for extra amusement, you talk about things that might possibly happen in the future? I do not understand."

"Not everything can be a big debate, Adrien."

"I just want to understand how you think. It is very interesting the way different people see the world differently. Like art. Painting. Both Modigliani and Picasso, by example, paint the same person. But both portraits look different. Which is the true portrayal of the person?"

Which indeed?

Chapter 8

The next morning I woke at nine. I was beginning to adjust to the time zone. I listened for a minute or two, yawning and wiggling my toes. Was Adrien rattling around the apartment? The only sounds that reached my ears were the sudden blare of music, probably from an open car window. The normal sounds of passing traffic. I stretched, thought about going back to sleep, and then forced myself to get out of bed. If I didn't get in contact with the lawyer soon, my parents were going to accuse me of ignoring their interests. I was still thinking that Mademoiselle's place was going to be a tiny rat hole tucked away in a small alley. If I had been a betting man, that's where I would have placed my money. But I was a girl and, for all intents and purposes, I was an accountant and much too aware of statistical odds to ever gamble on anything.

I gathered my clothes, a red polo shirt and khaki shorts, carried them into the bathroom, and took a bath. Normally, you'd never catch me soaking in a bathtub. I've never really felt clean in one because all the dirt and grime that's washed off has nowhere to go. It just gets redistributed. But I had no other choice. I was done in under 15 minutes, even though I shaved my legs.

Wandering from the bathroom to the kitchen, I thought that I'd run across Adrien somewhere, now that he was officially on vacation, but there was no sign of him.

With a few stops and starts, I was able to make myself an espresso.

I picked up one of the baguettes I'd bought the day before. It was just about the right length for a baseball bat and just as hard. I had pulled open the refrigerator door to eye the stale brioche when I heard the front door shut.

"Claire?"

"In here." I shut the fridge, hoping he would have brought something more appealing with him.

He had. But it's not what I expected. I was hoping for a *pain au chocolat*. What he'd brought was a very pretty dress.

"For you. To borrow."

"Umm…thank you?" Why had he thought I needed clothes? He's the one who had unpacked my suitcase. Maybe he was taking me out for breakfast.

To a three-star restaurant.

He was dressed for it, in a subtle pin-striped suit and understated tie. And the dress was certainly up for it. Made of a beautiful coral red silk crepe, it had a close fitting tank-style bodice with a deep sweetheart neckline. Then it dropped into a bias cut skirt. There was a slim black leather belt with a small buckle that rode the waist. It was the look the French do so well; a dress that could be dressed down with a jean jacket or dressed up with a glistening diamond necklace and four-inch heels.

It was simple. It was elegant.

And I didn't know until I'd put it on that it had no back. After all of the effort Adrien had gone to, for who knows what reason, I couldn't wear it because I didn't have the bra for it. My polo shirt and shorts would have to do.

"It is good?" I had heard him pacing the hall while I had been changing.

"Not really." I was looking at myself in the mirror, wishing I could have said yes. It was gorgeous. I had slipped my arms from my bra and shoved the straps back inside the bodice. I wanted an untainted view. There was something about that shade of red that put sparkle in my eyes and almost made me love my pale skin.

He flung the door open. "Something does not go right?"

I whirled around to face him, not wanting him to see the back of my bra through the nonexistent back of the dress. But I shouldn't have worried. He was smiling.

"You look lovely. This is good, Claire. Very nice."

"I can't wear it."

"Why not? It fits you."

"I don't have the right…things…to go with it."

His eyes trailed from my eyes all the way down to my toes and then his brow cleared. "Shoes. Yes, I see. Your running shoes will not do." He reached forward to grab my hand, and took me with him toward the door. "We will look at the shoes of my mother. She will have the right thing."

That was a statement I would never dispute. Madame Delaporte was always perfectly dressed. Never ostentatious, always elegant. "Smart casual," the bane of everyone who has ever been invited to an informally formal reception, was her specialty. But she probably didn't wear my size.

We were both right. She had a perfect pair of medium heels, but they were a size too big. "You must wear them. Just for one hour. You can have them off in the car."

"Adrien, I can't. *Pas possible.* Besides, I can't even wear the dress. I don't have a slip or hose." Or other things, like a strapless, backless bra. Although, if I ever owned a dress like this, I would certainly invest in one.

"A *slip?* You do not have panties? But of course you do."

"No. Not…" How embarrassing. "Not *un slip.* A slip, a short skirt you wear underneath a dress so the light won't show…things."

"This is not *nécessaire.* I do not know this slip. No women wear this in Paris. This is not a problem."

How would he know what women wore beneath their dresses? "But I don't have any hose."

"Hose?"

"*Collants.*"

"In the summer? No one wears this in summer. Are they not hot? They are called *collants* because they *colle.* They stick to your skin. Why do you want these in summer?"

Finally, a man who understood that pantyhose were the worst invention ever. "I still can't wear this."

"Why not? You are beautiful."

"Because I can't."

He picked the pair of heels up off the floor, grabbed my hand again, and pulled me out of his parents' bedroom and down the hall.

"So, you put on the shoes and I will get my keys and we will go."

"Okay. But first I have to take off this dress."

"*Mais tu es fou!* I call Solange at six this morning and wake her up just to make her find you something to wear. And it fits and you look beautiful and we are going to one of the oldest law practices in all of Paris. I know that you are American, but, Claire, you are also French! You must learn to be *correcte*…"

That was the closest Adrien had ever come to insulting me.

He must have seen something in my eyes, because after a pause, he added, "…*ma poule.*"

"I don't have anything to wear underneath, okay?"

"But we have just said—"

"A bra."

"A bra?"

"*Soutien-gorge.*"

"*Un soutien-gorge?* But you do not need one. Why would you wear one?"

Great. Just confirm what we already know to be true: Claire has no breasts.

"You are perfect."

And now my cheeks matched the color of the dress. I know he was only speaking hypothetically…but then again, maybe he wasn't. Because if he had borrowed this dress from Solange, then she had the same shape that I did. So I was caught between humiliation and humiliation: Adrien had noticed my lack of shape *and* I was wearing a dress he had borrowed from a former girlfriend. With whom he had probably done unspeakable things.

Interesting maybe, but unspeakable just the same.

By this time he had walked around me and seen my back. "But,

Claire, you have a beautiful back. You should want this to be seen." He had also seen the bra. "*Alors*, you go and take this off and then we will go."

What could I do? I took the thing off and then we left.

It took about 20 minutes of stop-and-go driving to reach the lawyer's office since it was on Ile St. Louis, in the middle of the Seine. We were obliged to cross to the other side of the river and drive along the *quais* to reach it. Finally, we drove over Pont Marie and then, after a confusing series of turns, the car plunged from dazzling sunlight into the obscure shade of *quai* d'Anjou. Its seventeenth-century townhouses were defended from the Seine by a row of flourishing plane trees.

Adrien parked the car along the building side of the street. After buttoning his suit jacket and tightening his tie, he came around to the passenger door to help me out and then started down the sidewalk at a fast clip. Usually I can keep up with him, but usually I'm not wearing heels that are too loose and too high. Adrien slowed his stride and offered me his arm when he saw me teetering. He led us to a building notable, even in the shade, for the dingy grime clinging to its stonework. It wasn't cold, but the absence of light led to a psychologically induced shiver.

Adrien pushed a button set into the stone framework of the huge anonymous black door. When it clicked, he pushed it open, and we stepped into a sterile entry hall composed of the same dingy stone. It led to an inner courtyard via another open arched doorway.

And there, it was cold.

I rubbed my hands up and down my arms, turning, stamping my feet. I caught a glimpse of myself in the entry hall mirror as I waited for him to find out, from the building directory, what floor the office was on.

Here was the surprise: I actually looked elegant. Which is to say, I didn't look at all like my normal self. My hair was the same straight shoulder-length brown. My eyes were the same gray-green. But the dress had added a tinge of color to my cheeks and wearing heels had lent stature to my height. I was standing straighter. Which had the benefit of thrusting out my chest. And I have to admit that the feel of silk against my skin—against all of it—felt luxurious.

We got into a cramped elevator set into a spiral staircase, and ascended to the third floor. When the door opened, Adrien gestured me through.

I lost my balance and stumbled. The building was so old, and the floor in the hall so warped, that it slid toward the stairs. A precipice.

He caught me around the waist before I could do myself any harm and then opened the only door in the hallway. Pressed me through it with a hand on my back.

My bare-naked back.

Which led to shivers and tingles that would be completely out of place in a law office. So I won't mention them. Because, honestly, what else could be expected from going around town wearing only one vertical half of a dress?

We stepped into a dim, dusty hall. I could just make out a reception desk if I squinted in the gloom. It felt cool up here too, but not because it was air-conditioned. There was a dry, musty smell that I've always associated with old books turning into dust. As we approached the desk, I realized there was a woman sitting behind it. When we finally stood in front of it, I realized it was not just a woman, but one of those lacquered, helmet-haired women of a certain age that pack the roar of a lion into a sturdy five-foot frame.

Adrien announced my name and stated my business.

She glared at us. "Monsieur cannot see you."

"Perhaps he could spare a few minutes."

"Not possible."

"Or even maybe just a moment."

"Out of the question."

"Because if he knew that Mademoiselle had come all the way from America on behalf of the will of Mademoiselle Dumont...?"

"Monsieur will be gone until the beginning of September."

"But really, it is such a small thing. The matter of the will and the settlement of the estate."

"Monsieur is very pressed for time."

"Surely such a small thing will take only two minutes."

"Today is his last day before vacation."

"Well, in that case, perhaps I will just leave my card." Adrien pulled one from his suit jacket and handed it over without any kind of flourish.

The secretary took one look at it, frowned, and then excused herself and tap-tap-tapped right down the hall.

When she returned, 30 seconds later, she escorted us back down the hall as if we were royalty.

The lawyer was standing, shifting from foot to foot, looking very apologetic. As apologetic as a bald-headed, stoic, 70-year-old Frenchman can look. He stubbed out his cigarette and hurried from behind his desk to greet us. Then he gestured with open hands to the two leather chairs crouching in front of his desk.

Adrien waited until I was seated before he sat in one. "About the matter of Mademoiselle Dumont?"

"Mademoiselle Dumont. *Oui.*"

"Mademoiselle Le Noyer is here about the will."

"Ah. The body has been taken south. If I recall, the estate was an apartment and all of her worldly goods. But these were to have been given to a *Monsieur* Le Noyer."

"And this is his daughter."

For the first time, the lawyer looked at me. As he did, his watery eyes sharpened and he took in an audible breath. "*Oui.* Yes. I can see this now. You have her face. Her eyes. So. You are the heir of your father?"

"No. I mean, my father is still living, but he is not able to be here."

The lawyer's interest in me faded and his eyes sunk back into their watery retreat. "The will is very specific. Everything was left to your father. Unless you have a power of attorney, I cannot just give you the keys to the property."

And, of course, he was leaving for vacation tomorrow and wouldn't be back for a month. Because I was in a dress with no back, when I uncrossed my legs and tried to stand up to leave, my skin stuck to the leather chair. Not for very long, but long enough that it felt as though I'd left half of it with the leather.

Adrien got to his feet after I did, but he didn't seem very interested in leaving. At least, not as interested as I was. "But I am sure one can do something." Of course something could be done. Adrien never takes no for an answer. "It is the least of things to have a form signed and express mailed to wherever one will be. And if a key is left with a trustworthy person and then that person is told when the necessary documents have been received…and then if one contacts the person and retrieves the key…" They traded hypotheticals for about five minutes before arriving at a mutually acceptable solution.

Figuratively speaking, of course.

I might have concentrated more on their conversation except that I was trying to decide whether we should go straight to the hospital so that I could have a skin graft or whether you had to make an appointment for things like that.

The lawyer shook Adrien's hand and then turned to me. He sighed and lifted a hand to his chest. "I never thought to see her face again. It does my heart good."

I offered my hand for him to shake, and he took it, but then he drew me in and gave me two *bises*. French air kisses. If I were making comparisons, Adrien's ears were much better than Monsieur's. They weren't stuffed with tufts of wiry white hair. But how harshly can you look upon someone who has just given you a compliment?

At least I think it was a compliment…or maybe Mademoiselle had been one of those people with a really great personality.

Just as long as she hadn't left any cheese molding in her cupboards.

We retraced our steps back down to the ground floor. As soon as we heard that formidable door thump shut behind us, Adrien pulled off his tie and stuffed it into a pocket. Then he shrugged out of his suit jacket and tossed it over his shoulder, releasing an invisible cloud of lime-scented cologne.

I'd never really considered lime a scent before. To me, it had been always been a color. To avoid. Like a green lifesaver or lime Jell-O.

Better just to do without.

But as a scent, lime had a lot to offer. It had zest and sunshine.

Warmth. The color orange. I know that sounds strange, but to me, oranges smell like yellow. And lemons should be blue.

There must be a short-circuit in my brain somewhere.

Or maybe it was just that I was staring into Adrien's eyes again. They were so impossibly blue. Like the wings of a butterfly I'd seen once on display at a natural history museum. They were so brilliant, so bright, that they glowed.

"*Ma poule?*"

"What?" His mouth was moving, but I couldn't hear any words.

"Have no worries. You will have the apartment soon enough."

"Uh, yeah. Thanks, Adrien. Well done."

"*Merci.*"

"I don't think he ever would have seen me if it hadn't been for you."

"Perhaps not. At least, not until September."

"What was on the card you handed the secretary? Can I see one?"

"*Bien sûr.*" Adrien carefully disengaged my hand from his arm. How had that gotten there? And then he reached around his other side, fished a card out of his jacket pocket and handed it to me between his elegant fingers.

It looked normal. Very plain, actually. His name, his company, his title. Dassault Aviation, Directeur of some under-bureau of something. An address in St. Cloud, west of Paris. His contact information.

But wait.

Aha! Just there, right after his name, was a comma and an *X*. Yep. An original *X*-man. That was Adrien.

My dress didn't have any pockets, or anything much else for that matter, so I handed it back. "Where are we going?"

"For a walk."

"Where?"

"*Bah*…here. On Ile St. Louis. Where else would we be going for a walk?" He tucked my hand over his arm and started humming a wispy melody.

Where else did I have to go?

We were walking away from the car along the *quai*, toward the western tip of the island. We were still in the shade, but after the dank interior of Monsieur's offices, it felt good to be out in air that was stirred by the breeze that wafted up from the river. It should have been delightful, but it wasn't. I stumbled.

"*Ma poule?*"

"My feet."

"Ah. We must fix this." He bent down on one knee. Placed a hand on my calf to lift my left foot.

I placed my hand at the back of his neck for balance.

"If we take this one off." He slid it from my foot and set it on the ground. "And then take this one off." With gentle hands, he set my foot down and I turned toward him so he could remove the other. Then he hooked a finger inside each heel and held them up to me.

I gave him a hand to help him up and then took the shoes from him.

"Better?"

"Ye-es." Was it legal to walk around a city in your bare feet? Was it sanitary? Did I care? Not enough to protest. The stone blocks of the *quai* were emanating the coolness of the shade. It was revitalizing. I hadn't walked around barefoot since...Carcans? Had to have been.

Lost in memories of the summers of my youth, I was so surprised when Adrien grabbed me around the waist and whisked me up into his arms that I shrieked and threw my own arms around his neck.

"*La crotte de chien.*"

"The what?"

"The dog..." he turned and gestured with his chin behind us to a tidy little pile of dog poop. I would have planted a foot on top of it had he not rescued me. "It is lucky if you step in it with your left foot. But only if it is not on purpose...perhaps you might have wanted the luck...?"

"No. Thanks."

"Not to mention." He continued down the street with me in his arms, not once breaking stride.

"You mean some people actually step in it on purpose?"

He looked at me, eyes twinkling. "Some people need a lot of luck."

"And if you step on it with your right foot?"

"Not so good."

"You could put me down if you want."

"A pretty girl? All to myself? In my arms even? Out of the question. Besides, we have come to the stairs. You might chip your toenail polish."

I stuck up a foot so he could see it.

"No toenail polish? Claire, are you sure your father is French? I will paint them for you myself."

I tucked my foot back under its mate. There was something about toes that was intimate. I couldn't imagine letting Adrien paint mine.

He walked down the stairs and then forward toward the tip of the island before setting me on my feet. Then he spread his suit jacket on the stones at the edge of the bank and offered me a hand as I sat down on it.

I dangled my feet over the edge.

He joined me, our hips pressed close.

We sat in silence for a long while, watching the water flow by and an occasional tourist boat pass. We waved at the passengers, who then pointed, hooted, and waved back at us.

Probably Americans.

Glancing around, I saw other couples walking the *quai* or cuddling along the banks. Adrien and I blended right in. Sitting close, our arms crossed behind us as props, we looked just like lovers.

Wouldn't it be nice to have a lover?

Not an illicit sex kind of lover. I am, after all, the world's last 29-year-old virgin, but just someone. Someone who loved me.

Someone to kiss.

"I should have brought champagne. I am a zero at romance."

"Save it for a girlfriend." Did he even have a girlfriend? Adrien had pulled an enormous amount of information about my private life from me, but I had yet to gain any information about him. Only one way to fix that problem. "Do you have a girlfriend?"

"*Moi?*" He started, turned his eyes from the river to my own. "*Non.*"

"Would you like one?"

He smiled, his eyes breaking into facets, reflecting the light. "Yes. You would volunteer?"

"No. You wouldn't want me."

"Why not?"

"Nobody else does. I'm very intimidating."

Adrien just laughed at me.

"I am." That's what my father says anyway. He says I show my intelligence too much and that scares people away. My mother says I'm too serious. She thinks I would be more approachable if I smiled more often. But she didn't come into contact with the whackos in the university district on as regular a basis as I did. Sometimes unapproachable meant the difference between being stalked or being overlooked.

"Maybe to Brian, but he does not know you the way I know you."

"I'm serious."

"Yes. And I am too. I was there the summer you discovered strawberries."

That was one for the *Carcans Summer Vacation Myths and Legends* book. My father still thought it was cute to mention it anytime he saw a strawberry. I was about six years old and gorged myself on them one night. I hadn't known they would provide a good case of the farts. And, scrupulously honest as I was, I couldn't let one pass without saying, "That was me."

"And do not forget that I was also there for the salt experiment."

The Great Salt Experiment. The summer I was eight, I was in love with a science book my father had given me. There was a chapter about the Dead Sea and how the high salt content of the water made everything float. That was extra fascinating to me because I'm one of those people who float for about three seconds before sinking, feet first. So one morning I stole the giant box of salt from the kitchen and smuggled it to the ocean later in the day, determined to test the salt theory.

I waded out from shore and then dumped it all into the water around me and floated. Or tried to. I had such unswerving faith in science that I just knew I would bob to the surface, given enough time. Adrien fished me out about a minute and a half into my experiment. I don't know what would have happened if he hadn't been around; the tide had carried me much farther out than I had planned.

"Thanks for rescuing me." He always seems to have been rescuing me from some stupid scrape or another. They must not have been very relaxing vacations for him. "How was it that you always happened to be around?"

"I saw you running toward the beach with a big box of salt. It was so big you had trouble carrying it. And I said to myself, Claire is up to something again. How could I not follow you? Being with you was more fun than being with anyone else. You were so creative and full of interesting ideas."

Interesting. That was one way of putting it.

"You were never afraid to try things. Like dying your hair."

"Bleaching." When I was 13, I had decided I needed a new image. Chiefly, blond hair. I didn't want to mention it to anyone because I was sure they'd tell me I couldn't, so I took some bleach from the kitchen, stuck my head over the bathtub, and poured the entire bottle over my hair.

The result was less than desirable.

Adrien had heard me sobbing in the bathroom. He wrapped a towel around my head, whisked me into town in his father's car, and asked the hairdresser to fix the mess. He'd never told a soul. That I had heard of.

"You'll be happy to hear that I've put my wild youth behind me. I'm a respectable woman now."

"That is too bad, because the child that was Claire made me laugh. A lot." He ruffled my hair with his hand and stood up, extending a hand to help me up too. "*Bon*. We must eat lunch and then we must think of another creative idea."

"For what?"

"For getting into your new apartment."

"We can't. Not until we have the power of attorney."

Adrien pursed his lips. "I would not say 'can't.' I would say 'not supposed to.'"

"If we're not supposed to, then we're not supposed to."

"Exactly, but that does not mean we cannot. It means we must be creative."

Creative must be the French euphemism for illegal and immoral.

Chapter 9

$\mathcal{A}$drien, I really don't think we should do this."

"Why not? It does not hurt anybody. The apartment will be yours, when? Tomorrow? The next day? So you see it a few days early. Not a big deal." He was already ringing for the *gardienne*. He jabbed me in the side with an elbow. "Look sad."

Look sad?

How about invisible? I'd much rather be anywhere than here, the lobby of Mademoiselle's apartment building. On our drive back to the Delaportes' apartment, over lunch, and on our walk over to Mademoiselle's building, I'd said everything I could think of to dissuade him, but he had a counterargument for every excuse I'd presented.

A young woman came to the glass-fronted door and pulled it open. She peeled rubber gloves from her hands. Pushed strands of blond hair from her forehead with the back of her hand. *"Oui?"*

By some sleight of body, Adrien maneuvered us both inside the front door. "We are here about the apartment of Mademoiselle Dumont. Claire is the cousin of Mademoiselle, and the death was very shocking to her. She is very sad, are you not, *chérie?*"

No. In fact, I was not.

I was trying hard not to laugh. There was really nothing funny about the situation, but the stress of doing something I knew I shouldn't seemed to be manifesting itself in a compulsive fit of giggles.

Adrien pulled a handkerchief from his pocket with a flourish and covered my face with it, managing to pinch me soundly on the nose.

As my knees buckled with the surprise of the sting, Adrien put a supportive arm around my waist. Hopefully my "Ow!" sounded like a howl of grief.

"Would you like to spend some time alone in her apartment? Would that do you some good? Just a moment. Stay here. I will get the key." She pushed open the only door in the hallway and disappeared.

"Ow! Why did you do that?" It was hard to whisper when what I really wanted to do was to yell at him.

"You could not very well laugh when you are supposed to be overcome by grief."

"Then why didn't you tell her I was hysterical instead of sad?" I was rubbing my nose with the palm of my hand. He'd given it a good pinch.

We heard the rattle of the doorknob.

Adrien whipped the handkerchief back up to my face and pulled me close to his body with an arm. "There, *chérie*. It will be okay."

The giggles were back.

He must have sensed them welling up inside because he turned my face toward his chest. I could smell his lime cologne again. I could feel my heart beat faster, my cheeks start to flush.

Maybe I really was becoming hysterical.

The *gardienne* came back, led us to an ancient doll-sized elevator, and then ran up the stairs to meet us on the third floor. There was only one door on the landing; the apartment occupied the whole floor. Things were looking up! It wasn't a rat hole after all. She opened the door and then gave us the key. "Just lock the door when you leave and return it to me."

Adrien pushed the door open further with his hand.

I grabbed his forearm and looked over his shoulder. My jaw dropped. I didn't know whether to laugh or to cry.

There may not have been cheese molding in the cupboards, but everywhere else, everything else was molding. Paint was peeling from the ceiling in long strips. Chandeliers were dangling by wires. Spiders had strung their scaffolding in the corners. The windows looked as if they hadn't been cleaned in years. The floorboards were scuffed beyond repair.

And that's only what I could see from the front door.

Adrien reached back and felt for my hand, taking it and pulling me forward.

I resisted, afraid to go any farther.

"Come inside."

"No." Because maybe when the power of attorney was signed and the lawyer gave me the key, the apartment would be different. Maybe it would be...clean. Or in a different building, on a different street. Maybe even in a different section of the city. Maybe this was all some huge mistake. Or maybe it was a punishment for sneaking inside. Maybe if we had just waited, it would have been...not perfect. It was too awful to have ever been perfect. But maybe it would have been better.

"We should look around."

"No, we shouldn't. We don't belong here." I didn't belong here. My parents belonged here. My dad would really get into this kind of thing. It would give him something to do besides golf.

"*Viens.* We have come this far. Maybe things are better inside." Adrien was an optimist, but even he didn't sound convinced.

If I were guessing, I would have said that it could only get worse.

He dropped my hand and walked forward through the spacious, but decaying, entry hall and into the double salon. He crouched behind a chair upholstered in moss green and deep burgundy silk and tipped it onto its front legs. He bent closer, rubbed at the frame with a thumb. "This is marked."

That was the only sentence that could have moved me from the front door.

In a flash I was crouching beside him, my hand on his thigh, looking at the signature carved into the underside of the chair.

Adrien and I had both been apprentices under our fathers' tutelage during those long vacations in the south of France. We'd spent precious hours poking around dusty antique stores and tacky flea markets learning how to tell when furniture was really "of the epoch," when it was a reproduction, or when it was a revival piece, made "in the style of" a certain era. We learned from experience when paint or gilt was original and when it had been applied to cover damaged wood. And we could tell at a glance whether an item was from France, Germany, or England.

The chair was definitely original, definitely from France, and definitely marked by its maker.

"RVLC." We looked at each other in disbelief, and then we sprang apart and hopped around the room tipping the rest of the furniture over.

They were all signed.

All four chairs, two armchairs, and a banquette couch.

"Roger Vandercruse."

"*Dit* Lacroix." Adrien's disbelief echoed my own.

What a find! Roger Vandercruse, or Lacroix, had been one of the master furniture makers who had worked for Louis XV. One of the greatest furniture makers of the eighteenth century.

We didn't touch the commode or *secrétaire*, but from their intricate, meticulous marquetry, Adrien guessed they might be Cressent or Boulle.

The apartment might be falling apart, but the contents were absolutely priceless.

My flirtation with depression had ended. I was the one to lead the tour of the rest of the apartment. It was like the best kind of Christmas. Or like opening wedding gifts from royalty. Mademoiselle had several large Sèvres vases and a complete service for 24 of Sèvres china. Turquoise-blue. Decorated with birds. Glimmering with gold accents.

She had silver Christofle place settings for 24. Baccarat stemware.

Adrien swore that the curtains moldering at the windows were made of Aubusson tapestry. The carpets beneath our feet puffed clouds of dust whenever we made a step, but their sheer size and vivid color, even underneath the grime, made me think they had been chosen for their quality as well.

There was a small library at one end of the apartment. It was lined with bookshelves and shrouded in dust. We peeked in the bathroom. That undid what excitement the previous half hour had created. After that, I needed a pick-me-up.

So Adrien did just that.

He pulled me away from the bathroom door, where I was trying hard not to weep, and then he carried me like a sack of potatoes into the bedroom. Did it cheer me up?

Not at first.

Sure, there was a marble fireplace. Yes, there were some interesting northern European paintings on the wall. But that was about it. No carpets. No gilded mirrors. None of the opulence that had been on display in the other rooms.

There was something sterile about it. Ascetic, although it was in better condition than the other rooms. It was cleaner. I had turned around and was about to walk out the door when I stopped by the commode and started fiddling with the marquetry chest that was resting on top.

The lid sprang open when I moved the latch. Inside were a collection of boxes and pouches, each stamped identically with the logo of a *joaillier*. A jeweler. I picked up a box and opened it.

I gasped.

Even in the pale light which filtered through the grime on the windows, the jewels inside glowed. A necklace and earrings made of shimmery green-and-silver moonstones.

Adrien came to stand beside me. He gasped also, but for a different reason. "But—they are a perfect match for your eyes, Claire." He took the necklace from the box, swept my hair forward across my right shoulder, and fastenened the clasp. Then he propelled me down the hall to the bathroom, flicked on the light, and stood me in front of the mirror. He scooped my hair back from my shoulder and then stood behind me.

It was uncanny. The stones mirrored the depths and nuances of my eyes.

"The exact colors. It is very…bewitching."

The way he said it was ambiguous in meaning. I couldn't tell if it had been meant as a compliment. The effect was startling. I seemed to be all eyes, like some pagan goddess. "You don't like my eyes?"

"I do not know. I have never been able to decide."

Our eyes met in the mirror. He must have seen the hurt in mine. You can't just tell someone you don't like their eyes. It's not like a bad haircut. There's nothing you can do to change them. Except maybe buy colored contacts. But that's a stupid thing to do if you have perfect eyesight to begin with.

He didn't like my eyes?

He clasped my shoulders, speaking to my reflection in the mirror. "They haunt me. They have always haunted me. I see them sometimes in my dreams."

I squinched them closed, trying to imagine them floating at me out of a dream.

I could see his point.

His fingers tightened on my shoulders. His hands felt like brands, burning into my skin. He swept my hair aside again, fingers gliding with the hair across my bare back.

I shivered.

He bent close to work the clasp. Unfastened it. Took my hand, turned it palm up, and deposited the necklace into it. Then he left.

Trotting down the hall, I joined him in the bedroom. He had picked up a pouch, poured the contents onto the top of the commode.

Black pearls.

He picked up another pouch, but this time the occupant nearly dropped to the floor. We both dove for it. Conked heads. But Adrien opened his fist to display a pin. A brooch. A small black cat, sitting on its haunches. It was pieced together from an intricate, tiny mosaic of black pearl, the facial features outlined in gold. A thick collar of a necklace had been made in stones of red, blue, and green, and it dangled an amulet with a scarab in its center. The eyes of the cat, a clear golden amber, winked at us.

It was delightful. Dignified.

A piece of jewelry that even someone like me could wear. So maybe Mademoiselle wasn't quite the stuck-up snob I had started to think she was. I slid the brooch back into its pouch. Returned it to the chest and slammed the lid shut.

"*Attends.*" Adrien reached out a finger to reopen the chest.

There was something not quite right about all of this. I put my hand over his to keep the lid shut.

He shrugged and went to open one of several large armoires shoved up against the far wall.

How could we have had a relative who had been so obviously rich? How could such wealth have escaped the notice of the family? My father might not see his relatives often, but I knew for a fact that gossip made its way across the Atlantic in regular intervals. "Who was Mademoiselle Dumont?"

"Aged 82? Of mysterious wealth? I do not know, but she had style." He flung the door of the armoire wide. "Look at these: Lanvin, Balmain, Givenchy, Dior, Chanel." The armoire he had opened contained only fancy long dresses and their matching shoes. For the most part, they were black, with an occasional gleam of emerald, silver, or electric cherry red.

I walked over to join him, curious at what the other armoires would hold. We soon found out: one for suits, bags, and shoes; another for blouses, coats, and hats. I pulled open the drawers of the commode: undergarments, scarves, and sweaters. Very nice cashmere sweaters in a bouquet of colors.

Considering that Mademoiselle had lived nearly a century, there weren't that many clothes. The surprise was that they dated to almost every decade of her life. There was a Lanvin ball gown that looked as if it came from the 1930s and there was a Chanel suit that might have been bought last year. Judging from the sizes, her physique hadn't changed in eight decades.

"Such style. Look at this, Claire." He was holding out a suit. He walked it over to me. "Feel this."

I obliged.

"They do not make wool this fine any longer. You could wear it this afternoon and be fashionable."

It was black, but then the French will wear black even during the furnace heat of high summer. I would have guessed it was from the 1950s with its Peter Pan collar and tailored jacket that became double breasted at the waist with its cut-away front. It was timeless. A classic.

Reaching down into a drawer of the commode, I pulled out a cashmere twin set. A long-sleeved cardigan of snowy white and a square-necked tank shell to match. Again, it could have come from any era of the last century.

"Where would she have gone in gowns like those?"

"Parties. Balls. She must have been a society woman."

"But how did she get into society? She wasn't born into it."

Adrien shrugged. "A man, perhaps."

"But she never married."

"You do not have to be married in order to go out with a man. Maybe she had boyfriends."

For decades of her life?

He shrugged again. "*Allons-y*. There is more to look at."

I had to run to keep up with him. I needn't have hurried because the kitchen turned out to be as bad as the bathroom: century-old fixtures and appliances from the dawn of the age of electricity. And of course there was no dishwasher...and no washing machine either?

"But of course not!" Adrien sounded indignant. "You would throw a Dior gown or a Chanel suit into a washing machine!"

"No." I might not win Ms. Fashionista of the Year, but I wasn't completely stupid either. "But she wouldn't have sent her underwear to the dry cleaners."

Adrien sent me a strange look. "She would have handwashed them. In the sink..."

Duh. Now I did feel like a moron because you can't watch a movie about the 1940s or '50s without the heroine feminizing the hero's bathroom by draping hose and bras on every conceivable surface for drying.

What would that be like? A wardrobe that could never be casually thrown into the washer and dryer? A whole household of things that demanded special care? We hadn't looked, but I'm sure her linens were actually made of linen.

We had wandered back into the living room. Were standing in front of the fireplace, surveying the mess.

"*Mystères et boules de gomme*. But one thing we know for certain: She had good taste in cigars."

"How would you know?"

"I smoke sometime. Cubans."

"But how would you know she liked good cigars?"

He turned and fiddled with a box on top of the mantel. It was a marquetry box with gold handles and gold lock. He opened it. On the inside of the lid was some sort of measurement device, a dial, with two vents flanking it. And there was an unfinished wooden tray which Adrien removed. Beneath lay a neat row of cigars.

"Here." He was holding one out to me to sniff. "One does not put bad cigars in a box like this."

"No, thank you."

"Only the very best ones smell this way."

Then that would place it just above the smell of wet dog and just below hot tar on my list of favorite things to smell. And it's not because I'm picky. Creosote and gasoline are among my top ten. "I don't like cigars."

"But have you ever tried one?"

"Have you ever eaten maggots?"

He looked offended. He also looked as though he wanted to try one. I hated to forbid him; he was a grown man. He was helping me. Maybe if he stripped, straddled the balcony, and promised not to talk to me for 48 hours until the smell dissipated. "You could…" I couldn't do it. "…take them home with you."

His eyes brightened. "Really?"

"Take them all." Foul, reeking, detestable things. "Enjoy them."

"Thank you very much." He began to open the lid again, but I motioned it closed. Every time he opened it, small puffs of odor leaked out. "Just take the box too."

He raised an eyebrow.

"Dad doesn't smoke." If he did, Mom would divorce him.

"That is a shame. A good cigar is like a fine *Armagnac*. Speaking of which…" He set the box on a chair and walked over to a *secrétaire*. He turned the key and let down the lid. Instead of revealing a desk, like the Delaportes', it revealed a bar.

He studied the collection. Picked up a bottle. "*Armagnac. Château LaBalle.* 1973 vintage. Aged in the finest black oak of Monlezun." He picked up another bottle. "*Cognac. Maison Surrenne.* 1946. This is legendary. One of the best ever produced. Part of it was forgotten for 51 years and only just bottled in 1997. But this bottle? In this place? It could be an original."

"What are you saying?"

"I am telling you that she, or someone else, had very fine taste. The very best taste in cigars and liquor. She had a mentor, and it was a man."

"You don't think she kept the cigars and the alcohol for general visitors?"

"Fifty euro cigars? Not for company. You only stock these if someone specific likes them."

"One of her boyfriends."

He shrugged. "Have you smelled this apartment?"

"I'm trying hard not to."

"It smells of many things, but it does not smell of cigars."

That was true. Thankfully. I'm like a shark when it comes to cigars. It only takes a molecule to start me retching.

"Whoever this supply is for has not been here for quite some time."

"And you think the cigar man was the liquor man?"

"Cigars and liquor go together."

"So there was a man, but she didn't marry him."

"She did not marry him, but they spent enough time together that she had a supply of his favorite things."

A romance. "I wonder when it started?"

"By the liquor? Some time after 1946. And it ended some time after 1973. But if you have enough money and the right connections, you can always buy a vintage from someone. So the dates do not mean everything."

There were clues to Mademoiselle's history. A whole house full of them. We just had to figure out how to interpret what we were seeing. But what else could place a date on a relationship? Everything in the apartment was an antique.

Adrien and I arrived at an answer at the same moment.

Chapter 10

𝕭𝖞𝕮

"The clothes!"

We rushed down the hall, tripping over our feet.

I began to open a drawer of the commode, but Adrien stopped me. "Those are classic sweaters and scarves. We will look at her gowns. One would only buy these if one had an occasion to wear them."

He pulled the dresses from the armoire and handed them to me. I laid them on the bed. There were at least 20. After he'd given me the last of them, he turned, to stand beside me.

"Now what?" If I had been more spontaneous, I would have thrown myself on top of them, to revel in the feel of brocades, silks, and satins. Feathers, beads, sequins, and lace.

"Now we put them back."

Great idea. Any others? Maybe we should count the number of sugar crystals in the sugar bowl. Or the number of grains of rice in a five-kilogram bag.

"We put back any from earlier than 1980, and we will see what is left."

We put some impeccably tailored, classic gowns back in that armoire. Five dresses were left.

The first was a one-shouldered pleated column dress in deep fuchsia.

"She must have had your shoulders."

I gave Adrien a look.

"She must have. To wear a dress like that when you are 60 or 70 years old?"

"What do you think? Eighties? Nineties?"

"It could be either."

We put it aside.

The next was also made of hundreds of tiny pleats, but the fabric was stiffer, and it was arranged in tiers. From a strapless bodice, the tiers formed a subtle 'V' of a peplum and then fell in longer tiers to the ground. "I'd guess 1980s."

"Early or late?"

I had a peplum dress in the 1980s, but when was it? "Mid-80s."

"Well, at least that is something. Next one."

He plucked a dual-length gown from the bed. It was stunning. A boat-necked dress in dark Prussian blue with tiny cap sleeves. The bodice was embroidered with an ornate gold crest. The skirt was long at the back and sides, but it had been slashed in the front and folded back to reveal a short gold underskirt.

"She must also have had your legs."

I shook my head. "I know this one. I saw the long-over-short look in some magazine. It was late '80s, early '90s." It had probably been a magazine at a beauty salon. Or the doctor's or dentist's office. The look was inspired by the 1700s. The models on the catwalk had worn Marie Antoinette-style wigs. How I had longed to own one of those dresses. I had wanted to be the heroine of my own fairy tale.

"I am impressed."

"I don't hate fashion, Adrien. It's just that there are more practical things to spend money on. If I had unlimited funds, didn't work at a university, and didn't live in perpetual drizzle, I think even you would approve of my wardrobe."

The next dress was a fantasy of feathers and heavy silk. Strapless. Tight-fitting bodice. Full, sweeping skirt. It could have belonged to either decade.

The remaining dress was the same. Of indeterminate vintage.

But we knew one thing for sure: She'd been escorted somewhere to something as late as the early '90s. From the '40s to the '90s. She had a relationship…or relationships…that had lasted 50 years.

And yet she had never married.

Why not?

And what would I do with all of this? My mother was much too tall to wear any of it. And I didn't have the career for them. But they were too priceless to just throw away. "Do you think that a museum would want these? Or maybe the design houses, for their archives?"

"What?" Adrien clutched a dress to his chest. "Give these away? You must not." Trust a French male to place more importance on clothes than an American female.

"Maybe your mother would want them? Or Solange?" Since she and I could wear the same size and since she obviously liked clothes, maybe she could take them and love them. Because they had been loved. All of these clothes. By Mademoiselle. There didn't look to be a loose thread or a moth-eaten hole among them.

And they were such lovely clothes.

I ran my hand across luscious silks, whispery taffetas, slippery satins. It was a little girl's dream come true. An entire wardrobe with which to play dress up. Where on earth had Mademoiselle worn these? There were what, 15? Twenty? At $5000 apiece?

Amateur historian that I was, I began creating scenarios for all of them, from a champagne-soaked ball in the 1940s to a prestigious charity auction in the 1980s. And during the 1930s, when France was in the throes of political corruption and upheaval, when the depression reached her shores? Mademoiselle had survived, even profited, that much was clear, but how? And where did she wear those fabulous dresses?

And during WW II? How many of those suits had known the sudden perspiration of fear at the sight of Nazi soldiers? Had any of the gowns been caressed by German hands? If only they could talk!

"They belong to you."

"To my parents."

"Your mother could never wear them."

"Well, I can't wear them."

"Of course you can."

"These? I would never wear gowns like these."

"*Jamais?* You should never say never, Claire. I will make you a promise. Do nothing with these now, and by the time you must leave France, if you do not want them, then I will find something to do with them."

"Fine."

I took a moment to move the jewelry box to the back of one the armoires. It didn't seem smart to leave it sitting where anyone could see it. I groped in the corner for space. Shoving some shoes aside, I felt a book. I pulled it out. It was leather bound. I flipped through it; it was a diary. I left the box in the armoire and took the diary with me. When I got up from my knees, Adrien had already started back down the hall.

We might have stayed a while longer, but I was feeling uneasy about being there and we still owed the *gardienne* the key, so we gave the apartment one last look and then pulled the door shut behind us.

I handed the diary to Adrien; he shoved it into his pocket.

When we reached the ground floor, I walked right off the elevator and out the front door. I had no intention of getting my nose pinched again, and Adrien was perfectly capable of returning the key on his own. I loitered in front of the building for about five minutes. Even if I hadn't known what floor the apartment was on, it would have been easy to guess. The windows on the third floor were the only ones that were dirty.

What was I going to tell my parents?

I needed to call them tonight because they were waiting for some kind of information from me. One thing was certain: I couldn't tell them I'd seen the place because we were supposed to have a power of attorney before being given the key.

So I guess I was off the hook for at least the next 24 hours.

What were my parents ever going to do with such a dump?

I would clean it, of course. And I could have the furniture crated and shipped to them, but then what would they do with it? They did not live near enough to Miami to get a fair price for the pieces. Especially after shipping was factored in.

So I'd have to do something with it here. Did they have garage sales in Paris? Somehow, I rather doubted it. And the prospect of liquidating such meticulously collected pieces was depressing.

It was a shame about the apartment. The building itself was in good shape. It was older than the Delaportes', but it still exuded a quiet air of luxury. Had Mademoiselle's apartment been taken care of, I'm sure it would be worth…quite a bit. But in its present state, "fixer-upper" seemed a little hopeful.

It was ironic.

My parents had been the ones with the highest hopes. I'm the one who counted on the molding cheese, of which there had been none, by the way. Even though I could say "I told you so," what I wanted, more than anything, was to be able to tell them that they had been right.

Or for Adrien to tell them that I had told them so.

Either scenario would work for me. And where was he, anyway?

I soon found out.

He was humming when he stepped onto the sidewalk. After catching me around the waist, he waltzed me across the street to a crazy rhythm.

Here's a little known fact about me: I can't lead and I can't follow. I'm hopeless when it comes to dancing. But dancing, the ballroom kind, is something I have always wanted to do. It might have had something to do with *Strictly Ballroom*, although I draw the line at any comparison with Fran. We may be similar in the way all dark-haired woman are, but that's it.

Anyway, Adrien didn't seem to notice that I can't dance. He twirled me around and I managed to keep my feet off of his, and by the time we reached the other side, I was laughing like I hadn't laughed in years.

"Bravo, Claire! You are a fabulous dancer. Very graceful."

"You have got to be kidding. I can't dance!"

"Nonsense. You just did."

"No, really. I can't."

"You, *ma poule*, are a ballerina."

"No, I'm not. Really."

"Well, then it must be your partner."

"I've never been able to dance with anyone." Not since seventh

grade when I could no longer stand on my father's feet. And let's just not talk about my awkward junior high school years when the idea of fast-dancing with a boy was nearly as terrifying as the thought of—gasp!—slow-dancing with one.

"Then you have not been dancing with people who know how to lead."

Bless his kindness. That was possible. Unlikely, but possible.

"*Mais, bon.* About Mademoiselle. The *gardienne* says that she was very healthy until just recently. Except for her eyes. She was going blind. Cataracts, maybe? But every day she went out for lunch. Always dressed well, she looked about 20 or 30 years younger. She never had visitors."

"At least not from a maid service."

"Perhaps she never saw how bad the apartment had become. And she never had mail."

"Never? What about bills?"

"*Jamais.*"

"Maybe she had a post office box?"

"Or some sort of financial manager. She might have had family money. We could ask the lawyer."

"When he comes back to work in September." Strange. If there had been family money, wouldn't my father have known about it? At least heard rumors of it?

Who was Mademoiselle?

We walked in silence down the street in the general direction of the Delaportes' apartment. Had we been moving any slower, we might have been accused of dragging our heels. But there was nothing to hurry back to, and the heat of the day was sloughing off into the relative coolness of evening.

We passed storefronts and bars.

We saw the odd tourist, stranded in the no-man's-land between Invalides and the Eiffel Tower. And that's when I began noticing the strangest thing. People were noticing me.

Men, that is.

Frenchmen. The waiters wrapped in bath towel-length aprons.

Unlucky professionals hurrying through the streets, trapped in Paris during August. Taxi drivers leaning out their windows.

And they weren't just giving me casual once-overs. Surreptitious glances over my shoulder revealed actual heads turning.

For me!

You see, the thing is, I'm not a head turner. I never have been. Except maybe that one Halloween in fourth grade when I decided to dress up as Medusa and had a "hat" of green nylon snakes wriggling out of my skull.

That turned quite a few heads.

And it's not as if I'd tucked the skirt of my dress into my panties by accident. In my experience, those kinds of looks are usually accompanied by snickers. At least they were in seventh grade.

These were looks of admiration. As if I were beautiful.

It had to be the dress.

I'm sure it cost a fortune, but maybe Solange could tell me where to buy one. For a weapon like this, I would be willing to pay any price.

Let's see…I could bring my lunch to work for the rest of my life. Maybe I could eat oatmeal for breakfast for the next 20 years. Or just go without. But then I would shrink to twig-size and the dress would be too big.

Fashion was a very tricky business.

It was probably best just to stay old Sensible-Shoes Claire. I'd had my brief shining moment in the fading afternoon sun. It would have to be enough. My personal budget didn't have room for any frivolities. Not for the next three years, anyway. Lattes, wallpaper paste, and newspaper subscriptions, yes. But not expensive dresses. My polo shirts and shorts would have to do.

But it seemed that admiration provoked an unconscious response. I noticed myself walking slower. Smoother. Holding my head up. My shoulders back. My mother would have been proud. And then I began to anticipate the glances. It was fun.

And, emboldened, I began to look back.

I received a cigarette salute, a raised glass of wine, and two horn honks.

Adrien finally broke off humming and sent a quizzical glance in my direction. Then he surveyed the street in front of us, threw an arm around me, and pulled me to his side. "Do not think that you are going to find someone else to take you out to dinner tonight. I have plans."

To my great disappointment, the glances became more covert. Adrien must have looked very much like my boyfriend. He was giving off all of those protective signals.

Hand on waist. Whisper in the ear. Kiss to the hair.

If he kept going, I'd happily drown in lime-scented cologne.

Oh, well. I'd enjoyed all ten minutes of it. I'm sure I'd remember it for the rest of my life. Paris, back when I was beautiful.

Chapter 11

❦

"So what does it look like?" Pots clanged in the background, and I thought I could hear water running in the sink. My mother could never do just one thing at a time, so she was probably cooking and washing dishes while she was talking to me on the phone.

"Paris?"

"The apartment."

I was standing by the phone in the Delaportes' living room, gnawing on one of my fingernails. That was odd. Either I was really hungry or very insecure. I had several bad habits—leaving coffee cups strewn around the house, eating ice cream straight from the carton—but chewing fingernails wasn't one of them. "Oh. Well, we're not allowed to see it yet. The lawyer needed a power of attorney, so he's going to fax one to you and Dad can fill it out and mail it back. He'll have to use express mail because the lawyer didn't want a copy. He needs Dad's original signature."

"So you haven't seen it yet?"

"Mmm?" She could interpret that anyway she wanted to.

"When will you see it?"

"I don't know. How fast can Dad sign the form and mail it back?" Honestly! Could I make it any more plain?

"Did you give the lawyer the fax number?"

"Yes. He'll do it just as soon as he can."

"Okay. Talk to you soon. We'll be here." Of course they would be.

The only reason I was in Paris was because they were there. That's why I was here.

Adrien was leaning against the door between the hall and the living room, watching me. "All goes well?"

"Fine."

He walked into the room and pulled a book from his pants pocket before joining me on the couch. "You would like this back?"

I took it from him and swept a hand across the smooth leather cover. "It's Mademoiselle's diary. It was at the back of her armoire. The one with the evening gowns. I didn't want someone to find it."

"Except for you, perhaps. So maybe this will solve the mystery of who is Mademoiselle. You are going to read it?"

"Do you really think I should?"

He shrugged. "Why not?"

I opened it. Flipped to the first entry. It was slow going. I had to work at deciphering her filigree handwriting. Adrien lost patience and finally took the diary from me. He began to read out loud.

1 January 1936

All the world will call me a fool for departing for the north, for Paris, in January. Why should I go at all? Perhaps the better question is this, Why should I stay? What would be the purpose? So that I can tend the vineyards, keep the geese, and stare at the sky? This is not for me. And the longer I stay, the more unhappy I become. The more unhappy I make everyone around me: my father, for doing such poor work; my mother, for having no interest in being married; my neighbor, for having no interest in marrying him. I have no idea of what I shall do, but I know I shall be more happy away than at home.

And if this is not the case, then I can always go back.

3 March 1936

I am established. Evidently, I have a very nice back. A back so nice that artists will pay money to draw it. And sometimes this takes them days. The longer, the better, in my opinion. I am getting paid

to sit or stand or lie on a bed and do absolutely nothing. The more nothing the better, since they fly into rages if I move.

17 May 1936

One of my portraits has won a prize at one of the national salons. But, of course, it is not me who is given any notice. It is the artist. I suppose that is how it should be, but even an artist must receive inspiration. From something. Or someone.

3 July 1936

I believe I am one of the only models who does not accept the attentions of the artist as part of the compensation. Please forgive me, but why should this be part of the arrangement? I have tried every way I can think of to say no, but I fear that I shall have to invent new ways. Or perhaps write my own dictionary and sell it so that people can understand. I have laughed at propositions. I have cried over them. I have, in one terrible instance, even run away from one. I have said perhaps another time. I have said never in my dreams. I have pretended not to understand and I have pretended not to hear.

18 August 1936

When does a back cease to be just a back? Some artists have painted me and never thought about me one instant. For them, I am just a back. A lovely back perhaps, but a back all the same. Some artists have painted me and I am anything but a back; I am a fantasy. But still the painting has nothing to do with me. My back is a springboard from which they create another woman entirely. Their mother perhaps. Or their first lover. Or their last lover. Maybe even their wife. And then for some artists I am not a back at all. My back is a pretense; it becomes something else. An object that becomes secondary to an idea. And then, for several artists, my back exists only so they can try to get me to lie down on it; there are not so many of these as one might think.

But enough of them that I have considered whether there is something else that I might do in Paris.

15 September 1936

There was someone new today. He came by the studio where I was posing to speak to the artist. I play games when I pose. When someone comes into the studio, when they begin to talk, I imagine what they must look like by their voice. I imagine where they must come from by the way they speak. Usually the voices belong to gardiennes or message boys or jealous girl-friends or other artists whom I know. The voice today was new. It sounded like cognac. A deep, rich amber. Smooth and rough at the same time. Cultivated. And it did not belong to a Parisian; it belonged to a northerner. From Belgium, I think. He tried to get the artist to take a break. To go to some party at the Ritz. I could have told him myself that the artist would not go. He is a dreamer, this one. My back is an idea. A grand obsession that he must excoriate before he can go back to living his normal life. The man went away before I had a chance to see him.

16 September 1936

He came back today. The man from Belgium. Tried to persuade the artist to go out for lunch. He did not succeed. But he stayed anyway. He sat on the stool in the corner for a long while before he left.

17 September 1936

The man returned. It was not to speak to the artist. It was to see me, I think. My back. I can tell when people are looking at me, even when I cannot see them. The artist, I get used to after a while. His glance becomes like a noise that is so constant I no longer hear it. Like the sound of the sea or the whisper of a breeze in the trees. The glance of this man—I have never felt anything like it! It is like an opera I once heard. I went with an artist once, before I knew what artists are like. This glance evokes emotion. Sometimes so strong, my heart catches in my throat. Sometimes so gentle, it makes me wish to sigh. But when the artist was finished, by the end of the afternoon, the man was gone.

18 September 1936

The man came back. He stayed all day. Even when the artist went out for a moment, he stayed. He tried to get me to turn around, but I would not. I did not want to lose the pose. He asked me if I wanted a blanket. I told him I was not cold. Asked if I wanted a cigarette. I told him I did not smoke.

19 September 1936

The artist has finished. The man did not return. I took my payment and left.

20 September 1936

I have taken another sitting. It begins tomorrow. It is for an artist I do not know. But the pay is very good.

21 September 1936

Today I went to the sitting. I went to the address which had been indicated and found it to be a small café. I was looking at the note I had received, trying to determine whether I had misread it, when a voice spoke into my right ear. It brought to mind the color of the best cognacs. I smiled and turned. It was the man. I was not so far off about his looks. In the sunlight his hair glinted russet and amber as it waved back from his forehead. He was tall and thin. He was not an artist; he did not have the hands for it. He did have money; he was dressed in a well-tailored suit. I told him he looked the way I thought he would. He said I did not look anything at all like he thought I would. I asked him how he had recognized me. He told me it was from the back of my head. I volunteered to turn around if it would make him feel more comfortable. He looked at me. Smiled. Said he could get used to my front too. We had a nice lunch. He drove me back. Walked me up to the door. I asked him what time he needed me to sit for him tomorrow. He told me at ten and would I mind very much if the sitting took place in the front seat of his car on the way to Chartres. I said I would not mind at all.

I yawned a monster yawn. Closed my eyes. Opened them and yawned again.

Adrien paused, looked at his watch, and closed the diary. He got to his feet and set it on the mantel. "Go and change your clothes. If we eat at Café du Marché on rue Cler, then we can walk to the *Tour Eiffel* and go up before it closes. But we must leave now, before you fall asleep."

Chapter 12

❧⁘❧

A walk to the Eiffel Tower sounded fun. I'd never had the chance to go to the top before. But it also sounded very touristy. "You don't have to do this just because I'm in town." It's probably like living in Seattle and having to go to the Space Needle or Pike Place Market anytime anyone came to visit. Fun to do once in a while, but it's not part of your routine. Plus, it's a pain in the rear to find somewhere to park.

"I have never been."

"Ever?"

"I have been there, yes, but I have never been to the top. I am a Parisian. I live here. I am not a tourist here."

Well, in that case…

Adrien grabbed his keys and we were out the door. We didn't wait for the elevator. Just took the stairs. At the ground floor, Adrien pressed the button on the wall to release the door. It clicked and we made our way out into the freshening air. I have to admit that summer evenings in Paris were luxurious.

Sumptuous.

A breeze from the Seine began to riffle through the air. The heat of the day was assuaged. The trees spread their leaves languorously. The traffic slowed. The noises softened. And all through the city, people came out. Mostly just to stroll because evenings lasted until eleven. A magical grace period between sunlight and twilight.

We walked our normal route along rue Saint Dominique in the direction of rue Cler. I thought about Mademoiselle. About the courage it would have taken to leave home. The strength it would have taken to throw off a future that had seemed certain. To push aside expectations and go to Paris without even knowing how she would support herself.

When we passed some real estate offices, I lingered in the windows to get an idea of the going price for an apartment like Mademoiselle's. After comparing the listings of three offices, I settled on the ballpark figure of 1,000,000. Dollars, euros? At that price, it was all the same. It was like winning the lottery! I couldn't breathe.

Seriously.

I'd only hyperventilated one other time in my life. Good thing I'd had that experience. Otherwise, I'd have thought I was having a heart attack. It's very scary, because you feel as though you can't breathe and then you get scared and then you can't breathe and then...Hadn't I read somewhere that the mind-body connection is a lot stronger than most people think? Strong enough that many people are able to stop their hiccups just by telling their muscles to relax.

It wasn't working.

Maybe if I could just force myself to cough. Wasn't that supposed to reregulate your heart if you were having a heart attack?

It wasn't working.

Of course, I wasn't really having a heart attack; it just felt like it. Maybe if I plugged up my nose then my body would have no other option but to make itself take a breath.

Okay, that was a bad idea.

"Claire?" Adrien was still looking at the sale announcements posted in the windows. "It looks like you could get one million for your apartment, but maybe not quite so much since it needs...everything. If you figure in the cost of materials and the cost of labor and..."

That worked.

He finally noticed that my lips were turning an unnatural shade of blue. "Did I say something? Are you ill?" He glanced at his watch. "You must be starving to death. *Allons-y!*"

Yeah, that was it.

We arrived at the café and didn't have to wait very long to get a table on the street. It was along a bench pushed up against the wall. A perfect size for two. And in a perfect position to people-watch.

At Adrien's suggestion, I decided on a *salade brique de chèvre chaud*. Granted, a salad with a warm pastry-wrapped block of goat cheese might not be everyone's bag of lettuce, but it sounded good to me.

Adrien ordered a *pavé* of salmon and a half-carafe of house wine.

The server brought us a basket of bread and two wine glasses, filling them both.

One million dollars.

Although, like Adrien said, it would need a lot of work to justify that sort of asking price. Maybe my parents could just sell it "as is." They'd still walk away with a giant, ostrich-sized nest egg.

One million dollars.

Maybe they'd even share some with me. My fingers, needing something to do while my mind was occupied, were fiddling with the stem of my glass. I picked it up and took a drink.

Sour.

I puckered and blinked. I'd liked the one I had at the Delaportes' better. I picked up a piece of bread and tore it into shreds. Took a bite.

Had another drink. I was thirsty.

I had some more bread. We waited a while. Adrien assured me it would be worth it.

Adrien picked up the carafe and refilled my glass. "Are you feeling well, Claire? You seem *distraite*. If I had known you were going to drink, I would have ordered a better wine. A full bottle even."

"This is fine. *Santé.*"

Adrien tipped his glass toward mine.

At that point, our food arrived and we started to eat. I cut into the cheese and snagged a piece of bread to put it on.

My head felt funny. My feet felt swollen. Was this what drinking felt like? Maybe it wasn't worth it.

"Claire, do you feel well?"

"I'm not sure. My head feels funny."

"Like it is buzzing?"

"Just a minute." I closed my eyes. I couldn't hear anything. I put my hands over my ears. Was there a buzz in there somewhere? "Nope."

"Are you sure?"

"No. No buzz. Just a hum. Like a bee. Or an air conditioner." And it seemed as though my eyes had slowed down. Way down. Like my automatic focus feature was on the blink.

"You drank too much before you began to eat. You will feel better in a while. Have some more bread." He slid the basket toward me.

"Why aren't you married, Adrien?" That might have sounded stupid, but he knew what I meant.

"Because I have never asked anyone."

"Never ever?"

"*Jamais.*"

"No one has ever asked me, either."

"What if I asked you?"

"Would you?"

"Of course. I love you."

The way he did when I was 17? "I'm serious."

"So am I." He smiled at me. He looked a little sad.

"Then why are you sad?"

"Because the girl I love doesn't know I am in love with her."

How could anyone not be in love with Adrien? "I'm sorry."

"As am I. What should I do?"

"Tell her." Just because I hadn't been lucky in love didn't mean everyone had to share my misfortune.

"I have."

"And?"

"She did not take me seriously."

"Well, how did you say it?"

He looked straight into my eyes. "I love you."

If I hadn't known him better, I would have thought he was saying those words to me. "It sounds like you mean it…"

"I do."

I would have told him he flirts too much. With everyone. And that maybe the girl didn't appreciate it, but it seemed to be a part of the whole culture. "Then she's a moron. Or she's just not ready to hear it."

"So you think I should keep trying?"

"How long have you been trying so far?"

"It seems like almost my whole life. I thought I had gotten over her, more than once. It is too impractical. For many reasons. But she always haunts my dreams. There is just something about her. Something very special."

As we ate, the restaurant filled. Soon, there was a line. The waiter took our plates away. Adrien ordered two espressos. Eventually, the waiter returned and set the espressos on the table.

Adrien unwrapped two sugars and plopped them into his coffee. Offered the bowl to me. "Sugar?"

Would they make it taste any better? I dropped first one, then two cubes of sugar into the demitasse. They turned from white to brown and then crumbled and melted away. I grabbed another package of sugar cubes and added two more.

Then I stirred the coffee with a spoon. It looked like syrup now. Did it taste that way too?

I took a sip. Then a swallow. Nope. Still tasted like espresso. I stifled a yawn. My head hurt. Not a searing, needle pain. Just a steady dull pressure that pulsed with every beat of my heart.

Adrien waved the waiter over and settled the bill. Then he took me by the arm and dragged me away from the café.

At least, that's what it felt like. My feet just couldn't keep up. There was a delay between when I told them to move and when they actually did. I don't think I looked funny, but I felt funny. As if my limbs were connected to my body with rubber bands. Not thin twangy ones; fat, thick ones. The kind that require a good pull before they expand.

He hooked an arm around my waist.

I lurched against him for a few steps, and then I threaded an arm around his waist. Held against his side, my gait steadied. And when my head was tucked into his shoulder, it didn't bounce around so much.

We walked down two blocks, back to rue Saint Dominique. Then we turned west and walked some more. Crossed avenue Bosquet. We made our way toward the Champs de Mars, and from time to time I could see the Eiffel Tower playing peekaboo with the buildings.

That lime cologne.

I could smell it. I started to sniff. I followed my nose to a place under Adrien's jaw bone and sniffed a big, long sniff. That's where it was coming from. I'd found the source.

"*Ma poule?*" Adrien sounded as if he were being strangled.

I allowed myself one more giant sniff, and then I put my head back into the spot on his shoulder.

His muscles tensed and he moved away from me, so I made a grab for him with my other arm.

He stopped dead in the middle of the sidewalk. Then he carefully gave my left arm back to me and we continued on. When we came to the Champs de Mars, he found a bench and sat me down on it.

He sat at the other end, his arm stretched along the back of the bench so that it almost touched my shoulder. But not quite. "You sit there and I will sit here and everything will be fine. Okay?"

I looked at him and smiled. "Okay, Adrien. I'm sure I'll feel better in a minute."

"Do you still want to go up the *Tour Eiffel?*"

"Sure. I'd go anywhere with you."

"...*que le Seigneur me donne la pitié.* You feel well?"

"Better." As we sat there a while, I became part of a softer, more intimate world. The sun had not yet set, but it was planning to. The shadows had lengthened, obscuring passersby. Streetlights were glowing. The Eiffel Tower was sparkling. It was a world that contained just Adrien and me. "Let's go."

"I do *not* feel fine. I need two minutes." He was looking at me as if I were dangerous. Contagious.

"Are you okay? Are you sick?" I scooted down the bench, placed a hand on his forearm.

He jerked it away as if I had burned him and jumped to his feet. "Yes. No. I feel well. *Allons-y.*"

So we went. We walked northwest, toward the river and the tower that loomed ahead of us. There was lots of activity, lots of humanity, but hardly anyone standing in line at the north pillar.

We went inside a small building and waited for about ten minutes, watching a gear and weight system pull the elevator back down.

The mechanics looked sturdy enough, although you can never be sure. I decided not to watch them anymore and concentrated instead on the head of the person standing in front of me.

At times I have been known to be afraid of heights.

I was really, really hoping that tonight was not going to be one of them.

We got into the elevator and were pushed, by the people behind us, straight forward. I was pressed against the back wall. Adrien was right behind me. There were windows, but that was fine because the only view was of the structure's ironwork. Then I blinked and we had moved past the gear housing and I could see straight through the structure. I saw the ground, the trees, the river at regular intervals as we glided up to the first level.

"You wish to get off here?" Adrien had cupped a hand to my left elbow and bent to whisper in my right ear.

How much courage did I have in reserve? Without knowing for certain, I thought I'd better just push on to the top and get it over with. "Let's keep going."

"As you wish." He moved from his position behind me to take a position beside me, his forehead against the glass as he strained to get the best view. "*Spectaculaire.* You must look while you can because to go to the top, after the second level, we ascend through the middle. There will be no view."

That was just fine by me.

I sent a look out the window every few seconds, nowhere near as interested as Adrien in the shrinking piece of earth beneath us. We finally reached the second level and exited the elevator. I might as well have stayed inside, because the first thing he did was find a "window" so that we could peer straight down at the ground we ought to have been standing on.

Leaning over that caged oval took my breath away.

I spent the rest of my time looking at the displays of the tower's construction and the hydraulic system that had been conceived to run the elevators.

We went back into an elevator and made a more conventional trip to the top. The other elevators had ascended at an angle to match the tower's structure. This elevator, running straight up the center, seemed almost anticlimatic. But it did serve to calm my nerves. We stepped out into an enclosed space wrapped by windows. Beneath the windows were panoramic photos labeling the sites to be seen in various directions. Above the windows, placed in their actual directions, were listed the distances to the world's most well-known cities. Milan, for instance, was 645 kilometers away.

Just a hop, skip, and a jump. But let's not talk about jumping.

"We must go outside."

"I don't think so. I wouldn't know what I'm looking at. It's dark."

"But that was the point, Claire. To see the lights of the city."

"And I can, see?" I'd pressed my nose up against the windows and I could see the lights. They were pretty. Lots of lights in the dark. All of the major monuments were illuminated, so that Notre Dame, Hôtel de Ville, the Arc de Triomphe, and Sacré Coeur were easily seen.

Could we go back down now?

"You cannot mount the *Tour Eiffel* and not go outside." He grabbed my forearm and tugged me along toward a set of stairs.

"I have to go to the bathroom." Never hesitate to use tricks learned as a child. Sometimes they work.

Adrien rolled his eyes. "*Bon. Par là.* I will wait right here."

Really, I did have to go. But I might not have needed 15 minutes in which to do it.

True to his word, Adrien was right where I'd left him, although he had company. He was leaning against the wall, arms crossed, talking to a blond woman dressed in a very tight halter-neck sundress. They were laughing when I joined them. She tossed her hair over her shoulder and whispered something in his ear.

He laughed and said goodbye. Watched her walk away.

I watched her walk away too, hoping she'd snap the heel off one of those teetering sandals and fall flat on her face.

It's certainly not as though Adrien was my boyfriend. He could talk to whomever he wanted. It would just be nice if it could be an ugly girl or someone's grandmother once in a while.

I cleared my throat.

"Claire. Good. We go now." He stood aside so that I could go first.

There was nothing else I could do but trudge up the stairs. I figured I would stay as close to the stairway as I could. Anyway, we were so high up that I was sure I would be able to see something without going too near the edge.

I was wrong.

The very top level hugs the center of the tower. To see anything at all you have to lean over the railing to have a view past the platform below. So I did it. For about five seconds. All in all, I was proud of myself.

"*Ma poule*, come see this."

"I already did."

"Not all of it."

"All I wanted to."

"Are you afraid?"

"Of what?"

"Me."

"No."

"Because I thought you did not like me."

"No." It was time to come clean. "I don't like heights."

I saw his teeth flash in the gloom. "Then I will hold your hand to keep you from falling. Come here. Just for five minutes and then we go back down."

As soon as I got within range, he wrapped his hand tightly around mine and dragged me toward the rail. "I will not let you go. Do not have fear. Just look. *La Seine.*"

The Seine. Winding through the city like a silver ribbon. From this height, we could watch the progress of the tourist boats as they lit the *quais* in front of them with spotlights. And we could see the bridges that had been stitched across the river, holding the banks together.

There was a slight breeze which fingered my hair and sent whiffs of Adrien's cologne in my direction. He put his chin on my shoulder to talk to me.

"You see that small arch? Here to the right? It is the Arc de Triomphe du Carrousel at the Louvre. And just here, the Arc de Triomphe."

That, I could recognize. Even at night the 12 avenues radiating from its base were visible.

"And to the left, out there? You see the square? It is the Grande Arche. At La Défense. They are in alignment. All of the three. You have the history of France from its past to its future."

I nodded. Barely. The soft whisper of his voice in my ear was doing strange things to my senses.

"And just across the river is Trocadéro with its fountains. And farther down the river, the Maison de la Radio."

"Wh-which?"

"The one in demi-circle." He left his place at my shoulder and walked around to the right. "This way."

I floated after him.

He was waiting at the railing, left hand extended toward me.

When I had reached his side, he brought his arm around behind me and then gripped the rail beside me. I was trapped.

"And here is Hôtel de Ville with the office of the mayor. And the Conciergerie where Marie Antoinette was held. You Americans have such a fondness for Marie. I have never understood this."

My brain didn't seem to be working as quickly as usual. He had to repeat his question. Which brought his mouth closer to my ear and made my vision go hazy. "Who? What?"

"Marie Antoinette. You Americans always take her side. Why is this?"

"Because it shouldn't be a crime to be stupid. She was an innocent girl caught up in an unjust system. It's not like she was the king. It's not like she was even French. Or wanted to be. Wasn't she German?"

"Austrian."

"Well, how would you feel if you had to be the Queen of Austria and everyone hated you just because you were French?"

"If I could live in Vienna and listen to the Boys' Choir whenever I wanted, I think that even I would not mind wearing a dress every day."

Ha-ha. "Seriously, how would you feel—living in a country that wasn't your own?"

"I do not know. I have never done it. And you?" He moved closer. His arm tightened around me.

"I don't know. My dad does it. But I don't know if I could." I'd always wondered if my dad had any regrets about leaving his country. About marrying an American. "I don't know."

Chapter 13

Adrien walked me back to the Delaportes'. He stopped in front of the door. Kissed me on the forehead. "Do not worry. You will feel fine in the morning. Next time will be better. We will have something to eat before. You will not drink so much so fast. It will be fine. You will see. *Bonne nuit.*"

I watched him walk away.

"I will see you tomorrow. Not too early, I think."

I closed my eyes. I could still see the twinkling lights of Paris. And I could still smell that lime cologne.

Next time.

"Bonne nuit." I said it to the darkness. He was already gone.

When I woke at seven, it was to the pounding of hammers.

In my head.

Tiny hammers held by little gnomes. They were doing construction work inside my skull. I closed my eyes, hoping they would go away, but that just intensified the pain.

Because now, instead of just feeling the headache, I could imagine it. With my eyes closed, the darkness of my vision pulsated with each strike of those hammers.

So I opened my eyes and stared at the ceiling.

That worked for a while. I counted the number of repetitions in the pattern of the molding. Swirling flowers mixed with leaves.

It wasn't the worst headache I've ever had. It was just very persistent. Insistent. Incessant. Staring up at the ceiling provided relief for what must have been ten minutes, but then it suddenly seemed larger than life. As though it were the only thing in the room. And if I stared at it anymore, my horizons would shrink to the four-square-foot space above my bed.

Pulling the covers over my head didn't help any.

But I might have stayed there the whole day anyway if I hadn't had to go to the bathroom. But I did, so I closed my eyes and started down the hall.

I might have made it if I hadn't run into Adrien.

"Claire?"

I cracked open one eye just the tiniest bit. And even then, the ray of light streaming into the living room, brightening the hallway, was blinding. "Adrien."

"May I help you?"

"I don't think so."

"*Un café?*"

"Maybe."

"I will make a *café*. You get dressed."

Sure. Save the easy part for yourself.

I hobbled to the bathroom. Hobbled back. Opened the commode drawer. Pulled out a pair of shorts. A shirt. It was red. I put it back. Sat on the bed, exhausted by the effort.

Adrien nudged open the door with his foot. He was holding out a steaming demitasse of something.

It was tempting, but it smelled like coffee. "I don't think so."

"It will help you feel better."

Adrien sat on the edge of the bed next to me. "Just one sip."

Isn't that what the devil said to Eve?

He held the cup for me, his long fingers almost wrapping around it twice.

I drank the whole thing in one long swallow.

Adrien picked up my hand and drew me from the bed, inch by inch, as if I were a child learning how to walk. "Come have something to eat."

He'd already cut and buttered a section of baguette for me. He sat across from me and extended a fist toward me, palm down. "Take these."

I held out my hand and two pills dropped into it. "What are these? Just because I drank a little too much last night doesn't mean I'm a drug addict."

Adrien held his hand out again, this time palm up. "Well, if you do not want two aspirin, then I can always just flush them down the toilet so that we will not be caught with illegal substances."

I was swallowing before he'd finished the sentence.

"You take a bath and then we go?"

"Where?"

"Outside."

The bath felt heavenly. The misty, moist bathroom air cleared my sinuses. And by the time I emerged, clean and clothed, if I didn't think of those gnomes, they didn't think of me either.

We headed out the door, and when we hit the street, we wandered. It took me a while to find the method in his crazy, directionless path, but then I realized that wherever we walked, it was always shaded. I was wearing sunglasses, but I still sent up a prayer of thanks for his thoughtfulness.

We strolled through St. Germain des Prés and then drifted into a multistoried Gilbert Jeune bookstore. I could have done without the bright yellow sign out front, but once I was inside, I was fine as long as I didn't try to concentrate too hard.

Adrien dug through a section of used French classics, and then he went over to a shelf of technical books.

I did more people-watching than anything.

And I noticed that no one was watching me.

What a letdown after yesterday. But really, what else should I have expected?

Dressed in my normal uniform of polo shirt and shorts, I might as well have been invisible. How shallow people are. That's what I wanted to think, anyway. But when I caught a glance of myself in the store's bathroom mirror, I took a long look.

I had to admit that the shirt and shorts didn't do much for me. Granted, I didn't have much to advertise in terms of curves, but I was thin. However, the blousing of the shirt and the bagginess of the shorts made me look as if I were ten pounds heavier.

Huh. I hadn't realized that before.

Maybe when I got home, after I'd paid off all my expenses and replaced my savings—in about 15 years, maybe—I'd buy myself more flattering clothes. Something in a vibrant shade of coral red.

I had a theory that as far as fashion goes, most women get stuck for 10 or 15 years in their college-era style. They keep the same general haircut. Stay with the same style of clothing. I could use myself as an example. I still have a pair of penny loafers in my closet back home.

And I wear them.

As well as some paisley challis skirts and a corduroy shirt. Or two. It's not that I don't know what's in style. I can spout off the up-to-date hemlines, silhouettes, and colors the way guys always seem to know which rugby or soccer star has been traded to which team.

And how many guys actually watch rugby or soccer?

I know all the rules; I just don't play the game anymore. I've given up. Because in my life, given the choice between new bedding plants for the garden or a new jacket, the plants win every time.

But I was in the capital of fashion. So maybe I could do something.

Learn some clever little trick that would instantly turn me into a fashion plate.

I glanced again at my image in the mirror.

Or maybe not.

As we were leaving Gilbert Jeune, Adrien pulled out his cell phone. Stood for a moment in the bright sun to make a call.

Until he saw me wincing.

Then we moved back underneath the awnings, and I looked at mounds of used books until he was done. They looked like college texts from the '70s. I wondered what happened to books when no one wanted them anymore. I wondered if authors ever crept around used bookstores buying up their books for 75 cents a copy. Collecting them like orphaned children. Or maybe they picked them up and put them down again as if they'd never even heard of the author. Or maybe they completely disowned them—never visited a used bookstore, as if they could pretend that people liked their books enough to keep them.

How sad to be an author of unloved books.

Adrien rejoined me. He stared at me, wondering, I'm sure, why I was clutching a copy of *Mushroom Spores and the Winds Which Spread Them* as if it were a 100-euro bill.

"You are going to buy this one? I did not know you have an interest in mushrooms."

"I don't." Then again, he'd seen me tipsy. So why wouldn't he think I'd be interested in hallucinogens? But, for the record, I felt really bad about putting it down.

We started off down boulevard St. Michel. "You are hungry for lunch?" He glanced down at me.

"Not very. But if you are, I could have something small."

We got sandwiches at a take-out store and ate them on a shaded bench across the street at the back of Hôtel Cluny. Adrien had a *rillettes*—pulled pork mixed with salty seasonings and lard—and I had a nice, mild chicken *crudités*, the *crudités* being plain old lettuce and tomato. It was just about right, except that when I was finished, I was still hungry.

Adrien must have seen me eyeing the store, because when he was done, he got up and bought a big fat nutella Belgian waffle.

There is an advantage to hanging out with someone who's known you since childhood, You don't have to inform them of your mania for creamy chocolatey hazelnut spread. Adrien passed the waffle straight to me.

It wasn't until the last bite, when he began to wipe at my face with a napkin, that I realized I had the goo spread all over my mouth. What might be considered cute at the age of six was undesirable at the age of 29. About three minutes of mortified scrubbing at Adrien's direction passed before I realized there was not, nor had there ever been, any chocolate on my face.

So instead of licking the last bits off my fingers, I dabbed them on his nose.

He blinked gravely. "Thank you, Claire. When I become hungry this afternoon, I will still have something to eat."

"Would you like me to shove some waffle up your nose to go with it?"

He considered for a moment. "*Non.* I do not think so. This will be fine." He grinned and then stretched his tongue up and licked it off. I could tell Adrien's true talents were being wasted at Dassault. "What do we do now? Behind us is the Cluny Museum. It has Roman baths and medieval artifacts."

I wrinkled my nose. I wasn't really big into medieval.

"The baths are very cool and shady. And upstairs are the famous Lady and Unicorn tapestries. They are in a special dark room."

I was, however, very big into cool and dark.

We got to the Roman baths eventually, but only after passing through a series of rooms containing tapestries and textiles. Flat, one-dimensional paintings. Stained glass. Then we plunged down a set of stairs and walked out into a vast, vaulted stone room. The *frigidarium*. And it was.

Frigid.

The cool air echoed the muted sounds of passing traffic, our shuffled footsteps, and the history of 2000 years. It was so vast, so empty, it was hard to populate the space with the activity which must have filled it when Paris was still a Roman settlement called *Lutèce*.

We made a circuit of the room, admiring the stone and brick construction. Then we went back into the Cluny Abbey structure housing the Middle Ages exhibits. We strolled past assorted heads, pillars, capitals, and sculptures from a variety of cathedrals and churches.

Saw lots of chests and caskets. Tiny ones. Medium-sized tabletop ones and big huge floor-sized ones. And then a display of toys. At the end of the last room on the ground floor was an interesting tapestry. On further investigation, it turned out to illustrate the stages of wine making. It also made my stomach churn. If I'm not going to eat toe jam, then why would I want to drink grapes that people had stomped into juice with their bare feet?

They didn't still make wine that way, did they?

Maybe not, but it looked as though all those people were having a lot of fun. It portrayed wine making as a community activity. As a social experience. One that appeared to be a pivotal event in their society.

Wine making as a community builder.

"You like this tapestry?"

"Yes."

"*Pourquoi?*"

"Because it looks like everyone is having fun."

"Is this such an abnormal occurrence in your life?"

Was it?

I examined some medieval toys while Adrien studied the tapestry. I tried to remember what day of the week it was. Traveling had really messed up my sense of time. It had to be a weekday, didn't it? It had to be. Adrien was on vacation.

But he wasn't, was he? If he were, he'd be in Carcans.

"You're not stopping yourself from going on vacation just because I'm here, are you?"

"Does it matter? Unlike you, I have six weeks to take, and I am required to take two of them consecutively. I am also required to be back at work in September. Besides, one does not have to leave home to take vacations."

"But if I weren't here, wouldn't you be in Carcans with your parents?"

He shrugged. "I might be."

"You *are* planning to go this year, aren't you?"

He shrugged again.

"You should. I'll be fine by myself. I speak French. And I don't want to spoil your vacation."

"It is not a big deal, Claire. I was only going to Carcans as I do every year. So this year, I will have a vacation from my vacation." He stood back from the tapestry and winked. "Because a vacation should be different than what I would do *normalement, non?* So, if I always go from Paris, then this year, if I want to have a holiday, I will do something different. I will stay in Paris. I have never stayed in Paris in August."

Me neither, so that made two of us. I didn't know whether to be happy or feel embarrassed about it.

I shrugged.

He shrugged.

We climbed the stairs and went up to the next floor.

Paintings.

After a while, the people all started to look the same. Pale, anemic, and wormy. The men might have been women, the women men. And then, mercifully, we came to the Lady and the Unicorn tapestries.

Adrien grabbed a plasticized brochure from a rack as we entered the room. I headed straight for an ottoman in the center of the room and claimed it.

The tapestries hung from the walls of the darkened room. They were pretty. A deep, rich red depicting the textile version of a pale, anemic, long-haired woman. And they were accented with colors of fathomless blue and glowing golden-cream. According to Adrien, of the six tapestries, five of them represented the senses. Although he wouldn't have had to tell me.

The woman was surrounded by mythical beasts and flags in varying stages of unfurling.

Adrien informed me that the flags signified the family who had commissioned them. "At least, that is what they think."

"Who thinks?"

"The experts." He held the brochure out toward me as if he thought I'd want to read it.

"What's the sixth one?"

"Love."

"Love?"

"That is what they say."

I didn't bother asking who said it. Why did they think it represented love? Apart from the subtitle "To My One Desire."

The lady was putting away a necklace.

Putting away a necklace is the equivalent of love? Why? Because it represented taking off all of her clothes? I knew medieval symbolism was strange, but this reminded me of my tenth-grade English teacher, straining to pull symbolism out of poems like "Roses Are Red." "Are you sure they say it's love?"

"Or they say that it could be she is renouncing the other senses."

The French are just weird sometimes. I can say that with authority and without being racist because I am half-French myself.

Sometimes I am weird too.

If it were love, wouldn't it be inscribed "To My One Love"?

I think the poor lady was being inundated with gifts from a knight she didn't love. Sure, he was poetic and romantic, thinking of gifts which coincided with the five senses, but she just didn't love him. Knew she couldn't live with him. The last straw was when he gave her a fabulous necklace. They should have portrayed her throwing it at him. But then that was a kinder, more chivalrous era.

In my opinion, she was a medieval Greta Garbo. What did she want? Her one desire?

To be left alone.

See? That fit the scenario. The problem with looking beyond what is obvious is that, oftentimes, you miss the point entirely.

I shared my theory with Adrien since he'd finally stopped offering me the brochure and started looking at the tapestries himself.

He started laughing and he wouldn't stop. When he could finally breathe again, he started to explain. "I have been here many times to this museum with Solange. She is a medieval historian."

That explains how he knew about the baths being cool and this room being dark.

"We came at least once a month because she wanted to solve the mystery of the tapestries—one of the great unsolved mysteries of medieval art. Who exactly commissioned them and what is the meaning of the sixth tapestry?"

"There is no mystery."

He started laughing again. "This is why I have missed you, Claire." He put an arm around me and gave me a squeeze. "You are irreplaceable."

Okay. If he insisted. But trust me, if you ever visit, there is no mystery.

Chapter 14

On Saturday Adrien appeared at the apartment with breakfast. This time I caught him off guard.

I was up.

And I was bathed and dressed. And it was only eight in the morning. I was becoming more adept at bathing in the bathtub. I used the same principle I use when I mop. Two buckets, or two tubs of water: one for cleaning and one for rinsing. I'd even made myself an espresso.

Twice.

The first one was too weak.

"Have you already eaten?"

"No."

"Good. Then we can have these." He brandished a small white bag in front of my nose. I was dubious, but I was also starving. Just how filling could half of whatever was in the bag be?

Very.

They were *pains au chocolat*. Squares of flaky pastry filled with tablets of dark chocolate. They were divine. And I figured if we walked about ten miles today, it couldn't possibly be of importance to the general shape of my figure.

And, in fact, Adrien had planned on doing some walking.

"I thought we could go to the market on avenue Wilson and then I could show you my apartment."

Sounded good to me. I grabbed my backpack and we left.

It wasn't long before I realized something was wrong. There was no traffic, pedestrian or otherwise. Paris was a ghost town.

"Is it a holiday?"

"*Non.*"

"Is there a strike or something?"

"*Non.*"

"A curfew?"

"*Non.*"

"Are you sure it's okay to be outside?"

"*Oui.* Is there something wrong?"

"There's nobody here."

"It is Saturday, and it is only eight o'clock."

"On a *Saturday.*" I was from the land of 24-hour home construction stores for people who worked 60 hours during the week and just as many hours on the weekend accomplishing home-improvement projects. If they weren't up by eight A.M. on Saturday doing something, then they were ill.

"*Oui.* A Saturday. The only reason to wake up so early is to be first at the market."

Which we were, by the way. Some of the vendors were still setting up. The covered market was located in tented booths on a median spanning several blocks of avenue du Président Wilson. It began near Pont de l'Alma and stretched up toward Trocadéro.

Outside the first tent was a mattress salesman and a furniture repairman. The European answer to one-stop shopping.

I was curious about what Adrien would buy for himself. I didn't have to wait long. He stopped at one of the very first booths. A *fromager.* He bantered with the saleswoman. She sold him a thick slice of blue-spotted Fourmes and a wedge of Brie.

We skipped the next stall, a *boulanger,* who, Adrien said, sold poor-quality pastries. I eyed them with a skeptical glance as I went by and they did seem overbaked and meager. The savory quiches less than savory.

We did stop at the next stand, a green grocer, for a nice long chat, as well as for some *salade*—he bought a big frilly head of red leaf lettuce.

A vine of ripe tomatoes and some *fruit rouges:* black currants, raspberries, and cherries.

We walked for a while before coming to a man who sold olives of all sizes and colors: black and green as well as the full spectrum of browns and even several varieties of white. Adrien bought several bags' worth, asking about the man's family in Morocco, before continuing on and switching sides to another *boulanger.*

I could see why he preferred to shop here.

The baguettes were nice and healthy, the croissants bursting with golden flakiness. He bought a baguette and two small *tartelettes* before enlisting my aid to carry his growing feast of food.

On we went to a butcher selling chickens. But only so that he could tell me the next butcher sold larger, plumper chickens at the same price. With roasted potatoes.

And so he did. And we bought one.

We stopped in at a seafood booth, my favorite due only to the variety of colors and textures. There were stacks of scallops on the half shell, bins of crabs with their spider legs hanging over the edges. Colorful pyramids of shrimp. A fan of sleek mackerel. He chatted with a young man behind the tables for a few minutes and then left without buying anything. All our purchases were complete by midmarket, but we walked the length just the same.

There was a lady selling socks.

A gentleman selling kitchen gadgets like mushroom scrubbers and garlic graters.

A table stacked with tins of foie gras.

An Italian delicatessen.

Another fruit and vegetable stand that had nice fruit on display but actually bagged overripe produce. I'd have to trust Adrien on that one because the smiling vendor looked honest to me.

After we'd done a U-turn at the upper end of the market, we stopped halfway back at a florist's, mostly because I couldn't make my feet keep walking. The bouquets were so gorgeous that I had to stop and look.

Along the ground were nosegays of roses in bright circus colors, puffy round bouquets of subtly shaded Hortensia, bunches of bright sunny gerbera daisies dotted with looped ribbons. They were all interspersed with greenery, but not of a kind I was familiar with.

No fern fronds here.

Used to bouquets built on a vertical or triangular axes, the sight of round, dense balls of flowers was entirely different. Refreshing. As if you could take a scrumptious bite out of one of them. Or play a psychedelic game of soccer.

On a series of tiered shelves above them were large black buckets filled with individual flowers. Long-stemmed roses of every color. Prickly masses of thistle. And on the chest-high counter, looking down upon all the other lesser flowers, were half a dozen orchids in pretty pale pinks and lavenders.

"What is your favorite?" Noticing that I was no longer trailing him, Adrien had turned around and come back to find me.

"White roses." That was my standard answer. Wise enough to recognize that they were already a flower, they chose to clothe themselves in the simplest of colors. Cool, elegant, pristine.

"Then why are you looking at the orchids?"

"Because."

Because everyone has something that they really want to possess but always talk themselves out of buying. For me, that something was the phalaenopsis orchid. There was something so achingly poignant about a plant that grew with its roots showing and turned out a series of fragile blossoms along the arc of a single branch. A branch so thin that it didn't look as if it could support the weight.

But they were also high maintenance.

They need bright sun, but not bright midday sun. They like temperatures in a range between 55 and 85 degrees, but not any colder and not any hotter. They also like humidity, but not too much of it. They like water, but don't want to drown in it. They can be encouraged to bloom again, but only if you prune them in time and if the season isn't too late.

I love orchids, but they could never survive at my house.

I have this secret fantasy that my plants grow legs at night and water themselves in the bathtub whenever they need it. And they scrounge around under the sink for plant fertilizer when they start to feel especially stunted.

And that's fine for ferns, ivies, and peace lilies, but I could never subject an orchid to my lifestyle of benign neglect. It just wouldn't be right. So I've talked myself out of buying one at least a dozen times.

It wasn't that hard since 30 or 40 dollars buys not one container but flats of pansies, an entire garden's worth of seed packets, or a bag of grass seed. Or three big tall bouquets of cut flowers that would take up enough space to make an impact in a darkish room of a small 1940s Seattle home.

"Claire? Would you like an orchid?"

"Yes. But you can't let me have one. I'd kill it in less than a week."

Adrien just laughed at me and asked what color I wanted.

"The white one with the blushing pink cheeks. But I can't have it. I can't be trusted."

"*Ma poule*, I can be trusted. I will check up on you, and if it starts to wilt, then I will confiscate it and put you on probation."

"But I'm not going to be here long enough."

"All the more important that you get what you like now so that you can enjoy it even longer."

It was ridiculous to even consider buying a houseplant I wouldn't be around to care for. "It's not like I'll be able to take it back to Seattle with me."

"It does not have to last forever. If it will bring you pleasure while you are here, then you must have it."

"Adrien, that's silly. Let's just get a bouquet." I looked down the stand at those masses of roses.

He hounded me, grabbing at the sack I was carrying. "Claire. Do not be *ridicule*. You are here for such a short while. You must make yourself happy."

That's what temptation does. It keeps presenting the same argument, over and over again, until it sounds exactly like what you've been thinking the entire time.

Adrien signaled an end to our argument with a nod to the florist and a flourish of euros.

My eyes squinched shut. I couldn't believe he'd spent that much on a ridiculously engineered flower that had no right to exist outside a hothouse. And certainly not anywhere in my house.

I vowed to enjoy every single one of its molecules.

Chapter 15

೫)ುಲ್

Before walking back to Adrien's, we redistributed the packages. I carried the orchid; he carried everything else.

I still couldn't believe I owned one.

It took a near miss with a car while crossing avenue Marceau in the direction of avenue George V before I could lift my eyes from the delicate petals of the single blossom. We stayed on the west side of the street, protected from the sun by those ubiquitous plane trees with their peeling camouflage bark. We passed a Givenchy boutique (on both sides of the street), the Chinese Embassy, an avant-garde beauty salon for men, and the American Cathedral.

I was in Adrien's neighborhood now. It was upscale, high fashion. A perfect fit. And convenient. It was just off the Champs-Elysées.

We waited in front of the red-and-black striped Hédiard *épicerie* for the light to change. Without noticing how, I found my nose almost pressed to the window, looking at artfully presented packages of chocolates and candies, cookies and nuts. Stacks of tinned *pâtés* and baskets filled with pyramids of fruit.

I detached myself from the window and went back to stand by Adrien. He was looking at the cars parked along the side alley in front of the Four Seasons George V. I spotted a sleek Lamborghini, a Maserati, and two racy Porsches.

But only after he pointed them out.

I've never had any interest in cars. Whenever I park at a mall, which is practically never, I have to think hard to remember what my own car looks like so that I can find it again.

When the light changed, we walked east across the six-laned avenue George V that had no lane markings save one stripe down the middle, and we found ourselves at one corner of a three-way intersection, just in front of an Hermés shop and an attached hat shop. And down from it, a tiny shoebox of a jewelry store.

I'm not a big fan of scarves, hats, or jewelry, so I had already sailed past it when I realized that Adrien had stopped in front of a nineteenth-century building. It was made of cut sandstone and had a balcony bulging out over the top of the front door.

He was punching a code into a keypad. "This is me." He held the glassed wrought-iron door open while I stepped through. At the back of the foyer beyond a wide modern glass door was a paved courtyard and an elevated bed planted with shrubs. Adrien hit a button to turn the lights on.

They cast a feeble shadow from the inside of an Empire-style suspended bowl chandelier.

He pushed the button to call a modern elevator. Farther down the hall were both the requisite spiral staircase clad in a red oriental runner, and the older, smaller elevator, nestled in the hollow of the stairs.

We rode the elevator all the way to the top. Sixth floor. Seventh, if you were counting American-style with the first floor at ground level. When we got off, I followed Adrien down to the end of the hall where he put a monster-sized key into the door and turned what sounded like the equivalent of 20 deadbolts to open it.

I stepped inside. Looked around.

I was disappointed.

No 12-foot ceilings. No moldings on the walls. No chandeliers. Instead, there were hardwood floors, burnished gold and reflecting light from a high gloss finish; they must have been new. The walls had been painted in matte white.

It might have been located in an old building, but Adrien's place looked modern.

And he was looking at me.

Just as long as he didn't look into my eyes.

If he did he'd know every thought I was thinking. So I started to look on the bright side of things. And that was the first thing. It *was* bright. Standing in the hall at what was the back corner of the apartment, natural light still reached me.

With the front door shut, the apartment fanned out before me. To my right, two closed doors and then, almost straight ahead, a room with at least one window. And then traveling along an arc toward my left, his bedroom with two windows. Uncurtained paned glass doors separated it from the hall. Left of the bedroom, off a crook in the hall, was another room. I couldn't see it, but the windows in that room had projected puddles of sunlight onto the hall floor. And last of all, far to my left, a galley kitchen with an open window at the end. It was this window that let in the sun which doused the hallway.

So maybe it wasn't elegant, but it was cheerful. I didn't have to dig too deeply for a smile before I turned to him. "Show me."

He started out toward the room straight ahead and then he remembered his packages. "One moment."

As I stood there, I heard him open the refrigerator. Heard the rustling of the packages. And then he was beside me, ushering me into his home. The room straight before us was an office with two windows projecting from the garret underneath the building's mansard roof. That uneven roof left only two walls without any angles and only one wall, the back wall, without a sloped ceiling. It was against this back wall that Adrien had placed bookshelves. Four of them. Glass-fronted and towering from floor to ceiling. I had trouble deciding whether to stop and browse through his collection or to continue on the house tour.

Being a cat-person, curiosity won and I opened a glass door to pry.

He was a collector of French classics. First editions, if he could find them. There were Zola, Balzac, Dumas. And other earlier, rarer works, such as Molière, Voltaire, and Racine. They were all, of course, leather bound. Some simply done, others tooled with gold leaf or hand stamped. I loved old books. Loved the mystery of who had read them, touched them before I had. "Where did you get these?"

"*Salons des vieux papiers.* Book fairs. In fall and spring. Vendors from across Europe fill convention halls with books, newspapers, postcards, posters. I go to every one." He pulled a slender volume from the shelf and offered it to me with both hands. "This is one of my favorites."

I took it and read the title. *"Histoires ou contes du temps passé, avec des moralités: Contes de ma mère l'Oye."* Stories of Mother Goose. It was by Pierre Perrault.

"Not from 1697—not an original—but it is an early copy. With just the eight fairy stories."

I'd never thought of him as a fairy-tale kind of guy. As a knight in shining armor or maybe as a handsome prince, but not as someone who saw any value in the actual tales. "You like fairy tales?"

"Yes. Because they are not just about fairies, are they? They are about dreams in common. Dreams that every person shares."

"Of handsome princes?"

His eyes glinted amusement. "Maybe. And of justice. Of trust and love." He took it from my hands and pushed it gently back into place on the shelf. "It was my first purchase."

I was looking at him in profile as he faced the shelves, and I was seeing things in him that I had never seen before. Then he turned and looked at me, and I found myself falling again into those brilliant blue eyes.

They were so luminous, so magnetic, that I found myself squinting. Against the color and the pull.

"You are surprised?"

I started to shake my head but found myself nodding instead. "I am."

He unfurled a smile. Shrugged. "So we learn something new about each other."

About each other? What had he learned about me?

He leaned in close. And then closer, his eyes passing back and forth between mine. And then they dropped down.

I followed his gaze to the place where it stopped. On the orchid, which I had set down on the floor. I picked it up.

"You like orchids. I like fairy stories."

Oh. That. I hadn't realized I was holding my breath until its release shook the solitary bloom like a hurricane.

Adrien removed it from my hands and sat it on his desk. "I will show you the rest of the house."

I was whisked down the hall and to the bedroom. It was large, but it had an awkward wedge shape. And the only long wall without slanting ceilings was covered by a huge thigh to ceiling mirror. The two garret windows were flanked with plum brocade curtains embellished with gold braid and the Louis Philippe-style bateau bed was draped with the same material.

I've always felt strange in other people's bedrooms, so I stood in the door, admired the directoire *commode-secrétaire.* How convenient to be able to put away your clothes and write a letter at the same time.

Then Adrien pulled me into the living room. It was a rectangle with one corner lopped off. Like the dog-eared page of a book. And on either side of the turned down corner was a garret window flung open to the day. These were hung with crisp white-striped sheers which swayed in the breeze.

The room didn't look large enough to be divided in two sections, but it was. The corner to my left was configured into a dining room with a small round table and two chairs. The glass tabletop rested on a four-columned pedestal made of black marble; the legs of the chairs repeated the motif. The remainder of the room featured furniture in a mix of styles. A recamier sofa, often mistakenly referred to as a fainting couch. A pair of Louis XVI chairs. And a directoire armchair.

It was a nice apartment. A work in progress, mixing modern and antique, but it was cozy in a formal sort of way.

Adrien left me in the living room with a bowl of olives while he went to fix lunch. There were three cabinets that had been built into the walls, so I opened the doors. They were filled, to overflowing, with books. Recent ones. Books on topics ranging from the history of Kosovo to the life of Winston Churchill. I lifted out several with the thought of borrowing them.

Then it was time for lunch. I could tell when the smell of roasted chicken wafted past my nostrils. When I turned around, I saw that

Adrien had already set the table and placed the food on serving dishes and platters.

I'd have to learn to volunteer my help more quickly.

While I sat, he put in a CD by some French singer that fit the mood; sunny, floating guitar and light percussion echoed by lyrics which seemed just as cheerful.

"I like your place."

Adrien nodded his thanks—I'd caught him in the middle of a mouthful.

"When did you buy it?"

"Let me think." He put his wine glass down and pondered for a moment. "It was in '97. Just before real estate prices began to mount." He sent a sly gaze in my direction. "I was very smart, you know. I could not afford this now."

I was surprised he could have afforded it then. "Why here?"

"In the eighth? Or in the attic?"

In the attic, but I didn't want to offend him, so I smiled and shrugged.

"I got tired of waiting for life to happen. I kept thinking I would get married and then I would buy an apartment. Or a house in the sub-urbs. But I have not. It is not smart to pay rent when I could own, so I decided to buy. And I like this area. The Champs-Elysées has every-thing. It is on a good metro line. I walk outside and I can watch a movie, buy groceries, or go to the bank."

He sliced a piece of chicken neatly from the bone.

"I might have liked something with Versailles floors or molded ceil-ings, and I could have had, but I also wanted space. What if I never get married? I do not want to spend the rest of my life crammed into a stu-dio apartment." He shrugged. "So I found a nice building that had apartments with good wood floors and molded ceilings, and I bought what I could afford: an apartment in the attic."

"That's what I did too."

"You live in an attic?"

"Uh…no. I mean, I got tired of waiting around for life to happen. I'd always wanted to own a house, so I decided to just do it. I couldn't afford to buy exactly where I'd wanted." The truth was, I could hardly afford to buy anything at all. What I'd really wanted was one of those cute Arts and Crafts bungalows that line the streets in places like Queen Anne or Wallingford. What I'd gotten was a small 1940s ranch in West Seattle.

It was cute.

The front door was flanked by two small round windows. It was in the shape of an "L." As much of an "L" as a two-bedroom, one-bath can make. And I figured in about 15 years, West Seattle would be the new upwardly mobile neighborhood of choice. Kind of like Ballard was now. So I'd have all the cachet without the astronomical mortgage.

"So what does this say about us, Claire?"

"We're realists. We might have had other dreams, other plans, but we're making do with what we've got. What else can we do? Otherwise, we might be waiting around for people who may never show up."

"Or it could mean that we have given up."

"I haven't given up. I'm just making myself comfortable until I get married. I'm waiting in style." If you can call living in a shoebox house with a suspect furnace waiting in style. "I'm taking a breather."

Adrien laughed out loud. "Ah. You are taking a break. Good for you. I, myself, have been taking a break for five years. Maybe I am ready to play again."

Five years?

At that moment I discovered something I didn't know about myself. I hadn't known that the thought of living my life, unchanged, for five more years was unbearable. I had thought I was doing fine. As well as can be expected for an unmarried 29-year-old. I wasn't like some people. I didn't constantly obsess about how my ovaries were aging and my egg supply dwindling. And I didn't need a man to be complete. I didn't define myself by my marital status. Or my job. So I knew I had my head screwed on right. I just hadn't known life could be so lonely.

Maybe I'd been wrong about things.

But one thing I knew without a doubt. I didn't want to take a breather. Not for five more years.

Chapter 16

꧁꧂

$\mathcal{S}$unday dawned bright and smoggy. Only I didn't know it until we were on the way to church and had topped the hill in Suresnes. As we turned the corner, I could see the city, spread out below us, beyond the green hedge of the Bois du Boulogne.

At least I think it was the city.

Vague shadows grew more indistinct in the distance and eventually blended into the steel blue horizon. I started thinking about what smog, breathed in on a daily basis, might do to a person's lungs. But then I stopped. Because what was the alternative? To stop breathing?

It hadn't harmed Mademoiselle any. Or at least not much.

I'd tried hard to remember what I'd worn the previous week to church, but with two pairs of shorts and a limited number of shirts, memories of my fashion choices were fuzzy. I crossed my fingers and chose a red polo and blue shorts.

Adrien was wearing a bright sky blue gingham shirt and white duck pants. He played the guitar again during the service, but sat next to me, going through a jack-in-the-box routine whenever it was time for a song.

I recognized many people from the previous Sunday's service, and after church was over they returned the favor by coming over to ask how my week had been. I quickly became immersed in a knot of conversation with other 20- and 30-year-olds about their social plans for the coming year.

Everyone was excited about some chocolate fair that was going to be held in November. Some people were advocating for the group to visit a wine show. Another wanted to try for cheap tickets some night to the *Comédie Française* to take in a classic French play. And someone was lobbying for a weekend trip to Bruges in Belgium, touting all the advantages of world-famous chocolate, lace, and beer.

Nice combination.

How come no one ever wanted to do stuff like this at my church?

Cynthia appeared and gave me two French air kisses alongside my cheeks. Then she stood back and searched my eyes. "So. How is Adrien?"

"Fine."

"Nothing going on?"

"Should there be?"

"Any seventeenth-summer sorts of things?"

"Shh!" I glanced around the room, looking for him. "No. And none expected. How was your week?" At that moment Adrien appeared and pressed his hand to my back. I only had enough time to send a one-size-fits-all wave over his shoulder before we were jammed into the bottleneck of people trying to leave through the front of the church.

Adrien clasped hands and offered greetings as he worked his way toward the exit, but his forward momentum never slowed. Short of throwing out an elbow or shoving people aside, I had a difficult time keeping up with him. Ten minutes later, after we'd made it out the door, I felt as though we'd accomplished a strenuous athletic feat. I was so hot and sweaty from the press of humanity that I felt that I should pour a bottle of sports drink down my throat.

Or dump it over my head.

"Is your house on fire?"

That stopped him in his tracks. "What is this phrase? I do not know it. And more—why would you say something like that?"

Someone had given me a flat tire and I had bent down to work my heel back into my shoe. "It means 'Slow down, Speed Racer!' Why are you in such a hurry?"

"I am sorry. All my excuses. But I would like to take you to the Musée Jacquemart-André, and if we do not hurry, we will only have one hour to dine."

Only one hour? The horror!

As it turned out, we had an hour and a half. And I have to admit, Adrien was right. It would have been nice to have had just a little more time to enjoy the atmosphere. The museum was housed in a nine-teenth-century private mansion. Its old dining room had been con-verted into a tearoom, the walls displaying seventeenth-century Belgian tapestries and ceiling paintings by Tiepolo.

The weather being warm, the seating spilled out onto the terrace adjoining the *cour d'honneur*. In the midst of such grandeur, I was the only one out of place, so I vowed not to look at, not to even think about, what I was wearing. Shorts and polos might be *de rigueur* for Americans in the summer, but certainly not for the French.

I might look French, with my dark hair and long legs, but I defi-nitely didn't sell myself that way. What I needed was a closet filled with Solange's clothes. Then people might actually start speaking to me in French. Throughout my week's collection of experiences, even when I spoke French, waiters and vendors replied to me in English. It was get-ting old.

"Do I look American to you?"

Adrien put down his glass of orange juice and looked me straight in the eye. "Of course."

"But I'm French."

"Your bones might be French, but your spirit is American."

"When I speak I don't have an accent."

"Yes, but your clothes and your hair, even your eyes, betray you."

"So how do I get rid of the traitors?"

Adrien shrugged. "Throw your clothes away. Do something with your hair. *Redresse-toi*...you must sit up, stand straight. You must believe in your beauty, because if you do not, then why should anyone else? Your good fortune was to have a French father, your bad fortune, to have an American mother. So you have the look, but you do not have the spirit. You see?"

No. I didn't see at all.

"Look at yourself."

Now that was what I'd been trying hard not to do. But it didn't matter because I could recite what I was wearing with my eyes closed: white ankle-length sports socks, mostly white running shoes, blue shorts, brown belt, red polo shirt. Tucked in.

No need to mention unmentionables.

So, like I said, I was no longer a fashion plate, but my clothes matched and they were clean. Or would be tonight when I threw everything in the wash.

"*Non*. Not at your clothes. Look at you."

At me? Pale white skin. Long thin legs. Average-height slender body. I'm all angles, except, of course, at my cheekbones, where angles in my round face would have come in handy.

My eyes, unusual. A green-gray that looked like cat eyes.

If I looked at myself cross-eyed, I could probably see my nose—Adrien had taught me that trick when we were younger—but it was spoiled by a scattering of freckles. What else can be expected with alabaster skin? And the rest of my body was generously dotted with moles in assorted sizes and colors.

I was inspecting some of those moles, those on my arms—something I should do more often—when I realized that I was hunched over the table, my arms crossed over my stomach. Looking down, I could see my legs. Touching at the knees, but then reaching back to wind around the chair.

It felt awkward. Probably looked awkward too.

As I straightened, I had to push my hair away from my eyes. I should have pulled it back that morning. It was blunt cut so that I could let it hang or pull it back in a ponytail. I could also braid it or twist it into an upsweep. In theory. In practice, I was strictly wash-and-go. I tucked a lock behind my ear, hoping it would hold back the rest.

What had Adrien been saying?

"You are beautiful, Claire. I do not know why you insist on hiding this from all the world."

I blushed. Beautiful. That would be nice if it were true because none of the lesser forms of beauty—cute, pretty, attractive, stunning—had ever been applied to me.

"Maybe if I hid your clothes you would have to buy new ones."

"At my salary, if you hid my clothes, I'd just have to go around naked."

"This would not be a bad thing."

"Maybe not for you, but it might be a little cold for me. Why does it matter to you what I wear? You should like me for me, not because I'm beautiful." Or not, as I'd already established.

"I do like you for the person you are. But the person you are on the inside must wear the person you are on the outside."

"But it's shallow to be so worried about looks."

He pursed his lips. Took a bite of pastry. Chewed and swallowed. Took another drink of juice. "Yes. Of course. Of course you are right. God must be very shallow."

I swallowed my bite of pastry whole. "I never said that."

"Yes, you did."

"I didn't. I said that it's shallow to worry about looks."

"And if one believes that God created everyone—both inside and out—then we must believe that in some small way he cares about our features. Is it such a difficult thing to believe?"

Was God allowed to care about the way I looked? I shrugged. During my week in France, I'd already determined that the safest route with Adrien was to stay uncommitted as long as possible.

"Claire? You do not think that God takes pleasure in the way we look?"

I shrugged again. How many more shrugs did I have left? I'd have to start using them more judiciously.

"How about this question, Does God take pleasure in flowers? In the sunset? In the endless undulations of the ocean?"

The soul of a poet and the mind of a heretic. Flowers…could I give him that one? God made the flowers. All of those proverbial "lilies of the fields" that were dressed in such splendor. Okay. I could give him that one. Sunsets? Sure. I had to start saving my shrugs somewhere. "Yes."

"Yes!" Adrien smiled. "Of course he does. If God is good, then he may only create good things. Beautiful things. God is the creator of beauty, yes?"

"Ye-es." I shut my eyes. He was going to pounce. Soon. Anytime now. I could feel it.

"He is the creator of your beauty, yes?"

I couldn't really say anything except yes, could I? "Yes?"

"So do you not think it disappoints God when you do not acknowledge the special beauty he has given you?"

"So you're telling me it's offensive to God that I'm wearing shorts and a polo shirt?"

"And running shoes."

"Running shoes? God has something against running shoes?"

"Are you running?"

"Adrien, I don't think God cares what I wear as long as it's clean and practical."

"*Non, non, non.*" He accompanied those "tsks" with a waving finger. "It is not what you wear. It is how you see yourself. You do not see the beauty, so you cannot acknowledge it." He looked at me carefully, speculating. "Perhaps, though, this is not your fault. Perhaps not." His face brightened. "I will pray for you." Then he dug into his eggs with a spoon.

"*You* pray for *me?* Wait a minute. Why?"

"Do you not normally pray for a person who has a misconception about God?"

"I don't have a misconception."

He patted my hand. Actually reached out and patted it! "*Pauvre* Claire. This is always what people say when they have a misconception. It is rather like being insane, do you not think so?"

"What is my misconception again?"

"That God is not concerned with beauty."

"I never said that. God created beauty. I believe that. I just don't believe that I offend him by...how I see myself." That should clear things up. I really hoped it would because I wanted to eat, not talk.

"You go to a museum, you go to a park. You stand in front of a picture or a statue. What are you doing?"

I started to shrug, but then remembered I needed to save them. "Admiring them?"

"*Exactement!* Admiring them. Why? Because they are works of art. You stand on top of a mountain, you stand in a field of flowers. What are you doing?"

"Admiring them." It worked last time. I was crossing my fingers that it would work this time. I was also eating the most incredible potato salad.

"Exactly. Paintings and statues are works of art. Mountains and flowers are works of art. Man has argued that he is the highest creation of God. How can we not call ourselves masterpieces? And what do masterpieces deserve?"

I was getting tired of this game. "Admiration."

"Exactly." Adrien flashed me a grin.

"People are God's masterpieces; we should admire them like statues." I'd finished with the potato salad and gone on to a salad of mixed greens with smoked salmon. Really good.

"Or paintings or flowers. Every woman wants to be admired, *non?* Brian, by example, did he not tell you how beautiful you were?"

"Brian could have cared less how beautiful I was. He liked me because I was nice and kind and good."

"He never said that you were beautiful?"

I shrugged. There was no point in holding them back now.

"And this was okay with you?"

"That he appreciated my inner beauty? Of course!" I wished Adrien would just shut up.

"Nonsense. This is rubbish based on Hollywood movies. Every woman wants a man to notice her beauty."

Was I really having this conversation? "Fine. So maybe you should appreciate...that woman over there with the pretty smile."

"*Oui.* Yes, I have been. And also the man sitting next to her. He has a very strong jaw, would you not say?"

"Did you do this when you were dating Solange and Véronique?"

"Do what?"

"Point out other attractive women to them?"

"Or they would point them out to me."

That seemed a little kinky. "And it didn't bother them?"

"Why should it? Other people were probably admiring them. Like people would admire your fascinating eyes or your long legs if you would notice them first."

"You don't think that's being just a little unfaithful to whomever you're dating?"

"Unfaithful! It is not like I wanted to have sex with them. I admire a flower, I admire a person. They are both created by God. Why should I look at one and ignore the other?"

"Fine. Look all you want. I'll just keep eating."

Adrien's lips curled and he winked. "I will still pray for you."

Pray for me! Me? I'm the one who'd known God the longest! "How can I prove to you that I don't have a misconception?"

"This is simple. Just change the way you see yourself. Or I will change it for you."

Chapter 17

❧

How many times in life can you say that you've had a warning when something bad is going to happen? Not a premonition, but a real warning?

I'd like to think that I'd be smart enough to pay attention when I hear one, but now I know that's not true because, in retrospect, Adrien gave me a very clear warning on Sunday. And now it's Tuesday, and I'm standing in the bedroom with a towel wrapped around my body and my hair is dripping onto my naked feet. I'm not wearing any clothes because I don't have any.

Not anymore.

Which is very strange because I did when I got into the bathtub. I had two drawers full. One for socks, bras, and underwear, and the other for shorts and shirts.

I opened both drawers again just to make sure.

They were empty.

I closed them and opened them again, just to make extra sure.

I looked underneath the commode, expecting to see running shoes, but they weren't there either.

"Claire?" Adrien called my name from outside the bedroom door.

I started to answer him, but my words were drowned by the beep-beep-beeping of the garbage truck on the street outside the building. I stalked towards the door and tried again. "You rat!"

"I think you mispronounce. My name is Adrien. A-dri-en."

"Give me back my clothes!"

"I cannot."

"Give them back right now. Just because you don't like them does not mean you can take them." I flung the door open, holding the towel together with one hand and extending the other. "My clothes."

"I am sorry, but I do not have them."

I swiped dripping hair back from my face. "Then get them."

"They are gone."

The funny thing about speaking a foreign language, especially French, is the presence of *faux amis*, or false friends. These are words which look and sound similar to your own language, but have different meanings. I shook my head. "You don't really mean gone. Try again."

"They are gone."

"Gone, gone?"

"Gone."

"You mean they're not here? Where are they?"

"I threw them in the garbage."

The garbage that the beeping truck had just taken away? Okay. That wasn't a *faux amis* and it wasn't funny. "Everything? You threw everything in the garbage?"

"*Oui.*"

"Not my jeans."

"*Oui.*"

No! My jeans had just come into their own. They were perfectly faded. Perfectly stretched out. Perfectly soft. I'd been working to make them that way for seven years. They were also a size four. I would never buy a size four anything again. But they were proof that I had, once upon a time.

"Even my shoes?"

"Pfft. The shoes are not important. You do not even run."

They were important to me. If I'd had the ability to put on those shoes, I would have kicked him in a spot that would have left future generations free from the menace of Adrien's offspring. As it was I stood there. Stupefied. There is no etiquette book that has a section on what to do when your host throws away your entire wardrobe.

"My bras?"

He shrugged. "You don't need them."

Well, thank you very much, Mr. Chivalry.

"My panties?"

He blushed. "There were holes."

"You looked?" That did it. I shut the door in his face. But it didn't make a very loud bang, so I opened it again and slammed it. Hard.

And the doorknob fell off and rattled across the floor.

Great. Just great. Because to get all my feelings out I either needed to swear at the top of my lungs or slam the door shut another 50 times.

"I can't believe you did that! Are you crazy?"

"Trust me, Claire. You will thank me for this."

"When? When I get arrested for streaking? Are you planning to keep me here for the rest of my life?"

"Why? Are you planning to stay?"

"You're so…arrogant…so…so…Arrogant…ARROGANT! I can't believe I ever had a crush on you."

"You did? When?"

"Give me back my clothes!"

"I regret that I cannot. But I do have the dress we borrowed from Solange."

"How convenient."

"Here." He tried to turn the doorknob. "Take this."

"I'm not wearing it."

"But you must."

"I won't."

"Don't be difficult."

"Then don't throw away my clothes without asking."

"Claire. Enough. Open the door and take the dress."

"I can't."

"*Oui.* You can. Just open the door and take the dress."

"I can't open the door."

"Why must you be so stubborn?"

"Adrien, listen to me. I can't open the door. The doorknob fell off. I can't open it."

He tried the doorknob again. And again. "And I cannot open this, either."

As he fiddled with the door, I looked around the room for something to throw at him, which surprised me, because I'm not the throwing type.

I stomped on the floor a few times, but it wasn't very satisfying without shoes. Which reminded me. "If I had running shoes, I could climb out the window and down to the street."

"I refuse to argue about this. It is *ridicule* to own a pair of running shoes when you do not run."

I got tired of standing around with no clothes on, so I decided to crawl back in bed. "A normal person would never have done this!" I pulled the covers over my head.

"Yes. Well, sometimes pain is necessary to create beauty."

I hopped out of bed and stomped to the door. "This isn't some reality makeover show, Adrien. And I'm not ugly!"

"Of course you are not. I never said you are ugly. I say that you are more beautiful than you think."

"But the point is, I don't care."

"Yes. Exactly. This is exactly the point."

"No, I'm saying I don't care. I'm fine with how I look. I'm fine with how I am."

"But do you not see, Claire, that you cannot be happy with fine?"

"I'm telling you that I am."

"But it is very offensive. To have been given something and not appreciate it? What if da Vinci had decided not to paint? Or Michelangelo not to sculpt? This would have been disaster."

"So you think if I get new clothes I'll have some gigantic impact on the world. And that if I don't I'll be committing some great big sin."

"Be reasonable, *ma poule.* I only wish to see you realize yourself fully."

I slid down the wall and sat on the floor. There was no point in arguing with someone suffering delusions. And my clothes were already gone. "Are you fixing it?"

"The door?"

"Yes."

"*Non.*"

"Why not?"

"Because it is broken. And all of the pieces are on your side."

My desire never to see him again as long as I lived vied with my uncontrollable impulse to kill him.

"Claire?"

"What do I have to do? I have the doorknob."

"There should be a small pin, maybe two, that held it in place."

I crawled in front of the door for five minutes before I found them. They'd come to rest in a crevice between two floorboards. And since I don't have long red pointy acrylic fingernails, I couldn't pry them loose. "I can't get them."

"You cannot find them?"

"I found them, but they're stuck. I need a knife or something."

I heard his footsteps stride down the hall. In a minute I heard them come back. "I am pushing it under the door."

A small paring knife appeared, handle first.

I grabbed it and pried the pins out. "Now what?"

"You need to fit the doorknob back in place and then slip the pins in the plate to secure it."

By the time it was back in place, I was ready to disassemble it and use it to bash him in the head. But I didn't. I exercised self control. I kept my hands to myself, reined in my rage, and put a lid on the explosive words that threatened to spew out of mouth. But only because I really had to use the bathroom.

Adrien caught up with me just before I reached the bathroom door. "Here." He thrust the dress at me.

I took it in with me and put it on. Let's just not mention how many things *didn't* go on underneath that dress. I actually took the time to pull my hair back in a French braid. I put on a smudge of eye shadow and a smear of lip-gloss, and debated about mascara until I thought I could stand to look at Adrien without wanting to place a choke hold around his neck.

I could hear him pacing back and forth down the hall in front of the door.

When I opened it, he froze. "So...maybe this was not such a good idea."

"I'm not talking to you ever again."

"But Claire—"

"Never."

He took me to boulevard Haussmann, nipping the Mercedes into a nonexistent parking space. When we got out, he started toward the Galeries Lafayette Department Store, but I went the other direction toward H&M. He might be high fashion, but my style could usually be found at stores like Target. It would serve him right if he lost me right there. But he was onto me before I'd taken two steps. He grabbed me by the elbow and tried to steer me. "Galeries Lafayette is this way."

If I had been speaking to him, I might have said, *H&M is this way*. But I wasn't, so I couldn't.

We had an arm wrestling match right there in the middle of the sidewalk until I realized that people were starting to stare at us, so I gave up. Suddenly enough that he nearly lost his balance.

I might be nice, but I can also be passive-aggressive.

We went inside. If I had been in a better mood, I might have enjoyed the turn of the century building with its tiers of wrought-iron balconies topped by arcades and its colorful stained-glass dome.

But I wasn't. He tried to get out of the doghouse by taking me to Angelina's tearoom on the fourth floor and buying me a hot chocolate.

It almost worked.

It was the best hot chocolate I'd ever had. Rich, smooth, thick, decadent, made to be diluted with whipped cream. I caught a smile creeping up to my lips, but I cut it off, swallowed the rest of the cup, and jumped to my feet.

He had started to smile also, but when I jumped to my feet, his mouth clamped into a straight line.

I felt a little bad, but then I thought of all my clothes on the way to the city dump and that justified my grudge.

He linked his arm through mine. "So, you will need maybe one pair of pants, two skirts, a sweater, several shirts, a jacket…"

In the car I had done a little strategizing. Not that any of this was my idea. Or even a good idea, but the simple fact was that I had no clothes. So I had to buy some. I was hoping I could leave Adrien in the sporting goods section, do a little speed shopping, and be done with the whole fiasco by lunch.

He had other plans. "Where do we go first?"

"Why don't you go look at tennis rackets or something and I'll meet you in about 45 minutes?"

He clucked like a mother hen. "There is no hurry. We have all day."

He kept saying "we" and he didn't look as though he was going anywhere. I needed to turn the expedition into "me." And fast. So I smiled up at him. Fluttered my eyelashes. "Let's start in lingerie." If you could believe the movies, the word "lingerie," when translated into "guy language," is pronounced "linger-hey-I'm-outta-here!" That's exactly what I was counting on.

But guys in France must speak some other language.

The lingerie department was divided into small boutiques. One of the smallest, the one toward which Adrien escorted me, featured portraits of almost-naked women on the walls.

The only thing more embarrassing than having to shop in a lingerie department is having to shop there with a guy who is not related to you by blood or by marriage.

"Go away," I hissed at him between closed teeth.

"I know I am not hearing you speak to me because you promised never to speak to me again. Never ever, if I remember correctly. So if I hear you, it must be my imagination." He picked up a black bra-and-panty set. "Try these."

Black? As if.

He put them down and then held up a set in white. There were beautiful. A white cotton eyelet demi-bra embroidered with connecting starbursts that laced up the middle and fastened in back. The panties were worked in the same embroidery with lacing in the back. He held them, an eyebrow raised.

"I am not Solange or Véronique. And I am not going to act out some fantasy for you."

He waved them in front of me as if I were a bull.

"Of course, it wouldn't hurt to just try them on." I tugged them from his grasp. "I will never forgive you. Ever." I snatched up the set in black from the table and went back into the dressing room.

Black could also be practical. In certain situations.

So I tried them on.

I'd like to say there's no difference between a $12 bra and a $70 dollar bra, but I'd be lying. The fit, the form, the materials. I had to admit that, at least on me, the difference was worth it.

The panties looked fine; I didn't bother to try them on. How different can an American small be from a French small? And I'm not one to stand around when I've made up my mind. I slithered back into the dress, dumped both sets into Adrien's hands and found two more sets and two extra pairs of panties on the way up to the saleswoman. And the whole time I was trying really hard not to remember that each bra was worth 70 euros and the panties worth 40. But it didn't take long for my subconscious to run the bill right up to 520 euros.

But my conscience was clear. I was not the one who had thrown away my entire wardrobe.

The saleswoman put the purchases into elegant pink-and-black boxes. Fastened them with ribbons. Put the stack into a bag with the lingerie brand plastered across its side.

I made Adrien carry it.

So I could try on clothes.

He soon proved to be worse than my mother was during back-to-school shopping. He would pick through the racks and hold up an item or two. I would take them, and several others of *my* choosing, into the dressing rooms and try them on.

After trying armfuls of pants, I found a pair that fit, even though they didn't have pockets. And they fit well enough to satisfy both my standards and Adrien's even higher standards. They were black cotton herringbone twill pencil legs.

Then we moved on to skirts.

If I had been talking to him, I would have told him that I would never wear a skirt in drizzly-rainy Seattle. Not when I walk ten blocks from the parking lot to my office and cruise the campus collecting and dispersing financial reports. But then, I wasn't talking to him, so I tried on at least 15.

And then two of them about six times each.

One was a trumpet-shaped knee-length black skirt. The other was a short ruffley flowery chiffon. It came down to this: Adrien thought my legs should be seen up to the thigh and I did not. He even recruited the saleswoman to come into the debate on his side.

I'm not a normal woman. I hate shopping, so I gave in to him and tossed him the skirts from the dressing room. It's not as though I would ever wear them more than two or three times. And he was paying, so why should I have cared?

After that, I thought I needed another hot chocolate, but Adrien had been scheming while I'd been changing, and he had other plans. He roped me into trying on white shirts. It wouldn't have been that bad, except that he kept handing me blouses with such low necklines that I would have needed safety pins to close the gaps. Or scotch tape. Something.

It's very difficult to argue with someone you're not talking to.

We settled on an elbow-cuffed shirt with heavy darting in front and back and a medium low shawl-collared neck.

And when he went up to the cash register to buy it, I noticed he'd found two sleeveless sweaters to add to the tab. The first was deep mulberry, the other green. It matched the flowery skirt. One of those light greens which change names every season. Citron, pistachio, honeydew—take your pick. Neither were colors I normally wore. And they were probably skin tight with V-necks that would plunge to my belly button.

Since he was buying the chiffon skirt, he bought the tank to match. It was made from tiers of pink chiffon.

If I were Adrien, I would have called it a day after that and given my credit card two aspirin, but he decided that I needed a black leather jacket. At that, I drew the line.

"Try this one. It would be perfect for you."

"Why? So I can be Claire the Biker Chick?"

"Just try one on. Just one."

"No. Absolutely not."

"Leather pants?"

That didn't even deserve an answer.

So we wandered around to a boutique within the department store that was selling cute tops. He took a pretty Marilyn collar off-the-shoulder top off the rack.

"Very nice, Adrien, but the neck would always slip down. What would I wear underneath?"

He raised an eyebrow.

"If you tell me I wouldn't have to wear a bra after you just bought four of them, I will personally buy another to strangle you with."

"But you have such nice shoulders."

Now that I was talking again, I was able to talk him into a knit sleeveless bateau top in coral and a black-and-white striped tank with a crossover neckline and wide black ribbed trim at the hem.

And a funny thing happened.

I realized that everything I'd been trying on fit. In the arms. At the shoulders. In the legs. I was used to having to roll up sleeves or constantly tug them down or turn up the hems of pants. I can't remember the last time I bought a shirt with shoulder seams that aligned with my actual shoulders. I could almost have been persuaded that shopping was fun.

But what did it mean if everything fit? Because it didn't look to me that Adrien was a biggest-bang-for-the-buck kind of guy. The clothes I'd been trying on were way beyond my means…so…I had a champagne body? Too bad I had a pork rinds budget.

As I left the dressing room, I prayed that these clothes would last the next ten years. It would take that long to earn enough money to replace them.

Adrien was talking with the saleswoman, but he stepped back from the counter as I approached.

"They are good?"

"They're good. But that's it. I'm through."

He waited until he'd paid before saying anything. And even then, he only said one word. But when he said it, I wanted to close my eyes and throw an adult-sized tantrum. The word he said was "shoes."

I hate shopping for shoes.

"I'm willing to go barefoot for the next two weeks."

"Bare feet? *Ridicule*."

"For the next four weeks."

He laughed.

I hate him, I hate him, I hate him.

And here's how much I hate him. I let him talk me into stilettos. Black stilettos.

I will hate him as long as I live.

But he also bought me some leather ballerina flats with a strap across the instep. Maybe I could get away with wearing the heels once and the flats the rest of the time I stayed in Paris.

When we got to the cash register, Adrien looked like a walking advertisement for Galeries Lafayette. I reached out before he had a chance to, and took the shoe bag from the salesclerk.

"*Alors*…it was not so bad, was it? We can look for perfume?"

"Don't press your luck."

"Is that to say that today was not terrible?"

"Not too terrible."

If he smiled, at least he had the compassion not to be looking in my direction when he did.

When we got home, I dumped the contents of the shopping bags on the bed. A pair of pants, two skirts. One shirt, two tanks, one top, two sweaters. Lots of embarrassingly expensive underwear. A pair of stilettos. A pair of flats.

What a day.

I had started out naked; I had ended up with a pretty decent wardrobe. A prettier and much more stylish wardrobe than I would have purchased for myself.

It was four in the afternoon, but I was exhausted, so I took off Solange's dress and climbed in bed. I know I should have thrown the underwear in the wash and hung up the pants and skirts and tops and put away the sweaters, but considering I still expected to open those drawers and find my own clothes, I thought I was coping pretty well.

As I was drifting to sleep, I realized one important thing that I'd forgotten to say in the midst of all the other words I hadn't been saying. I hadn't told Adrien, "Thank you."

Chapter 18

ঙ১৩

J was surprised that evening when I heard the doorbell ring. Or maybe I should say, I was surprised for the second time that evening.

The first time was when I tried on a pair of those how-different-can-an-American-small-be-from-a-French-small panties.

Very.

At least in the back. When I was growing up, "thongs" were sandals. And that's all I'm going to say.

But at least when the doorbell rang, I'd been up and gotten dressed. In the black skirt and the sleeveless light green funnel neck sweater. At least I think it was a sweater. It was so finely knit and so lightweight that I couldn't tell. For the record, it was a tight fit, but it also came down over my hips, so my official opinion on the subject was neutral.

I unlocked the door and pulled it open.

Surprise! It was Adrien. When he had dropped me off at the front of the building that afternoon, he'd said he'd leave me to myself that evening. But at some point he must have realized that he'd done a very bad thing when he'd thrown my clothes away.

He was standing there, one arm above his head, propped against the door frame. The other arm balanced what looked to be a pizza. A beer and a cola were clamped underneath his arm.

It was possible that I could learn to like him again.

"You are hungry?"

"Very."

"I may come in?"

I stepped aside so that he could come through.

But he didn't right away. He was looking at me. "You look very nice."

I blushed. I wished I'd thought to thank him earlier, but I'd been too busy being mad at him. "Thank you. For the clothes. For everything."

It was his turn to blush. Either that or the shadow cast by the door suddenly deepened. "I am sorry. I should not have thrown away your clothes. I had no right to do this. I just think that you are a very special person and I want everyone else to think this way also."

It was possible that I could learn to love him. "Why didn't you just say so in the beginning? I might have taken all those clothes down to the dumpster myself."

He laughed. Then he stepped inside and headed toward the dining room while I shut and locked the door. "Do not lock the door. I will just have to open it later when I leave." Adrien's voice came floating down the hall along with the smell of the pizza.

Old habits die hard. I felt safe in Paris, but locking myself into places—cars, houses, offices—has become ingrained. I'd never want to become a news item based on the fact that the one time I forgot to lock a door or window was the one time a rapist or serial killer found me. I can think of other ways to make the news.

Like becoming a millionaire or discovering a cure for cancer.

"I always lock doors."

"Even when you are going right back out?"

I'd read enough true-life stories in women's magazines to know that it only took about 15 seconds for a person to be killed. So going back into the house for ten minutes without relocking the door provided 40 opportunities for something bad to happen to me.

Adrien looked up from the plates he was setting in front of our chairs. "Has something happened to you before or are you just paranoid?"

"No and no."

"Please explain."

How can you explain living in a perpetual state of fear to a man? "I could be raped."

He frowned. "I do not think so. Not here in the seventh. Maybe

someone might try to steal something from you. It *is* August and rob-
beries go up when the city empties for vacation. But you are here in the
apartment and you turn lights on and off in the evenings. You should
be fine. And even if you are not, just give the thief what he wants and
he will go away. Would you like some?" He was holding up a slice of
pizza dripping with cheese.

Some people just don't get it.

And I could tell there was no use trying to explain. I just held out
my plate and took the piece of pizza.

He was halfway through his second piece before he spoke again. As
he did, his eyes never left his plate. "I am sorry also if I made you
uncomfortable while you were trying on lingerie."

"Well, I was. With all those pictures and…everything." And I'm not
married to you, and I'm not even your girlfriend, and why should you
know what kind of underwear I wear, anyway? Whew. Glad I'd gotten
all that off my chest.

Now his eyes lifted to mine. "The pictures offended you? What was
wrong with them? They are famous. By a famous photographer. They
are made into calendars every year."

Of course they were. And probably posted in offices all over France.
"But it's using nudity as a marketing tool."

"What is wrong with nudity?"

"What isn't?"

"The human body is beautiful. A masterpiece."

"To be admired like a flower or a painting."

"*Oui.*" He paused and then quirked an eyebrow at me. "Claire, do
you have a problem with nudity? Are you not comfortable in your
skin?"

"I like myself, sure, but I'm all in favor of clothing."

"What would you change about yourself if you could change anything at all?"

The real problem would be where to start. Breasts, thighs, weight?
Maybe I could even put in an order for fingernails that wouldn't bend
and tear like paper. "Just the normal things."

"Ah."

I kept waiting for him to say something else, but he didn't. So I nodded my head and tried to pretend I knew what he was "ah"ing about. But that just made me feel more stupid. "Would you care to elaborate?"

"You are not comfortable with yourself."

"Of course I am."

"You are not. When you ask a Frenchwoman that question, she would not change a thing. She may not be perfect, but she is happy with herself. With her own beauty."

"You're saying I'm not happy with my looks?"

"Are you?"

I shrugged.

"I think not. Because every time I tell you that you are beautiful, you do not accept this."

"Because I'm not."

"Why not?"

News flash: I'm not tall, blond, chesty, and blue-eyed. "You're just trying to be nice, Adrien. And thank you. I appreciate it."

"You see this? You still do not accept it. I should be offended."

"I'm not trying to offend you."

"But you are telling me that I do not know what beauty is when I see it."

He'd done it again. He'd backed me into a corner where I had to agree with him even though I didn't want to.

"Think about this. I live in Paris. Every day of my life, I see beautiful women. I think I know what beauty is. And if you keep trying to convince me that you are not beautiful, then maybe one day I will believe you. Do you want this to happen?"

"No." My answer might have come out more quickly than I'd planned, but then again, "no" is a small word, so it goes kind of fast. My scalp tingled with thousands of tiny prickles and I felt my cheeks grow warm. Adrien thought I was beautiful?

Adrien thought I was beautiful.

Chapter 19

$\mathcal{A}$drien thought I was beautiful. The idea would not stop spinning, twirling, pirouetting through my brain as I lay in bed that night.

It was a good thing no one had ever called me beautiful before. Because based on this one example, and the enormous distraction it had become, I wouldn't have graduated from college with a 3.5 GPA. Or high school with a 3.9 GPA.

Okay. I could stop smiling now.

Right now.

Anytime would be good. My cheeks were starting to cramp.

It's not as though it meant anything. He was basically a big brother. So he might think I was beautiful, but it's not as if my being beautiful required any action on his part. It was not as if he were going to ask me out on a date. Or give me an engagement ring.

Or anything at all.

But it did mean that there was hope. Because if he thought I was beautiful, then anyone might reasonably be expected to think the same thing. And with his educated opinion, I could extrapolate tens, maybe hundreds of anonymous Adriens around the world who might think the same thing.

Somewhere in the dark of night, while I was pondering my future from this new perspective, my eyes fluttered shut and stayed that way. Until the garbage trucks came by at seven thirty.

Garbage is picked up every day in Paris. Mail is delivered two times a day. I can't imagine what sort of madhouse that turns the post office into.

I spent the day at the apartment, reading one of the books I'd borrowed from Adrien. I had planned on calling my parents, but Mom called me first. Right when Adrien came over to get me for dinner.

She gave me the latest report on Dad's back. I didn't catch all of it because she was whispering. I had the feeling things were touchier between them than they'd been when I'd left.

Dad had been well into his take-care-of-me-leave-me-alone routine. He kept Mom busy doing things, such as fetching golf magazines, channel surfing, and finding "that advertisement in the paper three weeks ago about that used set of golf clubs." But when Mom wanted to try to help him do really important things, such as go to the bathroom or get dressed, he slapped her hands away and started yelling at her. In French, of course, because he always reverted to his native language when he was upset.

And it was perfectly understandable. For an engineer whose specialty is controlling the way things work, it had to be unbelievably frustrating not to be able to control your own body. So he controlled the only other thing he could: my mother. And when she tried to help him, reminding him that he was no longer master of his own body, he reacted in what I think was probably panic and attacked her.

I wish I could see myself so clearly.

Stepping into the ring that first night, I sent Mom out, fixed up a dinner tray for Dad, sat down beside him, and asked him to talk to me about golf.

It was not as insane as it sounded.

First, it's become his passion. Second, he used to be a professor and, prior to golf, the thing he best loved to do was teach. Third, my French is better than Mom's, so Dad could speak without thinking too much. There I was, a golf neophyte with nothing in the world to do but listen to him explain his beloved game. By eleven that evening, listening to him talk about how European golfers were neglected by the American media, I began to make plans to shoot myself in the head.

So if Mom were whispering, I listened as hard as I could and figured I'd catch up on all the gory details when I got back in country. Once she was done talking about Dad's health, she perked up. She talked a while longer before saying goodbye.

"Your parents are well?"

I started. I'd forgotten Adrien was there. "What?"

"Your parents?"

"Oh. Yes. Dad is doing better. They said to tell you 'hi.'" I turned around and faced him. How did he look so fresh and cool when it was 85 degrees outside? I was wearing my new white blouse. He was wearing a long-sleeved white shirt. Opened two buttons.

One button can't make that much of a difference, can it?

"Give me a minute and I'll find my backpack."

Adrien, one step ahead of me, was holding it in his hand. "In France we call this a *sac-à-dos.*"

"Backpack. Same thing in the States."

"This looks like it is meant for camping."

"Yeah, it is. Well, not for packing. For day-tripping."

He raised an eyebrow.

"On an urban hike. I got a great deal on it at REI." It was a small, low-profile pack meant for rock climbing? Skiing? Something. It was multicolored: bright purple with lime green mesh and orange pulls and toggles. It went with everything. That a clown would wear.

But then again, no one would ever steal it.

"A good deal? Maybe in Seattle, but not in Paris. I should have bought you a proper purse. I will carry it." He was standing there holding it away from his body. Had he never seen a backpack before?

"I can lengthen the straps for you."

"*Non, non.* I am not going to carry it on my back. I am not hiking; I am walking. To dinner."

"You're the one who volunteered."

He experimented with slinging a strap over one shoulder. Scowled. Made the straps as short as possible and grabbed the handle at the top. "We go." He fiddled with the pack in the elevator. Continued until we were halfway down the street. "Claire? I must ask you something."

"Sure."

"You had running shoes but not for running, and you have a

backpack that you do not use for hiking. Americans are so intent on going places and getting things done in the fastest, most efficient way. But what about beauty and style?"

Obviously he had never lived in Seattle. "I could buy a hundred-dollar pair of shoes, but they'd be ruined in the first rain of the season. And I could buy a leather purse, but it would get all spotted."

"Do all your sidewalks have puddles?"

"No, but—"

"You do not own an umbrella?"

"Yes, but—"

"You walk so fast that your umbrella turns inside out? You walk too fast to avoid puddles?"

"No, but—"

"It rains in Paris too. All winter long."

"Just let me finish! I would rather be comfortable and own things that aren't finicky. I don't have time to take special care of them. I wake up, I go to work, I come home. There's no time left."

He looked at me for a long time, staring deep into my eyes. His own eyes had turned a glinting, icy blue. "This is your philosophy of life? So maybe this is why you do not have a boyfriend."

"What are you talking about?"

"Boyfriends require special care and extra attention. You must go out with them. Maybe even dance with them. Check on them now and then to see that they are happy. Maybe it is good that you now have the orchid. You can practice caring for a plant before you start caring for a man."

I was stunned. I had never known Adrien to be so mean. So vicious. He was the one who volunteered to carry my backpack. It wasn't me. I pressed my lips together, trying not to cry.

We walked the length of avenue Bosquet and began crossing Pont de l'Alma bridge. Adrien pretending he wasn't carrying a backpack. Me pretending I wasn't crying.

And I wasn't.

Not really.

My eyes were overflowing a little. But it wasn't crying. Because I wasn't about to let Adrien see me cry.

And who did he think he was, anyway? Who gave him the right to criticize my life? And what authority did he have to tell me what to do? And wear? And think? It was surprising that I'd never realized what a big jerk he was before now. A big, arrogant, inconsiderate bully. He was a bully. A big mean...

I ran right into him.

Not because I was that childish, but because he'd planted himself right in front of me. See? A bully.

Stepping toward the side of the bridge, I tried to go around him.

He had longer legs and got to the railing before I did, cutting off my escape. "Claire? Is there something wrong?"

I refused to speak to him. Mostly because I knew that if I did, tears would come streaming down my face.

"Claire?"

I refused to look at him. If I did, he'd see that I was crying. Trying not to cry. But then I sniffled and he called my bluff.

"You are crying."

"No, I'm not." Tears were dripping off my nose and sweeping down my neck in a torrent.

He crooked an arm around my neck and pulled me into his chest. Hidden beneath his arm, the corners of my lips dissolved into my quivering chin. My shoulders deteriorated into twitching, trembling bird wings.

I am not a person who cries gracefully in languid ice-skater poses with elegant sniffs. I squeal. I squawk. I sob. With red-rimmed eyes and big faltering snot-sucking snorts. Knowing this about myself made my humiliation even worse. Made me cry even harder.

And the whole time, Adrien just stood there, his arm wrapped around my neck, sheltering me.

At first, I didn't want anything to do with him. Didn't even want him near me. If he'd been a teddy bear, I would have tossed him over the bridge into the river. But only after prying his eyes out and pulling the fluff out of his head. And then I remembered my teddy bear lessons. To get a hug, you have to give one. The image had barely become a thought when my I unpeeled my arms from my waist and wrapped them around Adrien's.

"I am sorry. Please forgive me." His hand was stroking the hair back from my forehead.

I buried my head deeper into his chest and nodded.

"I am always too impatient. But there is time. Right now. We must enjoy it, or we lose it. The things we can see and say and do today may be gone tomorrow. And if it makes life happier, better, more fun, then what is the harm? Buy running shoes, Claire. Or backpacks, if you insist on these things. But do it in Seattle. You live too earnestly. This time is my time and Paris is about the joy of living. *La vie est trop belle pour s'enerver.*"

Life is too beautiful, too wonderful to get yourself so worked up.

He circled his other arm around my waist and drew me close. I could have stayed in that embrace for the rest of my life.

He sighed. Kissed the top of my head. Tucked me tighter into his arms. "You are worth special care. I too wake up, go to work, and come home. But there is all the time in the world for those one cares about."

I tilted my head, looked up at him.

"Ai-ai-ai. Do not look at me with those eyes." He was squinting. "They are too bright. Eyes washed with too many tears."

I closed them.

He planted a kiss on each eyelid.

"Do you understand what I am saying? Love is an investment. To love someone you have to know them. And to know them, you have to spend time with them. Time is a gift you give someone."

He loosened his hold on me. I turned and settled into his side.

It was comfortable there, against the railing, watching the traffic go by. Nobody gave us a second glance. I'm sure we looked like one of those anonymous pairs of lovers that infest Paris, draped across each other, with nothing to do all day but kiss and ramble through the streets.

He placed a hand under my chin and tipped my head up. His head leaned down toward mine, eyes shining. They were searchlights. Beacons. And his words kept echoing in my head.

Time.

Time is a gift you give someone.

That's right. Who knew me better than Adrien? And I'd known him forever.

My eyes locked on his and a tingle shot up my spine.

He leaned closer. He was going to kiss me.

And I wanted him to. My cheeks flushed, my hand clutched at his waist.

Just in time I remembered what had happened the last time I'd wanted him to kiss me. At the last second I saved myself. I tucked my head into his shoulder and his kiss landed on my forehead. I pulled away from him. "Thanks. For all the time you've been spending with me."

His eyes went dark.

A corner of his mouth lifted. His hand left my chin and patted my cheek. "We will be late to dinner."

I straightened and swiped at my nose with the back of my hand.

Adrien handed me a handkerchief. What a gentleman.

As we walked, my thoughts revolved around Adrien and his mystery woman. The one he'd loved for forever. The one who wouldn't take him seriously.

I could sympathize.

Adrien was my mystery woman. Man. Fixation. As many times as I'd told myself I was over him, I wasn't.

Would I ever be? Was he going to stay stuck in my heart forever? Like the pencil lead I'd jammed into my palm in the sixth grade?

At least I was further ahead in my obsession than he was. I'd never told him I loved him. Because if I had, I'm sure he never would have taken me seriously, either.

What was I going to do about him?

The whole thing was unproductive, wouldn't lead anywhere, and was a big fat waste of time. If I could have, I would have hopped on a plane. Because I knew where this would lead. And I was not interested in going there.

Yet again.

We'd crossed the bridge and were waiting on a small concrete island at the edge of the six-way Place de l'Alma intersection. Adrien grew tired of waiting, grabbed my arm, and plunged into the cars. He almost caused an accident. Several of them. And he single-handedly created a chain reaction of honks that had spread right around the intersection by the time we had stepped back up onto the sidewalk.

We hoofed it up avenue George V. Crossed several streets. He was walking as though he was on autopilot. At warp speed. But then it was his neighborhood.

Suddenly, he took a right and I nearly swung off into outer space.

"We're not running a marathon."

He stopped. Pivoted on one heel. "Excuse me?"

"If I still had my running shoes, I could actually have put them to use."

"Oh. Forgive me." He turned around again and started off at a marginally slower pace.

"Are you okay?"

He didn't turn around, but he did answer me. "It is nothing at all. Just an *idée fixe* that I shall have to throw away."

"Oh. Because usually when you walk, you hum."

At this, he turned. "I do?"

"Yes. Or sing."

"Mphf." He walked a few more steps and then began to hum. I recognized the tune as *V'la l'bon vent*. Not one of his usual merry tunes. It was about three ducks bathing in a pond. The king's son comes to hunt and shoots one. Something about him aiming at a black one, but killing the white one instead.

And all the feathers blow away in the wind.

It was then that I saw what he meant about being late for dinner. The restaurant was Le Relais de l'Entrecôte and already there was a line 15 people deep. We waited for 45 minutes. I should have brought a book because Adrien didn't say one word.

I glanced a couple times at his face, but it was lifeless as any spider who has ever dared to enter my house.

And over dinner, he brooded. Twice it looked as if he was going to say something, but then he climbed back inside himself and stared into his wine.

Obviously, something was wrong. It seemed as though I was supposed to apologize, but I didn't know what I'd done. So then I decided maybe he was supposed to be apologizing, but I couldn't figure out what he'd done. Was he sick? Had his mystery woman shot him down again? I finally gave up trying to figure him out. The food was too good to be spoiled by a brooding hen. There's nothing that makes me hungry like a good cry. And this restaurant provided the perfect cure. About two minutes after we were seated, a waitress came to our table. Unlike other restaurants we'd been to, all the servers there were women. And they were all dressed in "French maid"-style, black-and-white uniforms. Maybe that's why they were all women.

She asked us two questions, What we wanted to drink and how we wanted our steak cooked.

And then she left.

It seemed that she'd forgotten to ask us something. Like what we wanted to eat. But Adrien wasn't saying anything. Still. So I leaned back in my seat and decided that whatever happened would happen. And he could sort it out.

What happened was wonderful.

The waitress returned and brought us wine along with a basket of bread. Typical start to a French meal. But then she came back. And brought us both a salad. Which was strange, because I hadn't ordered one. But I wasn't complaining. It was good. Made of spindly crunchy designer lettuce, sprinkled with nuts, and spiked with vinaigrette.

Even before we were done with the salads, steak appeared. With fries. And they were not hefty home fries carved from super-sized potatoes on steroids. These were fries without an attitude. Honest-to-goodness droopy dwarf fries made from real potatoes. And that wasn't even the best part of the meal. The best part of the meal was the steak. It was beyond belief. My knife cut through it like butter.

I'm not exaggerating.

When I popped the first bite into my mouth, it melted like butter. Really.

And the waitress spooned sauce on top of everything. A better-than-béarnaise sauce that could only have been whisked up in heaven.

That good.

And here's the very best part. I'd finished all my steak and was spearing the rest of my fries onto my fork when the waitress came by with seconds. More steak. More fries. And I, who never go back for seconds at an all-you-can-eat buffet, ate it all. Every little fry. Every morsel of steak.

If I ever have to be executed, that's what I'm going to ask for as my last meal.

What an experience. And it only lasted about 45 minutes. Mere seconds compared to the hours-long meals we'd been having. Fast food, French style.

I wish I could have said Adrien enjoyed it as much as I had, but I couldn't tell. It's a good thing it was over so quickly, otherwise I might have missed not talking about whether beauty was simplicity or simplicity was beauty, or some other philosophical trick question. But we were out the door and walking down the street before I confronted the silence.

"If you're not feeling well, I can walk myself home."

He didn't turn, didn't twitch, didn't respond.

"Adrien?"

Nothing.

I stopped walking.

He kept plodding down the street.

"Hey! Adrien!" My voice bounced off buildings, windows, doors, and cars in the small street. Turned the heads of dogs and people.

"Claire?"

I jogged down the street toward him. Or started to. Those wimpy fries had developed an attitude once they'd reached my stomach. "What is it?"

"What is what?"

"What is going on with you?"

He shook his head, as if he were trying to snap himself out of something. "Nothing." His eyes skewered my heart. "I just want you to know that I have enjoyed my time with you also. You are a very special person. You deserve only good things."

Now why should that have made me feel so sad?

Chapter 20

ℬↃℭ℞

Adrien telephoned me the next morning.

"My secretary just called. She said Mademoiselle's lawyer received the power of attorney. He is releasing the keys to you today."

"So there are some French people who work in August."

"*Bah...oui.* She took her vacation in July."

Of course she had. For the whole month, I suppose. If I could do it all again, I'd choose to live my life in France. "When am I allowed to pick them up?"

"Whenever you want."

"Where are they?"

"With the *gardienne.*"

"The—?"

"*Oui.*"

Great. I was hoping I'd never have to see her again.

"You would like me to come...?"

"Oh. Uh—" I'd never really thought about him not coming. Since my arrival, I'd assumed we were in this together. But maybe not. This was his vacation. Maybe he didn't want to spend it all with me. In fact, it was probably better if he didn't, since I wanted to keep my crush under control. In a week, I should be able to talk myself out of it. I just needed a little time. A little space. "If you have other plans, I'm fine. Really. I know how to get there. I can speak French."

He sighed. And it wasn't a normal sigh. Not even a heavy sigh. Was it frustration? Irritation? Exasperation? Defeat? Maybe I was just being hypersensitive. A carryover from his weird mood the night before. "When would you like to go?"

We arranged that Adrien would pick me up at ten. I bathed and dressed in the pants and coral top. I spent the rest of my time tidying the apartment. Which entailed putting books and magazines back on the shelves I'd taken them from. Straightening the bath towels. Wiping down the kitchen counters. Sweeping the front hall.

It was while I was sweeping that I saw the orchid reflected back at me from the mirror above the fireplace in the living room.

I would never hear the end of it from Adrien if I let it die!

Leaning the broom against the wall, I left the dustpan on the floor beside it and filled a watering can with water. Bottled water. Because according to Adrien, orchids can't tolerate the salts in normal tap water. I watered it in drops, not wanting to shock its fragile system. As I did, I noticed Mademoiselle's diary sitting next to it on the mantel.

When I was done, I replaced the watering can, mopped up the stray driblets of water, and coached the plant on what to say if Adrien ever checked up on me. Then I took the diary, tucked myself into an armchair, and read it for a few minutes while I waited for him.

12 October 1936

It has been three weeks since my last entry. It is because I have taken a vacation. From life. I have been to Chartres, Vaux-le-Vicomte, Chantilly, Reims, Provins, and a dozen other cities within a half a day's drive from Paris. I have gone to all those places with B. Now, he wants to take me to Belgium. To visit Bruges. For the weekend. Should I go? Or maybe I should stay? If he were with me right now, I would have no choice but to go. He can talk me into anything. Riding a barge down the Canal St. Martin or a donkey in Normandy. Going to a big band club or dining at the Ritz. I think it best that I do not see him again until I decide. I will tell him this. Tonight.

13 October 1936

I told B. I told him I could not see him until I made a decision about Bruges. He said that was absolutely the correct thing to do, but that it did not stop him from being able to see me. He had hired me to sit for him, had he not? And so he drove us to Montparnasse, near my room, so he could buy some paints and a brush and a canvas and then he took me back to his suite in the Ritz so he could paint my back. Because then, of course, I would not have to see him. Until after I had made a decision. So I decided. I said yes.

The entries from 1937 through the first half of 1940 were a running list of people, parties, and places Mademoiselle went with the mysterious B. It appeared that they hung out with a list of who's who in European royal families.

Well, good for her.

I didn't admire her choice. I thought it had been the wrong one to make, but that didn't stop me from admiring the verve with which she lived her life. And I reminded myself that at some point, her heart would be broken. Because she had never married. Not B. Not anyone else.

The intercom buzzed, so I went to the bedroom to grab my backpack, set the diary on the commode, and ran downstairs to meet Adrien.

We reached Mademoiselle's building just after ten that morning. The *gardienne* recognized us. She looked a little surprised when we told her why we were there, but she gave us the keys. Deposited the group of them into Adrien's hand.

"Excuse me, but are these all of them?" he asked, flipping through the keys, which were attached to a bare metal ring.

"*Bah...oui.* You have the front door, the back door, the box for the mail, and—" She gave a little cry and disappeared, only to come back waving an additional key and a flashlight. "For the *cave*." She walked us to the back of the entry hall and gestured into the gloom of the court-yard beyond. "Down the stairs. She has number seven. And you will need a torch."

We certainly did.

Walking down those stairs was like walking into an Indiana Jones movie. Powdery cobwebs. Vaulted cellars with thick wooden doors. The drip-drop of water. A damp, dank smell. And a suffocating darkness.

I hooked a finger through one of Adrien's back belt loops so that he wouldn't get away from me. He was wearing that cologne again. And we were so close I could feel the heat from his back. Friends. We were good friends. I tried to get my wayward heart to stick with the program. Ended up singing a Brownie song to myself in my head; something about making new friends and keeping the old.

We turned a corner and went deeper into the dark. I was sure there were rotting skeletons of people who'd gotten lost down here ages…centuries…ago. People hiding from the Revolution. Or Napo-léon. Or the Germans—once, twice, three times—in the last 150 years.

I shuddered and bent two fingers around the belt loop.

Adrien found door number seven. He wrenched the lock from the latch and pushed open the door.

Or tried to.

The thick boards, hung a century or two before, had swollen from the constant moisture. It creaked open about a foot and then refused to budge. He put a shoulder to it, and then I joined him with mine but it was no use. So we slid inside.

I let him go first.

He was exploring via flashlight by the time I pushed my way in behind him. There wasn't much to see. One wall was buttressed by a wine rack. Another by wooden shelves containing wooden wine boxes. And that was it. "That's it?"

"What did you expect?"

Old trunks. Old pictures and clothes. Broken-down furniture and discarded lamps.

"This is not an attic, *ma poule*. It is a *cave*. It was built for storing wine. Stone construction, under the ground. It keeps a constant temperature." He was wiping thick gray dust from a row of bottles. He bent down, using the flashlight to read the labels. Some of them had already decomposed, leaving only strips of paste to mark their presence.

"*Lafite-Rothschild.*" He had turned to grin at me, eyes shining. "She had *Lafite-Rothschild.* Both 1982 and 1988."

Good for her. "Can we go now?"

"*Non.* Let me finish looking." He stumbled around the cellar mumbling like some crazed maniac. I could only make out a word or two. "*Latour. Margaux. D'Yquem.*"

Was this going to be like following my dad around a hardware store? Promises of "in a minute" and "just give me two seconds," which turned into an hour or more.

I would rather have watched a golf tournament.

I would have gone back upstairs if I weren't certain dozens of skeletons and ghosts were waiting for me just outside the door.

The good thing was that if Adrien were impressed with Mademoiselle's wine collection, then my father was sure to be impressed too.

"These no longer have their labels. They are useless." Adrien was holding two bottles out toward me. "We might as well drink them."

"Sure. Fine. Can we leave?" I'd just remembered something. Where there are cobwebs, there are usually spiders. From this basic premise, I deduced this equation: Many cobwebs equal many spiders. And once my imagination had hidden thousands of spiders away in the farthest reaches of the darkest corners of the cellar, I began to imagine I could see them.

And feel them.

And the only thing worse than a real spider is an imaginary one. Or ones. Because they're huge and hairy. "I really need to go, Adrien."

"I can take these? This is fine?"

"You can take anything you want. Let's just go."

We squeezed through the door, Adrien padlocked it shut, and we made it to daylight in 20 seconds flat. At least I did. He, holding two bottles of wine and a flashlight, was a little more conservative when it came to taking the twists and turns of crumbling corridors at high speed.

I waited for him by the elevator in the foyer.

He handed me the bottles and went to return the flashlight to the *gardienne*. They chitchatted for a couple of minutes until I got tired of waiting and made a point of pushing the button for the elevator.

Time was wasting.

The sooner we got this over with, the sooner I could get home to Seattle, the sooner I could stop thinking about Adrien.

The apartment really was as bad as it had seemed. In fact, it was worse. In the morning light, I could see things I hadn't noticed last time we'd been there.

Awful things.

We went into the living room. I sat down in one of the Louis XV chairs. It puffed a cloud of dust.

Adrien's chair did the same.

I began to compose a mental list of cleaning supplies I'd have to buy. I'd seen Mademoiselle's broom closet, and it was filled with half-used cleaning products of unknown age.

All I could think about were my parents, who were so excited about what this inheritance would be. "I think they should sell."

"It could be fixed. Renovated."

I looked around. Tried to see past the dust. The cobwebs. The peeling spirals of paint. "It should be beautiful. It should be like your parents' place."

"It must have been at one time."

"She might as well have been living in a slum."

Adrien smiled. "Yes, but there are no slums in the seventh *arrondisement*."

"You know what I mean. If she was short on money, why didn't she sell it? Move out of the city?"

"And you, who constantly proclaim yourself to be short of money, why do you not sell your house?"

"It's the biggest investment I have. I couldn't afford to buy another, so I'd end up paying rent again. And that's why I bought it in the first place. Anyway, I still have to call my parents and tell them about this…" Pit? Mess? Slum? "…place."

"And the tax."

"What tax?"

"The inheritance tax."

Big deal.

"It may be taxed up to 60 percent."

Huge deal. "Sixty percent of what? Peeling paint and cobwebs?"

"Sixty percent of one million euros or of however much the apartment is valued."

That was $600,000. The cost of my small house. Times three and a half. My parents could not afford to pay $600,000.

"In fact, it could be much more. You will have to have the furniture and the art appraised. Maybe the books in the library. The jewelry."

"So they can tax us on that too?"

"Yes."

"That seems a little unfair."

"Your parents do not have to keep these things. They can have them sold and then pay the tax out of the proceeds."

I groaned. "I can't tell them about the taxes. It's like saying, 'Guess what? You won the lottery! But wait—before you get a million dollars, you'll have to pay six hundred thousand.'"

"Or more."

"Pessimist."

"Would you like me to speak with them?"

"You'd tell them?"

"If you wish it."

He was looking at me strangely. The way you'd look at someone if you didn't think you were going to see them again. "You're not dying or anything, are you?"

"Not that I have noted. Apart from the normal."

"I'll see you again, won't I?"

"For dinner, if you want."

"No. I mean after this. When I go back to Seattle."

"I do not know."

Of course he didn't. And I didn't know, either. But I wanted him to say yes anyway. I couldn't imagine years growing into decades and never seeing him again. This couldn't be the last time. An irrational panic bound itself around my heart. The constriction of a claustrophobic future. Of the hollow years to come.

"Is this so important? That you see me again?"

"Yes."

His smile started in his eyes and finished at his lips. "Then you shall."

We left the apartment. Locked it up and went to lunch.

Adrien hummed all the way.

We decided to eat dinner that night at his apartment. It was to be a simple dinner of things we'd picked up on rue Cler before heading across the river to his place. A baguette. Slices of pastry-wrapped *pâté*. Delicate lamb chops and ratatouille. A carton of fresh raspberries and a container of *fromage blanc*.

Adrien called my parents before we ate.

I perched on the chair in his office and watched him speak from behind his desk. It was a directoire desk with two drawers on each side and supported by slender legs. The chair I was sitting on was a comfy round-backed bergère armchair, upholstered in natural-colored canvas. A colorful handwoven Moroccan carpet in brick red with black and yellow embroidery covered the floor.

"It is not in good shape...it will need painting at the least. Maybe new floors...the lawyer has accomplished all the paperwork. What is left is to pay the inheritance tax...on both the property and the possessions...it can be very high. As much as 60 percent. In fact, I would count on it." He glanced up at me. Frowned.

My parents must not have been taking it well. I got up from the chair and began to browse through his books again.

"You can sell, of course, but the tax must still be paid…I can arrange appraisals…I would guess around one million euros. For the property. For the furniture and jewels, I do not know…"

"Yes, that would be six hundred thousand euros…yes, I agree…I can see what they suggest…yes, of course…it is no problem." He hung up.

"They didn't take it well."

"*Non.* They may have to sell. It will depend upon the appraisals."

I knew they might, but that hadn't stopped me from wishing they wouldn't. "If it were fixed up…it's just sad. To think of her living there. She must have loved it. And then my father inherits and sells it."

Adrien was watching me intently.

"I mean, don't you think?"

"*Oui.* One could do quite a lot with it. One could live there if one wanted to."

"But that would take six hundred thousand euros, wouldn't it?"

"*Evidemment.*"

Chapter 21

&ƆCȢ

$\mathcal{A}$drien prepared the food in the kitchen. He refused to let me help, so I tried out his recamier sofa. It was backless with two scrolled ends of equal height. Two neck-roll pillows had been piled at one end. It was placed in front of the living room area window and used to hold back the curtains. There was a stack of books on the floor beside it, waiting to be read.

I sat down, took my shoes off, and swung my feet up. And I was sitting straight as the letter "L." Not so comfortable. So I fluffed up the pillows and then wriggled down a bit until my head rested on top of the scroll.

Not so bad.

I reached down and plucked the book off the top of the pile. Read *100 Years of Flight*.

I put it down and reached for the next one.

Sun Tzu's *Art of War*.

Next.

Something in French. *The Enterprise of the Third Type*. Hmm. Star Trek? Nope. Business.

I dropped it in my lap, leaned back, and closed my eyes. A slight breeze drifted in through the window. A ray of afternoon sun caressed my arm.

I purred.

Adrien came in and out. I heard him put plates on the table.

Silverware. I recognized the soft pop of a wine cork. I heard it all, but I was too lazy to move.

Until he whispered in my ear, "You must try this."

I opened one eye, focused on the glass of wine he was offering, and shut it again. "Not today."

"You do not have to drink. Just taste."

I opened the eye again. "What's the difference?"

"Tasting only requires one small sip. Maybe two."

He'd already destroyed all my theological arguments in favor of Prohibition. I'd already gotten tipsy. Once. So there was no point in resisting. I opened both eyes, took the glass from him, and put it to my lips.

"Wait!"

I almost spilled it all over myself.

Adrien sat at the opposite end of the couch and then swung his legs up beside mine. How cozy. My feckless heart began to beat a staccato rhythm, even though I knew he didn't mean anything by it.

"We begin." He held his glass up to me in a salute. "*Santé.*"

"*Santé.*"

"So, first we swirl the wine."

I swirled.

"This is to release the aromas. So now we smell." He dug his nose into the glass so far that it almost hit the bottom.

I sniffed. From the top.

"Not like that, Claire. Like this." He did his deep-sea diver imitation again. "Try it like this. How does it smell? A general impression."

Fortunately, my nose is small, so I didn't have to swan dive into my glass. It smelled like...wine. "It doesn't smell bad."

"Exactly. Not so strong, rather pleasant. Very good."

Beginner's luck.

"So now we must smell with more precision. No swirling. Just smelling." He looked at me from over the brim of his glass, his eyebrows urging me to jump into the game.

I took another sniff.

"*Non, non, non.* You must smell it quite strongly. The aroma must make it into your sinus cavities."

I hadn't voluntarily tried to insert anything into my sinus cavities since I'd seen Adrien snort a spaghetti noodle up his nostril and cough it down into his mouth. Then he'd taken up each end and flossed his nose. I'd thought it was really cool. I must have been about six. So I did it too.

I furrowed my nose deeper into the glass and pretended I was a vacuum cleaner.

"What do you smell?"

Besides my eyeballs? "It smells fruity."

"Yes. But what kind of fruit?"

It wasn't bananas, mangoes, or papayas. It smelled like a berry. "Raspberry?"

"Ah—close. Blackcurrant. Now we swirl again and smell. What is this one?"

I swirled and smelled. It did smell different than before. But between decaying garbage and cotton candy, there were tens of thousands of things it might be.

Adrien smelled again, deeply. "This is fabulous."

"Fabulous." I was trying hard not to laugh. He was so serious. So earnest. So cute. So not my boyfriend.

"What is it? I will give you a hint. It grows on the ground." He was looking at me expectantly.

What was I supposed to do with that information? Be happy that I didn't have to consider anything that grew on bread or out of my armpits?

I took another sniff. This was worse than taking a geology final. Essay Question Number One: Describe this rock. Um, it's very heavy.

"It is violets! So now we taste."

I put the glass to my mouth and took the tiniest of sips. It wasn't bad. Quite good actually.

"Wa-it."

"What? Did I do something wrong?"

"You must…" he was holding up his hand in front of his mouth. It was moving in a vertical circular motion.

"…sing?"

"Non."

"…what? Do I have bad breath?"

"Non. You must…"

I hate charades.

"…swing it around your mouth."

"Swish."

"Yes. Swish."

So I swished.

"How does it feel?"

Warm, tart, thick. The liquid puckered my cheeks. I grimaced. "I don't know."

His eyebrows furrowed. He looked concerned. Took a sip. Swished. Pondered. "I think this is a good one. Very balanced. You see, there are four factors which must be considered. Alcohol against softness. Acidity against astringency. So, if you take and label the four sides of a paper with each attribute and then mark the intensity of each one, then you can connect the dots and interpret the balance of the wine."

And he kept on going. I felt like someone watching the business segment on CNN. Blah, blah, blah, Microsoft. Blah, blah, blah, General Electric. Blah, blah, blah, uptick in the downtrend.

I had no idea what he was talking about.

And instead of zoning out to ticker prices scrolling across the bottom of the television screen, I was becoming hypnotized by the sunlight glinting plum-colored stars off the wine in his glass. His feet, which were bare, leaned against my hip. A warm, fuzzy feeling invaded my body, and spread a pink flush across my cheeks. I knew then that, on the graph of my accumulated crushes on Adrien, this one was going to be an outlier. One of those that makes the trend shoot skyward. Like Mount Everest.

It was going off the charts.

I was going to need help.

I put the glass to my lips. Took a long swallow.

"I think this is a very good wine. Maybe we should just enjoy it."

I needed to break the spell. To do something. Say something. Anything. "Do you have a *cave* too? Like Mademoiselle's?"

"*Oui.* Of course. They come with the apartments."

"And you have wines like this in it?"

"*Non.* Not this good. But I go to wine fairs, in the spring and fall, and I buy some. A few new cases every year."

"How do you know what to buy?"

"I buy what I like. One tastes, at the fairs. I go the first day to try *aperitifs.* I go the second day for white wine, the third for red wine, and the last day for *digestifs.*"

And the day after that for an entire bottle of aspirin.

So we sipped. We talked. About everything. Books. Politics. Ideas. The Roman Empire and the Russian Empire. America and France. Now and then I jabbed him with a foot just to make a point. And he would grip my toes or squeeze my calf to make his.

He told me where he'd gotten his furniture. At antique fairs in Paris.

"And Claire, there is this one, the *Foire nationale à la brocante et aux jambons.*"

"The National Antique and Ham Fair?"

"*Oui.* Yes."

"They sell antiques and ham? At the same time?"

Adrien grinned. "Yes. I swear to you. It is wonderful. Normally I spend the whole weekend there. It is huge. And it is outside. At a fairs ground."

"A fairground?"

"*Oui.* And one may find absolute trash or priceless treasure. There is nothing like it. It begins next month. At the end of the month. If you would be here, I would take you."

By the time I finished my glass—yes, I did it, I drank the entire thing—I agreed with him about the quality of the wine. And this time, I didn't drink too fast. I had sipped the wine over the course of an hour. No hums. No headache. I hoped that also meant no gnomes.

He held up his empty glass. "Just one last thing. The longer the taste lingers in the mouth, the better the wine."

I'd finished my glass a half hour earlier and I could still taste those blackcurrants. The taste was so strong I could have sworn I'd actually eaten a whole bowl of them.

"We might just have drunk a *Méo-Camuzet*, but we will never know."

"You could say you did. I won't tell."

He winked at me. "I might."

"You should."

As we had talked, the breeze coming through the window had thinned as it jettisoned the warmth of the sun. The shadows had lengthened. The color of the room had aged from sunlit yellow to a cream-washed gold.

I turned and dropped my legs over the side of the couch, leaned out the window and hooked my elbows around the iron railing. Across the street, over the tops of the buildings, I could see the top half of the Eiffel Tower. It was silhouetted against a fiery peach sunset.

I heard a rustle and turned to find Adrien beside me, one leg dangling on the floor, the other folded out beside him. He was almost encircling me.

My heart zoomed into outer space until I yanked on its leash.

"My heart is happy that you are here."

I almost choked. "Mine too."

"Did you feel this way with Brian?"

Had I? "No. But I didn't really know him. Not like I know you." I turned back to the window. The peach was fading into a cerulean blue which deepened into midnight blue and blended with the rest of the universe. "He was a nice guy. Not brilliant like you are, but he was smart. And funny. He was nice."

"He was nice. This is the best thing you can say about him? Because if someone asked me to describe you, I would use many words, but nice would not be one of them."

I turned right around to face him and found myself practically sitting in his lap. "Are you saying that I'm mean?"

"*Non.*" He reached out and swept a lock of hair away from my forehead. But his hand didn't settle back on the couch. It gripped my chin and turned my face up toward his. "But nice is the very least of who you are. And not the first description that would come to mind. I am very glad that Brian was nice, but nice is not enough. Not for you."

I was imprisoned.

By his eyes, by his hand, by his words.

Each word that he spoke added to the mass of the words that had come before. They hung heavy in the air until they burst as they dropped into my heart.

Adrien.

What I wanted was someone like him. Why couldn't there have been an American version? Someone who could pronounce the letter "h" and knew the difference between football and soccer?

I knew my crush on him was hopeless. I'd been living in a prolonged state of hopelessness for…most of my life. Yep. Mount Everest. I was well on my way to the top and in desperate need of oxygen. I didn't blame him for it. I'm sure women fell in love with him all the time. But there was no need for me to add myself to the official list. And it was sweet, the way he looked after me as if I were his sister.

Sister and brother. Adrien and me.

That's why there had been a Brian.

Brians were real. Not everyone could be as brilliant as Adrien. As charming as Adrien. As successful, as funny, as handsome as Adrien. It wasn't fair to compare. And I never had compared my boyfriends to him; all two of them. As far as "Brians" go, my Brian had been at the top of his class. And that had been good enough for me.

Adrien was still holding my chin.

I couldn't look him in the eye, so I shrugged. Smiled. "Sometimes nice is the best of what's left. I'm pretty old, you know. Almost 30. The good guys have all been taken."

"Not all of them." He took his hand from my chin, got up, and pulled me with him. "*Bon.* We must eat."

We had dinner and then Adrien walked me home.

We passed lovers. Scores of them. They were holding hands. Kissing. Strolling down avenue George V. Crossing the Pont de l'Alma bridge. Striding up avenue Bosquet. The tourist bureau must pay people to pose in amorous positions. "Visit Paris and have the most romantic kiss of your life."

I should sue for false advertising.

It was a perfect summer night. Languid. A breeze still stirred the air. Sacré Coeur glowed in white purity on top of Montmarte hill. The Eiffel Tower glistened.

If my life had been a movie, I would have poured out a confession of my unrequited love right there in the middle of the sidewalk and thrown myself at Adrien's feet. And he would have swept me into his arms and kissed me passionately.

But my life is not a movie.

It's reality TV. There is a difference between what I want and what I can have.

I don't mind taking risks for love. Calculated risks. But I wasn't willing to risk my friendship with Adrien for a drive-by kiss. I mean, Adrien in love with me? What were the odds?

Although, if I could find a way to kiss him just before the plane took off, and if I could guarantee that I would never have to see him for the rest of my life…well, maybe.

Chapter 22

Adrien couldn't come by the next day until after lunch; he said he had some paperwork to do. Which was just fine with me. My poor heart had been working overtime. It needed a break. So I called Cynthia.

And I told her I needed help.

She hopped on the metro and was at the apartment in under 20 minutes. She kissed me on both cheeks and then looked into my eyes with a probing glance. "So what's the problem?"

"Adrien."

"Ah."

"Remember when I said I used to have a crush on him?"

She nodded.

"I still do. It's like…malaria. It lies dormant for a long time and then, just when I think I'm over him, I have a flare-up."

"A flare-up. Are you talking candle or bonfire size?"

"I'm talking Great Chicago Fire of 1871."

"Devastating?"

"Totally."

"And this would be so terrible because…?"

"He's Adrien!"

"I know."

"Half the population of Paris is in love with him."

"Guilty. I liked him myself for a while. But he's so flirty. They all are. Or at least very gallant."

"See! So you know what I'm talking about. He flirts with everyone. The warm hand on the small of your back?"

"Yep."

"The gaze that penetrates deep into your eyes?"

"Yep."

"The listening intently to every single word you say as if you were the only one on earth who mattered?"

"Yep."

"The draping of an arm over your shoulders?"

"Yep."

"Holding your hand?"

"Nope."

"The smoothing of your hair back from your face?"

"Nope."

"The attempts at kissing you?"

"Nope."

We stared at each other for a long moment.

"Really?"

We both asked the question at the same time. My heart went streaking into orbit. Again. I was getting tired of it doing that whenever I thought of Adrien. Which was practically...all the time.

I was too old for this.

I took a deep breath. "This is why I need help. I'm blowing everything out of proportion. I've known him forever. He thinks of me as a little sister."

"In most countries in the world, you'd get thrown in jail for kissing your sister."

"You're not helping. Tell me all the reasons this would never work."

"Are you sure you don't want it to work?"

"Why don't I just buy you a flamethrower?"

"Look. Let's go for a walk. We'll go to Ladurée. Have some *macarons*. Sip some espresso. Get some perspective. Sound good?"

Sounded great.

I went into my room to grab my backpack. But after the recent debacle, I thought twice about using it. It didn't go with what I was wearing. And would I really need my day planner, an entire tin of Altoids, three pens, a map of Seattle, a pair of mittens, Kleenex, aspirin, and five elastics for my hair? But what were the options? Carrying my money around in my shoe?

Maybe Adrien had a point.

I slung my backpack over a shoulder and we left.

We walked down avenue Bosquet, across Pont de l'Alma bridge, up George V toward the Champs-Elysées in silence. Every time I began to speak, she shushed me. "Just...*sois zen.* Stay zen. Deep breath. Peace. Calm. Relax."

We got to Ladurée and were seated upstairs in an elegant salon. Ordered espressos and assorted flavors of *macarons* before I exploded. "It's hopeless!"

"Are you sure?"

"He's Adrien!"

"The last time I checked, he wasn't married."

I just shook my head. "Okay. Give them to me. The reasons it won't work."

She let out one of those puff-cheeked French sighs. The ones reserved for insane people. Or idiots. "You live in Seattle; he lives in Paris."

"Right."

"He's flirty. He's French."

"Yep. Right." This was good. This is exactly what I needed.

"You project this brother/sister thing onto the relationship."

"Right. Absolutely."

She leaned back. Took a sip of espresso. Ate another *macaron.* "I think raspberry are my favorites."

I blinked. "And...?"

"Dark chocolate are pretty good too."

"Cynthia! Reasons. The other reasons!"

"There aren't anymore."

"There have to be."

"There aren't. You've either got to sweat it out or you've got to tell him. Your choice."

"I can't tell him."

"Why not?"

"I just can't."

When I got back to the apartment, Adrien was waiting for me. "Would you like to take a walk?"

"Sure. Yeah." Why not? Anything to distract myself.

"I spoke with a general contractor about the apartment. He is a friend. On Monday he will meet you at nine o'clock to see what must be done. Provide an estimate. You can call your parents—"

I opened my mouth to protest, but he'd already read my mind.

"—or I will call your parents and we can decide what they would like done."

I opened my mouth to thank him, but he went right on talking.

"I have also made an appointment with a real estate agent. To have an idea of the market value."

I tried to thank him, but he wasn't listening.

"I have also made appointments with an antique dealer on *quai* Voltaire. He specializes in Louis XV at the top end of the market. And I asked Sotheby's to send information on placing things for auction."

This time I grabbed his arm and made him stop. "Thank you. Very much. I would never have found these people on my own."

He smiled down into my eyes. "It was nothing, *ma poule.*"

The walk turned into a hike. He wanted to poke around the *bouquiniste* stalls near Notre Dame. But I didn't know that at first. If I had, I might have suggested taking the metro. As it was, we walked east. Past the American Church. Past the Assemblée Nationale. Past even Musée d'Orsay before crossing the *quai* Anatole France and drifting along the sidewalk that perched above the Seine. Dozens of dark green boxes lined the stone wall. When opened, with their lids propped up, they revealed mini shops filled with books, postcards, magnets, and posters.

At first I slowed and stopped in front of each booth. But then I realized that Adrien had a route. He was a bee on a mission, zipping around several vendors at a time, only to stop and linger at particular stalls. Always asking the same questions. Did they happen to have any first-edition Victor Hugo? Did they know of anyone who did?

"It is not likely that I would find one here, but one never knows."

He was in between stalls, and I was trying my best to keep up with him. "Do you come often?"

"One time or two times a month." He gave me a wry grin. "Maybe three times when the weather is fair."

Like I said. A man on a mission.

The stalls dwindled as we approached Notre Dame. We studied it from across the river.

"You want to go inside, Claire?"

"I don't know." Masses of people were streaming in and out of the doors. Crowds jostled on the parvis in front of the cathedral.

"Have you ever been?"

"No."

"You should. It is one of the finest examples of Gothic architecture in the world."

"Have you ever been?"

"*Non.*"

We were leaning on the stone wall at the edge of Pont au Double bridge. Watching the water curl and unfurl as it glided past.

"What would you like to do tomorrow?"

I shrugged. I had no idea. No plans.

There was something flashing in his eyes, but I couldn't decide what it was. Irritation? Amusement? The sun? "Then you do not mind if I spend the evening with Solange?"

"Solange? Perfect. You can return the dress to her."

"Perfect."

If I hadn't known better, I might have thought he looked disappointed. But what was I supposed to say? It wasn't as though he was in love with me. He could date whomever he wanted.

But hadn't he broken up with her?

Were they getting back together?

Was she a busty, blue-eyed blonde?

Adrien pushed off the wall and began walking across the bridge.

I followed him.

We walked toward the cathedral. It became more imposing with every step. It wasn't my idea of a beautiful building. It was immense. Solid. Grand. Stoic. But not beautiful. Too many straight lines? Too rigid? Looking at the cathedral, one could see quite plainly that Christianity was serious business.

And that was probably the point.

Inside, it was enormous. Filled with people. None of them were speaking, but there was still an echo. At first glance, it appeared empty. But then what building wouldn't that had such vast volumes? The middle was sectioned off by wooden gates. Chairs were arranged in large rectangular groupings, leaving both a center aisle and side aisles open.

It was a somber place.

I felt like a mouse, scuttling through someone else's world. Small. Insignificant. As if I didn't belong.

There were tiered shoulder-high candelabras. A glassed-in priest's office offering confession in different languages. Tucked between the ribs of the buttresses, along the outside walls, there were chapels. Most were dedicated to saints by specific families or guilds. There was some beautiful stonework and woodwork.

And those gorgeous stained-glass rose windows. They left drops of gumdrop-colored light on the floor.

I hadn't realized how dark it was inside until we pushed out into the open again. I also hadn't realized that I'd been tiptoeing, trying to be as quiet as that stray mouse. I stepped from the cathedral's shadow into the sun.

Shivered.

"Thanks, Adrien. Now I can say I've been there. It was very…large."

He burst into laugher. "It is not my cathedral. You can say whatever you wish about it."

"It was empty."

"Yes. In more ways than one, *non?*"

I was disappointed. It had been a cathedral for centuries. A holy place. You'd think there'd still be some leftover vibes around. Not that I believed in cosmic energy or ley lines or whatever it was New Age pagans traveled to places like Stonehenge to feel. But shouldn't there have been something? Some extraspecial connection to God? Wasn't I supposed to feel as though I had earned a holiness badge for visiting?

We walked around the river side of the cathedral and to the park at the back. We sat on a bench and watched pigeons strut and children play tag in front of the fountain.

Adrien stretched his arm along the back of the bench and turned toward me. He tilted his head and stared at the cathedral. "It was built for the wrong reasons."

"Can there be a wrong reason for building a cathedral?"

"The bishop was jealous of St-Denis Basilique. North of Paris."

"He built a cathedral so that he could have one too?"

"*Non.* He built it so that he could say he had built a cathedral too."

"It had nothing to do with God?"

"Nothing at all."

"So if people come here thinking that they'll find God…?"

"Maybe they will find him. He does not play hide-and-seek with us. But you could find him just as well in a metro station or a bar, *non?*"

"Maybe not in a bar."

"But God is everywhere."

In theory God's omnipresence worked for me. I could imagine him in my house, in my church, at the grocery store. On Mount Rainier, at Alki Beach, on Bainbridge Island. I could talk to God, I could admire nature with him, but I wasn't quite willing yet to drink a beer with him.

Adrien studied my face as I thought about what he said. "You think there are some places where God is not?"

"Well—no."

"But there are some places where you would not be if you were God."

Exactly. "Yes."

"Well, thank God that God is God." He got to his feet and held out a hand to help me to mine.

It wasn't until we were nearly halfway home that I realized I'd been insulted.

I stopped in the middle of the sidewalk along the *quai*. "What did you mean when you said that about God?"

"I meant that you are a snob, Claire."

"What!"

"You are a snob."

"I understood what you said the first time. And I am not."

"But you are. If you were God, there are some things you would not do. There would be limits to your compassion."

"What kinds of limits?"

"You would not meet people in a bar. You would not make friends perhaps with a person who was having an affair. You would not sit beside someone when they went into the Moulin Rouge for a cabaret show. You would not go to a lecture on Druid religion. You would not sunbathe on the *Côte d'Azur*."

"Topless? Of course not."

"See. This is what I mean. You are a snob. A religious snob."

"Would *you* do them?"

"Of course. Why not?"

"A lecture on Druid religion?"

"It is where I am going with Solange tomorrow evening."

"*Druid* religion?"

"They are not going to tie me to a table and make me drink blood. Just because I listen to a lecture does not mean I will believe everything that I hear. In any case, we are not talking about me, we are talking about you."

"I am not a snob."

"But, you see, you suspect me of some kind of heresy every time I speak about God. You think perhaps my faith is not so strong because it disagrees in some cases with yours."

A snob? I couldn't be. Was that possible? "I'm not a snob."

"Then convince me."

"How?"

"Do one of those things. The one you would be least likely to do."

"I will *not* sunbathe topless."

"Then the next one you would be least likely to do."

"I am not going to the lecture with you. I can't. Because it's a date. And you didn't ask me. You asked Solange."

"Then do the next worst thing."

"Refresh my memory."

"Make a friend with someone who is having an affair. Go to the Moulin Rouge. Go to a bar."

"You're daring me to do one of those things? This is ridiculous. We're not in junior high school." And that was the whole point in my opinion. I wasn't a girl anymore. I was a woman. And Adrien wasn't responding to me like one. He was responding to me as if I were an adolescent. He was daring me to do something. Well, I wouldn't. If I wanted him to treat me like a woman, then I needed to start conversing like one.

"I did not think you could convince me."

"Do you honestly think I'm a snob? Really?"

"Do you think you are?"

A prude? Maybe. Probably. Yes. But that didn't make me a snob. "What's your definition?"

"I think that you have beliefs about God that you think others should share, but sometimes those beliefs are incorrect. I cannot say whether it is because you are American or whether it is because you are simply mistaken in your beliefs."

I was trying very hard to be mature. To not take everything he was saying personally. But it was very difficult! "Like what?"

"Like having fun."

Having fun? Having fun was a priority in elementary school. In junior high. But I'd never heard it included in Sunday school curriculum. "So I'm snobby because I'm not fun?"

"*Non, non, non.* It is because you think that faith cannot be fun."

"Just so we're clear, Jesus went through a lot of pain—which was not fun—in order to establish the Christian faith. I don't see the fun connection anywhere."

"It was before that. Long before. It is everywhere. Think of...the creation. The mind which created volcanoes and thunderstorms and fields filled with flowers."

"Volcanoes are fun?"

"Of course. Think of the thought which conceived them. A grumble of the earth, a splitting open of the soil. A spitting of lava...fire, flames, cinder everywhere!"

So he criticizes me for spiritual heresies while he describes God as a pyromaniac.

"And then ash flies into the air, darkens everything. Clouds form. Huge thunderheads that growl and convulse and rip apart, sending torrents of rain to the earth. But every drop of water contains a particle of ash. And that water and that ash fall onto a meadow and fertilize the earth, and the creative work of destruction gives breath to a field of flowers. You see?"

"No."

"*Non?*" Adrien folded his arms across his chest. "God could have done the same thing more efficiently, but instead, he created poetry and community among all living things." He frowned. "If you cannot identify with my God, then what is your God like?"

"My God doesn't mess around like yours does. He's too busy. And so was Jesus. He spent his time taking care of people. And then he died. A terrible death."

"*Oui.* This is true. But how did he spend his free time? Do you remember?"

I opened my mouth. And then I shut it. Reminded myself I was trying to be mature. "I don't recall."

"He attended a wedding. He made friends. He did many things that very religious people found offensive. The very worst, I think, in their opinion, was that he did not like them. He chose other, different friends."

"And I suppose you think that's because the religious people weren't very fun."

"*Bah...oui.*"

"But they weren't fun because faith is serious. It takes work."

"Of course. But what do you think heaven will be like? We will not be working any longer. There will be nothing left to be done. So we will be able to see the true nature of God, *non?*"

I nodded. I could agree with that.

"Do you not remember how heaven is described? It is a *fête*. A party."

"I don't think it was meant to be a literal interpretation."

"Claire, you miss what I am saying. Earth is God's creation. So in its original state, it was an extension of himself. Is it so difficult to think that we may have been created to enjoy it? That one of our purposes is to celebrate? You lack a *joie de vivre*."

Joie de vivre. Joy of living. I'd have to work on that. I'd put it on my spiritual to-do list. Right after acquiring patience and self-control, loving my neighbor as myself, and walking humbly with God.

"You do not agree?"

"What do you want me to do? Paint a smiley face on myself?"

"*Non.* I do not mean to insult you. I just thought you might wish to know this about yourself."

"Are you done assaulting my character? Because I would like to go home."

He threw his hands up in the air. "Fine. Forgive me."

"No! All you've done since I've been here is wish that I were different. But I'm not. I'm me. And that's all I can ever be. If it's not good enough for you, then go hang out with Solange or Véronique or…the other one. The one with the family castle in Provence."

His lips quirked. Then straightened. "Virginie. And I am not trying to change you. I am trying to see your faith. I want to know that the God you believe in is the same God that I believe in. I do not think he is, and I do not like your God very much. So which one of us is right?"

He took my hand in his.

"Which one? I would not try to change you. I love everything about you. But you do not see everything about you that I do. So how do I show these things to you? Obviously not very well. So I am sorry."

He turned my hand over. Looked at it. Then looked up at me. "I think that if you thought about God a little more, then you would try a little less, and you would be more happy. Less earnest. Do you not want to be happy, Claire? What is it that you want from life?"

I started laughing hysterically. I couldn't help it.

What do I want?

I want to trade my life in for the opposite version. The one where I majored in history in college. The one where I was a high school teacher. The one where I was already married to Adrien instead of trying to dissect him from my heart with a dull-edged knife.

I wanted a do-over.

That's what I wanted.

But I would never tell Adrien. What would be the point?

Chapter 23

ॐ৩ৎ

We agreed to take a break from each other the next day. It seemed best. And anyway, Adrien had his date with Solange.

Did you hear that, heart? Solange. Not you.

I gave him the dress when he dropped me off after our...discussion.

Okay, I flung it at him. Along with ten euros so Solange could have it dry-cleaned.

After he left, I poured myself a bowl of cereal, cried my eyes out, and went to sleep.

The next morning my eyes were glued shut, encrusted with tears. I felt my way to the bathroom and bathed them open. Then I sat on the edge of the bathtub and stared at myself in the mirror.

Was I a snob?

I tried not to think about the things Adrien had said on our walk home.

Like that strategy had ever worked before.

Was I a snob? Did we believe in different Gods?

I do not like your God very much.

Well, I didn't like his God either. He had entirely too much fun for someone who was in charge of the universe. What was wrong with taking life seriously? It was usually considered the mark of a mature person. Life was too short to screw up. Everyone knew that. Some people just chose to ignore it. Or didn't get it.

So I was okay.

Wasn't I?

What if I'd gotten it all wrong? What if I was supposed to have been enjoying life this whole time? What if I was supposed to have been having fun instead of working hard, paying my bills, being a good Christian, causing no offense to anyone.

Having fun.

Was that supposed to be a goal in life? It certainly wasn't a virtue. Not like being kind or honest or gracious. Was it? Was life really about pleasure? Because I'd always thought it was about dedication. And perseverance. About preparing for pain and hardship. Not that I'd had much, but I was certainly ready for it. Statistically speaking, it should be knocking at my door any day now. That's one of the reasons I held on to my job; it had good health benefits. And that's why I had my faith, right?

Right.

And on I went, debating with myself all day long. I was ready to flush myself down the toilet. I'd wanted a *break* from Adrien. I hadn't wanted to become him.

I went out for lunch, walked up to Invalides, and strolled the grounds. Anywhere that I could go for free. I ended up in the severe inner courtyard. It was paved with gray stones, lined with gray shadow-filled cloisters.

Not a flower in sight.

Yes, it was nice that Louis XIV had provided food and shelter for his injured soldiers, those invalided out of the army, but it couldn't have been more depressing. I sat on my hands on the wall of the cloister. Thought about thinking about Seattle. My house. My job.

Thought about Adrien instead.

Bounced my heels off the stone wall until I realized I was in the process of shredding my new flats.

Splendid.

I stalked out into the sun and down the avenue de Tourville, through the intersection at Place de l'Ecole Militaire. Then I ambled down rue Cler, stopping at Picard. I picked up a couple frozen dishes for emergency dinners: *coquilles St. Jacques, cannelloni Bolognese,* seafood tagliatelle, Thai turnovers. Picard only sold frozen food, but after having the cannelloni for dinner, I decided it was better than many restaurant meals I'd eaten in my life.

And cheaper.

After dinner I went into the library and picked up a novel, a French translation of an American bestseller. I sat in the library, glued to the book, until midnight. Dozed off and on in the chair after that.

Went to bed at two.

My eyes fluttered open on Sunday morning.

I sat up and threw off the sheet. Stomped toward the commode. And there, sitting on the top, smirking at me, was my backpack.

Adrien had made me paranoid.

And the combination of colors was giving me vertigo. What had I been thinking when I'd bought it? It was obvious that I hadn't been.

So I snuck over to Mademoiselle's and stole something out of her closet. Technically and theologically, it wouldn't have made the grade as an actual theft. But it sure felt like it.

It wasn't that I was tired of lugging the backpack around town. Not really.

I wanted to be looked at.

Noticed.

I craved the admiring looks I'd received while wearing Solange's dress. And I wanted to know it wasn't her taste that made the difference. I wanted to make sure it was my own bad taste in bags that had kept anyone from giving me a second glance.

I have a vain, frivolous heart.

I chalked it up to temporary madness due to involuntary imprisonment in Paris. It's not as though I was planning to stuff the contents of Mademoiselle's armoires into my suitcase and pretend they were mine. I just needed to borrow one purse. For a few days. Weeks. Besides, what was she going to do? Rise from her grave and poke me in the eye?

So I pulled open the doors of the armoires and went to work, dumping purses from their dust bags and ultimately selecting a black satchel bag that was about a foot long and five inches wide at the bottom with four little gold studs for feet. I couldn't put it over my shoulder and had to hold it by the handle, but it was the roomiest of Mademoiselle's purses. It had two thin little straps that looped around the top flap and fastened in the middle like a belt. It also had a lock.

Who puts a lock on their purse?

If someone's going to steal it, a lock is not going to stop them from taking anything. It would take about five seconds to cut into the bag with an electric bread knife. And if someone's going to take it around town, don't you think they'd want instant easy access? For metro money? Or a mint? Or one of five pens?

I took the lock off and left it on the dresser.

Then I scooted back to the Delaportes'.

I was in the living room inspecting the orchid when I heard a key turn in the front door. Adrien's head emerged; his eyes found me. He opened the door wide and stood there. "I come in peace."

He took his hand from behind his back and presented me with a bouquet of roses. At least a dozen. White.

I rummaged around in the dining room, looking for a vase.

Found one.

As I entered the living room, I saw Adrien's reflection in the mirror over the fireplace. Saw him stick a finger in the orchid that was sitting on the mantel. Checking up on me? Making sure it was wet but not too wet? Well, it was and it wasn't. But only because I'd seen it yesterday morning in passing and taken pity on it.

"How was Solange?"

"Well. And how was your day?"

"Fine."

"You are ready?"

"Yes."

I'd left the purse by the door, so I just scooped it up on our way out.

We took the elevator. After arriving at the ground floor, Adrien pressed the door button and held it open for me. "Did you do some borrowing this morning?"

"The purse?"

"*Oui.*"

"Yes."

"Any reason why you picked this one?"

"It was big."

"Hmm. You know what kind of purse this is."

"A big black one?"

He grinned and put a fingertip to the tip of my nose, just like he used to do when I was a kid. "An Hermès. A Kelly Hermès."

"It's pretty nice, don't you think?" The style was growing on me. It wasn't dressy and it wasn't casual. It was just about right.

We had reached his car. I waited while he opened the door. Buckled my seat belt as he closed it. Hung on to the purse as he raced down the street.

"So. Since you do not mind talking about money, do you know how much this purse costs?"

It was probably a couple hundred dollars. But then again, it wasn't really mine. So who cared? "Two hundred?"

"Times five thousand. Ten thousand euro."

I wrapped both my arms around it.

He slid a glance in my direction. "Normally, they come with a lock."

"Really?"

"It is too bad this does not have one. People collect these."

So maybe I'd sneak back into Mademoiselle's tonight and get the lock. I didn't have to use it to lock the bag shut. Maybe I could just clasp it around the handle.

And look totally stupid.

But no more stupid than I looked carrying a 10,000 euro bag that was apparently missing its most important part. If I still had my shorts or jeans, then I could empty the bag, lock it, and carry only the most essential of my essentials in my pockets.

But then I wouldn't need a purse, would I?

So maybe I'd sneak back into Mademoiselle's that night and trade it in for a cheaper, more easy to navigate model. It was way too big. Like wearing a suitcase around my wrist.

Maybe when we got to church, I'd just leave it locked in the trunk.

When we did get to church, I didn't want to be that obvious about it, so I tried to shove it under the seat.

"You are not going to take this with you?"

"Just checking to see if it could be considered carry-on luggage."

The problem with this purse, the most irritating problem, was that it couldn't *be* hidden. It might not be too formal or too casual, but it was conspicuous. I couldn't just tuck it under my arm. Couldn't toss it over my shoulder.

It demanded attention. Required special treatment. This was not a purse that could be tucked underneath a chair.

It spent the entire service on my lap. Like a cat. And when we stood up to sing? I clutched it with both hands. As though I were standing on a train platform, waiting for the express to Brussels.

Borrowing this purse was not the best idea I've ever had.

It ranked right up there with trying to drive from Seattle to Portland the day before Thanksgiving and fueling the ride with a super large latte. My kidneys still cramped whenever I thought about it.

As soon as the service was over, I tried to make a dash down the aisle and out the door so I could toss the purse into the car and be rid of the responsibility.

I wasn't fast enough.

Cynthia found me.

"Wow. Great purse."

"It was my…aunt's." One of these evenings I would diagram Mademoiselle's connection to my father and determine exactly what sort of relative she was.

"They say those things will last for decades."

Marvelous. Just what I wanted. To walk around for the rest of my life with my wallet locked inside a $10,000 purse. Ten thousand dollars? I could buy a new car with that kind of money.

Another woman walked up and joined us. Kathy? Katie? Christy? I couldn't remember. "Is that a Kelly? Did Adrien buy it for you?"

"No. Why would you think that?"

"Because…well, I figured…I mean, aren't you guys going out? You come with him every Sunday to church…"

Cynthia was saying "I told you so" with her eyes. Then she winked. "So how's the apartment business?" She looked as if she really was interested, so I gave her the real interesting version.

"It's awful. I just got the key on Thursday. It's worse than I remembered. I don't know what's going to happen. It needs a lot of work, and my parents will probably end up selling it."

"They don't want to live in France? Isn't your dad French?"

"They can't afford the inheritance tax. Six hundred thousand dollars. If Adrien's right, that's a minimum."

Cynthia whistled. "I hope I never have a fairy godmother die and leave me her apartment."

Kathy/Katie/Christy gave my arm a squeeze and group-hopped, talking to other friends.

Cynthia glanced around the room. Lowered her voice. "How are things with A?"

"'A' what?"

"A, Adrien."

"Oh." The last time I'd spoken in code was in the eighth grade. And then it was about a guy we'd referred to as TDH. It was short for tall, dark, and handsome. Even though he wasn't tall or dark. But that was part of the code. "He's fine. I'm still sweating. Buckets."

That's when Adrien found us.

"Have you told Claire about the fall retreat?" Cynthia pinned Adrien with her eyes as if he were a dead bug stuck on a bulletin board.

"She will not be here."

"When is it?" With the amount of work the apartment needed, I might end up dying in Paris of old age myself.

"Toussaint."

"God bless you."

Cynthia howled. Tears welled up in her eyes. When she finally quit laughing, she told me what the joke was. "Toussaint. All Saint's. November 1. It's a national holiday. Kids have the week off school. So the church is going to Brittany for the weekend. We're staying in a *gîte*. A bed-and-breakfast sort of place."

That sounded fun.

"And it's too bad you won't be here over Christmas. We're going to Val Thorens. Skiing."

"I don't ski." Never wanted to. Never will.

"But you don't have to. That's the best part. Last year I played cards. Shopped. Talked. Drank hot chocolate. I never put on a ski once. I don't like snow. And at least six other nonskiers are going this year." She leaned in, whispering, "I started signing people up in June. Adrien's going too. He actually skis."

He would. He probably had skis that matched his pants that matched his jacket that matched his gloves.

"I wish I could go." I surprised myself by meaning it.

We stopped by the market near the church. We each bought things to stock our respective refrigerators before we drove back into the city. Most of my purchases involved the baker. Adrien's revolved around the *fromager*.

I asked him to make a stop at Mademoiselle's.

While he sat in the living room, I went into Mademoiselle's room and reassessed her other purses.

I pulled out everything she had in black.

There was a quilted leather purse with a chain link shoulder strap. Not my style. An envelope style clutch made of vinyl printed with the letter G. A dainty little trapezoid "grandmother" purse with a gold frame, kiss clasp, and single short handle. I set the Kelly beside them.

There were no good options.

While I was sitting on Mademoiselle's bed staring at the purses, daring one of them to call my name, I became aware of Adrien standing in the door, watching me.

"They are all good choices. All classics. All quite expensive."

"I wish you'd thrown my backpack away too."

"I would have, but I could not find it."

"It really doesn't work as a purse."

"You could save it for hiking."

"I would if I hiked."

"Why not take this one?" He walked over the pile and picked out the grandmother purse.

"You think?"

"Why not? If you do not like it, you can come back and trade." He glanced at me, put the purse down, and picked up the Kelly. "Or you could just keep this one." He was taunting me.

I snatched it from him. "I'll keep it. All my stuff's already in it."

He sat down on Mademoiselle's bed and watched as I put all the purses back.

"*Alors*, about…this woman."

"Solange?"

"*Non.* The other."

"Oh. The one you're in love with?"

"Yes. This one."

I hoped my heart was listening. Maybe this was what it needed. To hear about Adrien's one true love. In detail. Maybe then it would listen to what I was trying to tell it. "What about her?" Tell me everything.

"*Alors*…if you were her, what would I have to do to make you take me seriously?"

Erase every memory of that summer when I was 17. If I were going to take Adrien seriously, I'd have to get over my fear of humiliation. "You'd have to make it safe for me."

"What do you mean by safe?"

"You would have to make me believe that I'm the only one you've ever loved. Or at least the only one you love right now."

"And why would you not think this?"

"I don't know. Maybe…I've seen you…kissing someone else. At some point in time."

"Where might you have seen this?"

"I don't know. Where have you been kissing girls?"

"You have never met any of my girlfriends, have you, Claire?"

"Well, has she?"

"Who?"

"Whomever it is that you're talking about."

"Oh. *Non*. I do not think so."

"How many girlfriends have you had?"

"Pfft. Several. Some. What does it matter?"

"It might matter to this girl. How could she take you seriously if she knows about all the others? Or suspects there have been others? Why would she think she's different from anyone else who's come before?"

"But she is."

"Then that's what you have to make her believe."

"How?"

"I don't know. You're the one who's in love with her." What would I want him to do if she were me? "Kiss her."

"I have tried."

"What does she do?"

"She does not let me."

"Maybe she doesn't think you mean it. Or mean it enough."

"Why would she think this?"

"I don't know, Adrien. Maybe she's a moron. Are you sure she's worth it?"

"I am certain of it."

"Well, good luck."

Chapter 24

ॐ

Mauvaise nouvelles." The general contractor was shaking his head mournfully. As if a close relative had just died. A closer relative to him than Mademoiselle had been to me.

Just because "bad news" sounded prettier in French didn't make it any more palatable. I didn't know that anything else could be wrong with the apartment. I followed him down the hall and into the bathroom, where I found many possibilities.

The peeling linoleum didn't really count; I figured it was just cosmetic. So maybe it was the claw-footed oval bathtub, which had been pushed away from the wall? The sink, which was no longer resting on its pedestal? The mirror, which had been glued to the wall but was now lying in pieces on top of a paper bag? Or maybe it was the toilet, because, although there had been one, there was no sign of it now.

The bathtub won, but only because the man was gesturing toward it, the corners of his lips turned downward. *"Regardez."*

Well, I was looking.

It may not have been the best of tubs, but it had been serviceable. I had planned on allocating a half day to scrubbing and bleaching it and then I had thought it would work just fine. I didn't get it.

I glanced at the man.

He gestured down toward the floor.

Oh my.

There wasn't one. Not anymore.

He told me that the floor near the tub was soft, so he pushed the tub away from the wall and tore away the linoleum to find the problem. Most of the time, he assured me, in buildings this old, a soft spot in the flooring is just a matter of replacing a rotting board or two.

It wasn't very reassuring, because it looked as though a good dozen boards weren't there anymore. It had probably been a leaky pipe. And figuring that the plumbing in the building dated from the turn of the last century, it was really very, very *mauvaise nouvelles.*

The list of renovations just kept getting longer. Repaint the apartment, rewire the electricity, replace the appliances. And now the bathroom would have to be refloored.

If anyone deserved a break, I did. So I dodged fallen streamers of paint, skirted around humungous dust bunnies, and walked right out the door. I'd already given the contractor a key. Adrien had come and gone. No one needed me. I was superfluous. Except when it came to hearing about ever-increasing scopes of work and sums of money.

That was when I came in handy.

I left, threatening that I would never come back. I must have walked for 15 or 20 minutes; by the time my head cleared and my gaze sharpened, I had already marched past Invalides and its golden-domed church, and I was peering through an iron gate at the gardens of the Hôtel Biron and its Musée Rodin.

I decided to go in. Why not? The last time I'd visited, I'd been too busy talking with Cynthia to look at any of the exhibits.

I did a full circuit of the gardens but wasn't really into them. There were lots of flowers in bloom. Lots of picturesque vistas, if you like your gardens posed. Lots of statues. I saw *The Thinker,* towering over tall clipped hedges. In spite of its sober setting, I stuck with my original opinion. Rodin's inspiration was clearly acquired while sitting on a toilet.

I came to the conclusion that Rodin hadn't been a happy man.

Thoughtful, introspective, brooding, depressed, but not cheerful. Definitely not. And by looking at his statues, I was being pummeled by his emotions on a day when I had more than enough of my own. The contrast between the placid, serene, well-ordered gardens and the intense statuary was too much drama for me.

Maybe I wasn't into sculpture.

Maybe I'd wasted five euro.

I went inside.

The farther into the museum I went, the more stunning the sculptures became.

Literally.

I was surprised that I didn't remember any of it. Inside, the scale of the sculptures and their moods fit the setting. The rooms were laced with antiques and original carved-wood panels. They were accented with huge, ornate mirrors. But the walls were painted in subdued colors and the windows, by times plain to the point of utilitarian, at others paned and wreathed in ironwork, let in streams of light. The effect was breathtaking.

No more so than in room four. Walking into it, I saw a parquet wood floor. A white chair rail with wainscoting beneath. The room itself wasn't anything special. But the works of art on display were. Because, aside from *The Hand of God* (Rodin had a thing for hands) and other works, it displayed *The Kiss*.

This one I remembered. Before, I had been embarrassed. Somehow, looking at it with Cynthia had felt like watching an R-rated movie with my mother.

Now I was fascinated.

The sculpture was sitting on the floor, an island of marble interlaced with eerie flesh tones. It wasn't encased in glass or sheltered in a corner. I was free to walk all the way around it, so I did. And here's what I decided: it wasn't a normal classical kiss. There was no mastery here of male over female. It wasn't about power. Just a shared passion. A mutual possession.

Were they in love? Beyond love?

I stood there and stared.

What can I say? It seemed to symbolize everything that was wrong with my life.

It was a statue with a two-person composition. A man and a woman. So, right from the start, the imagery was all wrong for me.

It was about passion. They say that as long as you have one, and it doesn't have to be a job or a person, then you can find meaning in life. I don't have a passion. Even my cat died about three years ago.

It was sensual. Remember old Sensible-Shoes Claire? Need I say more?

It reeked emotion. Whereas I am an unglorified accountant.

It oozed fulfillment of a dream. The ownership of my own abandoned house in Seattle was still 28 years away.

It was everything I wanted and nothing that I had.

Was it wrong to be envious of a statue? Maybe not wrong, just weird. And all of a sudden, I felt like a voyeur. A *voyeuse*. Clearly this was an intimate moment that was meant to be private.

But, then again, it was a statue. And statues were meant to be viewed.

And maybe that's where Rodin's genius lay. Bringing life out of stone. But then, it wasn't life. Not really. It was emotion. He wrung emotion from the stone. It wasn't so much that he wanted it to look alive. It was much too rough; in places, unfinished. He wanted it to feel alive. And it did. Those two representations of people did a better job of acting than many A-list Hollywood actors.

How did Rodin do that?

The technical side of my brain went to work as I paced around the statue again. They were nude; that had to be a part of it. I couldn't see any tricks; there weren't any gimmicks. Was it in the pose? The languid, draped arm, the clench of fingers on a thigh. The spasmodic curl of toes.

They evoked the suggestion of passion.

Maybe that was it.

I looked more closely and discovered that in their move toward each other, there had been a hesitation. It was conveyed through the position of their bodies, as if they had been drawn together reluctantly, but were now about to turn toward each other wholeheartedly.

How did I feel about that? About them? Two naked people about to...do what naked people usually end up doing.

I assume.

But it didn't seem to matter what I thought. I wasn't part of their world. Anyone viewing the statue would feel the same. It wasn't about me; it was all about them. Rodin didn't intend to solicit my opinion or anyone else's. He hadn't provided any commentary on their story. No cues as to whether this was an ill-fated romance or a tale of happily ever after.

And I needed to know the story. Desperately.

Looking around the room, I found a plastic panel with detailed information.

I scanned quickly, looking for the good parts. I didn't care when it was created or for whom. It didn't matter where it had been displayed. I wanted to know about *them*.

What I discovered was surprising.

It was meant to be part of the *Gates of Hell* grouping, in which Rodin would illustrate scenes from Dante's *Inferno*. To represent the sins of the flesh, he chose the story of two real people, Paolo and Francesca, who had lived in Italy in the thirteenth century. Francesca had been wed to Gianciotto Malatesta, Lord of Rimini, to cement peace between their families.

She was young and beautiful.

He was ugly and deformed.

So that she wouldn't balk at the union, Gianciotto's younger hand-some brother, Paolo, was sent to complete the marriage by proxy. Nothing might have happened had not Gianciotto left Francesca in his brother's care while he went away on business. As it was, they enter-tained themselves by reading romances, and inspired by those words, their love became too passionate to remain chaste.

They were caught when Gianciotto returned. Francesca was killed accidentally while trying to keep her husband from stabbing her lover. And then Paolo was killed too. Their eternal passion had been turned, in an instant, into eternal damnation.

Boy, those romance novels can be dangerous.

Rodin had stripped the scene of its setting, its time period, even its clothing. He had sculpted the couple at the moment they became aware of their feelings for each other. Their first kiss. To the sculptor it hadn't been a very interesting subject. He didn't expect it to stimulate thought.

I begged to differ.

My own musing began the moment I saw the sculpture. What would it feel to be kissed like that? Was it okay to be kissed like that? To want to be kissed like that?

I took my thoughts down to the museum's café, Le Jardin de Varenne, and sat down at one of the tables set out between rows of chestnut trees. Sitting as I was at the back of the garden, I could better appreciate it because it seemed to have retreated from an insistently serene foreground to a pleasant background.

My previous thoughts of renovation and financial insolvency had been replaced with an intriguing glimpse of love. And I was famished for it.

And for food.

I eat, therefore I am.

I hadn't eaten since breakfast. I ordered an Orangina and an *Assiette Provençal*, which turned out to be a large salad with tomatoes, cucumbers, corn, tuna, sweet peppers, anchovies, and olives. I'm not a big fan of small salty fish, so I picked off the anchovies and rolled them up in my napkin.

Brian never kissed me the way Francesca and Paolo kissed.

But then, he was a pastor. Not that his choice of profession made him less sensual, but I'm not sure that he could have devoted his entire being to me. A kiss like that would seal a person off from the outside world.

Adrien could probably kiss like that.

I choked on a piece of lettuce and took a swig of Orangina to wash it down. Where had that thought come from? Wherever it had originated, I knew without a doubt that it was true. Adrien was a person who would pour his entire being into…whatever he was doing. I wondered what it would be like to kiss Adrien?

A real kiss.

I finished my food. Collected my purse. And about the purse. I'd made peace with it. We now coexisted in a state of mutual acceptance. I shared my seat with it. Strictly 50-50. Which meant that I was a little cramped, but I also didn't have to hold it on my lap and coddle it.

As I walked out of the gates and back toward the Delaportes', I hid my thoughts about kissing, about Adrien, in the deepest, darkest, shadowiest recesses of my mind.

And I tried to replace them with thoughts about the apartment.

Adrien was waiting at the Delaportes' when I got there.

"Claire! Is everything fine?"

"Hmm?" Have you ever noticed how lips can seem alive? Apart from the words they say and the face they're attached to?

"Are you okay?"

"Yes. Fine. I went for a walk."

"A four-hour walk?"

I shrugged. "You talked with the contractor?"

"Yes. I have a breakdown and estimate of work right here." He strode down the hall toward the library. Came back waving a document. "Some things cannot wait. They provide hazards. Like the bathroom. Others things, like the floors, do not have to be done right away."

"When can we kiss—"

Adrien's eyebrows leaped to the top of his forehead.

"Kick. When can we kis-ck, kick this into gear? Get it into motion. When does he think he can start? If we want the work started. If Dad and Mom want to. Before they sell. If they sell." I sat down on a chair in the living room. Crossed my legs. Took a deep breath. "When can he get started?"

Adrien opened his mouth, started to say something, and closed it. He sat down on the couch. "He does not know. It is August. It may be difficult for him to contact his best people. And then…" He shrugged. "It may cost more if you expect them to start this month."

"They have to start this month! I have a job in Seattle." I threw my hands up in frustration, and when they came down, they landed on my purse. Which was on my lap. Honestly! It was worse than a cat. Always sneaking onto my lap when I wasn't looking. I put it down on the floor. On the oriental carpet which covered the floor. Next, I was going to start buying cans of premium-grade tuna for its dinner.

"Maybe you should quit."

"Quit what?"

"Your job."

Why? He wasn't making any sense, but I decided to play along anyway. "Okay. Then what would I do?"

"Whatever you wanted."

Like he had a personal connection to the Job Fairy.

"You are under too much stress."

I almost laughed out loud, and then I reconsidered. Almost cried. The University of Washington was as laid-back a place to work as any I'd ever seen. Except that I had the wrong job. People my age were supposed to have found their passion in life. They were supposed to have acquired their dream job. Yes, I had a head for numbers. Yes, my job was easy, but I wasn't bounding out of bed in the morning to get to it.

I still had to use an alarm clock.

And the snooze button.

Do whatever I wanted… "Well, 'whatever I wanted' would have to pop up the very next day. Because I have a mortgage on a house that still needs a new furnace, a new water heater, and a new roof sometime in the next two years. And I have to eat. And buy gas for my car. And maybe buy a coffee once a week. That leaves about 50 dollars left over at the end of every month. So thanks for looking out for my happiness, but I think I'll hang on to the job that I have."

For the first time ever since I'd known him, Adrien looked abashed. "I am sorry. I should not have interfered. We should call your parents."

Or something.

I dialed the number, Adrien talked to them for a while, and then he handed the phone to me.

"Claire! Hello." There was an underlying note of stress in Mom's voice. Not strident enough that I would have confiscated the knives from the kitchen, but present enough that I would have warned Dad to be on the lookout for a sponge bath which might be freezing cold. Or a bowl of soup that might be boiling hot. "How are you?"

I'm slowly going insane. The apartment is falling apart as we speak. I want Adrien to kiss me, and he wants me to quit my job. "Fine. I'm fine."

"Well, if you talk to the Delaportes, tell them we say 'hi.'"

"Okay. I'll tell them."

I hung up the phone and saw Adrien sauntering down the hall toward his parents' bedroom, a book in his hand.

I followed him.

He was lying on the bed reading, but he looked up as I stepped into the doorway. "*Oui?*"

"What did my parents say? About the apartment?"

Adrien closed the book and sat up. "They wish to sell."

That was sad. Much as there was to scorn about the place, it was still a grand old dame. It felt as though they were planning to disown my grandmother. I sat down on the foot of the bed. It's not as though I thought they'd keep it, could afford to keep it, but they hadn't spent that long agonizing over the decision, had they?

"You are disappointed?"

"A little. But what else can they do? Six hundred thousand euros is a lot of money."

"Yes."

"It could be really fabulous. If you could take the time to do it right…do they want to sell it right away or have it worked on?" If they sold it right away, I could be back in Seattle by next week. I might still have time to enjoy the best two days of the year: the ones without rain.

Maybe I'd get another cat.

Maybe I'd take my backpack for a hike.

Or buy new running shoes and take up running.

"They want the best price, so they wish to have work done but can spend no more than thirty thousand dollars."

"So we'll have the bathroom done?"

"And the painting. Would you like me to call the contractor?"

"Please. How long do you think they'll take?"

"For an apartment this size? And with all the moldings to paint? Two weeks. Maybe three. It will get done."

"I know." But the prospect of spending two or three more weeks in the company of Adrien was alarming. And exhilarating. I had no idea how I was going to survive.

Chapter 25

Adrien called the contractor. The contractor called his crews. They were all willing to work but, as Adrien had suspected, they were not willing to do it without an increase in their normal wages. We would be able to have all the necessary work done, but barely. Nothing else could go wrong.

It started well enough on Tuesday.

Adrien had a duplicate key made and passed it to the contractor. By the time I arrived, the painters had visited each room, taken down all the curtains, corralled all the furniture in the middle of the floor, and draped it under canvas. They were mounting scaffolding in the living room. The carpenter had scraped the linoleum away from the bathroom floor and was pulling up floorboards. There was a growing pile of mushy timber in the hallway. At the same time, the plumber had replaced the toilet and was spreading new grout between the tiles on the wall.

I was impressed. They were industrious. Efficient. Everyone was working hard. I envisioned being able to fly home in two weeks.

And then they took a two-hour lunch.

"This is normal." Adrien was trying to calm me down.

"Maybe if they're Spanish and are used to taking *siestas*."

"Everyone takes two hours for lunch. I take two hours for lunch when I am working."

"I don't. I eat my lunch at my desk in front of my computer. It takes about ten minutes."

Adrien looked at me in horror. If he'd been Catholic, he probably would have crossed himself. "Americans are so unhealthy." He muttered something and then placed a hand on my arm. "Claire, relax. The work will get done."

"But it can't take all year. We have a budget." Budgets were my world. Budgets were my bane. They haunted me. I've been known to wake up in the middle of the night fighting off phantom charges. Batting away frivolous expenses. I sweat off at least five pounds a year over budgets. If I ever get an ulcer, budgets will be the reason why.

"It will not take all year. They have said it will take two weeks. We have a job to do also. We must choose new flooring for the bathroom. New linoleum. We can do this now if you like."

It was more of an order than a question.

But it was a good idea. I would have picked up a paintbrush, climbed the scaffolding, and started painting had we waited much longer for the painters to come back from lunch.

Adrien rifled through the carpenter's tools and found a tape measure. He took measurements while I drew a diagram of the bathroom and wrote them down.

Then we drove west, out of town, to Vélizy-Villacoublay. There was a *centre commercial art de vivre*. A sort of a collection of factory outlets centered on the theme of housewares. There were several furniture stores. Bookstores. Stores selling silk flowers and others selling assorted knickknacks.

Also a store for *bricoleurs*. Handymen.

The first thing I did was fill a shopping cart with cleaning products, buckets, a broom, a mop, and a dustpan. Everything I thought I'd need. And even some things I hoped I wouldn't. Like mouse traps. Then we found the section for flooring and looked at samples. Whatever else can be said about me, I'm a traditionalist at heart. I vote Republican unless the candidates are raving lunatics or hopeless dweebs. I like plain Hershey's kisses—not Hugs—without almonds. I was against M&Ms adding any new colors to their candies. And my favorite flavor of ice cream is vanilla.

So is it any surprise that I picked a simple pattern made of large black and white squares? Adrien saw it first, pointed it out, and I kept flipping back to it. The whole decision took less than ten minutes. Then we were free to look at everything else.

There were doorknobs and light fixtures. Drawer pulls. Moldings for walls and ceilings, and for placing above chandeliers. There was a section for kitchens, a section for gardens. We hopped from one to another. Fingering merchandise, picking it up, turning it over, investigating how gadgets worked. And over time, one thing became apparent.

We had the same taste.

In everything.

The things I thought were ugly, he thought were hideous. And we pounced on the same treasures at the same time. We might have been twins when it came to decorating; our similarities were that pronounced.

Traditional in living spaces, we both went modern in the kitchen.

There were some drawer pulls I might have bought. They were elongated brass teardrops set on a hinge. Almost like miniature door knockers. I remembered how many drawers I had on my dresser, but not how many drawer pulls they had. I suspected that the longer drawers had doubles, but I couldn't be certain.

Adrien was standing beside me, watching me flip the sample up and down.

"Very nice. Elegant."

"I know. I'd buy them, but I don't know how many I need."

"So guess. If you need more, I can mail some."

"Really? You wouldn't mind?"

"It is not so difficult to come back and buy them."

So we left the store with a roll of linoleum and a bag filled with cleaning supplies and drawer pulls. When we reached Mademoiselle's, the painters were just finishing for the day.

The plumber and carpenter were long gone.

Adrien drove me up to his place. We went to Noura Traiteur, a Lebanese restaurant, for dinner. It was just across the street from his apartment and up one block. All the sun-drenched flavors of Lebanon in a stylish, modern atmosphere.

We planned to meet at Mademoiselle's the next day at eleven, see how the work was progressing and then go somewhere for lunch.

Boy, did we go somewhere.

When I arrived, Adrien was already there, talking with the *gardienne*. He stopped talking when he saw me. Smiled. *"Chérie. Tu es arrivée!"* He opened an arm and pulled me into the conversation, letting his hand drop to my waist.

And left it there.

That's when I remembered that the *gardienne* thought we were together. Lovers. And the thought that I could legitimately steal a kiss from him entered my head.

But then I shoved it to the back of my brain.

If I were going to steal a kiss, I wanted to do it in private.

I shoved it back into my brain. Again. And added a kick.

"And today is Wednesday…" the *gardienne* said, sighing. *"Normalement* on Wednesday, Mademoiselle would come down and wait for a taxi at eleven thirty. Every Wednesday, the same thing."

"Where did she go?" Adrien beat me to the question.

The *gardienne* frowned. "I do not know. She never said. I would speak with her sometimes. But only about the weather…you know… and the worst is that I never get to see my uncle anymore."

And that would be because…? Was this uncle B? The mentor? The cigar and liquor man?

I could feel Adrien straining forward, wanting to know the same thing.

"My uncle drove the taxi."

Obviously not the same guy.

"She did not like to use the telephone, so he would just come and pick her up. Every Wednesday. He is the one who got me this job. Mademoiselle Dumont mentioned one day that the *gardienne* was getting frail. He mentioned that I was looking for a position and…" She shrugged. Then she gasped. "And it was horrible. The Wednesday after she died, he came. Just like normal. He did not know."

"Today is Wednesday. Could you call your uncle? Ask him to take us wherever he was taking Mademoiselle? We know almost nothing about her. Maybe in doing this we will learn something." Adrien was quick. And clever.

"*Bonne idée.* Of course."

Fifteen minutes later, a taxi pulled up outside the building. The driver got out, came to the door. He was a short, bald, barrel-chested man. He reached out his hands to me.

"You are the *cousine* of Mademoiselle Dumont?" He looked up at me, his eyes swimming in tears.

I nodded, tried to take a step back.

He followed, grasped my hands. "All of my *condoléances.* She was a true lady."

Adrien slid an arm around my waist and detached me away from the driver. "We would like you to take us to the same place you took Mademoiselle on Wednesdays."

"To the Ritz? As you wish."

He bundled us into the back of the taxi before I could think of anything to say. We were going to the Ritz. At least I was wearing my skirt. And I had my purse. Which was perched on my knee. I put it away to the side, near the door, and pushed close to Adrien.

I put a hand on his shoulder to whisper in his ear.

He bent his head toward me.

"We don't know what she did there. Who she met there." Maybe she had been having some sort of tryst.

Adrien turned his head. We were facing each other at eye level. His eyes twinkled at me. "Every Wednesday at lunchtime? *Evidemment,* she ate lunch. What else would she do?"

The taxi driver put my mind at ease. "A true lady. Imagine. Going to the Ritz for lunch. Every Wednesday. I would ask her what she had, and she would tell me the most wonderful things. Made me hungry to hear about it, even if I had just eaten my own lunch."

The taxi raced neck and neck with other cars as we crossed the Pont de la Concorde, heading straight for the ornate gilded fountain in the middle of the square. At the last second, he pulled to the right, leaving my head reeling as we skidded over the cobblestone street. Another five minutes and we were gliding into Place Vendôme as if we owned it. He pulled up in front of the Ritz as if he had every right to be there.

We got out.

The driver called out to us. "I will pick you up at the normal time?"

Adrien and I looked at each other. He winked at me, and then putting a hand on the roof of the taxi, bent down. "When would that be?"

"At two."

"Yes. Thank you."

He took my hand in his as we walked up the steps. He must have known I was thinking about running away.

Place Vendôme is the most elegant of the elegant places in Paris. An obelisk stands at the center and million-dollar jewelry stores like Bvlgari and Cartier ring the circle of the plaza. Most of them have bouncers that stand just inside the doors and scowl. But the biggest jewel of them all is the Ritz Hotel. If it takes courage just to window-shop in front of the jewelry stores, then it takes a miracle to be able to walk up the steps of the Ritz as if you belonged there.

And I didn't.

That's when I remembered my purse.

I wielded it in front of me, daring anyone to turn the $10,000 purse away at the door. I might not have deserved to enter that hallowed hotel, but I was pretty sure they'd let the purse in.

They did.

We spun right through the revolving door. It spit us out into a tiny lobby that almost looked like a back entrance. I would have turned around and walked out, but Adrien seemed to know where he was going.

He marched right up the tiers of steps and down a long hall flanked by vast seating lounges. In one were a group of children crawling all over the ottomans and sofas. Their unconcerned mothers were sipping wine and chatting as if the children were a figment of our imagination. In another area, two men were talking, a laptop computer set on a table between them. At the end of the hall was the entrance to a restaurant.

Guarded by a man standing behind a carved podium desk.

"Monsieur?"

Adrien pulled me forward, even with his side, never releasing my hand.

I'd been hiding behind him.

"This is Mademoiselle Dumont's *cousine* from America. Mademoiselle died recently."

The man inclined his head.

"It has just come to our attention that Mademoiselle Dumont dined here on Wednesdays. We know almost nothing about her, so we would like to meet her friends."

The man turned toward me. Bowed. As much as a person can bow without moving a muscle. "But, madame, she dined alone."

"Alone?" That didn't fit my picture of her at all. I was expecting a gaggle of old women chattering around a table. "Are you sure?"

"Quite certain. But perhaps you might wish to speak with the monsieur who served her? I may seat you at her table?"

"Her table?"

"We have held this in reservation, hoping that she was ill and would return soon. When the weather was fine, she dined outside. This suits you?"

"Yes. Thank you." I even smiled at the man. Anyone who would hold a reservation for weeks after an old woman died couldn't be all that scary.

We followed him through a gilded dining room with sky blue accents and a painted ceiling and out into a courtyard garden. The tables were set simply with white linens that floated in the breeze.

There were giant stone vases planted to overflowing with flowers. Ivy tumbled down the walls. There was a statue at one end. A Grecian woman, holding up two fingers. If they'd been carved farther apart, I would have surreptitiously returned the gesture.

Peace out.

A middle-aged man in a tuxedo approached our table. His dress was impeccable. His demeanor professional.

"Welcome to l'Espadon. You are the *cousine* of Mademoiselle Dumont?"

This man wasn't scary at all.

"I am. She died a few weeks ago."

"I am very sorry to hear this. I looked forward to serving her each week. She was a *grande dame*. A real lady."

"What did she order?"

"Whatever I suggested." Then he winked. "But I knew she did not eat fish and she preferred not to eat fowl, so it was usually beef, pork, or lamb."

"Did she ever eat with anyone?"

"Never. I served her for 20 years. Maybe 30."

Wow. He looked a lot younger than he must have been. We asked for his suggestions.

"Mademoiselle usually ordered from the lunch menu." We picked up the menus, took a look. It was 68 euros and included cheese, dessert, and coffee. A real bargain by Parisian standards. "The *joue de lotte* is especially nice today."

Monkfish? Maybe. I guess we were stuck since we asked for his advice.

He left us so that we could look at the menus.

Adrien and I looked at each other with raised eyebrows.

I'm the one who said it first. "This is unexpected."

"Quite."

"She dined alone, at the Ritz, for 30 years. Every Wednesday." It seemed that if you were going to go to the Ritz, you'd want to do it with someone. Otherwise, why bother? What did it mean? "She wasn't a total recluse, or she wouldn't have gone out for lunch...right?"

Adrien shrugged.

Could you be antisocial and go out to lunch at the most prestigious hotel in town at the same time? What had happened to B? "Who was she, Adrien?"

"I wish I could tell you. More than you know."

When I arrived home that evening, I grabbed the diary, sat on the bed, and read for a while. The last time I'd picked it up, I'd read through the chronicles of a socialite's life before the war. I was a little fuzzy on the events of WW II in Europe, but as I read through the entries from the early months of 1940, I began to get nervous.

And then May 1940 came.

It was excruciating knowing what was going to happen and knowing that they hadn't the slightest idea. There was nothing in the diary that communicated any knowledge that Paris was about to be occupied. B went up to Belgium to visit his family, and Mademoiselle stayed behind in Paris.

9 May 1940

We have no more chocolates. We have days without meat. Days without sugar, days without liquor. And three days each week without pastries. But still. The weather is lovely. Horse races at Auteuil, which had been suspended since September, have begun once more. We have gotten used to this war, I think. And if it never comes to Paris, it is not so bad a way to live.

10 May 1940

There are rumors that Germany has invaded France and Belgium. Nobody believes them, of course, but I am worried all the same. It was one thing to support Britain in declaration war to protest the invasion of Poland. But to have the Germans invade France? B has gone north. He is not to return until next weekend. I am hoping that he will call.

11 May 1940

It is true about the Germans. They have invaded. Luxembourg and the Netherlands also.

12 May 1940

Have tried to ring B. Cannot get through.

14 May 1940

Have sent a letter to B.

15 May 1940

The Netherlands has surrendered.

16 May 1940

I read the newspaper this morning, expecting to read of the German onslaught in other countries. But I find they are in Ardennes, at Sedan. This is less than 200 kilometers from Paris. How did they get from the border to Sedan without anyone to notice?

I left the apartment to take a walk, to clear my head, to calm my fear, and I see all around me evidence of the Germans' invasion. I am used to seeing cars with license plates from Moselle and Vosges, to the east; refugees from the border with Germany. I am not habituated to seeing cars from the north, from Meuse or Aube. And worse from Seine-Saint-Denis and Val d'Oise. Too close! I feel this war closing around me. More close, more quick, than a nightmare.

18 May 1940

The Germans have taken Antwerp.

19 May 1940

I joined today, with a crowd of others, at the *Cathédrale Notre-Dame*. We offered prayers to Sainte-Geneviève for the salvation of Paris. God listened to her once before and stopped the advance of the Huns. Maybe he will listen to her again. In this I hope, because God no longer listens to us. Where is B?

24 May 1940

Ghent and Tournai are taken.

26 May 1940

Calais has fallen. Paris has become emptied of people. As if someone pulled the plug on a drain. I want to flee also. I would go anywhere. But not without B.

28 May 1940

Belgium has surrendered.

31 May 1940

Have received a note from B. He tells me to go south, back to my family. He will meet me, and from there we can go to Spain. Must pack. Must hide so many things. All of my friends have gone. I shall entrust the most valuable of things to Marie-Pierre. She is, perhaps, not the best of cooks, but she has become a loyal employee. At least she has not run away like the others.

13 June 1940

I am home.

14 June 1940

We are told the Germans have entered Paris.

22 June 1940

France has signed an armistice with Germany and the government has moved to Vichy. I am now a citizen of only half my country. At least I live in the better half; the Germans have the north and the west. Had I left Paris any later, I might have been trapped. At least now I am in unoccupied territory.

For an entire year, there are no entries. Then she started again.

15 June 1941

Have heard nothing from B. Must assume he is dead.

16 June 1941

Fed geese. Worked in vineyards.

17 June 1941

Did the same.

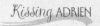

18 June 1941
Jean-Claude came to visit.

20 June 1941
I have had news of a colony of artists near Marseilles. Refugees from Paris. And among them, some of my former employers. They dare to exhibit their work; work the Nazis have called degenerate. How I would love to be there. But I do not want to be associated with scandal. Not anymore. I want to survive. The maps tell me I live in "Free France," in "Unoccupied France." But still everyone looks to their backs. The walls have ears. The forests have eyes.

The rest of June and July recorded the daily tasks she accomplished and the frequent visits of Jean-Claude, a neighbor.

And then, on September 1:

Have received letter from B! He is alive. He is well. And on the way to the eastern front. He has become an officer in the Légion Wallonie. Will fight beside the Germans against the Bolsheviks.

And after that, it was back to business. I flipped through the entries. Nothing caught my eye until November of the next year, 1942.

We are no longer free. We are no longer unoccupied. The Germans have come.

28 November 1942
The Germans are the worst kind of blight. The worst type of plague. With them they have brought fear, hate, deceit, and betrayal. The faults we have had the habit of overlooking in our neighbors have now become their biggest assets. The use of that which once hindered them in society has now become the best

method of survival. This one cheats? That one gossips? This one lies? The Nazis give gold for such straw.

18 December 1942

We must now hide the geese in the farthest corner of our land. Germans steal whatever they find. And who would not want a plump goose for Christmas? That the Christ was born into such a world as ours. It is no wonder that he left it.

I flipped through pages filled with geese and vineyards. Jean-Claude and his vows of love. And then, the worst entry of all.

7 August 1943

The Germans uncovered an underground network in our village. Jean-Claude was part of it. He was betrayed by a *collaborateur.* Tortured. Shot. Plain, honest, dull Jean-Claude. Unexciting Jean-Claude. Jean-Claude, who claimed he loved me more than his goats. Flatterer. Those goats produced the best cheese in the region. He may not have had any imagination, but he had vision. And courage. The same Nazis who shot Jean-Claude were the same Nazis B agreed to fight with. One man did nothing to deserve to be killed. One man did nothing to deserve to be recruited as an officer. I used to think hell was a more sophisticated cabaret than I had yet to experience. But I was wrong. Hell is not an experience. Hell is an entire world from which there can be no escape. This world is become hell. And hell has no heart.

I flipped through more pages. Flipped right through the Germans' surrender in 1945. She never heard from B again. Is that why she never married?

August 1945 is a running list of neighbors' sons who returned from the war. And those who did not.

And at that point, my eyelids wouldn't obey me anymore. They kept falling shut. So I put the diary back on the commode, brushed my teeth, and went to sleep.

Dreamed of all the movies I'd ever seen about WW II.

Chapter 26

It had been the worst day of my life. Why? I'll make a list.

1. Adrien wasn't around. There was an emergency at his office. And it bothered me that it bothered me. Because I was supposed to be over my crush by now.

2. The painters weren't working today. Because yesterday, Thursday, was a holiday and tomorrow was Saturday. It didn't make any sense to me, but I was still supposed to pay them as if they were working.

3. The Rodin Museum was closed. Due to a strike.

4. The Berthillon ice cream store was closed. Due to the fact that it was August.

5. I stepped in dog poop on the way back to the Delaportes' apartment. With my right foot.

Worst day of my life?

Okay, maybe I was exaggerating. Most frustrating day of my life. That was more accurate.

I closed my eyes and took a deep breath.

Stole another glance at the couple necking not three feet from me.

I wished someone were kissing me!

My ideal kiss would be passionate. It would be my fingers wound in his hair. His hands stroking my neck. It would be closed eyes and heavy sighs. It would be me floating and him grounding me, caressing me, and when I opened my eyes, I would know that he loved me.

And not some woman named Solange or Véronique or Virginie.

Gaaaah! Why wouldn't Adrien stay confined to the back of my brain?

I was supposed to be thinking in hypotheticals, not about Adrien in particular.

I sighed. And then I did it. I admitted to myself that certain things were true.

My crush was not temporary or malarial. It was a long-term, permanent condition of my being.

And I wanted to be cured. I didn't want to go into denial again. The best way to do that would be to know what he thought of me. I needed to create a moment-of-truth situation. Something that would provide the catalyst for a change in our relationship.

And the sculpture of *The Kiss* flashed into my head. I thought of Paolo and Francesca and I then knew the solution. The best way to determine Adrien's feelings toward me would be to kiss him. And the best way for Adrien to clarify his feelings for his mystery woman would be to kiss me. I'd be doing both of us a favor.

And then I would know if he liked me. Or not, as the case would probably be. But then at least I could tell my heart, "I told you so," and I could get on with my life.

I needed a kiss.

And I didn't care anymore what it took to get one.

I also needed a haircut. I discovered it when I got back to the Delaportes'. While I was preparing to scrub the poop off my shoe, I had pulled my hair back in an elastic and looked at myself in the mirror. And I thought, *I'm prettier than this.* I'd never had a thought like that before. But the more I looked at myself, the more I realized I was right. There ought to be something that could be done to my hair.

A ponytail with locks falling forward can be a nice look on some people, those who have ruler-straight hair. Kind of a country music star, "my hair's too cool for a pony tail" look. On me, it just looked undone. My hair defies classification. It isn't straight enough to be straight and not curly enough to be curly. Someone once told me that it's wavy, but that implies some sort of symmetrical consistency.

On Saturday I took a chance and headed toward a salon I'd seen on rue Saint Dominique, just past avenue Bosquet. It hadn't seemed too intimidating. And it wasn't. They even offered me an espresso while I waited.

Then they helped me into a robe and sat me on a chair. That's when the fun started.

It began with 15 minutes of them trying to convince me to have my hair colored. A pair of men descended on me, picking up locks of my hair, and letting them drop. "It is a nice color, madame, beautiful. But if you had a few highlights, some red perhaps, and then a few lowlights, of *chocolat* maybe, then it would be even more beautiful."

I finally told them I had a boyfriend who liked my hair exactly the way it was.

Liar, liar, pants on fire.

But then, I might have a boyfriend who liked it. If I could ever work up the nerve to kiss Adrien. Or trick him into kissing me.

So after I convinced them to leave my hair color alone, I had to talk them out of a perm. And not just one perm. Three. I negotiated down from a full-on curly perm to a body wave to a roots-only. And then to nothing.

I said I was allergic to chemicals.

I might be. You never know.

And then we discussed styles. It was on the tip of my tongue to just tell them to shorten everything five centimeters, but I didn't.

I really wanted to be beautiful. Didn't I? Besides, I'd already spent half an hour talking about what I didn't want. I might as well spend ten more talking about what I did. But I didn't know what to say because I didn't really know what I wanted other than a change. A complete and total change. In the end I gave up, frustrated. Said the only thing I could say.

"I want to look…beautiful."

They both clasped their hands in front of them and sighed.

Then they spun me around, brought out the shears, and went to work.

I saw lots of hair, long lengths of it, drift to the floor. So I closed my eyes. For better or worse it was being cut and there wasn't a thing I could do about it. At the very worst, I could always grow it out when I got back home. I'd figure out some joke to make about Parisian fashion. And buy a hat.

I could always buy a hat.

I looked good in hats. And if I bought quality, and if it were black and went with everything, then I could wear it for the next three years. A hat. That's exactly what I would do.

I realized I was losing feeling in the ends of my fingers because I was clasping my hands together so tightly. I took a deep breath. Released them. Just concentrated on breathing in and out.

About 45 minutes later, after a coordinated assault with two deadly curling irons and clouds of hair spray, they brushed off my forehead and neck, pulled off the robe, and spun me around to face the mirror.

My breath caught in my chest.

I was beautiful.

I'd said that's what I'd wanted and I'd meant it, but I hadn't thought they'd be able to do it. They had. I looked sleek.

Imagine me looking sleek!

I looked elegant. I'd have to get rid of all those sensible shoes in my closet back in Seattle.

I looked…I really looked beautiful.

They'd cut a fringe across my forehead. Heavy at the top, it ended just above my eyebrows with an uneven edge. As if they'd snipped tiny inverted *v*'s into it. Then they'd layered and angled and shaped the rest of my hair into a modern pageboy with the faintest of upturned ends. Not in the least trendy. But very fashionable.

Now I matched my new clothes.

I hoped I'd be able to do it myself because if I looked like Old Claire tomorrow, I knew I'd dissolve into tears.

I bought every single product they suggested. I paid the bill and then tipped them about 40 percent. They deserved it.

And you know what the very best thing was? I walked down the street, holding my head high, my shoulders back, my purse hanging from my fingertips, and I saw things. I saw people look at me.

Twice.

Three times even.

And it felt great.

And as if that weren't enough, Adrien had a reaction that was the cherry on top of the cake.

I heard his key turn in the door late that afternoon and I ran, on tip-toe feet, to meet him. He opened the door, saw me, and dropped his briefcase. Right on his toes.

Poor man.

"Claire! You look beautiful. Fabulous. Enchanting!" He took my face between his hands and brought it up to his face is if he were going to…kiss me, kiss me, kiss me…and then he let my face go abruptly and kissed my cheeks.

I glanced down, trying to hide the disappointment, embarrassment, sudden shyness in my eyes. I discovered that his briefcase was still perched on his toes. I reached down to pick it up and found my hand closing around his.

We straightened. Still clasping hands, clasping the briefcase. "You brought work home?"

"I was not certain you would be here." His eyes were doing wonderful things, roaming my face, cataloging my features, making me feel beautiful down to my toenails.

"Here I am."

"Here you are." He glanced down, so I did too.

I was still holding on to his hand. I let go.

He sighed. "There is so much I have to do…you deserve to go out tonight to show off your beauty. But we have a new contract. It must involve a new permanent weekend shift. If we cannot negotiate with the union at *la Rentrée*…" His voice was hoarse. His shoulders slumped. He looked exhausted.

"I'll order pizza in. I'll read while you work."

He looked relieved. He set the briefcase by the door. "If you are okay with this."

The pizza was delivered half an hour later. We took it into the dining room.

"What is it you're working on?"

"A contract. Dassault is launching a new technology. Unmanned combat air vehicles. We must be ready for demonstration at the air show next June. And we will not be ready if we cannot get the *syndicats* to be more flexible."

"The syndicate?" I knew the French were socialists and that their industries were inextricably linked to their government, but I had no idea they worked so closely with the mob.

"*Oui. Syndicat.* You call them 'labor unions'? Is this the right term?"

I smiled. "Yes."

"There is something funny? Because I could use a joke."

"In America, the syndicate is the mob. I thought you were trying to work with the mafia."

He smiled. "*Non.* Only Americans work with the mob. The evils of capitalism."

"Like there aren't any evils in socialism."

"There are some. But not so many."

I snorted. "High taxation? Government control of private property? Redistribution of wealth? Socialism is the first step toward communism."

"And capitalism is so pure? It is based on selfishness. It operates best when there are no controls and when every person looks out for his own interests."

I was already shaking my head. "That's only the theory. In operation, it's much less cutthroat."

"Oh. Then that excuses why your Native Americans and inner-city citizens have Third-World health care. And why the life expectancy in socialist Europe is higher than in capitalistic America."

"What does health have to do with economics?"

"Exactly my point."

"There's no connection."

"But there should be. There is in socialism."

"Which is why it's such a menace. Government reaches into every aspect of life."

"To care for its citizens—"

"—who might just be able to care for themselves if they worked hard enough."

"Socialists are unwilling to subject their poorest members to the whims of the economy. The stock market does not always go up, you know."

I knew. Too well. "And for this you tax yourselves at the highest rate in Europe?"

"Yes. And for this we get excellent health care, free education, skilled workers. Quality of life."

"And those who should be rewarded most, who have the brains and the resources to build companies and get rich, have their money taken away from them and redistributed to people who don't deserve it."

"Why do they not deserve it? Because they are sick and cannot work? Because they are poor? Because they are disabled?"

"We take care of people in America too."

"But not at the start. At the end. But only if enough is left over and only if Americans remember to be generous. Socialism takes care of people from the beginning."

"But that's not government's role. Because when government gets involved in caring for people, then the people who want to be cared for have to meet the government's requirements. It sets you up for censorship, fascism, racism…government shouldn't run the people, people should run the government."

"For the people. People should run the government for people. Not for profit or money. What is the goal of government? Is it not to make life better for its citizens? And is not the best measure of that the way in which we care for the least of our citizens?"

"That's the role of nonprofits. And churches."

"But then there are still all those Native Americans and inner-city poor, are there not? Maybe you do not have enough churches in America."

I just couldn't win. There was no point in arguing. It was like tearing off a scab. Why keep doing it when it was just going to keep on bleeding?

What had started the conversation anyway?

Adrien's work. The reason why he was so tired. I put my frustration on hold for a moment and looked at him. Really looked. Into his eyes. They were red. His eyelids were drooping. He was tired. "A new contract. So what's the problem with the union?"

"They want to work more hours."

"*More* hours?" I must have been in the twilight zone. When has a union ever asked to work more?

"We have a 35-hour workweek while you, in America, have a 40-hour week. How do we get the same amount of work done that you do? We must hire more people. For this contract we cannot afford this, but we still need more people. So we must find a way to do the work more cheaply."

This was basic economics. I could follow the idea, but I still didn't understand why the unions wanted to work harder.

"We cannot pay a Frenchman less than the union wage, so we must find someone who is not French."

"You have to send the jobs overseas."

"Exactly."

"And the union will volunteer to do more work if you will keep the jobs in France."

"Yes."

"So if it's their great idea, what's the problem?"

"VSD. *Vendredi, Samedi, Dimanche.* We want a new weekend shift. *En permanence.* And for a Frenchman to work the weekend, every weekend…"

Oh. I could see why that would be a problem.

We finished the pizza while I tried to keep my mouth shut. As much for Adrien's sake as for mine.

After dinner he worked at the desk in the library while I read, curled up in an armchair. I fell asleep.

When I woke, he was kneeling beside the chair, rubbing the back of his hand along my cheek. "Claire? I must go now. It is late."

"How late?"

"Nearly midnight. I am sorry."

I yawned and stretched. "I'm fine."

I walked him to the door, trying to keep my bleary eyes from falling shut.

"I will pick you up for church tomorrow."

I nodded. Walked down the hall and fell on my bed fully clothed.

I dreamed the whole night. Dickensian visions of sad, decrepit people with rotting teeth and claws for hands. They couldn't walk. They couldn't talk.

They just held out empty cups. And everybody kept walking by.

Chapter 27

Talking with Cynthia before church, I was finally able to get a handle on where she lived.

"In a falling-down building in the first. But the apartment's great. It's fabulous."

Of course it was. She had my life in reverse. Everything I wanted but nothing I had. I admired everything else about her. Why not her apartment too? "Ready for school? When does it start?"

"Teachers' first day back is Thursday. The kids come back next week."

"I've always thought it would be fun to teach."

"Then why don't you?"

"My degree's in business."

"So get another degree."

Another degree? Four more years of college. Twenty more years of debt. Yeah, great idea. "I don't think so."

"That's what I did. I talked myself into studying economics when I should have been studying languages and history. Wound up in some high-pressure finance company in Miami. So I quit and spent three years getting my Master's of Science in education. Got certified as an elementary school teacher."

"You quit your job and just decided to do something else?" Cynthia had always reminded me of someone. Now I knew who it was. She reminded me of Mademoiselle. They were both brave. Both courageous. Both had the strength to look at life and make tough decisions about what they wanted.

Cynthia was laughing. "I did! And I love what I do. I'd rather be teaching than at home. I used to come home from work dragging, ready to roll into bed at eight o'clock. Now I'm at school for eight hours, and I feel like I could work eight more. It's energizing."

Energizing. A job you really wanted to do. Wouldn't that be something?

"And you're the lucky one."

Me? "Me?"

"You said your dad is French, right? So you're considered French. I had to go through a stack of paper 20 feet high to get residency status and a work permit. All you have to do is show up and hand out copies of your birth certificate."

"But I'm an American. I have an American passport."

She shrugged. "Nothing to stop you from being French at the same time."

I looked around the church, made sure Adrien wasn't within hearing distance. "Cynthia? It's about A. I have to do something. Tell him. Something."

"What are you going to say?"

"I don't know. Do you think I really have to say anything?"

"No. You could just throw yourself at him."

I frowned. That's not what I had in mind.

Her eyes narrowed. "Or maybe there's a way to make him say something first. How'd he like your haircut?"

I blushed. "Fabulous. Enchanting."

She grinned. "Meet me in front of Ladurée on Tuesday morning at nine thirty."

Adrien came along then and detached me from the group.

Later that morning, I found myself thinking about Cynthia and her passion for teaching. What would it be like to have a passion?

Could you kiss someone with passion if you didn't have a passion of your own?

What if that person were your passion?

Passion.

My life seemed to consist of shades of gray and types of drizzle.

People like Cynthia, people with passion, existed in multicolor. Maybe I was just a gray personality. Like Eeyore. But who wants to be Eeyore? Who wants to live with Eeyore? Maybe I was doomed to a colorless existence.

A life without passion.

What if there never was anyone?

Could I survive with a string of cats? Would that be enough? Somehow, I doubted it.

Something needed to change. I needed a new perspective.

Be careful what you wish for.

We ended up spending the afternoon at the Picasso Museum. But it didn't start there. It started with the falafels.

We had falafels for lunch. And I finally learned how to pronounce them. At least in French.

Falafels.

They're one of the things I've known about forever but never tried. And they were great. Much better than they looked. So that was the first thing.

The second was the museum itself.

The Picasso Museum is housed in a seventeenth-century mansion. I would have walked right past if Adrien hadn't hooked my elbow and pulled me in through the gate. Upon entering, standing just inside the lobby, it looked like everything an old mansion should. A black-and-white parquet tile floor. A switchback staircase enclosed by an ornate grillwork banister. Intricate moldings above the doors and on the ceilings.

As we climbed the stairs to the first floor, everything looked in order until we entered the first room of exhibits. After that, I couldn't see past Picasso.

That was the third thing.

I had come preparing to hate him. I'm a big fan of the Northern

European school of painters. Those dour, sober painters who cataloged the fourteenth through seventeenth centuries. I'm into realism.

It still amazes me that I was able to stand in front of paintings with disarranged features for three hours and not laugh my head off.

But it was fascinating.

I learned things I'd never known about Picasso. He had started out normal. His paintings looked like real people. He was even married. To a Russian ballet dancer.

I found out later that he was also a sculptor.

At the end of our visit, looking at the paintings he accomplished at the end of his life, it looked as if he hadn't cared anymore. Like he slapped anything onto a canvas, daring someone to tell him he'd stopped trying.

But I also discovered that I liked him.

Not as a person, but certainly as an artist. His disjointed faces and figures somehow made sense to me. Although I couldn't begin to understand his obsession with women, I did come to understand how he saw each of them.

Marie-Thérèse, the blonde, was represented in gentle, rounded, ineffectual lines. He might have been sleeping with her, but it didn't seem that she had much impact. A shadow that snuck into bed with him now and then.

But Dora Maar! She was the opposite. All angles. Brittle. Sharp, dramatic colors. Love her or hate her, you had to feel something about Dora. Then there was Françoise. An artist herself. Strong. The mother of two of his children. And lastly, Jacqueline. His long-necked muse. His serenity and peace. His nurse, maid, secretary, lover.

After three hours I could tell at a glance which portrait was of which woman. It had to do with the features he highlighted. The colors he used. But it also had to do with the emotions the paintings evoked.

And what about me?

What if Picasso had known me? What if he had painted me? I know he would have featured my eyes. But what other colors would he have used? What feelings would the paintings have portrayed?

I knew the answer almost before I asked the question.

Loneliness. Solitude. Detachment.

And that's not the way I wanted the portrait of me painted.

I wanted to be Dora Maar without the mental problems. I wanted to be Françoise without the kids. Or maybe with just one of them. But I didn't want to be Marie-Thérèse; I wanted to matter. I wanted someone to look at me the way Picasso looked at Jacqueline. But I didn't want to be a doormat.

As it was, I probably wouldn't have registered as a splotch on one of Picasso's canvasses.

So something had to change.

And I realized then that it had nothing to do with my job. Nothing to do with Adrien.

It had everything to do with me.

I had been building a life for myself based on things I didn't want or need. I didn't want to work as an accountant. I didn't need a house. I'd based life on the fear of what I might not have—money, a job, a house—instead of basing it on what I wanted.

I'd tried to be smart, to accept the opportunities that had come my way, but I'd given up my dreams in exchange for stability. How stupid was that?

I'd done everything the way people tell you that you should. I'd looked after my financial interests. I'd planned years and decades in advance for retirement. I made sure I had health care and car insurance and I had my furnace checked every fall.

I was a model citizen.

But I didn't want to live a life thinking about things that I wanted. I wanted to have them. Was that inconsistent with my faith? Wasn't I supposed to be content with the things I had?

That's what I'd thought. That's what I was doing. I was building my life based on what I had, not on what I wanted to have.

But that's not what Mademoiselle had done. She hadn't liked her life, so she'd made a new one for herself. Not that it had turned out happily or that it was a life I would have chosen. But she'd made a change. It was possible. With enough courage, enough conviction, it was possible.

Maybe I was just having a midlife crisis. In my late-twenties. Did that mean I'd have a latelife crisis in my seventies?

Was wanting to have things, different things, wrong? Did it mean I was ungrateful for the things I did have?

Was I stuck?

That's the question I most wanted answered. But it's also the answer I was most afraid of knowing. What if I was stuck?

We stopped at a Chinese *traiteur* near the Delaportes' for takeout. At the apartment, Adrien got out plates and serving spoons while I opened cartons. I offered him a packet of chopsticks and kept one for myself.

Adrien waved his away. "I am hungry. Better not to use these. Forks are more efficient."

Something he couldn't do? That he admitted to? "It's easy. I'll show you. No forks tonight. We're eating with chopsticks."

"No forks?" There was a gleam in his eyes. "If you insist."

Showing someone how to use chopsticks from the opposite side of a table doesn't work very well. So he picked up his plate and came around to my side.

"How did you learn to do this?"

"I don't know. I just did."

"So how is it again?"

"Here." I picked up mine to show him. "You even them out at the ends and then put them in one hand."

They clattered onto the table.

"Let me do it." I evened them out. Put them in his hand. "The point is to hold the chopstick nearest you stable and let the other one do all the moving. Got it? Like this."

He picked them up to try and they slipped away from his fingers.

"It's okay. Try again. They should only touch at the ends."

I watched as he tried. They fell.

"The other ends. Where they pick up the food. Like you're pinching something. Try this. Hold one fixed between your thumb and your ring finger. And hold the other chopstick with your pointer finger, long finger, and thumb. See?" I demonstrated by popping a slice of lemon chicken into my mouth.

"You are taunting me."

"No, I'm not. It's easy. Try it again."

He tried again and failed again. For having such long fingers, he was amazingly clumsy.

I picked up his chopsticks and took his hands. I positioned the chopsticks inside them and then held his thumb and forefinger, moved them up and down. "See? Easy." I picked up my own chopsticks and picked up a piece of sweet-and-sour pork. I was hungry. It was good.

"I cannot do it."

"Sure you can. It just takes practice. When you're really good, you can pick up a single grain of rice."

He tried again. This time he was able to pick up a piece of chicken. But it fell before it made it to his mouth.

"No problem. *Encore.*" I picked up the piece of chicken and ate it while he was trying to grab a piece of pineapple.

"These are not *évidente.*" He finally jabbed the piece of pineapple with the end of a chopstick and put it in his mouth.

"That's cheating."

"Not if one is hungry. In this case, it is survival." He set his sights on a piece of pork and chased it around the carton for a full minute before giving up. "I cannot do it. If we cannot eat with forks, then you must feed me." He licked his lips, closed his eyes, and opened his mouth. A moment later an eye popped open. "I am hungry, Claire!"

"Okay, okay." I fed him a piece of pork. He opened both his eyes. Chewed. Smiled and opened his mouth again.

I snagged a piece of pineapple. Got it halfway to his mouth. Glanced at his eyes.

They were fixed on mine.

Glanced at his lips. They looked so…delectable. So soft, so full, so kissable. They were lips made for kissing. You could just tell.

I dropped it.

"Ah. Not so easy, is it?"

I picked it up. Tried again. Dropped it in his mouth. And I couldn't avoid his eyes. Somehow, between his mouth and the cartons of food on the table, I got hung up on his eyes. I picked up the carton of rice and shuffled some onto my plate and some onto his. Then I picked up a portion for myself. It trickled away from the chopsticks halfway to my mouth. My fingers wouldn't work right anymore.

But Adrien was quick. He picked up his chopsticks and lifted a single grain of rice from the table. Offered it to me.

"You know how to use chopsticks? You already knew how? This whole time!"

"You are a very good teacher."

I opened my mouth to reply and he dropped the rice in. "I can't believe—"

"Please, Claire. Not tonight. I am too tired to fight you off. And I would not want to fail."

"Fight me off? You mean fight me, right?" I really couldn't tell. I was looking into his eyes and I was seeing…things. But then maybe it was Picasso's influence. I'd probably be seeing "things" for the rest of the week.

"As you say." He was too busy eating to look up from his plate.

Chapter 28

After dinner he took the cartons down the hall to the kitchen. I shoved the chairs under the table. Thought again about being stuck.

Adrien came back, went into the living room, and put some jazz in the CD player.

The crazy syncopations brought the disjointed figures of Picasso's women to mind. I thought about them. Wondered again which one I would have wanted to be. Decided I would rather Picasso not have noticed me at all.

The phone rang me out of my hazy reverie and jolted me straight into the present. Finally, it stopped ringing. But then I heard Adrien's footsteps come down the hall.

He appeared in the dining room. "Claire?"

"Mmm?"

"The telephone is for you."

"Thanks." I pushed past him and picked up the phone in the living room.

"Hello?"

"Claire?"

The voice belonged to a male, but he wasn't my father.

"Yes?"

"This is John." My boss. I was busted. "Why am I talking to you in Paris?"

"It's rather complicated."

"Did your father die?"

"Uh, no."

"Is his back still broken?"

"Yes."

"And the reason you went to Florida was to help your mother take care of him."

"Yes."

"So did he move to France in the last three weeks?"

"No."

"So I'm asking you again, why am I talking to you in Paris?"

"I did go to Florida to help my mother, but the day after I arrived, we were notified that a relative in Paris had died and that she had left her estate to my father. Obviously he couldn't fly over and take care of the paperwork, so he asked me to do it."

"And that takes three weeks?"

"It shouldn't have, but the will left him an apartment, and once I took possession, I realized that it's…" there had to be a word invented that would describe Mademoiselle's apartment. "Okay, the building was constructed in 1697. My father's cousin owned her apartment since 1946. She changed absolutely nothing since the day she bought it, and the last years of her life she was blind. So, I have to have it rewired before it bursts into flames, repainted before I die of lead poisoning, and floors rebuilt before I fall through to the apartment below. That's why you're talking to me in Paris."

"How long does all that take?"

"It should take about three weeks, but it's going to take about two months since nobody over here works in August."

"Come again?"

"I don't know, John. Two more weeks? Three?"

A very long, very heavy sigh made its way across the phone lines. "Forgive me if I don't sound sympathetic. You realize that school starts again next month."

"Yes."

"And that I really need you here, Claire. And that the reason I'm working on a Sunday is because you're not here to do the things you usually do."

"I'll be back as soon as I can. I swear."

"You've used up all your vacation leave?"

"Yes. I still have some sick leave."

"Well, you'd better hope you don't have to stay more than three months. Here's what we'll do. We'll put you on leave without pay. If you use one day of sick leave each month, then you'll keep your insurance benefits active. Sound good?"

Good? It sounded great. What a relief! "I really don't think I'll be here that much longer."

"Let's hope not."

The moment I hung up the phone, it rang again.

"Hello?"

"Claire?"

"Mom?"

"Hi, honey. I think I might have done a bad thing; I just wanted to warn you. Someone called and I was playing solitaire on the computer and they asked for you and it was a man and I gave him your number and then he said his name was John."

"John is my boss."

"I'm sorry."

"It's okay. Everything's been worked out. How's Dad?"

"He's getting better. He starts therapy next week. That will get him out of the house."

"Give him my love."

"I will, honey."

I placed the phone back on the receiver and turned around just in time to see Adrien disappearing down the hall toward the kitchen.

I played with the band of my watch. Saw that enough grime had collected between the links that it was leaving black stripes on my wrist. I was in danger of turning into a zebra.

When he came back bearing espressos, I asked him if he had any Q-tips.

"Any what tips?"

"Q-tips? Cotton swabs? For cleaning?" I mimed sticking something into my ear and twirling it around.

He set the espressos on the coffee table and then walked toward the bathroom. When he came back, he was holding out an honest-to-goodness Q-tip.

"Do you have any more? Five or six?"

"Of course."

"And some alcohol?" I was following his rapidly disappearing back.

"I was thinking of a *café*, but if you would rather have a *digestif*, I will not complain." He was joking, because when I caught up with him, he was holding a half dozen Q-tips and a small bottle of alcohol. "What do you intend to do with these?"

"Clean my watch." Probably not the answer he was expecting. It's one of my little idiosyncrasies. I can't stand to see dirt between the links of my wristwatch. Know why? Because technically it's not dirt. It's a collection of dried, dead skin cells. My dried, dead skin cells.

Gross.

He stood there for about two minutes while I swabbed away at my watch, trying to clean out the tiny nooks and crannies.

Then he took it away from me. "Stop. There are people who do this for a job, Claire. They are called *joailliers*. Jewelers. We will go find one. We must have the jewelry from Mademoiselle appraised, and so we will take your watch with us." He was rubbing my watch dry between the folds of a towel. Then he held it out to me. "Do you…clean your watch… often?"

I took it and shrugged. Only at the first of every month, along with turning my mattress, checking my smoke detectors, and cleaning the fridge. But you'd never catch me saying that, now that he suspected I was strange. Borderline obsessive-compulsive.

"*Bon*. Tomorrow we will go to the jeweler and leave with him all of the jewels from Mademoiselle for appraisal."

"Leave them!"

"How else do you expect to have them appraised?"

"They couldn't just do it while we wait?"

"The entire box?"

Okay. Maybe not.

Adrien left soon after we finished our *cafés,* wishing me a good night's sleep before disappearing into the night.

Fat chance. I had to figure out a way to bulletproof his Mercedes before we took Mademoiselle's jewels in for appraisal.

I wandered into my room, spied Mademoiselle's diary, and started to read it. I didn't put it down until I was finished.

1 January 1946

And so, I find myself where I first started. Ten years ago. I have just reread what I wrote then. I might as well write the same. I shall quote myself because nothing has changed. "All the world will call me a fool for departing for Paris in January. Why should I go at all? Perhaps the better question is this, Why should I stay? What would be the purpose? So that I can tend the vineyards, keep the geese, and stare at the sky? This is not for me. And the longer I stay, the more unhappy I become. The more unhappy I make everyone around me: my father, for doing such poor work; my mother, for having no interest in being married; my neighbor…"

At least this time I know what I will do. I still have my back. And I suppose there are still artists who will want to paint it.

1 April 1946

I was sitting today for an artist when one of his friends stopped by. He opened the door to the studio and walked over to the painter. I heard his steps. He took off his coat, draped it over a chair, and then gasped. Called my name. It was B.

8 April 1946

And so this is what happened. The Légion Wallonie started with 1500 men. By March 1942, they had lost half. They began with 22 officers. Only 2 were left. The légion fought in the Caucuses and in one action lost 854 of 1000 men. They were refitted and reinforced and restructured a half dozen times. By May 1945, only a few hundred men were left. B let himself be drawn into the légion because of his hatred for the Soviets. By the time the war ended, he hated himself for fighting beside the Germans. There is little left of the man I once loved.

16 April 1946

B has asked me to go to Bretagne with him. I cannot say no.

20 April 1946

He is no happier here. He spends hours at the ocean. Walking the shore. Staring.

21 April 1946

He has told me what has happened in Belgium. How his family has imposed their will on his future. There is nothing I can do and there is nothing he will say. I have no voice in the matter. I can do nothing until he asks me to.

25 April 1946

He has asked me.

3 May 1946

I did it. I said yes. What else was there to say? I might have said it last week when he first asked me, but I needed to be sure of my own mind. Apart from my body. Because I cannot think when he is near. I cannot talk. I do nothing at all but fall into his arms. And then, I am lost. Like the finest of watercolors. They run into each other, merge, and become something else entirely. Something unexpected. Unforeseen. But wonderfully beautiful all the same.

And then it started again. The same kind of catalog of people and parties and places that occurred before the war. She was swept back into his circle. At least he asked her to marry him this time. But if she married him, then why was she referred to as Mademoiselle?

I scanned the pages. There were entries about dances. Politicians. *Haute couture* fittings.

And then there was this:

14 February 1952

He has asked about children. I told him I have not decided. Others have children. It might not be so bad. But I enjoy too much the time I spend with him. I do not wish to share it with anyone else.

Then more parties. Decades worth. And then these:

3 April 1990

Mathilde has died. B is inconsolable.

23 May 1992

I find my patience has deserted me. It has been two years since Mathilde has died.

2 September 1995

It has been five years. I told him today to leave. Or that I would leave. One of us must go. He said he would. I did not expect anything else; he has always been a gentleman.

Who was Mathilde? His mother? His sister? Mademoiselle had never mentioned a Mathilde before these entries. Mathilde had to have been someone important or B wouldn't have mourned her death for five years.

3 September 1995

B came tonight. With a necklace. Sapphires and diamonds. I

nearly cried. He does not know me at all. Perhaps he never has. I told him he could come back when he was ready. That everything would still be here for him: the cigars, the whiskey, me. But when he came, he would have to come with a larger gift than these. I do not think I will ever see him again.

14 October 1996

He has died. And he has taken my heart with him. But then I have already taken what I wanted from life. Is God punishing me for this? Or perhaps I am punishing myself. The years were good and filled with love. But if I had had a daughter, what would I tell her? What is love worth? Maybe I made the wrong decision. I probably did. Who is to say that I could not have made a life with Jean-Claude? At least for a little while. Or that there should have been someone else? Or no one else at all? Was it worth it? Who can say?

There were no other entries.

It made me sad to think that Mademoiselle would look back on her life and wonder whether she made the right choices. But then I had been doing the same. My advantage was that I was doing it early instead of late. There was still time for me to make changes. I'd already ditched my Jean-Claude. And after spending the summer in Paris, I didn't think I'd ever regret that decision. But what about Adrien?

How much was his love worth?

And how much of myself was I willing to give to find out?

Chapter 29

Adrian came by at nine the next morning, and then we walked over to Mademoiselle's. The weather was sunny but brisk; a warning of autumn's imminent arrival. He was wearing a sage green golf jacket. I was wearing the white blouse. And I was shivering by the time we got to her apartment, so I decided to borrow one of her sweaters. Maybe even keep it if I liked it enough.

I was becoming a hardened criminal.

The painters were already at work in the living room, so we dodged paint cans and went down the hall to her bedroom.

All of the furniture had been moved to the middle of the floor and draped in overlapping canvas tarps. We had to remove five to find the right armoire. I dove deep into it trying to remember exactly where I had hidden the box. My fingers fumbled over the top and then grasped it. In the daylight it looked smaller than I'd remembered.

Adrien knelt beside me. I swung the top open and breathed a sigh of relief. Everything was still there. I would have loved to have taken those beautiful things from their boxes and pouches, one by one, and just look at all of them. Spend time with each piece. But it seemed a little...indiscreet. A little too much like pawing over them.

I was sure that watching the jeweler do it would be just as satisfying.

Adrien picked up a pouch, dropped the contents, the cat brooch, into his hand, and then folded the cloth and put it into his pocket. "So we can look up the address."

He gave the cat to me. "You might as well wear it."

My eyes blinked wide open.

"It is not like it is worth five thousand dollars. And it matches what you are wearing."

But then, almost anything matches black pants and a white shirt.

"These have all come from the same jeweler," he said, "so we take them there for the appraisal. Do you think she had a phone book? I can look it up."

"I've no idea. Where would she have kept one?" Or a phone, for that matter.

Adrien looked while I found a sweater. A cardinal red cashmere. I'd never owned a cashmere sweater before. Didn't even technically own one now.

I pinned the brooch to my shirt and went into the bathroom to see how it looked. The cat's amber eyes winked at me in the mirror. Once I'd repinned the brooch straight, it seemed like a lot of trouble to take it off, so I left it and joined Adrien by the *secrétaire* in the living room.

The phone had been hidden inside behind the liquor. He began a series of *oui, oui, oui*'s and *non, non, non*'s in apparent answers to questions coming from the other end of the line. Then he hung up. "You have the box?"

I lifted it in reply.

"Then we go. We will take the metro. The shop is on rue St. Honoré. In the first." He started toward the door, but then he stopped in the hall when he realized I wasn't right behind him.

Standing where he left me, I was clutching the box to my chest. "How much do you think they're worth?"

"I do not know. I am ignorant of jewelry. I know nothing. This is why to have them appraised."

Now that wasn't true. At least not according to the Rolex watch he always wore.

"*On y va?*"

"On the metro? Just like that? Is it safe?"

He looked at the box. "Why not? What is wrong with it? It is quite solid."

"Someone could steal it. Or we could set it down and forget it. Or it could…fall onto the metro tracks and get run over…or…"

He put a hand to my cheek and patted gently. "Claire. How many people do you know who can read your mind?"

"You." It was out of my mouth before I'd consciously formed the thought.

He smiled a smile that curled up from inside him and burst onto his lips. "This I did not know! *Bon*. Well, it is your good fortune that I do not want to steal from you. And everyone else who is in Paris today cannot know what this box contains because they cannot read your mind. You have just said so yourself. There can be no danger." He held out his hand to me. "We go."

"Walk?" I felt stricken with terror. Tightened my hold on the box.

"I will protect you, *ma poule*. With my body if I must. Come, they are expecting us. It is very simple. Straight by metro from Ecole Militaire to Concorde, and then we walk. Would you care for me to hold this box?"

"Please."

He accepted it as if he were a knight and I, his lady. At least anything that happened to it between here and there was his responsibility now. But then he set the box down and took the dangling sweater from my elbow.

"A very nice color. Allow me?" He did some folding and placed it around my neck. Twisted the arms, looped them together, and it was magically draped around my shoulders. If I had tried to do the same thing, it would have looked like a noose.

He picked up the box and we headed for the metro.

We only stood on the *quai* for a few minutes before the air began to stir, gusts of warm train-generated wind mixing the stale air with a confetti of abandoned metro tickets and dust. I closed my eyes against the onslaught.

After the doors hissed open, we entered the car and found empty seats facing each other. Four seats in fact, because we sat in the area— divided by the center aisle—where two-person benches faced each other.

The doors slid shut.

There was silence for a moment. The train jerked forward, seemed to slip back, then steadily gained speed. We raced off through the darkness of the tunnels, swaying gently.

I glanced over at the box Adrien was holding. Looked at the other passengers in the car. Couldn't everyone hear the way the jewels were clinking together?

Of course they could.

They were just pretending they couldn't.

A gypsy came and planted himself right next to our seats. Yawned and began to squeeze the breath out of his accordion. If it were any other morning, I would have pelted him with coins to make him go away, but this morning, I was happy to have his company.

Overjoyed to have him standing there blocking the aisle and access to our seats.

I was almost certain that a pair of disheveled twentysomething guys were checking out the box. But now, with the gypsy, there was no way for them to get to it short of climbing over the seats and throwing Adrien out the window. Even then, they'd have to have a knife or other sharp object to shatter the glass, and that would take a lot of time and effort, and it wasn't that long a ride, so we arrived safely.

We got off at Concorde and lagged behind, so that the stream of people flowed around and passed us.

Except for one guy.

He ran up behind me on the steps leading from the metro. He was wearing a black leather jacket and sunglasses. You know the type. The kind that look as though they're looking for something.

Something like the box.

A less paranoid person than me might point out that most of the men that morning were wearing black leather jackets and sunglasses, but then they weren't trying to protect a box filled with jewels, were they?

So, at the top of the metro exit, the first man was joined by a second man. And that man was also in a leather jacket, and he was also wearing sunglasses! And he was carrying a big cardboard box—just the right size to fit our box into, close the flaps, and run off with!

He stopped Adrien to ask what time it was. See—that's how tricky thieves are. They were planning to distract us and then rob us.

But I wasn't going to play along. I didn't even give Adrien time to answer. "It's time enough to know what you're up to!" And then I tugged on Adrien's arm to get him to follow me.

Only Adrien wasn't expecting that. He was still looking at his watch. So when I grabbed his arm, he dropped the box.

And time froze.

Adrien tried to catch it.

The man holding the cardboard box dropped his box and tried to catch it.

The man's friend tried to catch it.

I just stood there.

The first man caught it and then handed it to his friend while he picked up his box.

The friend handed it back to Adrien.

I just stood there. I was pretty sure I'd had a stroke because I could not move. Or speak or breathe.

But the box was back in Adrien's hands. It hadn't broken, hadn't spilled its contents, hadn't come unlatched. The men had been given the opportunity to rob us, and they hadn't taken it. How could I have thought they were thieves? They looked like Rick Moranis and Jeff Daniels. Can you imagine Rick or Jeff ever stealing? Anything?

Well, maybe. But the movie would have been a comedy, and they would have been tripping over themselves trying to steal…whatever it was…and they probably would have turned themselves in to the police in the end.

So the box had been safe the whole time.

It was just my imagination that was scary.

They talked to Adrien as we walked down rue St. Florentin and then turned right onto rue St. Honoré, although they avoided me as if I were deranged. It turned out that their box was filled with old books they were taking to a bookseller.

"Are there any Victor Hugo?" Adrien couldn't quite keep the eagerness out of his voice.

"*Oui.*"

"Any first editions?"

"*Non.*"

"*Dommage.*"

And right in the middle of the block was the jeweler's. It was a small shop with only a tiny display window, but inside that window were two fabulous necklaces. Confections of multicolored diamonds. Who knew they came in purple and blue? It was that kind of store.

I was glad to be wearing that cat pin. Because if it weren't for that, I wouldn't be wearing any jewelry at all. I've always thought that walking into a jewelry store without wearing jewelry is like walking into a shoe store without wearing any shoes. You sort of have to be wearing what they sell in order to be taken seriously.

That's why I don't frequent jewelry stores.

There was an old man standing sentry behind the store's single counter. He had to have been at least 75.

Adrien wasted no time in approaching him. He set the box on the counter and opened it. The man's posture changed. He went from a contented cat, lounging in the sunlight, to a hunting cat, ready to pounce. Every muscle in his body appeared ready to spring upon the box.

"I may...?"

Adrien gestured toward the box and the man withdrew a pouch. It contained a box. He touched the latch to let the lid spring open.

He sighed.

The box showcased a dream of a necklace made of platinum scrolls and varied colors of rubies. They ranged from the lightest of pink to a single brilliant electric red stone that must have been at least three carats. There were earrings to match. "This one was created for a beautiful Valentino gown. The same color as that Mogok ruby in the middle. A 3.5 carat. And perfect. Did you know a ruby of this size is much rarer than a diamond of equal size? A five carat ruby is nearly priceless."

He took another box, springing the latch. A matching set of earrings, bracelet, and necklace. Emeralds. Victorian-looking. A thick stiff collar to be worn close to the throat, but so lacy it appeared ethereal. "For these, she had a dress designed."

He pulled open the strings to a pouch. A slither of pearls poured out into his hand. "The pearls!" He undid the clasp and pulled them straight along the counter. "A perfectly matched set. Round. Ten millimeter. Very high luster. White. There should be earrings to match."

And he was right. Later, he found them.

On he went, opening boxes and pouring from pouches. Mademoiselle was a lady who knew her gems. Everything was first class. Opals. Peridots. Aquamarines. Until he got to the sapphires.

He flipped the lid open. Frowned. Pushed it shut. "She never liked sapphires and diamonds. Not together. She thought they were cold. They were given her. Was there nothing else?"

Adrien and I looked at each other. Puzzled. Until, in looking around, my eye caught the winking gaze of the cat. I unwound the sweater from my neck and adjusted the blouse. "There was this."

"Ah, yes. There it is." The jeweler smiled at it, as if it were his favorite child. "Mademoiselle Dumont's Bast."

"Pardon?"

"Bast. The Egyptian cat goddess. She commissioned it in 1947. Was almost never seen without it. We used only the very best black pearl, ruby, emerald, and gold. Yellow diamonds for the eyes. She started a trend among her set for Egyptian motifs the first season she wore it. But she had the only Bast." He began to laugh and had trouble stopping. It must have been an inside joke because it wasn't funny to me.

Or to Adrien. "What is the significance of Bast?"

The jeweler stopped laughing and stared at us. "The duc de Bastogne."

As soon as I heard the name, I knew I'd discovered the identity of B. The identity of the cigar and liquor man. The man Mademoiselle had fallen in love with before the war. The man she had married after. I opened my mouth, started to speak, and stopped. Something wasn't right. Something didn't fit. "So they were...?"

The jeweler looked at me for a long moment. Then he pursed his lips, shook his head, and refused to say more. He packed up the box and handed it to us. Placed a slim file folder on top.

And that was it. He didn't speak another word. Kicking us out the door would have been more polite.

So we left.

"Adrien, I've read through Mademoiselle's diary. The man she fell in love with? The one she met at the studio? She called him 'B.'"

"As in Bastogne?"

I shrugged. "They lost each other during the war, but then after, they met up again. They married."

"Married? You are certain? She said they married?"

"He asked her. She said she told him yes."

"Then why do we still call her Mademoiselle?"

"I don't know. He died in 1996. Maybe she reverted."

Adrien was already shaking his head. "*Non.* If one marries a *duc*, then one has some sort of title. And there would not have been a marriage without your family knowing of it. I do not think they ever married, Claire."

"She loved him. He asked her. She said yes."

"I do not think a *duc* would have been allowed to have married her, *ma poule.*"

"What do you mean, allowed?"

"We French are not like you Americans. We have classes in our society. And we do not move between them. When a *duc* must marry, then he must marry within his class. Remember that your Mademoiselle came from the south, where she had been feeding geese and working in the vineyards. And when she came to Paris, she did not stay at the Ritz. She worked as a model."

"So?"

"So they did not marry."

The metro was more crowded on the way back, but we were still able to get seats. We peeked in the folder the jeweler had given us.

They were bills of sale.

I flipped through and did a rough calculation in my head.

Adrien did a rough calculation in his head.

We both gasped and stared at each other. "Two million euros!" We ran all the way back to the apartment.

Adrien's apartment.

He Googled "duc de Bastogne." We spent more than two hours surfing the Internet.

There was a lot of information about a man named Emile, duc de Bastogne, but he was too young to have been the cigar and liquor man.

"The duc's son?"

Adrien shrugged. "Or his grandson or nephew. Titles always pass to a male."

There was information on the history of the duchy. Bastogne is a region in Belgium. And someday, if there were a nuclear explosion in Brussels and everyone else in the royal family died, then Belgium's crown would pass to a duc de Bastogne.

There was lots of information on the Battle of the Bulge and the Battle for Bastogne during World War II. Sketchy information on the duchy's castles in the region.

And that was it.

"She knew a duke." You'd think someone in the family would have gossiped about her if she moved in royal circles.

"So it would seem."

I was trying to fit this information with everything else I knew about Mademoiselle. "She wasn't…I mean…I read her diary, the rest of it, and she said she'd married him."

"Your father, related to a *duc*? Surely you would have known this."

Chapter 30

❧

Adrien had warned me he would have to go back into work on Tuesday, but he thought he'd be back in Paris by the late afternoon. Which gave me most of the day to spend with Cynthia.

I met her in front of Ladurée. We had espressos and *macarons*. It was starting to become a habit. An hour later, I crunched into the last bite of a lemon *macaron*. Let it dissolve on my tongue. "So what's your big plan?"

"The big plan is to get him to notice you. If he notices you first, then you won't have to do anything, right? He'll do it all. All you'll have to do is sit back and wait for the kiss."

"And this is going to happen because…?"

"Have you ever heard of Sephora?"

"No."

She looked at me and pressed her lips together. "Maybe that's just as well."

We left the restaurant, crossed the Champs-Elysées, and walked down the sidewalk. She suddenly pulled me into a store. It had two bouncers guarding the entry and a long ramp which led down onto the shop floor. On the left we passed an area lined with books. I was surprised but pleased that Cynthia wanted to spend the morning in a bookstore. I couldn't imagine how that would help me out with Adrien, but I was ready to give anything a try.

It was when I turned to thank her that I realized exactly what kind of store it was. The wall to her right was lined with alcoves, and those alcoves were occupied by perfume and cologne bottles and boxes. There was music pulsating in the background and designer lights glowed from the shelves, ceilings, and walls. As my gaze swept down the ramp and into the store, I realized that almost all the walls were lined with perfumes and colognes. It was enough to make my nose start to tingle. The rest of the store, separated from the perfumes by a line of black-and-white striped columns, was crisscrossed with shelves that were packed with nail polish, lipsticks, eye shadows, and every other artifice known to females. "This is your big plan? Makeup?"

"No. *Maquillage.*"

"You can call it anything you want, but I already have one of each back at Mademoiselle's apartment. I already wear makeup. I'm wearing some right now."

Cynthia sighed. Frowned. Sighed again. "It's not that you don't wear any. It's that I can't tell that you're wearing any."

"I know. It's the natural look." After I'd broken up with my first boyfriend seven years before, I'd paid good money to change my image and guarantee that my makeup would look so subtle that it would be indiscernible to the naked eye. It was exactly the look I wanted.

"It's a schoolgirl look. And I thought you wanted Adrien to notice you."

"I do. I just don't want him to mistake me for a clown."

Cynthia threw an arm around my shoulder, escorting me off the ramp and into the store. "He won't."

It turned out that she had called and made an appointment for me to have my skin diagnosed and makeup applied. For free. She walked right up to the front counter. *"Ici Mademoiselle Le Noyer…qui veut être Madame Delaporte. On peut faire quelque chose pour l'aider?"*

I could have strangled her. She'd basically told them I had designs on Adrien and asked if there were something they could do to help.

The clerk clasped her hands to her chest, smiled, and said "Q*uelque chose? On peut faire tout.*" Something? We can do everything.

They did everything for about two hours. While I sat and listened and nodded. Said *oui, oui, oui* and *non, non, non* at appropriate intervals. Watched myself turn from a pale, dark-haired girl into a pale, dark-haired woman with vivid red lips, defined eyebrows and raccoon-ring eyes. The clerk used odd colors like white, chartreuse, and a violent violet. Applied 37 coats of mascara to pull off *Le Look*. With a flourish she handed me the mirror for an upclose inspection.

I was surprised.

I had expected to look like a Pollard painting. But I didn't. I looked… different.

I blinked at myself in the mirror. Tilted my head. I looked like me projected onto the pages of a fashion magazine. I looked…good. Maybe even head turning.

Maybe it would work.

Before we left, Cynthia led me over to the perfume wall. "You don't wear perfume do you?"

"Certain kinds give me a headache." And make my nose run.

"But it also creates a sensory memory, so you're going to buy some. You are going to have a signature scent and whenever Adrien smells it, he's going to think of you. So what do you want your perfume to say?"

"I've had a crush on you since I was five? Is there any way on earth you could ever maybe possibly feel the same way? Theoretically speaking?"

She was already shaking her head. "No. That's not it."

"It's not?"

"No. You want to say, 'I'm a woman. Take me seriously.'"

"So we're looking for a serious perfume?"

"Yes. You want something mature. Something aggressive. Something like this." She was holding out a bottle of 24 Faubourg. She reached for my hand. "Give me your wrist."

I pulled it back from her. "No. I don't want any."

"Yes, you do. And this is the one. Trust me."

"Not until I smell it first."

She held out the bottle as if she was going to give it to me, but at the last moment she pointed it toward my wrist and squirted. The tester must have been broken because it poured out like a fire hose. And it was a heavy perfume. Exactly the kind that gives me a headache. It majored in scents of amber and jasmine.

But I recognized it. From somewhere. It wasn't my favorite smell, but it had happy connotations. It made me think of warmth. Of laughter. It wrapped my body in feelings of mellow laziness. And then I began to sneeze.

"I'm so, so sorry."

I sneezed again. "A serious perfume? This is going to give me a serious headache!"

"Here. Here's a tissue."

I took it, sneezed into it.

"Not for your nose! For the perfume."

Oh. Of course. I applied it to the still-wet places on my skin. Sneezed again. "Bathroom." I sneezed. "Have to wash it off."

She grabbed my arm, pulled me up the ramp, and ran me down the street. We found a bathroom in one of the malls along the block. I scrubbed at my arm with soap for five minutes.

"Is it coming off?"

I dried my arm with a paper towel. Took a sniff. Felt a sneeze coming on. Froze. Waited. It never came. "I think it's fine now."

"I'm so sorry."

"I'll take a bath tonight. After...Adrien. And then everything will be fine. It's not a big deal." Not as long as I didn't think about what I was going to say to him. Or about what he would say to me. Or about whether or not we would kiss. "This isn't going to work."

"It is going to work. You look beautiful. Gorgeous. Stunning. Now let's go buy a new dress."

I was already shaking my head. "No more new clothes."

"Just one dress. Something sexy."

"But I'm not sexy."

"I know! That's why we have to make you that way."

She drug me out of the mall. We crossed the Champs-Elysées. As we walked up the sidewalk, my spirits began to lift. Heads were turning in my direction. Maybe everything would be okay. Maybe Cynthia was right. Maybe her plan would work. We went into a small women's boutique. She pounced on a black silk dress and pulled it from the rack. "Try this one."

"Black? Are you sure?"

"As in Little Black Dress? Of course I'm sure. Black says 'I'm serious.'" She had already waved over a salesclerk and they were both pushing me back into the dressing area.

I took off the chiffon skirt and the sleeveless green sweater I was wearing. Put the dress on. Or tried to. It was slippery. Fluttery. Didn't seem to have any seams on it that I could see. I got it over my head. When I finally got it on straight, I turned to look at myself in the mirror. I wasn't sure I liked what I saw.

The dress was cut on the bias, so it clung. It was a wrap style, so it had a V-neck that slipped lower every time I moved. The sleeves were ruched at the top and then slit. There was a small, hardly worth mentioning seam that held them together, and then they fluttered open, revealing my shoulders, before they joined together again at an equally insignificant seam. The dress had a front slit to midthigh. Adrien would like that. It also had a long scarf, which might come in handy. Maybe I would be able to use it to tie the dress together.

I wound the scarf around my neck, pushed back the curtain, and went out into the shop.

"Perfect! That's it!"

"It feels like it's falling off my body."

"Looks like it too! Adrien won't be able to resist. You look terrific!" She turned to the salesclerk. *"On va la prendre."*

Nice of her to ask me whether I actually wanted to buy it or not. Especially since this time I was paying.

She followed me back to the dressing room. "Do you have shoes?"

"Would stilettos work?"

"Absolutely! I wish I could be there to see his face!"

I changed back into my skirt and sweater. Bought the dress. We walked back to the Delaportes'.

"So, what should I say?"

"Don't say anything at first. Wait to see what he says."

"And then?"

"Just go with it. Whatever he says, just…see where it takes you!" We had reached the front door. Cynthia grabbed me by the shoulders. She was beaming. "Go for it. You'll do great. Don't talk too much. Remember, you want him to be the one to start the conversation. If all else fails, just kiss him. That'll take care of everything. So…good luck!" She air-kissed me and then she was off.

Leaving me standing there. Staring after her. Wishing I could go too.

I spent the rest of the day trying not to move my face too much, certain that if I did, all the makeup would crack and fall off.

I nibbled at lunch. Spent a few hours staring off into space, wondering what the outcome of the evening would be. Hoping, praying that Adrien would like me. Love me. Fearing that he'd listen to me, smile, and then pat me on the cheek the way he used to when I was little.

Just before 5:00, when I couldn't stand the suspense any longer, I went into the bathroom and played around with my hair. I used some of Madame Delaporte's hairspray to make it do what I wanted it to. Thought I did a pretty good job.

Looked at my watch. It was 5:30.

Anytime now.

I sat on the couch. Got up. Put on a jazz CD. Sat down. Felt all those random syncopations tap-dancing on my nerves. Got up. Put on a classical CD. Sat down.

It was 5:45.

I leaned my head back on the couch. Closed my eyes. Tried to take deep, calming breaths. Woke myself up snoring.

It was 6:30.

I stood up. Stretched. Paced. Wandered into the library. Did mental translations of all the titles into English. Sat in a chair. Stood up.

It was 7:00.

I walked into the living room, pulled the windows open, stared out onto the street. Watched the cars go by. People come and go. Realized that I would never be able to hear Adrien come in over the noise from the street. Pushed the windows shut and latched them.

It was 7:15.

I stood by the door, ear pressed up against it. Trying to detect his coming. Didn't hear anything. I opened the door and watched the elevator buttons, willing them to light up, signaling his arrival.

Nothing.

I walked up and down the stairs between the fourth and fifth floor in my bare feet. Counted the steps. Recited "One, two, buckle my shoe." Got to "big fat hen" when I heard the door downstairs click shut.

Raced back to the Delaportes', scrambled around looking for my shoes, ducked into the bathroom to check my hair and makeup, straightened the dress, and then went to stand by the door.

Thought that might look too eager. I arranged myself on the couch.

And waited.

And waited.

And realized it must not have been Adrien.

It was 8:00.

He'd never been this late before. Had he gotten stuck in traffic? Had there been an accident? Had he been killed? On the very night I had decided to declare my love? Could fate be that cruel?

I felt like screaming. Decided to eat instead. If he showed up, then he could join me. In fact, I was sure that because I had made the decision to eat, he would probably show up right then.

Right now.

Nope.

I ate.

I cleaned up.

I sat down on the couch again.

No Adrien.

I reviewed the things that Cynthia had told me to do. Don't talk too much, just go for it, and if all else fails just kiss him. Okay.

He called at 10:00. "Claire! All my excuses. I have been at work and probably will be until midnight. I must come back in the morning. I am so sorry, but I may not see you until Thursday."

"That's fine."

"*Alors,* you are fine? You have had a good day? *Bon. Bonne nuit, ma poule.*"

"*Bonne nuit.*"

Well, I'd done it. I hadn't talked too much; I'd gone with the flow. Too bad I hadn't had a chance to kiss him. I hung up the phone and went into the bathroom. Stared at my face in the mirror. That wonderfully sexy, wonderfully serious face I would never see again.

I washed the makeup off, brushed my hair out, and went to bed.

Chapter 31

❦

I didn't speak to Adrien for two more days.

He was busy with contracts and *syndicats*, socialism and saving the world from the evils of capitalism.

That left me with the painters. But they weren't a talkative group and they didn't need me for anything. I could have cleaned, but I was afraid I'd find things better left unseen. Like mice or rats. And every time I stepped into Mademoiselle's I could feel the fumes paralyzing my brain cells and my IQ going into decline.

So I found a tourist map of Paris and circled everything I'd always wanted to see.

I started at Père Lachaise cemetery and communed with the dead. I saw Jim Morrison's grave, but only because I'd gotten lost. I also passed by Chopin and Delacroix. Héloïse and Abélard; a miniature Gothic cathedral entombed their love.

Another example of a couple who got into trouble reading books.

The cemetery had been placed on a hill. With the temperature cooling and a breeze pushing back the haze, I had a panoramic view of Paris. Lime and chestnut trees lined the broad avenues between the divisions. Their branches cloaked the alleys that wound through the graves.

At times it seemed much more a park than a burial ground. At other times it felt like a city for the dead; many of the monuments lining the streets looked like houses. For very small, very short people.

I left refreshed. And that's saying a lot for a cemetery.

The cemetery was my furthest venture east. My next stop was the Bastille.

The storming of this prison became a symbol of the French Revolution. Ninety-nine people died and all the prisoners, all seven of them, were freed. It was just as disappointing to me as it must have been to the revolutionaries.

There's nothing there anymore except a monument to memorialize the event.

So I hopped back on the metro and went to the Conciergerie. The prison where Marie Antoinette was held until she was beheaded. Looming over the Seine, it looked medieval on the outside, its round towers topped by slate-tiled dunce caps. Its lifetime as a prison had begun in 1391. And inside it still felt dour and gloomy. Its stone walls and floors absorbed any warmth in the air.

Any hope in the soul.

I toured it as quickly as possible and got back outside as soon as I could.

The good thing is that I had purchased a combination ticket for Sainte Chapelle. So I stood in line to go through the metal detector at Palais de Justice, and then walked into the courtyard. The church is surrounded by the law courts. But on a clear day, light could still penetrate the complex, and inside, the stained-glass windows glowed, luminous from the sun. I sat on a bench for an hour and watched the windows move as the colors changed. Watched their vivid shadows waltz across the floor.

From there I walked back to the Delaportes'. Paris on foot is different than Paris by car. I could feel the breeze in my hair. I could smell the fresh bread from the *boulangeries*, the sweet roses as I passed a florist. I could stop and look at the stonework on the buildings I passed. Read the blue plaques that were posted to explain a building's place in Paris' history. Nearly every block had one. I could dawdle along the *quais*. I could sit on a park bench and have my vision dappled as sunlight filtered through the trees.

As I walked I was beguiled as I have never been by Seattle.

And Seattle is a pretty city.

When the sun is shining, it showcases natural beauty. The unique interplay of mountains and ocean. Of tall majestic trees and snowcapped peaks. Seattle is green. It is growth and vibrancy. It is a people attuned to their environment, combating rain with giant mugs of coffee and umbrellas, and celebrating the sun with crazy riots of flowers and Frisbees and volleyballs. Seattle is a comfortable city. It lets you do whatever you want, as long as you let others do the same.

Paris is a beautiful city.

An elegant city, it showcases magnificent architecture, grand vistas, and impressive avenues. Cream-colored stone and soaring arches. Graceful arcades and dignified churches. Paris is white. It is discreet and understated. It is a people so used to her beauty and the grace of her architecture that they themselves have become beautiful. A people so familiar with the symmetry of her buildings that their thoughts have become famously ordered as well. They celebrate winter by swathing their necks in colorful scarves. They welcome summer by dining *al fresco* in sidewalk cafés. And everywhere, they kiss. Paris is a beguiling city. It seduces you. Makes you want to become just like her.

As I walked, I fell in love with Paris.

And I continued the love affair the next day.

By Thursday evening, Adrien's work on the new contract had been completed.

On Friday, he took me out to lunch to celebrate.

He told me we would be going to the Plaza d'Athénée for lunch. The way he said it sounded like a warning.

I wore the short chiffon skirt and matching tank. I put on ten pounds of makeup and tortured myself with an eyelash curler trying to recreate *Le Look.* And in celebration of second chances, I had even decided to take my life into my hands and wear the heels. I can't imagine anything sexy about tottering around town on stilettos, but I guess there's a market for that sort of thing, because as we drove to the restaurant, as we waited for traffic lights to change, I noticed lots of women wearing them.

And not wearing panty hose. Or slips.

Just three more things for Adrien to be right about.

What's the fun in life if you already know everything about

everything? There aren't any discoveries left to made. No embarrassing situations to be a part of. No apologies to be made.

I had the feeling that if I could try it, I might like it.

We drove across Pont de l'Alma, up avenue George V, down the Champs-Elysées, and then turned onto avenue Montaigne. Had I known where the restaurant was, I might have suggested walking to save Adrien from having the car valet parked. But since I was a catastrophe on heels, I suppose it was all for the best.

He pulled up in front of a standard Parisian stone building. But this one had red flowers dripping from every balcony and cheerful red awnings shading every window. The front entrance was overhung with a deco-style opaque glass fan.

Inside it was anything but standard. We stepped from the revolving door into an oval portico ringed by columns and carpeted with an oval oriental rug. Passed through engraved glass doors and into what might have been an old ballroom.

It glowed.

It was understated with cream walls, cream molding, just the right amount of gilding to be tasteful without being overdone. Huge mirrors reflected light from huge windows. There were Louis XV chairs with curved lines, upholstered in pastels. There were modern touches too. A bright orange clock on a mantel that was a masterpiece of *avant-garde* elegance. Huge chandeliers veiled in cylinders of gauzy fabric, each projecting a hologram.

But even then it wasn't intimidating. Not until they brought the menus and I discovered that there were no prices listed.

None.

"Adrien, I think they gave us the wrong menus." I leaned across the table to show him mine. "No prices. It must be a draft copy."

He looked at me over his menu. "Everything is just as it should be."

"I don't think so."

"I have invited you to dine with me, so I am paying, and it is only me who needs to know how much I will pay."

"Can we trade menus then?"

He folded his together, set it down on the table, and placed both of his hands on top of it. *"Non."*

"I can't just take a peek?"

He clucked at me as though I were a little child. "I will give you one hint. You may order anything you like."

Fine. I wrinkled my nose at him before I took up a defensive position behind my menu. What to order? This was much more difficult than it sounds. On a date I usually throw out the least expensive and the most expensive items on the menu. Then I ask what my date is going to have, and if that doesn't sound good, I try to beat or match the price.

"What are you going to have?" It was hard to look sophisticated when I was whispering from behind a menu, so I finally just spread it out flat in front of me. "What are you having?"

Adrien sent a bland look in my direction. "I have not yet decided. I was thinking of the chicken or the fish."

Hmm. Neither of them looked bad...

"Or maybe the beef or the lamb."

Those looked better...

"But, you know, this pork looks very nice. I just cannot decide. What do you suggest?"

Okay. It was official. He was mocking me. It looked as though I was on my own. Chicken was a safe, cheap bet, but the beef dish sounded better. Of course, there was mad cow disease to consider. And if the restaurant were also considering it, then their meat had probably been imported from Chile or Antarctica or somewhere fabulously expensive. So no beef. There was always fish to consider. But then, I didn't really care for fish. So that left the pork or the lamb.

Pork or lamb?

I don't cook pork for myself because in seventh grade I saw a picture of a trichinella worm and have ever after suffered from a trichinosis phobia. So that left lamb. But how might lamb fit into the overall pricing structure on a menu? More expensive than chicken, I'm sure. Less expensive than lobster? Probably. So, lamb it was. Now I just had to decide on a starter and dessert.

I snuck a look at Adrien.

He was watching me.

I smiled.

He smiled back. "I will say it again, you look lovely. And you are wearing 24 Faubourg."

I was? I glanced down. Realized the skirt I was wearing was the skirt I'd worn to Sephora. Cynthia was right. Perfume prodded the senses! Maybe her plan could still work. "Yes."

"Ah. My mother used to wear this one. But she switched about ten years ago."

Or maybe it wouldn't. Cynthia had been going for serious? Mature? Well, she'd succeeded. Those sensory memories I'd had were from vacations in Carcans. Of course they had conjured up warmth and sun and lazy summer days. And now Adrien had just associated me with his mother! Okay. All was not lost. I just had to think. Fast. I smiled again. "You look nice, too. Handsome."

"Really? I have never thought of myself as handsome."

Starting to laugh, I sputtered to a halt when I realized he wasn't joking. "But you are."

"I do not think so. My nose is too big and my eyes are too close together. I have a funny smile." He had folded his arms, propped his elbows on the table. "I am what you would call goofy."

It was hard not to burst into laughter. "No. You'd have to have big ears to be goofy."

"Well, there, you see? I am nothing at all."

"No. There's something about you, Adrien. Something very special."

"Pfft. This is what all the girls say. Why should I believe you?"

Because I could bask in the glow of your eyes for the rest of my life? Because my heart sings whenever I see you? Because my body has a built-in Adrien-detector that tells me whenever you get within a hundred yards of me? "Trust me."

He was staring at me with those blue eyes.

I felt myself blush. My eyes darted down, looking for refuge. I picked up the menu to shield them. Besides, I still had to decide on a starter: soup, salad, or fussy-fancy appetizers? And dessert: something chocolatey, fruity, or custardy?

At least Adrien handled the decisions on wine. He refused to let me not drink, and when the *sommelier* came with the wine list, I could see why. It was bound into a book and it was two inches thick. I'm not kidding.

Adrien asked for suggestions, and the *sommelier* asked what we had ordered. They discussed several options before Adrien decided. Then he ordered champagne too.

"I don't—"

"I do not care. Today, we drink champagne."

Champagne? At lunch? Champagne was for bubble-headed women wearing black dresses and smoking cigarettes from long slender cigarette holders. In elbow-length gloves. Or wait. Maybe I was thinking of Audrey Hepburn in *Breakfast at Tiffany's*.

I closed my eyes and shook my head.

When I opened them, the champagne had appeared along with an appetizer. But not the one I had ordered.

"It is an *amuse-bouche*. To amuse you while you wait for what you have ordered." Adrien raised his glass.

I raised mine. I took a small sip. Felt my eyebrows rise. It was wonderful.

A wonderful start to a wonderful meal.

The food was excellent. From my soup to the lamb to the cheese (all five of them) to the fruit *charlotte-glacé* to the tiered plate of chocolates and *petits fours* to the coffee. And it all looked as wonderful as it tasted. Bright, fresh colors. Contrasting textures. It was cuisine meant to please all of the senses.

And the service was even better than the food. I think there were eight people who waited on our table, but I'm not sure because I never caught them doing it.

My water glass was refilled.

My napkin was replaced when I went to the bathroom.

Plates were taken away, silverware added.

And I never saw anyone do any of it.

The wine Adrien had chosen matched our food perfectly. Or so he said. I just know that every time I took a bite of lamb, I wanted to follow it immediately with a sip of wine. Each one made the other taste better. I only had one glass, but I made it last.

And then he ordered us each a glass of wine to go with our cheese selections. I had a port. He had another red.

By the time we were done, I never wanted to eat again. I didn't want to spoil the experience. It was the best meal I have ever had. Will ever have.

But I had been inspired. I might just think about learning how to cook something besides grilled cheese.

Once we were back in the car, I couldn't contain myself any longer. "How much was it?"

"Claire! This is very indiscreet. A man invites you to lunch and you share wonderful food and wine and have good conversation and the way you sum it up is by how much it costs? Does it matter?"

"No." Because I could always ask Cynthia at church on Sunday. She'd know.

Chapter 32

అ౨౧

*B*y the time Sunday came, I almost forgot to ask.

We were running late, so we elbowed our way through the crowds into church. Then after the service, all of humanity tried to squeeze into the church's one all-purpose room adjacent to the sanctuary. Between little kids streaming like a river to the table with cookies, and the congestion of groups that insisted on talking right inside the door, I couldn't even see Cynthia, let alone start a conversation with her.

But the little kids ate all the cookies, the *grandes dames* of the church moved into the kitchen for cleanup, and I snatched the last Styrofoam cup and a few leftover drips of coffee. By the time I turned around, Cynthia was beside me. She grabbed my arm. "You never called me! What happened with A?"

"Nothing."

"He didn't kiss you? Doesn't like you? What does 'nothing' mean? It didn't work?"

"It might have, but I never saw him that night. He had to work late."

"We could do it again. This week after school."

"No."

Between telling her about the progress on the apartment and exchanging thoughts on the singles group and the special charms of Paris, it almost slipped my mind. But I caught a glimpse of Adrien through the crowd and I asked.

"Plaza d'Athénée? Did you go for lunch or dinner?"

"Lunch."

"Did you have wine?"

"Champagne before, a red with lunch, and more with cheese."

"Coffee after?"

"Yes. And all these little pastries and chocolates. I didn't think I'd be hungry for at least a week, and then before I knew it, I'd crammed about four into my mouth..."

"Then it probably cost about six hundred."

I choked on the coffee I'd been sipping. "Six hundred?"

"Euro. Six hundred euro."

"That's six hundred dollars!"

"Well, give or take a few dollars with the exchange rate. Are you sure he wasn't trying to...seduce you? Or something?"

"He never even held my hand. Never even tried."

"Don't give up. You have to try again. The dress won't let you down. You have to promise me that before you leave you'll give it one more shot."

I promised.

Then Adrien appeared at my elbow, sporting his guitar case and asking if I was ready to go.

"Yes. Sure. Fine."

Cynthia and I crashed foreheads when I tried to give her a hug goodbye and she tried to give me French kisses. One of these Sundays I would figure out who did what by way of greetings and goodbyes.

Adrien surprised me by dumping his guitar in the car and then turning around and walking me to the Chinese restaurant across from the church. "We are meeting the pastor and his wife for lunch."

Oh.

I'd been looking forward to a quiet afternoon at home. A chance to observe Adrien up close. Maybe get personal. Take a walk just before dinner. But then, I had to eat lunch sometime, didn't I?

The pastor and his wife were a study in contrasts. Adam was tall and blond with a "gentle giant" manner; Deborah was short and angular. Dark-haired, dark-eyed, and intense. She was quiet, but she wasn't subdued. She had opinions. Not that she was arguing them with anyone, but I got the feeling that, once established, no one was going to talk her out of them.

The waitress came and we ordered. She disappeared and then came back with spring rolls and tea. We wrapped the rolls with mint and lettuce leaves and then dipped them into a sweet sauce. We had all ordered our Chinese favorites to share four ways.

While we were eating, I decided to get a theological expert's opinion on drinking. Because even though Adam was a pastor, he didn't come across the way Brian had. Didn't project the same careful, cautious earnestness. "How do you deal with drinking? As a pastor in France."

"Oh, the same as everyone else. Just take a glass, put it up to my lips and swallow." His kind green eyes were teasing me. He shrugged. "Everyone in the ministry seems to have a different approach. But in France, it puts up more of a barrier to a relationship if you don't drink than if you do. Last week we were invited over to some French friends' for dinner. The first thing they did was uncork a bottle of wine from their region. It was made in their hometown. How could I say, 'I'm sorry, but I don't drink'? They were honoring me by sharing themselves with me."

That was a point I hadn't considered.

"My predecessor always said that he didn't drink, although he'd always add, 'If you open up a bottle of wine and pour me a glass, I'd have to try some just to be polite.'"

"It's just strange that wine is so much a part of the culture here."

"Maybe it's strange that it isn't part of the culture in the States."

"So you don't think there's any theological reason not to drink?"

"Is there a theological reason to drink?"

"So you're saying…?"

"That there are some areas on which the Bible is silent. That there are some parts of religion which are cultural, not theological. And when that's the case, how much importance should be placed on them?"

"But getting drunk?"

"There can always be too much of a good thing. Drinking too much alcohol leads to getting drunk. Too much food leads to obesity. Too much of anything upsets the balance in life."

"But what about Christians who think it's wrong to drink?"

"What about Christians who don't like the ties I wear? Drinking is not a moral question. It's a lifestyle question. Many people derive great pleasure from wine and the way it compliments food, just as many people derive great pleasure from running marathons."

Adrien seemed to be having a lot of trouble getting food to stay on his fork. He kept pushing sweet-and-sour pork around his plate. Mixing it up with rice. Pushing it around again. He and the pastor had a lot of thoughts in common.

"So what do you think about politics and the church?"

Adrien must have been on the brink of catching a cold. He had a sudden onset of a coughing fit.

"I don't think you have to be a Democrat or a Republican or even a socialist. In fact, there are probably a lot of Christians who are communists. Some people argue that the early church was based on communist ideals. Early monastic communities certainly were. Communism with a small *c*—that's the idea that goods should be held in common. Communism with a big *C* is the idea that this should be accomplished through revolution. There probably aren't many big *C* Communists in the church in general, but I'd bet there are a lot of small *c* communists. The theory is not inherently bad. It's the application that needs a lot of work."

Mmm-hmm.

"And in fact, we actually do have a couple Communists here at the church."

"Big *C*?"

"Big *C*."

Our drive back into town was quiet. I was trying to find a place for Communism in my spiritual landscape. Decided that I simply didn't have any room for it at that moment. I was also still trying to grasp how much money Adrien had spent at lunch on Friday.

Six hundred dollars.

Adrien had spent $600 on lunch and he hadn't even told me. Hadn't warned me. Who spends $600 on lunch? I mean, you could feed about 200 people for Thanksgiving with $600. Or you could buy 20 new coffeemakers for the church. Or buy a whole herd of cows for a tribe in Africa. Or a plane ticket. Or even buy a really beat-up car.

Adrien nosed his Mercedes into a parking space and then killed the engine. He pulled the keys out of the ignition and placed them on the dash. "Claire? Is something wrong?" He hooked his right leg around the stick shift and turned to face me. His hand played with the head rest on the top of my seat.

"Did you spend six hundred dollars on our lunch at Plaza d'Athénée?"

"Why do you need to know?"

"So you did."

"It was my money. Why does it concern you how I spend it?"

"But six hundred?—On one meal? Normal people don't do that. Think of what you could do with six hundred dollars."

"I did. I am not poor. Just because I take you to Plaza d'Athénée does not mean I will have to beg on the streets."

"But it's frivolous!"

"Frivolous?"

"Irresponsible."

"Because I am not meeting my responsibilities? Which ones? I own my apartment. I own my car. I will never miss this money."

"But think of all the other people you could have given it to."

"Like who? The *clochard* who begs on the corner? That would be very irresponsible, would it not?"

"Yes, but that's not what I mean."

"Ah. I see. You are saying that you are not worthy of a nice meal in a nice restaurant?"

"No. Yes. No."

"So you are saying that you enjoyed the meal, but you just would rather not have enjoyed it with me?"

"That's not what I'm saying and you know it."

"So maybe we should not have had anything to eat at all on Friday. What should we have done instead?"

"You're twisting my words."

"And you are twisting my character. You are saying that I should do something charitable with such a large sum of money. I am saying that I do something charitable with various sums of money all the time. And that is my business. If I choose to buy lunch instead of a new suit, I should be able to do so."

"But it was just food. We still had to eat breakfast the next morning."

"Maybe for you it was just food, but for me, it was a memory I will always keep."

Okay. That was very sweet. But still. "Six hundred dollars? Was it honestly worth it?"

"Claire, you decide. If you have to ask if it is worth it, then obviously, to you, it is not! I apologize for having taken you. It was a big mistake. I will never do it again."

I got out of the car. Slammed the door shut. Stalked to the building door and punched in the code. Pushed through.

But I couldn't slam the door on him.

In the first place, it would have been rude. In the second place, it had one of those pneumatic things that resisted when you tried to hurry it along.

So he caught up with me. But he didn't say anything.

We rode up the elevator in silence.

We went into the apartment in silence.

I went into the bedroom, and kicked off my shoes. In my next life, I'll be a punter, because my left shoe ended up hitting the wall on the far side of the room. I spent about ten minutes trying to rub out the mark it made on the wallpaper. I succeeded in smearing it into oblivion with a small amount of spit and a large amount of elbow grease.

Then I sat down on the floor.

I had to face the facts.

I was a shrew.

A rude, ungrateful, pitiful shrew. Maybe I didn't agree with Adrien's expenditures, but it had been a nice meal and he had invited me along. It wasn't my money. It was his. And I was pretty sure no one would ever invite me to a $600 meal again.

I got up and adjusted the waistband of my skirt. It had gotten hitched around during football practice. Had I been telling myself the truth, I might have said that I was feeling ashamed of myself. As it was, I pretended that Adrien needed some space and I crept into the library to pick out a book.

Taking *Stupeur et Tremblements* by Amélie Northomb from the shelves, I tucked myself into an armchair and began to read. But I didn't get very far. It just didn't feel right to be quarreling with Adrien.

Not when I had caused the quarrel.

So I closed the book around my finger and tiptoed down the hall. He was sitting on the couch with a book in his lap. Staring out the window. Breezy jazz skipped from the CD player.

I put my hands behind my back and shifted my weight to the outside of my feet. Curled and uncurled my toes. How do you apologize for causing an argument when you still think that you're right but feel bad about making the other person feel bad? Because they were generous and you were…a shrew?

I walked to the end of the couch and cleared my throat.

He turned his head and looked up.

"Can we be friends?"

"Friends! When have we never been friends? We have always been friends, Claire." He pulled me down onto the couch and nestled me into the crook of his arm. He kissed me on top of my head. "Always."

We read for about an hour. He with one leg propped on the other and his hand along the back of the couch. Me with my back against his side, and my knees drawn up on the couch.

Then he began to play with my hair, picking up a lock and tickling the back of my neck with it.

I swatted at his hand. Kept on reading.

He raked his fingers through the back of my hair.

I turned my head so he'd have a better angle. It was giving my scalp tingles.

When he was done, he began tugging at the ends of it.

I turned around, ready to say something. But whatever it was disappeared. We were eye to eye. My face not two inches from his.

"Claire?" His lips were whispering my name. Enticing me closer. I lifted my gaze to his eyes. That clear blue had suddenly gone smoky. His hand moved from my hair down to my back. His fingers spread, then tensed, pulling me closer.

I placed a hand on his chest.

He took it in his own. Put one of my fingertips to his lips.

And then we heard a key turn in the lock.

Chapter 33

Adrien raised himself from the couch.

I froze. Petrified. No one else had a key to the apartment.

I watched in horror as the door edged open. A woman's head popped inside. *"Cou-cou! Tu es ici, mon enfant?"*

No one else had a key to the apartment except for Adrien's parents. Because, if we were splitting hairs, it was their apartment.

Adrien hurried to the door, took a suitcase from his mother, and kissed her cheeks. Shook his father's hand.

I left the book on the couch. Got up. Approached the door with dragging feet.

Madame Delaporte spied me first. "Claire! *Ma petite!*" She smiled, grasped me by the shoulders, and kissed my cheeks. She was just as elegant as I'd remembered. Even after having traveled all day, her black pants hardly showed a crease. Her sky blue blouse, with flutter sleeves, still fluttered. And her hair, that blond head of meticulously arranged hair, hadn't moved. Not for a quarter century. At least not that I could tell.

"Claire! *Ça fait longtemps…*" Adrien's father stood me off at arm's length, shaking his head. *"Regarde comme tu es belle!"*

I flushed. It's not every day someone calls you beautiful. I'm sure he was just being nice. He looked a little older. A few more wrinkles on his tanned face. A bit less hair. But the collar of his yellow polo was folded with precision and the navy blue sweater tossed over his shoulders knotted with *élan*.

"*Tu ne penses pas, Adrien?*"

Adrien looked across his parents at me. I could have sworn he blushed. "*Bah…oui. Elle est très belle.*"

I blushed. It's not every day two people call you beautiful.

Monsieur Delaporte hauled the suitcases back to their bedroom while Madame busied herself in the kitchen and Adrien poured drinks.

I stayed in the hall until Adrien's dad came out of the bedroom. He placed a hand at the small of my back and propelled me into the living room. "*Dis-moi tout.*"

Tell me everything.

So I did. I sat down on the couch. He sat down in an armchair. I left out the parts about Adrien throwing all my clothes away. Didn't mention communism or socialism.

Adrien gave us both a drink.

I took a sip, grateful for something to do.

He made one for himself and then sat down on the couch with me.

Monsieur made sympathetic noises as we told him about Mademoiselle's apartment.

Snorted in derision when Adrien told him about the contract at Dassault.

Adrien asked about their vacation.

His father shrugged and "pffted" and gesticulated as he recounted the month's adventures. He asked about my parents. About Dad's back.

I updated him on their adventures in Florida.

Then we all rose when Madame came in and announced dinner.

I don't know how she did it. I don't know where she had hidden the ingredients. But she was able to serve a roast chicken with potatoes, steamed green beans, *tabbouleh*, and raspberries with cream for dessert.

During dinner, Adrien and his parents conversed with the finesse of true artists. They talked about religion and sports. Africa and Asia. The stock market and predictions for the coming grape harvest. Just as any neophyte in the presence of the great, I sat and watched. Humbled. In awe of the masters.

Adrien stayed until ten thirty.

I got up when he got up, and then I realized I wasn't going anywhere. At that point it was too late to sit down, so I walked him to the door.

He put a hand to my cheek. "*Bonne nuit,* Claire."

"*Bonne nuit.*"

"My parents will take care of you. This is good timing. I go back to work tomorrow."

"But you said you finished the contract."

"*Oui.* But vacation is over. Tomorrow is *la Rentrée.*"

"Oh."

"So I will see you. Perhaps tomorrow night." He turned around and left.

How come I felt as though I'd just been abandoned?

I closed the door. Turned around. The Delaportes had gotten up and were collecting the coffee demitasses.

"*Si tu as besoin de n'importe quoi, n'hésites pas de demander,*" Adrien's mother called out over her shoulder as she carried the tray of dishes down the hall. Did I need anything? If I had, I'd figured out where it was weeks ago.

His father, heading in the opposite direction, paused to give me a kiss. "*Bonne nuit, chérie.*"

"*Bonne nuit.*"

The next morning I woke to the smell of coffee.

That was a nice change.

And to the sound of water filling the bathtub.

That was not.

There's a difference between staying in someone's house and staying in someone's house while they're there.

In the first instance, you can develop a routine and exist independent from the world. In the second case, you have to fit yourself into someone else's routine and someone else's world. Not that I was complaining; it was kind of them to let me stay. But I did feel out of place. I was constantly trying to do the wrong thing at the wrong time.

Like go to the bathroom.

Or take a bath.

Or go to the kitchen. Or the living room. Or the library.

The only place I could be sure of not interfering with their habits was when I was in my bedroom. But that didn't feel very polite. And I couldn't imagine surviving another week or two trapped in there.

It wasn't that I didn't like the Delaportes. I did. I'd never known them to be anything but fun and generous. Willing to laugh at the slightest invitation. But I had always known them in the context of my parents. The Delaportes were my parents' friends. And though that friendship extended to me, it had no depth. At least not on my side. They knew my entire history. I knew...nothing about them apart from the summers we'd spent together. After the conversation we'd had the evening before, there was nothing left to be said.

So I did the only thing I could. I told them I was moving into Mademoiselle's apartment and I gave them her phone number in case they needed to reach me.

I had no idea how I'd be able breathe paint fumes without sacrificing brain cells. I didn't know where I'd sleep or if I'd be able to light the stove without setting it on fire, but I figured it was worth a try.

How bad could it be? It would only be for a couple of weeks.

It wasn't that bad.

The toilet and the bathtub worked. The oven hadn't rusted shut, although I did singe the hair on my right forearm trying to warm up a quiche. The refrigerator would have fit better in a doll's house, but it was big enough to hold a box of milk, a head of lettuce, and a couple tomatoes.

It wasn't that bad, but it wasn't that good.

The week Adrien went back to work seemed as though it lasted for a month. Armed with a broom and a mop, I cleaned my way through Mademoiselle's bedroom, the kitchen, and the dining room. I chased dust bunnies until I was gasping for breath. I swept, scrubbed, and scraped away years' worth of grime. Dusted china and polished silver. I made trips to the dry cleaner's with armloads of curtains. Called a rug cleaner to come over and pick up the carpets.

I even got brave and decided to clean the library. Taking all the books from the shelves, I started from the top and dusted each bookcase. Then I dusted the books—covers, spines and pages—and then put them all back. It took an entire morning, but I made a discovery. At least I thought I had. Mademoiselle owned a collection of Victor Hugo. I didn't know enough to pronounce them first editions, but I had my suspicions. And I couldn't wait to show them to Adrien.

We had planned to have dinner together every night that week, but it didn't work out that way. Every afternoon he would call and apologize profusely for standing me up. By the time Friday rolled around, I had forgotten we'd ever had a standing arrangement for dinner.

The painters had finished the living room that morning, so I supervised the unveiling and replacing of the furniture. When they came back after lunch, they disassembled their scaffolding, moved it across the hall to the dining room, and set it up again.

While they were setting up, I made sure all the windows were wide open. I was tired of smelling fumes. Actually, I had been tired of smelling fumes on Tuesday. Now, on Friday, I couldn't even smell them anymore. I considered tying one of Mademoiselle's scarves around my throat so that my head wouldn't detach itself from my shoulders and float away into the sky.

I needed a break.

Once my feet had hit the pavement, they walked me to the Musée Rodin. I didn't protest. I paid the entrance fee, wondering if I could buy an annual pass. Then I spent an hour looking at *The Kiss*. And another hour sipping an espresso in the café, fantasizing about kissing.

On the walk back to Mademoiselle's, I tried to decide what I would have for dinner. I had narrowed it down to gyros or a specialty *crêpe* from the *crêpe* guy on rue Cler. I planned on taking my food down to the *quai* to eat.

I walked in the door, placed the purse on the floor, and went into the living room. I was going to plop on the couch and rest for half an hour before heading out again.

But the couch was already occupied.

"Adrien!" I was so happy to see him sitting there that I jumped onto the couch beside him and gave him a hug.

He pulled me onto his lap and returned the favor, ruffling through my hair with his nose.

"Tonight and tomorrow I am all for you, *ma poule*. What is the one thing in Paris you have always wanted to do but never have?"

It didn't take me long to tell him. "Let's go to the Louvre."

"The *Musée du Louvre* it is."

I reached over and took a short glass from his hand. Sniffed it. "What are you drinking?"

"Bénédictine. Try it."

I lifted the glass to my lips. Took a sip. "Mmm." It was thick and syrupy. Smooth. It tasted of all kinds of spices. Cinnamon. Cloves. Thyme. Coriander.

Adrien took his glass back and then dumped me from his lap. I stood in front of him, between his knees. He looked up at me. "What do we do for dinner?"

I smiled at him. "Gyros or *crêpes*."

He smiled back. "And then what?"

"Walk along the *quai*."

We walked over to rue Cler and watched as the *crêpe* guy made two *crêpes sarrasins* just for us. He poured the thick buckwheat batter onto a round flat iron that looked like a frying pan without any sides. Then he spread it into a circle with a flick of a utensil that looked like a push broom without any bristles. He cooked first one and then the other, loosening them from the iron when they were done, folding the first and moving it off to one side. When the second *crêpe* was done, he loosened it, flipped it over, and cracked an egg onto it. When the egg had begun to lose its translucence, he scattered first gruyère and then feta cheese across the top, and then followed with a layer of chopped toma-toes and salt and pepper. When the cheese had melted, his deft hands folded it into a rectangular package and slipped it into a paper sleeve.

Then he did it all again. My stomach was running on aromas from the *crêpe* stand and it had started to growl. At least we didn't have to walk far. Two blocks over to avenue Bosquet, three blocks down and then across the *quai* and we were at the river. Instead of going left past the Alma Marceau RER train station, we went right and walked through the gravel paths of the greenbelt to find a bench to sit on. We found one just short of a playground, protected from the sun by an overhanging tree.

We ate.

We watched children skip away from their parents and run up to the playground gate. Watched them climb up the equipment. Plummet down the slide, jump to their feet, and do it all over again a dozen times. Then they would race away down the path, only to be replaced by other children who would climb and plummet and do it all again.

And again.

We saw a pair of children, a boy and girl, become involved in a game of rotating beads of different colors which had been threaded on a three-foot by three-foot grid. A sort of three-dimensional tic-tac-toe on a very grand scale. They took turns, casting sly glances at each other before selecting which bead to rotate. The boy was probably ten, the girl several years younger. They played, quiet but intense, for about five minutes before the girl swept her palm across the grid in a blur of color and motion. The boy stood gaping.

It was the one move he hadn't expected.

Then he spun around to catch the little girl as she ran away.

Adrien and I burst out laughing, sharing the little girl's triumph and the little boy's dismay. I glanced farther down the path and saw the chil-drens' parents laughing too. They didn't look much older than Adrien and me.

I glanced at Adrien out of the corner of my eye.

He was a picture of mirth, his blue eyes radiating happiness.

I glanced back at the parents. They were still laughing, their posture mirroring our own.

They could be Adrien and me.

The father rose, calling the boy off the chase. He walked toward the play equipment, let the girl jump into his arms, and then swung her up onto his shoulders.

I could picture Adrien doing that.

The mother picked up her purse, and then joined the boy on the far side of the playground. She stooped down to speak to him.

His sullen eyes began to sparkle. He smiled. Then he placed his hand in his mother's and they walked over toward the man and the girl.

Her father set her down, she stuck her tongue out at the boy, and they sped away down the gravel path.

Father and mother linked hands and strolled after them.

I had made a nice life for myself in Seattle. I had a job. I had a house. I had a church. Assorted friends. Maybe none of these things were anything I could brag about, but I was content in many ways. As I watched that family, the thought crept into my head that there was more. That maybe even I could have more. Life could be better. There could be a small family. Someone to laugh with. Someone's hand to hold.

I glanced at Adrien.

He was looking down the park after them. His gaze had turned wistful. His eyes met mine.

A tingle crept up and down my spine.

That's what he wanted. For all his playfulness, for all of his flirting, he wanted those things too. And when I conjured this vision, when I inserted myself into that family, the hand I was holding was his.

Chapter 34

❦

There was something insubstantial and new in the atmosphere as we walked back to Mademoiselle's. A vision, like a mirage, shimmering between us. But what if it proved false? What if I were mistaken? What if, when I reached out, I found there was nothing there but my imagination?

Then I would lose part of the accumulated history of my life. The relationship I had with the person who knew me best would disintegrate, dissolve into a nothing of stilted conversations and awkward silences. My purgatory would be living with an eternal blush, my mind forever fixed on that one evening in Paris when I actually thought that Adrien and I could be lovers.

Friends *and* lovers.

Isn't that what everybody wants? We were already friends. Had an easy relationship with 25 years of shared memories. How hard would it be to reach out and take his hand?

Piece of cake.

A mere half step away from friendship, it could always be taken back. I could think of at least three ways off the top of my head: a) Oops! I slipped, b) My hands are always so cold—I'm borderline Raynaud's, c) Oh! Is that *your* hand? I'm so sorry.

Piece of cake.

So I should just do it, right? What's the worst that could happen? He's my friend. And the French are so touchy-feely. To him it's not going to be a big deal. It's not even going to be a little deal. In fact, the gesture would be so small that I might as well not even make it.

I would have plunged my hands into my pockets right then if I had any. But I was wearing my new pants. Enough said.

I glanced at Adrien. He was watching the traffic light. Waiting for it to change. I glanced down. His hand was loose at his side. Just hanging there. If I moved mine six inches...not even six. More like four. What's four inches between friends? Maybe if I started, he'd read my mind and meet my hand halfway. In that case, I would only have to navigate two inches. From my side to his side.

My hand had had enough of my dithering and made a move on its own.

I watched, fascinated as it opened up, reached out and slipped into...

Nothing.

The light had changed. Adrien was moving. He called an *Allons-y* out over his shoulder. I had to run to catch up.

But what if...?

"What if" occupied my thoughts for the rest of the evening. My dreams for the remainder of the night. I woke a dozen times at the prelude to a kiss.

In the morning I woke from the last of those dreams. The final variation on the theme. My lips felt tingly, but numb. Longing to be kissed. And I didn't want to get out of bed. Because what if last night had just been pretend? What if it were all in my head?

At least I could be thankful that it was still all in my own head and that I hadn't shared any of it with Adrien.

I stumbled down the hall. Took a bath. Dried my hair. Took some time putting on makeup. Got dressed. Then headed for the kitchen.

Stopped when I came abreast of the living room. "Don't you knock?"

Adrien was reading a newspaper in an armchair, but he folded it into a neat rectangle when I appeared. "I did. You did not answer. So, breakfast first? Then the Louvre?" He started down the hall, expecting me to follow. And I did. Because my heart was telling me I would follow him anywhere.

On my side, at least, things had changed.

We were out the door by nine and on our way to the metro. It was a crisp morning. I can't say that I was disappointed because I've never been a sun goddess. My skin had never produced a tan in its entire life. The best I could ever do in summer was to turn a darker shade of pale.

Autumn was my favorite season. Cool enough for sweaters but warm enough for walks outside. It crossed my mind that I would probably like Paris in the fall. The thousands of trees would make for a glorious tramp through leaves.

It was a shame that I would miss it.

I shrugged and threw myself into the task at hand: catching up with Adrien. "*Attends!*"

He was two steps ahead of me but stopped. He was humming *La Marseillaise* when I caught up to him. "*On y va.*"

I realized that the Louvre would be crowded. It was one of the top tourist sites in the number one tourist destination on earth. I just didn't realize how crowded it would be. We took the metro to *Palais Royal— Musée du Louvre* and went above ground so that Adrien could show me the glass pyramid entrance outside. Then we ducked into the mall beneath the museum, the Carrousel du Louvre, and waited in line at the underground entrance. At least it was shorter than the line snaking into the pyramid above ground. We passed through security, my purse was X-rayed, and then we waited in another line to buy tickets.

Adrien sent me to the information booth to get a brochure guide while he was waiting.

He joined me a few minutes later.

"French or English?"

"One of each."

I handed him the one in French and kept the one in English.

He plucked mine from my hand and replaced it with his. "So we can both practice our languages. What do you want to see first?"

I rattled them off. "*Mona Lisa, Venus de Milo,* and the *Victory of Samothrace.*"

He unfolded the brochure, which turned into a map, and spent a few moments orienting himself. Then he put a hand to my waist and threaded us through the crowd. It was almost as good as dancing. He looked like the only person who knew where he was going.

Went into the museum through the Sully wing.

We started with *Venus.* She was captivating even on approach because she could be seen, long before we reached her, glowing white toward the end of a series of rooms.

She looked cold.

After that thought popped into my head, I had trouble thinking of anything else. She also looked awkward, her front foot lifted as if she had decided to go up a staircase sideways. But the most disappointing thing was that she didn't look real. People talk about her as though she's the ideal beauty, but I couldn't picture her as a real person. We walked around her and then did a loop through the rest of the Greek, Etruscan, and Roman antiquities. There were some impressive statues of Melpomène, the muse of tragedy, and of Apollo and Diana.

Then we climbed a switchback staircase to see the *Winged Victory of Samothrace.*

She has the best location in the Louvre: towering at the top of a staircase. I climbed to the top and looked at her from three angles; that's what everyone else was doing. I decided that a head wouldn't really have added much to her charms. The explanatory notes said that she was meant to represent a naval victory at Rhodes and was envisioned at the moment she left the ground. Otherwise known as Nike. Blah, blah, blah. Important thing was the movement in the sculpture. For the first time, movement was suggested in stone. It looked like the wind was blowing her dress.

I took a look.

Yes, that was true.

We spent a minute longer on *Victory,* and then Adrien directed me right and into the Italian Gallery. We walked straight past lots of paintings I would have liked to have spent more time on: ethereal Botticellis, mysterious da Vincis, and on and on for what seemed likes miles until we came to a separate room at the bottom of the endless gallery. On a wall by herself, behind glass, was the *Mona Lisa*. And she was not as impressive in person because she was so much smaller than I'd assumed.

We waited for a few minutes, hoping to be able to have the chance to look at her by ourselves, but there were too many people. And they were all taking pictures of her. With their flashes on.

"It will serve them right." Adrien was throwing darts at the tourists with his eyes.

"What will?"

"They will develop their pictures and find that they have taken a picture of their own flash. It bounces off the Plexiglas and back into the lense." He was scowling. "And the light reflects back onto the other 20 canvasses in the room which do not have the protection that she has."

I turned to look at the room behind us. It was just as he'd said. I could even see the flashes reflected from several of the paintings.

"They should either confiscate cameras or they should place *La Joconde* in a room by herself. In ten years all these paintings will be ruined. That is why there are *cartes postale*."

Adrien was usually so easygoing, but he sounded embittered. I'd seen enough of the *Mona Lisa* anyway, so I slid a hand around his arm and propelled him back the way we'd come, taking a few extra glances at select pictures on the way.

By the time we'd once again reached the *Winged Victory*, his good nature had been restored.

"Where to next? Asian? Eastern? African?"

I didn't want to miss the chance to see Rembrandt, Vermeer, and all the other European artists I'd heard of, so we chose the Northern European paintings. Which meant more stairs.

We found a room, a gallery, dedicated to Rubens' paintings of Marie de Medici. They were huge, all 24 of them, and filled with a fantasy of allusions to Greek gods and goddesses. I walked past them as if I were on a conveyor belt. We only had one day and I wanted to see as much of the Louvre as we could.

"Minute, papillon!" Adrien stopped me. Recalled me. Asked me not to flit from painting to painting like a butterfly.

We ambled through the Northern European gallery. All 45 rooms. It started innocuously with two-dimensional jewel-toned medieval art based on biblical scenes. Then it moved into the more voluptuous early-Renaissance art, still based on biblical scenes. And then we moved into the sixteenth-century paintings from Holland.

I'm not sure why, but my cheeks felt as though they were chapped. My breathing was running ragged. I spotted a window in one of the walls and make a beeline for it. It looked out onto rue de Rivoli. The juxtaposition of people in modern dress and sleek speeding cars was like a ladle of cool water. My eyes took giant gulps. I closed them and took deep breaths.

Everything was fine.

I opened them and turned back toward the paintings. The figures seemed to writhe and sway. All those sinuous curves, the gilded ornate fabrics. The flirtation of shadow and light. I was drawn toward a depiction of *David and Bathsheba* by Jan Massys. I stood in front of it, transfixed. Eyes roaming from the impossible pale silver tones of her skin to the rich dark reds and golds of David's cloak and the maidens' dresses. Bathsheba was obviously about to bathe. Or maybe she had just finished bathing.

I couldn't decide.

But she was naked.

I saw the languorous way she was sitting. The darting angles of the messenger and the dog.

My eyes too were darting. Up and left to the castle roof. To the palm trees and the city in the background. But always back to Bathsheba. She was glowing with the glacial virtue of...and I was aware the instant that Adrien came and stood behind me.

I felt his breath fan my hair.

I heard him shift, felt his hip bump my backside. Little prickles started percolating on my scalp.

The thing is, I didn't know what to do. Or say. I mean, what sort of intelligent conversation can you make when you're staring at a portrait of a naked woman about to be seduced by a king?

Nothing came to mind.

So I stood there and began to tilt my head back and forth. Isn't that what art people do? So I tilted and then added a "hmm" for good measure. I was still stuck. Maybe if I backed up, as if I were planning to look at it from farther away…and if I kept on backing up, eventually I'd wind up back at the apartment.

Good plan!

I started to turn around and swung right into Adrien.

He put his hands out to steady me. It worked for my feet. But my heart felt as though it had careened over a cliff.

I played the only card I had. The female one. "Is there a bathroom around here?"

"If we go back the way we came, and at the corner of the building we go straight instead of right, we can see a few French paintings and find a bathroom."

Whatever it took to get me away from there.

So we went back in time to those pious religious paintings with sagging bodies of Christ and then went straight and—wham! Just when I'd started to feel normal again, I was confronted with *Gabrielle d'Estrées and her sister the Duchess de Villars*. No big deal, just a couple of aristocrats, except that they were both naked. They kept staring at me with knowing looks. I put my head down and just kept on walking.

So. For the record, by the time we reached the bathroom we'd seen some very nice work by Poussin. And I did, in fact, have to go.

Lunch was restorative. We left the museum and went to the food court in the Carrousel. While we ate couscous with hot, hair-raising condiments on the side, I lectured myself. Sternly.

I was visiting an art museum. The largest art museum in the world. If I'd become a little emotional, it was just because art was meant to evoke feelings. Eventually all the aspects of art that you subconsciously notice, like the sinuous curves and the subtle allusions, the colors—rich reds, brassy golds, contrasts of blue and orange—had to produce a psychological effect too.

Didn't they?

I'm the only person I know who would rather spend a day at the Picasso Museum than at the Louvre.

By the time we'd finished lunch, I was prepared to tackle the Louvre again. Besides, we had decided that we were done with paintings. Time for sculpture

We entered through the Denon wing on the ground floor, went up one level, and finally came to something worth seeing. Michelangelo. His slaves. *Dying* and *Rebelling* are sculptures which are fused with the stone. And they were powerful. Those were statues I could appreciate.

It's not that I'm against nudity in art.

There was a very beautiful seated *Nymph with a Scorpion* in the same room. I could admire something like that. There was a statue called *Friendship*. A standing nude. Perfectly benign. And there was a breathtaking *Pysche and Love*, joined in a tender embrace, and I was fine with that.

I thought.

Nope. My cheeks flamed. The tingles attacked. And that's when I figured out my problem. I was frightened by the thought of a touch. Afraid of a kiss.

A kiss?

How can anyone be afraid of a kiss? Two sets of lips touching. And if one person doesn't like it, then it never has to be done again. We're not talking major lifetime commitment.

But I was afraid.

Adrien was probably an expert and I was a low-level amateur. And I really wouldn't want to know that he didn't like kissing me. How humiliating. Better just to not kiss at all. Then I could imagine it to be anything, everything I wanted.

By midafternoon, I wished I were Adrien, because then I would just know if I liked me and I wouldn't have to analyze myself to death.

We hopped on the metro beneath the Carrousel. It was so crowded that we had to press our way inside and fight to hold on to the vertical bar in the center of the car. Adrien and I stood shoulder to shoulder, but his arm was longer, so as we glided along, I kept bumping into it.

Finally, he switched hands and used his free arm to move me around in front of him and then he wrapped it around me. I didn't have to hold onto the bar anymore, because I was tucked under his arm.

I liked it there. It was safe.

The only thing that made me move was the fact that we had to transfer metro lines. By the time we got back to Mademoiselle's building, my emotions were a muddled mess and I was exhausted.

Adrien called the elevator, the tiny old one, and when it arrived, I went in first and backed up to the wall. Adrien came in, farther than he had to, so that the door could close. But when the door closed and we began to lift, he didn't back up. He stayed where he was, pressed right up against me.

I felt a frisson of…something. If I had lifted my eyes, just a little bit, I could have seen his eyes. As it was, there was something fascinating about the one unbuttoned button on his shirt.

There must have been, because I couldn't make myself look away.

"Claire?"

I tried to answer. I did. But all the words disintegrated before they reached my lips.

I felt his fingers reach out to tuck a stray lock of hair behind my ear. Then they tiptoed down my jaw to my chin. He lifted it up.

My eyes lagged behind, but they finally locked with his.

They were so blue, so inviting, that I found myself diving right in. And I wasn't swimming in them long before I realized that he was feeling exactly what I was feeling.

He gripped my forearms and pulled my hands to his waist.

He didn't have to tug very hard, because I was already leaning toward him. He lowered his head, and then we were jolted toward the back of the elevator.

Adrien caught himself with his hands and I peeked out from beneath his arm.

The elevator had stopped. The door had opened. The moment had gone.

We had arrived.

Adrien glanced at me. His lips quirked. He pushed away from the back of the elevator and got off, holding the outer door open for me.

I slipped by him into the hall, pulling my key out as I went. I'm not a glib person, and for the hundredth time that day, I couldn't think of anything to say. In fact, it was possible that I would never speak again.

I didn't have the courage to do what I would have liked to, so I prowled. Up and down. Back and forth. All around Mademoiselle's room for about five minutes trying to talk myself into going into the living room and talking to him. And telling him everything. I threw open the windows and leaned against the casement, watching the traffic pass. Realized that I couldn't hide forever. Realized I didn't have the courage to talk to Adrien.

About anything.

So I scoured the library, looking for something to read. Paused when I came to the Victor Hugo collection. Should I, or shouldn't I? Not yet. I pounced on a Jules Verne that didn't look too fragile and plucked it from the shelves. If I couldn't be a functioning person, at least I could nourish my brain. So I sat in one of the armchairs and spent the next five minutes trying to get cozy before realizing that it was a hopeless cause. Because regardless of my lack of nerve, I was lonely.

And Adrien was sitting in the living room. By himself.

Like a forlorn child, I wandered down the hall, book clutched in my hand.

He looked up as I approached. He was sitting at one end of the couch. And he wasn't doing anything at all that I could tell. He stretched his arm along the back of the couch and raised his eyebrows in a question.

That was all the invitation I needed. I put the book on the floor, and then I curled up on the couch and rested my head on his thigh. Closed my eyes. I wasn't sure what he would do, but it was the best I could offer.

After a minute I felt his hand on my hair. Tentative. Testing. Conforming to the shape of my head. And then he started to stroke my hair. Run his fingers through it. It was really nice.

I closed my eyes and dreamed in Technicolor of all the art we'd seen.

Chapter 35

When I woke, it was six and the sun had begun its decline.

"What do you miss about Seattle?"

I yawned and rubbed my eyes. Had I been carrying on a conversation in my sleep? What was it he had asked? "Seattle?"

"You must be anxious to get back to all the things you have been missing."

I was? "I still have a couple weeks." But there must have been something that I missed. I thought for a full minute before I figured out what it was. "Mexican. I miss Mexican food."

"Then you must have some."

Suspicious, I sat up and turned toward him.

He was smiling.

After I had mentioned it, I discovered that I was hungry for Mexican food. I began to get excited by the possibility while he searched through the phone book for a restaurant. Until he told me where he'd found one: Les Halles.

Generally, Paris is a safe city. I could probably walk anywhere in the seventh at night, even in my nightgown. But Les Halles was a different story, according to Cynthia. What she'd described evoked images of purse snatchers and muggers. Of dark alleys and grimy characters. I'd never been there and I really didn't want to go.

Adrien laughed at my fears. "Maybe it is this way after midnight, but it is only six o'clock. It will be light until at least ten."

I told him I'd only go if he'd promise to leave the restaurant no later than nine thirty. I mean, I didn't miss Mexican food that much. I'd made it up. He was the one who had insisted that I must be missing something.

So I did my best to be inconspicuous. I dressed all in black. Those slender pants. A silk shirt I borrowed from Mademoiselle, with darts that made it cling from the bust down through my waist. I meant to blend in with those dark alleys and shady characters, but one look at Adrien's eyes told me I hadn't succeeded. He made it seem as though I were wearing a sparkling evening gown.

We got on the metro, and even though we had to switch lines, it seemed as though we were taking a special express. I blinked and all of a sudden we were there. He had to take me by the arm to drag me off the train. I hid behind him on the escalator out of the station.

As soon as we stepped out onto the pavement, I grabbed his arm and didn't unhand him until we reached the restaurant. By then we had twisted and turned through so many alleys that I would never have been able to find it again, even if someone asked me at knifepoint.

But we arrived and I relaxed.

Then I looked at the menu. I'd never even heard of half the things on it. But I was game. Adrien was trusting me to order, so I picked two things from each category, not certain what we'd be served.

It turned out that most of the dishes had sauces. Not mole or green sauce. Not even enchilada or hot sauce. They had French-style sauces that never should have been introduced to Mexican food. And the seasonings were way off. There might have been cumin somewhere. It seemed that every once in a while I got a hint of its ghostly presence. But there sure weren't any chiles. Or chile seasoning. Not even any cilantro.

It was like trying to compare an Andy Warhol painting with a velvet Elvis on the basis that they were both colorful. And the thing is, I'm not even a Mexican food connoisseur. I have some friends who know the difference between Mexican, Tex-Mex, and something they call Cal-Mex. And they're willing to fight about which kind is best and why.

I've never told anyone this before, but when I think of Mexican, I think of Taco Bell. I don't need anything fancy or authentic. Just a basic chicken or bean burrito. In a pinch I can even be happy with a frozen microwaved version. So I guess I was a reverse-snob. And I was disappointed by this Frenchified high-class version of Mexican.

Adrien, however, was delighted. "I know why you miss this. It is really good, Claire."

I tried to give him a smile. "Yeah. Thanks for finding this place."

"We will have to come back."

"Yeah. Sure."

At least they had real desserts. We ordered something with cinnamon and chocolate and it was fabulous. Maybe we would have to come back soon.

Adrien glanced at his watch and then began to signal for the bill. "It is nine thirty."

So…?

"I promised to be leaving here at nine thirty."

"Oh. Oh! Thanks." Geez. I hadn't expected him to take me so seriously.

"You enjoyed this? Yes?"

"Yes. Thank you."

"At your service. You can find almost anything you desire in Paris. No need to miss your home."

He was right. I'd seen a store advertising Russian caviar next to one displaying merguez sausages in their windows. But what else did a person expect from the culinary capital of the world? For some reason he thought this was important to me.

So I acted as though it was.

The next morning, he picked me up for church.

When we arrived, it seemed as if the whole city had decided to show up. It made for a rather cramped but lively service. Afterward, Adrien reminded me why it was like this.

"*La Rentrée.* Everyone is back from vacation."

Everyone and their brother. And sister. "Do you see Cynthia?" I was standing on my toes trying to see over all of the bobbing heads that filled the room.

"*Non.* You might try the other room."

I rolled my eyes. That was like saying, *If you ever get the chance, the view of earth from the moon is great; don't miss it!* But I found her. Eventually. After getting hung up in several other conversations.

Though she was barricaded against the wall by two knots of people, she elbowed her way through to me and drew me aside.

"How was your week?"

"Fine. Adrien's parents came back. I moved into Mademoiselle's."

Her eyebrows came close to hitting the ceiling. "They don't like you?"

"No. I mean yes. But it's just easier that way. How's school?"

"How's A?"

"Good. Fine. We kissed almost. Almost kissed. Twice."

"What? Fantastic! What do you mean by almost?"

"We were on his parents' couch, in his parents' apartment, and his parents came home. That was a near kiss. Then we were in an elevator. He made a move. The elevator door opened. End of kisses. Attempted kisses. That's it. Do you have any advice?"

She glanced over my shoulder and her eyes grew wide. "A is coming."

"Then make it quick."

"Okay. Next time he starts something, finish it."

"That's it?"

That's when Adrien joined us. He kissed Cynthia's cheeks and engaged in conversation for a few minutes, but his eyes were drifting and his feet were shuffling. I could tell he wanted to leave.

"We have to run. Have a good week." I leaned in to kiss her. "I'll catch you next Sunday."

Adrien kissed her goodbye, put an arm around my waist, and led me out the back door. "My parents wanted us to have lunch with them."

I glanced at my watch. Lunch? It was one o'clock. No wonder he was in a hurry.

He helped me into the car and sped toward town. As he drove he glanced several times in my direction. Started several times to speak. Stopped. Finally spoke. "I have an offer for you. You do not have to say yes, but I would like you to."

"It would help if I knew what it was."

"My company is having a *soirée*, a gala, to celebrate *la Rentrée* at the *opéra*. I would like you to come with me. It is the *Le Nozze di Figaro* by Mozart. The twelfth of September. It is at the Opéra Bastille, but…"

"I've never been to an opera."

"Jamais?"

"Never."

"Alors…you would like to go?" He wrapped and rewrapped his hands around the steering wheel.

"Yes."

Once I had agreed, there was the question of what to wear.

We knew right where to go. Later that afternoon, after lunch, Adrien drove me back to Mademoiselle's. We headed straight toward the armoire. I was getting ready to open one when he stopped me. He handed me the box of jewels.

"Perhaps we should match jewels to the dress."

"You want me to wear her jewelry?" Were those necklaces and earrings insured? Would there be a bodyguard?

"Yes. I would consider it a favor to me if you were to wear the moonstones."

"They aren't the fanciest…"

"But they fit you. And when I think of you after you leave, I would like to think of you wearing them."

I was flattered. And I was touched. How do you refuse a request like that? I didn't. Couldn't.

So what went with green-and-gray moonstones? Not red or inky blue, but that didn't stop me from trying on those gowns. Less obviously, not black either. At least not according to Adrien. He said it would drown the stones, lessen their luminosity.

He was the expert.

So I was left with a gown of silver lamé or steel gray. Neither of which would have been my first choice.

The silver lamé was, well, made out of silver lamé. And the steel gray dress had feathers. They sprouted from a sequined and beaded bust and had attached themselves in clumps to a long, sweeping hem making me think that it might be possible to fly. But when I put it on, I knew it had been made for the necklace. The green tint of the feathers was exactly the color of the moonstones. So what choice did I really have? And, hey, I'd never worn feathers before.

So, that done, we went for a walk. Ended up at the Eiffel Tower. Walked across Pont d'Iéna and up to Trocadéro. Stood on the plaza and watched as the Eiffel Tower gained brilliance with the setting of the sun.

And I wondered if those near kisses had just been my imagination.

Chapter 36

ᘒᑯᘓ

I was melancholy that week.

I watched the painters move through the apartment. Tackled the bathroom and the living room with buckets and broom. I saw the apartment begin to reflect some of its former glory. Realized my time was running out.

And I thought of everything I would be missing. The *Foire nationale á la brocante et aux jambons*. Adrien would have to hunt for his treasures all by himself. The wine fairs. The book fairs. Those châteaux on the Loire we hadn't had time yet to see.

The fall retreat and the Christmas ski trip.

The *Salon du chocolat*.

There were too many things left undone.

But there was no reason to stay. The apartment was now airtight. It would soon be squeaky clean. The *gardienne* would look in on it regularly. Mom and Dad would fly out for Christmas, hoping to oversee a sale.

I had loved being in Paris.

But I could come back.

I had my own friends in Paris now. I could stay with Cynthia. I could come back for summer vacation. Take leave without pay even and extend my two weeks to a full month. I could afford it. It would be something to look forward to for the entire year.

Or maybe, if I got my teaching certificate…

No.

I'd decided not to be tentative anymore when it came to life. Mademoiselle and Cynthia were my new role models. *When* I got my teaching certificate, I would have entire summers off. I could have a real summer vacation and spend it all in France if I chose to. I could do whatever I wanted.

But right now, my life was in Seattle. There were things to do. There was my house and my job.

By Thursday, I was sure I'd imagined the thing between Adrien and me. The whole thing. Everything. Every time I'd thought he had shown any interest in me.

He picked me up for the opera at six. When I opened the door and saw him, all of the air left my lungs.

He was dressed in a tuxedo. By the way it fit his shoulders and his arms, I could tell that it wasn't rented. I swallowed. Hard. Couldn't think of a thing to say. Why should wearing black make his eyes even more blue? And his hair glossy? And how could his skin look so smooth? How could he be so suave? This was not the Adrien I was used to.

All of a sudden, he seemed like a stranger.

He was looking at me intensely. Intently. There wasn't a shade of a smile on his face. He was serious.

Seriously good-looking.

And then I saw myself reflected in his eyes. I wasn't a gawky woman playing dress up in feathery frou-frou. I was a creature of the night. I was a fantasy.

He offered me his arm and covered my hand with his as we stepped into the elevator.

He helped me into the car, tucking in all my feathers, and closed the door. Then he strode around to the driver's side. It was a quiet ride to Bastille. His eyes roamed in every direction but mine. There was a gleam of sweat above his upper lip. And he'd cleaned the car; the recently vacuumed smell still hung in the air.

The last time I'd felt so nervous was at my senior prom. I'd had the luck of being asked to go by a boy I actually liked. We hadn't talked much over dinner. We hadn't talked much at the dance or on the way home.

In fact, we really hadn't talked at all.

And then we stood in front of the door to my house, shifting from foot to foot, trying to think of just one of the thousands of things we hadn't talked about all evening. And I remember wishing that he'd kiss me. And then he lunged forward with his arms out and I thought, *Well, I guess a hug is better than nothing.*

So I'd given him a nice church hug—medium pressure, two pats on the back—and then said goodnight and let myself in the door.

This is how naive I was. How naive I am. I never realized until about five years ago that the poor guy probably *had* been trying to kiss me.

So tonight I was making sure I paid attention to all the signals.

When we reached the parking garage, Adrien opened my door and took my hand to help me up. Then he put his other hand around my waist. He was so close that I could see the prickles of whiskers just starting to appear beneath his skin.

I released his hand and bent down to pull all of my feathers out of the car. Wearing the dress was like trying to walk six dogs at the same time; one of them was always lagging behind. And once I got all the feathers out, I had to step behind Adrien to accommodate them all.

But he had been saying something, hadn't he? "What?"

He dropped his hand from my waist and offered me his arm. "Nothing. The least of things. Shall we go?"

Taking his arm, I used my other hand to lift my skirt. And we were off.

In my entire life, I've been to zero operas and one ballet, *The Nutcracker,* in Seattle. With the set and costumes designed by Maurice Sendak. So I'm not an expert on opera houses, but I thought this one should look less like an office building. It was high contrast. Steel, glass, and white gleaming stone with a never-ending staircase mounting its levels. But Adrien took me straight up to the seventh floor and there we strolled the semicircular hall, looking at the panoramic view of Paris at night.

Other couples were doing the same. I noted that I was the only one with feathers. I'm not sure whether that made me fashion-savvy or just plain dorky. I had to keep remembering to look into Adrien's eyes. Because whenever I did, I felt transformed.

"Thank you for coming with me tonight."

"Thanks for asking me." I attempted to lean over the railing and look down, but feathers being what they were and my chest being what it wasn't, I decided that being veiled, however thinly, was preferable to a view below.

Adrien glanced at his watch. "We need to find our seats." He put a hand to my waist to turn me around and we descended several floors. To my surprise, we didn't enter the performance hall through the main lobby area, but instead ducked into a side hall and then into a discreet door. The door opened into a box of seats overhanging the main floor.

Wow.

There was a sober mix of black and dark wood in the performance hall. Futuristic glowing levels of seats that projected out over the ground floor. And full-blown lighting, like space-age sails, above.

The box was already filling with people, most of whom Adrien stopped to greet as he maneuvered me to our seats. He introduced me each time as a dear old friend from his youth.

We sat down.

From the first strains of the overture, I discovered that I was better educated than I had realized. I knew this opera. From movies or cartoons or something, the music was familiar. It wasn't long before I forgot that men and women weren't supposed to be able to sing so high or long or loud. And I got involved in the story.

A story of double and triple intrigues. Of a count trying to seduce his wife's maid who is marrying a fellow servant who has previously pledged himself in marriage to…his own mother?! It was frivolous. It was fun.

We stepped out of the box for a break at the intermission. Adrien found me a seat on a low leather chair and then fought his way through the crowd to a bar. He brought back two flutes of champagne and stood beside me as we both watched the crowd.

And then I saw someone watching me.

I'd seen him in our box too. I reached up for Adrien's free hand and gave it a tug. "Do you know that man?"

He bent toward me. "Which one?"

"The short one with the red cheeks who keeps staring at me."

Adrien straightened at that remark and looked in the direction of my nod. "Ah, *oui*. He's the Prince of...*quelque chose*...Prince of something. I will remember in a moment."

"You mean like the Prince of Wales?"

"*Non, non, non.* Not of royal blood. He is from one of the old families. Belgian, maybe? Dutch?"

"Why would he be staring at me?"

"Because you are beautiful."

No. That wasn't it.

A woman knows when a man finds her attractive. It was something else, and I wished I knew what it was.

"Shall I take this for you?" He was holding out his hand for my empty glass.

I let him take it, closed my eyes for a moment, and took a deep breath. When I opened my eyes, Adrien had returned. But he had been shadowed.

"*Excusez-moi*, Mademoiselle, Monsieur Delaporte."

Adrien turned and then bowed towards the intruder.

I turned toward my right, toward the voice, to find a leprechaun at my elbow. The man with the red cheeks.

"I have seen this necklace before and I have seen your eyes before, but not on you."

My heart leaped. "Did you know Mademoiselle Dumont?"

"Ah—then you are a relation?"

"She was my cousin."

"*Oui.* I see. I was sorry to hear of her passing."

"You knew her well?"

"How well does one ever know someone else?"

"What I mean is that I know nothing about her. She left her estate to my father. And he broke his back and so he couldn't come to France, so I did instead—" I knew that I wasn't making any sense, but I was so eager for information about Mademoiselle that I wanted the man to know that my interest was legitimate. And most of all I wanted to talk to someone who had known her. Someone who could tell me the things her diary hadn't.

"Well. It is good to see that her eyes live on in you. They were celebrated, these eyes of hers. Of yours. Very special."

"Who was she?"

"She was an artist's model in the '30s. And it was not for her eyes because no one could paint them. They were very disturbing. It was her back. Everyone painted her back. And one day when she was sitting for a painter, the duc de Bastogne walked in. And that was it. He fell in love with her back before he even saw her front. It was a legend in their circle of society."

I already knew all of that. "And?"

"And that was it. They were lovers until he died."

"But they got married, right? After the war?" I hadn't had time to show Adrien the diary, but this was even better. Maybe he'd believe me if he heard it from someone else.

He looked at me with reproachful eyes. "I said they were lovers. He was married. Not when they first met, but after the war he married. To some useful Fleming from an old family. Because he was Wallonian, you see. French-speaking. So for the family business it was useful to be married to a Dutch-speaker. Clothilde? Mathilde? Something. It was a shame. They hardly spoke the language of the other."

"He was already married."

"Yes. But he lived here, in Paris, for the business. Went abroad in the summers with his family. Went home for the holidays too, I suppose. That is how it worked."

"How what worked?"

"The arrangement. You know. Have a family. Have a mistress. Best of everything."

"A mistress." That wasn't what I had in mind at all.

"*Oui.* There would have been an agreement and a contract. If he lived in Paris, then he needed someone to help him entertain. A place to sleep. Someone to attend functions with. So she would have been given an apartment. An allowance for clothing and other expenses."

Like eating lunch at the Ritz every Wednesday.

"That was an era. And she was the last of the honest courtesans. Not a tramp like so many of the others."

"But she died alone."

"Yes. Of course."

"But they were happy? Until…Mathilde died? His wife?"

"*Oui.* Until his wife died."

"What happened then?"

"One never really hears, you know, but they never went out together again. As a couple. Perhaps she expected him to marry her. Although she should not have. One never marries a mistress, you know."

I felt the impact of that decade-old blow as if it had been directed at me. Which explained the state of the apartment. Maybe she'd given up. On love. On life. "But—" I wanted her to be the nice little old lady I'd come to know. I didn't want her to be a sensuous vamp. An opportunist.

But then, I didn't want her to have been betrayed by her lover either.

The worst of it was that I felt betrayed. Kicked in the stomach by my oldest friend. Kicked in the stomach, punched in the nose, and then thrown out of a speeding car and left for dead.

I wanted out of the dress. I wanted out of the opera.

The man kept talking and I kept nodding, but I wasn't listening anymore. Adrien must have known it. He took my hand, made apologies to the prince, and walked me away.

The lobby was emptying as people returned to their seats. In a few minutes time, we were the only ones left outside the performance hall.

I walked over to a wall and leaned against it. "She was a whore."

Adrien tsked. "Not a whore. She was the mistress of a powerful man."

"She was a kept woman."

"Yes."

"She was a prostitute."

"Claire, be practical."

"I am. She slept with a man and he paid her. Maybe not in dollar bills, but in jewelry, clothes, and furniture."

"*Non.* She might have had the furniture before she met him."

"You're laughing at me!"

"*Non.* I am not." Adrien slid a glance in my direction. "Yes, I am. *Ma poule!* This happens quite often. Sometimes even today people must not marry for love, but for position." He put an arm around me and drew me to his side. Then he reached out his free hand and turned my chin up toward his face.

"But that's wrong. Or if they do, then why do they have to take other people's wives. Or husbands?"

"I do not know. I never finished the diary. So you tell me. Why did Mademoiselle do it?"

"Because she couldn't help herself."

"She was in love."

"But at the end, when she was old, she didn't know if it had been worth it."

"She had regrets?"

"He was all she had. She gave up everything for him. Her life was about him. But he didn't marry her. And then he died."

"And she had nothing?"

"She had lots of things, but she didn't have anyone to love her. She was sad, I think. Lonely."

"Ah. Because he was not willing to give up his position for her?"

"You'd think if he really loved her…"

"Perhaps he gave her what he could. All the love he had to give. The prince was right. She should have known they could never marry."

"Then she should have said no when he asked her." What I had mistaken for a proposal of marriage had been a proposal to be a mistress.

"Yes. Probably she should have."

"I thought she was brave and generous and honest and…" and looking into Adrien's eyes took the righteous indignation right out of my sails. "And I liked her. She had the courage to change her life." She had inspired me. I had wished, more than once, that I could be like her. But not anymore.

"She was. She was all those things. And you can still like her. What is not to like? She slept with a man to whom she was not married. Multiple times. But how many times have you done things you wished you would not have done? Was she any worse than you are?"

"But—"

"*Ma poule.* Enough." He took his hand from my chin and wrapped it around me. Pulled me to his chest and put his chin on top of my head. "You know what?"

"What?"

"You have proved it to me. You are not a snob. Now you can say that you have made a friend with someone who is having an affair."

Yes. I guess I could. I was disappointed in her choices, but I still liked her. And I really did wish I could have known her.

Chapter 37

The next evening Adrien stopped by. I hadn't heard from him all day. I had dinner on my own. It was raining. Had been raining hard all afternoon, so I'd dashed down the street into a bar. Had a *croque monsieur* and dashed back. I'd been holed up in the library ever since.

I hadn't been expecting him and the doorbell scared me.

Tiptoeing close to the door, I was hoping that whoever it was would go away if they didn't hear any noise from the apartment. Just when I'd thought that's exactly what had happened, I heard the rattle of a key and I watched the lock turn.

It was Adrien. Holding my orchid.

What a huge relief!

He looked surprised himself when he saw me standing so close to the door. He glanced at his watch. Frowned. "You were just about to go out?"

"No. Just about to answer the door."

"Ah. I can come in?"

"Yes. Of course!"

He gave me the orchid. "You left this."

I had. It deserved a better mother than me. So I'd abandoned it on the Delaportes' mantel. But that didn't stop me from being its advocate. "You took it out in the rain?"

"I had an umbrella." He protested my accusation by shaking it in the hallway and leaning it up against the door.

I set the orchid down on the floor and I held the shoulders of

Adrien's coat while he shrugged out of it. And then I was left wondering what to do with it. Seventeenth-century apartment buildings don't have the convenience of front hall closets. "I'll just…hang this in the bathroom."

I found him afterward in the library, staring at the bookshelves. At the bookshelf. He blended into the room with his maroon-colored roll neck sweater. He turned toward me as I came in. "She has them."

"Has what?" I asked, trying not to smile. I was running fingers through my hair, attempting to undo earlier damage, prying apart the locks that had dried in clumps.

"Look at these." He took hold of my hand and pulled me toward the shelves. "Look at all of them! Victor Hugo. First editions, all."

To share his excitement was a privilege. But after an hour of explanation as to why this printer was more important than that one, or why that novel had gotten better reviews than this one, I'd had it. "Can I get you a drink?"

"What?"

"A drink? Would you like one?"

"*Oui.* Yes. Thank you."

I left him alone with his beloved books and tried to remember what kind of alcohol Mademoiselle had kept in the apartment. There were a half dozen open bottles of liquor and several decanters that were all but full. But I never trust anything that I haven't opened myself, so I picked up an unopened malt whisky branded "The Macallan" in one hand and a couple short square glasses in the other.

When I returned, Adrien was still crouched beside the bookshelf, devouring those antique volumes with his eyes.

"Whisky?"

He turned toward me, eyes glazed.

"Would you like some whisky?"

"*Oui.* Thank you." He scrambled to his feet. "I will pour." He opened the bottle, lifted it, and then looked at the label. "The Macallan? Claire, are you sure you wanted to open this one?"

"Why? Would you rather have something else? There were some

open bottles, but I didn't know what they were or how long they'd been open."

"This is the Macallan. It is the *haute couture* of whisky."

I closed my eyes and sighed. I'd learned my lesson. "Just pour me a drink and don't tell me how much it costs."

Adrien's lips bent with amusement. "As you say."

He handed me a drink and then served himself. "To Mademoiselle?"

"To Mademoiselle."

We clinked and then sipped. He sat in one of the old armchairs. I curled up in the other, legs underneath me. It wasn't that bad.

For whisky.

By the third sip, I couldn't taste anything anymore.

"I am sorry I did not reach you in time for dinner."

I shrugged. "It's okay. I was busy all day. The work is almost done here. The bathroom's finished."

"I wanted to see you tonight. I have seen you almost every night for one month. More even. It did not seem right to go home without saying *bonne nuit*."

I knew what he meant. The French only say *bonne nuit* to those they see immediately before going to bed. And for a month—longer—that person had been him. He was part of my bedtime routine.

"You have everything you need?"

"Yes." I had my new clothes and some of Mademoiselle's clothes. And a little black dress I might as well just throw away. What more could a girl ask for?

Adrien downed the last of his drink.

I unfolded myself, set my glass down on the desk next to the phone, and then sat back down in the chair. Maybe I'd finish it later. Or maybe not.

Adrien cleared his throat. "About that woman."

I blinked. That woman. Not Solange. The other one. The one he was in love with. Had been for…forever. Was that fair? Was it really fair to monopolize someone's heart without even acknowledging it? Without even giving him the decency of a serious response to his declarations of love? I'd had it with that woman. "I don't want to hear about her anymore, Adrien."

"Why not?"

"Because I don't like her. I don't think she deserves you."

"Really?" He sat up straighter in his chair. Crossed his arms over his chest so that just his thumbs were peeking out. "Why not?"

"Because…how many times have you told her you loved her?"

"Twice, at least."

"See? And she doesn't take you seriously. How many times have you tried to kiss her?"

"At least three."

"If she doesn't get it, she doesn't get it. It's time to move on. It's not fair of her to keep your heart on hold. You deserve someone who's going to take your love seriously. Someone who's going to return it." Someone like me.

"You are right. So what do you suggest I do?"

I looked at him.

He was looking at me. Waiting. For some kind of advice. Like I had any to give.

"Do you really love her?"

"I do."

"Then give her one more chance. But you have to say it straight out. No flirtiness. No subtleness. You have to make sure she gets it this time. And then leave it up to her."

"And what do I do if she does not love me?"

"Then look for someone else to love you."

"Like who?"

It was time. If I didn't say it now, I never would. And then I would be in the same position as Adrien. Waiting, endlessly, to be taken seriously. How could I give him advice if I couldn't follow it myself? "Like me."

"Like you."

My eyes zoomed down toward my lap. Crept over toward the bookshelves. Came to rest on the glass of whisky sitting on the desk. I'd done it. I'd said it. Now it was up to him.

But he didn't say anything. Nothing.

Had I not made myself clear? Did I have to say it all over again? I snuck a look at his face.

He was staring at me. Watching. Waiting. For something.

What was love worth? At this point it was worth everything: my pride, my future, my friendship with him. So I made my humiliation complete. "You could look for someone like me. Because…I love you."

"Then I will do as you suggest."

I was confused. Which suggestion? The one about confronting the woman or the one about finding someone else?

He rose from his chair and walked over toward mine. He took my hands in his own and pulled me to my feet. "Claire, I love you. I have loved you for most of my life. I have thought, at times, that I was over you. I have thought, at times, that this could never work. But you have always held my heart, so I am giving you one last chance." His eyes held mine. "Do you understand what I am saying?"

I was starting to.

He raised our hands to his lips. Began to kiss my knuckles. His eyes were still watching mine.

The effect of his lips against my skin was electric. Like a shock that traveled through my body, leaving tingling trails of numbness in its wake. My eyes fluttered closed.

Adrien unclasped our hands and pulled me close. He nestled his head against mine, moved his forehead toward my temple, his nose grazing my ear as it slid down toward my cheek.

I was assaulted by the full force of his cologne. My knees were begging to collapse.

His nose moved toward mine, caressing. They danced around each other. A slow, impossibly slow, waltz. He leaned into my forehead again and I opened my eyes, looking straight into his. My toes were curled so tight that my arches were cramping. I held fistfuls of his sweater in my hands. His lips were just millimeters from mine.

His eyes were watching me.

Then his arms tightened behind my back. Pulling me closer, pulling me up.

I watched his eyes shut. My eyelids fluttered closed again.

And finally his lips were on mine.

My fear dissolved and all my insecurities took flight. They disappeared in a giant whirlwind that reached deep into my soul, carried my heart away, and entrusted it to Adrien. We teetered together on the edge of love, his lips doing all the asking until mine finally answered.

He'd done it again.

He'd found me.

I hadn't even realized I was lost.

And that's what it was like kissing Adrien.

About the Author

❧ ♥ ☙

$\mathcal{S}$iri Mitchell graduated from the University of Washington with a business degree and has worked in all levels of government. As a military spouse, she has lived all over the world, including Paris and Tokyo. With her husband and their little girl, Siri enjoys observing and learning from different cultures. She is fluent in French and currently mastering the skill of sushi making.

If you are interested in contacting Siri, please check out her website at

sirimitchell.com.